MW00648656

HELFYRE

MARIEL POMEROY

Copyright © 2022 by *Mariel Pomeroy*

All rights reserved.

The characters and events portrayed in this book are fictitious. Any similarity to real persons, living or dead, is coincidental and not intended by the author. No part of this book may be reproduced, or stored in a retrieval system, or transmitted in any form or by any means, electronic, mechanical, photocopying, recording, or otherwise, without express written permission of the publisher and/or author.

ISBN: 979-8-9855446-9-5

Cover art and design by: *Saskia Hubmann*

Editorial Design by: *Saskia Hubmann*

Edited by: *Taylor Robinson* at *Taylored Text LLC*

Published by: *Mariel Pomeroy*

TRIGGER WARNINGS

"Helfyre" is an adult fantasy romance that contains graphic violence, general dark themes, swearing, and sex scenes– some of which include dubious consent– **and should in no way be misconstrued as a depiction of a healthy relationship.**

You're not broken, your soul simply demanded room to grow.

—M

MEET MY
MONSTERS

Calmani Deities

Old Brite Gods

Aether (Ay-ther)
Theia (They-ah)

Old Dark Gods

Manāt (Man-aht)
'Amm (Ahm)

Children of the Gods

Children of 'Amm

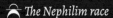 *The Nephilim race*

Avarice
Leviathan
Sirens
Varcolac
Shadow Heretics
Syraphem
Shifters
Wraiths
Shayṭān

Variety of dark creatures that populate *Aljira* and parts of *Lyria*

Children of Aether + Theia

◇ *The Mithra race*

Dioscuri

Malek

Fae

Brite Heretics

Nymphs

Shifters

Moyrai

Variety of light creatures that populate *Keloseros* and parts of *Lyria*

Children of Manāt

Kaymaat

Children of the Kaymaat

Helren

Djynn

Other creatures that live in *Lyria*

SCRIPT
+
WORLD

Lujha

⌒ *Nephilim language*

Athiran *(Ah-tee-rahn)* - Finally

Ahid *(Ah-heed)* - Calm

Taelma *(Tah-ayl-mah)* - Orders

Ma hi *(Mah Hee)* - What is she

Natye *(Naht-yay)* - No

Čist *(Shisht)* - Derogatory term for the Mithra

Sa'aqum 'ida laem tafeal *(Sah-cuhm ih-da lay-em tah-fa-hyell)* - I will kill them if you didn't.

Sayyid- Master

Ghabuin *(Gah-shun)* - Idiot

Ant hurun.aid tulum-*(Aunthu-ruhm. Aiid tuh-luhm)* - You are free. Kill them.

Sho byaal hon *(Shoh bee-ahl hone)* - Her kind isn't welcome.

U tebya umy roht *(Ou teb-yah uu-mee roht)* -You have a smart mouth.

Dreske *(dreh-shkeh)* - Derogatory term for shifter

Asmaht *(Ah-sh-maht)* - Shut your mouth

Altajue walaisla *(Alta-sheh Wah-lays-lah)* - Step down

Lay man almun *(Lay man Ahl-muhn)* - It's not possible

Mithrek Morta *(Mithrek Mortah)* - Angel of Death

Hal ant malnunje (*Hahl aunt mahl-nuhn-sheh*) - Are you fucking insane?

Gjóssa

-◇- *Mithra Language*

Glykó skýs (*gl-ee-koh sh-ish*) - Sweet dog

Skotá (*Sh-kot-ahh*) - Derogatory term for the Nephilim

Gamsió (*Gam- ee-sou*) - Fuck you

Majte (*Mah-sh-tsh-yeh*) - Honey

Angeloj (*An-gel-osh*) - Angel

Thélo (*Th-eh-loh*) - More

Boríte nare kánete (*Bo-ri- teh nah-reh kah-neh-teh*) - You can do this.

Ágos ganto (*Ah-gnosh gahn-toh*) - Holy fuck

Pajdí (*Pah-shdi*) - Child

Kóri (*Koh-ree*) - Daughter

Mamá (*Mah-mah*) - Mother

World

Vortex - A way to travel between realms as well as within the realm

Eyrid - coin

Epísmos - Seat of power in Keloseros

Alshaytan - Seat of power in Aljira

Siada - The lords in charge of different Aljiran territories

Nahr Alnufus - the River of Souls

Glimmer - The Fae's ability to travel through space

Shadow - The Avarice's ability to travel through their shadows

Solas -The energy that powers Aljira

Magyck - Both magic used by Brite + Shadow Heretics, as well as the word used to describe different creature's abilities or powers.

PRONUNCIATION GUIDE

Names

Aheia - *Ah-hey-uh*

Arioch - *Ari-ock*

Ophion - *Oph-ee-on*

Lúc - *Luke*

Tariq - *Tarr-eek*

Shiron - *Shy-ron*

Emryn - *Em-rin*

Aylee - *Ay-lee*

Karyme - *Car-ee-may*

Aljira - *Ahl- hee-raw*

Kal -*Call*

Siraj - *See-raj*

Mazikeen - *Maz-eh-kee*

1
Chapter

Aheia

Under the setting sun of the desert, Aheia's fear felt like hot kernels of sand and the caress of impending shadows. She recognized it in the way it gripped her neck and hurtled her heart into a rhythm that had her lightheaded, though the taste on her tongue was foreign. In days past, fear had churned Aheia's stomach like the rotten meat she'd been forced to eat to survive. Before that it had lived in the stale waters of stagnant streams, and yet further back it had sounded like crunching leaves when there shouldn't have been a soul for miles.

She'd learned a lot about fear in her time on the run, discovered how it lay dormant in common places and actions, waiting for movement or thought to jolt it awake. It had been an emotion she knew well, even before she escaped her home in *Keloseros*. A different version of the same invisible monster.

Though she couldn't focus on that now, knew that it would slow her if she did. After all, there was a very real monster, the kind with claws and teeth, sifting through the sand behind her, the kind that would kill her if she let it.

Aheia whimpered, grappling up the side of a dune with her hands, the sand cutting underneath her fingernails as angry tears rolled down her cheeks. She could see the *Varcolac's* shadows drift into view from the corner of her eye and knew the creature was toying with her, though she didn't understand why. Her legs were doing their best, but even at a full sprint on sand that gave way under her footsteps, she was slow in comparison to the being that was part wolf and part ancient *Calmani* magyck. It should have caught her hours ago, but instead, it followed her, the same distance at all times, even when she slowed. It was almost like it was corralling her towards the *Aljira* border instead of trying to chase her away.

She wiped the back of her hand across her eyes, keeping her gaze trained firmly on the shroud that rose in front of her. To most people, the border she was racing towards meant death—the entrance to a realm that dealt in darkness and gambled with souls unapologetically—the place that mortals called *hel*. To her, it was the closest thing to salvation she'd ever seen.

The dark onyx that separated Aljira from the mortal realm bisected the tangerine-painted sky and dark red sands, like a static disruption of nature. The thick wall of magyck and wards coiled and rolled like ominous thunderclouds as if the border itself was alive.

She was so close now that the proximity to her destination coaxed vicious thoughts from the back of her mind. They showed her scenarios of what might happen if she fell into the hands of Ophion's men, the painful death that she'd endure at the claws that sifted through the sands behind her, and relief at the prospect. It was the latter that scared her most because acceptance of death was what preceded surrender. If she gave up now the murder, the blood, the exhaustion... all would have been for nothing.

It seemed as though Aheia's life had boiled down to two narrow paths in front of her: either death in the mortal world on her own terms, or crossing the border to Aljira into a realm she'd been taught to fear. She hadn't let herself consider being dragged back to Keloseros as an option. Never again would she let Ophion lay a hand on her. Never again would she smile when she wanted to cry. Never again would she be so *weak*.

The thought of the bright gleaming streets, the frivolous and decadent parties, and the snakes masquerading as appointed royalty triggered memories that now lived in her nightmares and silent moments of solitude. It was as if the past loomed just behind her, and whenever she moved, it moved right along with her, just as ready to rear its head as her fear.

The thick blood that haunted her nightmares dripped onto the sand in front of her, marrying reality with her past in a way that had her struggling for the truth.

There had been so much blood in her short life, the good tainted by the bad long ago. It left her unable to separate the memories she held close to her heart from the looming darkness and cold, frigid ice she carried in her veins. The two things, good and bad, had coalesced into something gray and opaque while time slipped through her hands, as she lost track of its passing.

Aheia was only 28 in mortal years, but the immortality that she was born with made her life up to this point seem like it had passed in the blink of an eye. Though she'd never minded time before, never noticed how slowly or how quickly it moved. Not until now, now that she spent her days running from Ophion's bounty hunters. Now it felt important. Now time was the only thing that mattered. The strands themselves had her trapped in an hourglass, fighting against the onslaught of granules that were threatening to bury her with every passing moment.

Aheia strained to push up on her hands, looking up towards the edge of the sand dune. The blood had disappeared–though she knew it would always follow her–only to be replaced by an ominous cloud of shadows that drifted into view, blocking out the sun. Aheia ground her teeth together, silent tears streaming down her face as she struggled to her feet and continued across the desert, the Varcolac close behind.

The air burned her throat and strained her chest as she gulped down oxygen, willing her lungs to do their job. The heat pressing in around her was stifling, teasing beads of sweat from her hairline that ran down her neck, chapping her lips and cracking her skin. It was a foreign feeling compared to the winter she had left behind in her realm, but so was the mania, so was the exhaustion, and so was the person she'd become.

Her knees buckled as she tried to clear another red dune, her feet slipping just enough to throw her to the ground, the sand sticking to the cuts on her skin.

Give up.

The words in her mind shifted at the first sign of failure, sounding every bit as tired, desolate, and hopeless as she felt.

Just give up.

It was as if she wanted herself to fail, the darkness in her veins whispering lies into her ear. She knew they were lies, had heard them before, but it was hard to remember their duplicity when the words sounded so sweet.

It would be easier if you just let it eat you.

It was a strain to make herself accept otherwise, to tell herself that she could make it... that she couldn't give up now.

"No," Aheia ground out against her own self-deprecation.

I will make it. Crossing the border is enough. I will be safe there.

The distance between Aheia and the barrier slowly broke down to mere breaths as she ran, her feet screaming, her joints aching, her lungs straining in her chest as the border became so close she could see her reflection in it.

Her image shifted as if she'd stirred up a placid liquid, the ripples running over the surface over and over again, pulling her reflection apart. The *Dioscuri* in front of her was distorted, her features moving with the dark swirls until the magyck pieced her back together.

Aheia stretched her hand out, fingers grazing against the magyck just as pain blossomed in her ankle and her body was jerked down against the ground. The impact left her sputtering, choking on kernels of sand while gasping for air. She looked down to find the Varcolac's teeth buried deep in her skin, red blood running together with the dark sand underneath.

Aheia couldn't scream, couldn't find her voice amidst the pain, gasping down air so quickly she became dizzy. Her body slid against the sand, the granules scratching over her arms as dark, cracked claws pulled her further from the border, hope dwindling in her mind with every passing moment.

You're done. You're dead. You're–

"NO!" she rasped, tears falling angrily, kicking and clawing at nothing but smoke that swallowed parts of her body and shielded the creature inside. It hurt, Gods, it hurt. But death would hurt worse, and she couldn't get this close only to fail. This wouldn't be her downfall.

I'll never be weak again...

She threw the words around her mind with a vengeance, adrenaline surging in her veins as she sunk her hand into the inky blackness in front of her, trying to find purchase in the shroud. Her fingers seared as if she was holding her hand over an open flame, agony eating at both ends of her when the shadow creature bit down harder. She pulled herself forward, fire crawling up her arms, the pull on her legs threatening to tear her in two.

"Gods, please, no!" she screamed, twisting her body, almost up to her elbows into the next realm. The pain was blinding, her vision pulsing with slow red lashes that obscured her view in dizzying intervals as the Varcolac screeched.

It was that momentary reprieve, the creature letting go of her leg, which gave her the opportunity to force herself further, feeling her numb fingers slide against rough stone. The border swallowed her forearms, then her shoulders, and she inched into the darkness in front of her, the fire searing her skin.

"Someone." It was a whisper. A plea. A prayer.

She continued, her head pushing through the barrier, her eyes closed tight.

Breathing became impossible.

The screams choked up in her throat.

Her tears evaporated the second they hit her cheek.

At least I'll see her again.

Her heart wrenched in her chest at the new acceptance that settled into her bones. If this killed her, she'd see Andromeda, her mother, again; something about that realization eased the pain. After all, it was only physical. Physical pain she could bear. She'd borne it all her life.

The angry red lashes that streaked across her vision were pulsing violently, breaking up the complete darkness that surrounded her.

I miss you.

Her mind stuttered, teetering on the edge of reality, swaying over a dark abyss that seemed to be calling her name, when the pain suddenly stopped. The invisible fire vanished from around her as air rushed into her lungs, and her leg throbbed in agony. She groaned, curling on her side, blood hot and wet running down her calf as she peeled back her eyelids and promptly wished she hadn't.

Of course, the monster could follow her into Aljira. *Of course.* She had been so desperate and so tired that she hadn't given much thought to what would happen after she crossed the border. She tried to blink away the red haze, her fingers scraping against solid ground as she scratched her way forward.

Not like this. I won't die on my knees.

Aheia looked over her shoulder at the creature, watching it crawl through the shroud ominously, the magyck dripping around it like a waterfall. She put more space between them, the pain in her leg a reminder of what the Varcolac could do, of what it would do. She pushed up onto her feet, her joints aching, the wound at her ankle throbbing with each movement.

Her footing was unsure as her injured leg gave out under pressure, the ground shifting beneath her with every step. She couldn't see anything past her own hand in front of her. She could only feel–feel the panic, the smoke on her legs, the way her lungs burned–until suddenly, a new warmth engulfed her. It didn't burn the same way the magyck of the shroud had, but it stung her wounds enough to draw a hiss from between her lips.

She blinked her eyes slowly, the darkness around her thinning slightly, penetrated by soft amber light. Her feet found new ground, strong and sturdy under her, as the warmth seeped into her body, stroking over her cold center. She groaned, the pain in her leg bringing her to her knees again, the crack of bone against rock filling the silence around her as her bruised, dirty fingers dug into grouted stone for support.

"*Athiran.*"

A deep accented voice wrapped around Aheia's shoulders and squeezed, forcing her eyes from the ground in front of her, as her hand slipped with surprise. She gasped softly, looking around for its source as the sound of one simple word sank into her skin.

She was met with a stare that spoke of burnt secrets and gray ash, eyes that were flecked with embers, dark and angry. His gaze felt like a touch, like the rough slide of hands against her skin and the promise of tight grips and harsh words.

Her mouth went dry as she took in the *Nephilim* in front of her: the leathers he wore tucked into his boots, the black shirt, and the dagger-studded holster he had slung across his chest. His blades were black to match all the other dark elements of him–the curls that fell across his forehead, the eyelashes that framed those striking eyes, and the ink that painted his skin. Tattoos wound their way up the side of his neck and his arms, tapering down his fingers, and they reminded Aheia of shadows–she wondered if the art continued across the rest of his body.

She swallowed, pushing back onto her heels with a sudden need to gather herself. Settling onto her feet, she straightened up as best she could, taking a step forward. He watched her, his attentive gaze making her eerily aware of her movement, as she tried to put as much strength into her uninjured leg as she could.

His stature was just as intimidating as his stare: thick arms corded by muscle, hands big enough to close around half of her ribcage, and fingers adorned with half a dozen rings that looked forged in hot fires. And yet, it wasn't his size that filled the space between them, it was something in his presence.

It was dark and commanding and made her wish for real clothes, a step stool, and the powers she'd been born with. But instead of finding light at her fingertips, she found nothing but shadows on either side of her, with no way out.

The Nephilim tilted his head slightly, his muscular arms crossed over his chest, his stare making him look every bit the predator his exterior suggested.

She trailed her gaze over the hair he had pulled into a loose bun at the nape of his neck, and across his shoulders, noticing shadows stuttering from underneath the fabric of his shirt. It looked like fog on a lake in the hours just before sunrise, soft tendrils seeping towards her and whispering across her skin.

An Avarice

This Nephilim wasn't just another *Leviathan*, but a demon that could bend shadows to his will just like Dioscuri could bend light.

Her heart hammered in her chest, the danger at her back feeling like a faraway thing as she stepped closer, drawn in by his gaze. She was intrigued by something that lingered behind his eyes–past the flecks of orange that made his stare scorching, past the gray getting swallowed by his black pupils, past the anger she found there. He looked at her as if her very presence offended him, and for the first time in a long time, she felt the heat–heat she'd chased all of her life and never had much success holding on to–creep into her cold limbs.

It licked up her entire body as the Avarice watched her, his gaze so heavy she didn't know how long she could bear it.

"Will you help me?" she asked her mind losing grasp on reality with the amount of blood she'd shed.

The demon in front of her curled his lip as the Varcolac slowly closed the space between them.

2

Chapter

Arioch

He had, of course, heard the rumors of the *Mithra* royal from Kelo-seros: a thankless Dioscuri brat, on the run from her dear family. At least, that's how they'd framed it. Whispers had traveled through his court, but he hadn't paid them much attention. Not until the whispers turned loud, telling stories of evasion, murder, and unimaginable travels. It had piqued his interest enough to start paying attention when news of a bounty reached his border. Ophion was offering a gross amount of *eyrid*, which might have enticed others, but Arioch didn't need coin, nor would he ever work with those Mithra *Čist* after what they had done to his family.

He didn't think she'd make it, frankly. He didn't think she would clear the Red Sea; didn't think he'd see her in his Borderlands alive. But when he was proven wrong—which didn't happen often—he began watching her. There was something about the intensity that he saw in her pale blue eyes, even in the face of danger, that made him want to find out what made a privileged little goddess run so furiously and endure so much pain.

He'd sent one of his Varcolac after her, the kind of creature that made people scream and beg for mercy, because of a singular thought that pulled at his mind.

Will she falter in the face of death?

Arioch was delighted when she didn't. No, she hadn't faltered, nor had she turned back, even when he'd given her a chance to, staggering the shadows just enough to give her room to evade them. But instead of receding towards the Neutral Lands, she'd run towards Aljira, looking at his border like it held her deliverance. No one had ever looked at his realm quite like that.

Aheia stood across from him now, holding herself steady as her right leg bled. He watched the deep red *drip, drip, drip*, onto the rock, the shadow magyck that slithered underneath his skin writhing at the sight.

The prospect of toying with the little Dioscuri shouldn't have riled him like it did, but the fact that he saw hope in her eyes–hope as she stared him down from her small stature–was delicious. He wanted to crush that hope, wanted to smother it in his shadows until she realized that she'd made a mistake coming here, until he saw the fear in her eyes in recognition of who he really was.

The fact that she'd sought his realm screamed of desperation, it told him she was out of options, and had found herself facing her very last one. She'd ask him for a favor–they all asked for favors–and he'd grant it to her, for a price.

And then he'd play and see exactly what she meant to Ophion. There was a reason she ran, and there was a reason the Malek, the winged verities that held power in Keloseros, had her chased. Those blue eyes of hers had half of Lyria after them, a little goddess fallen from grace, and he knew they'd come knocking eventually.

On top of that, it wasn't just the balance between Aljira and Keloseros that he'd be fucking with, but the frail politics in his own realm on top of that.

Though the conflict it would cause to have her stay with him might just be worth getting to twist her up into tiny knots and dangle her out of Ophion's reach.

"I need a favor," Aheia whimpered, the noise stroking down his spine as if she was running her Gods damned fingers across his skin.

"Do you, now?" His lip quirked slowly as he watched her limp closer, her eyes pleading.

Arioch willed the Varcolac in tighter, watching her response carefully. It was calculated, all of it. The chase, the taunt, the pain. He needed her fear of what lay behind her to be greater than what she faced in front of her.

"I don't deal in charity."

"I have eyrid." Her hands shook as she unfastened a pouch at the side of the piece of cloth that was barely holding onto her body. She uncinched the top, wavering slightly on her uninjured leg, the pain threading into her focused expression. The pouch yielded a few pieces of coin, as well as bright white and blue crystals, all of which might have enticed a Nephilim that wasn't him.

He took a step closer this time and picked up one of the jewels, turning it over in his fingers before dropping it back in her hand. "No."

Her eyes widened, but it wasn't the fear that caught him off guard. It was the anger.

"What do you mean, no?" She cleared another step. "My payment is as good as anyone's."

Arioch raised his eyebrows and let his expression fall into soft amusement. "I don't want your jewels." He gave her a slow once-over, and then looked behind her at the shadow creature that he'd halted in its tracks, just for a moment. "You know the way out."

Then he turned on his heel, his body buzzing with awareness at her every movement. She needed to be pushed further, clean across the edge of reason that protected her from the request he was about to make.

The Dioscuri behind him shifted, and he heard a soft noise–not quite a whimper, not quite a groan–but every bit of it enticing. He wanted to see her face the next time she made a sound like that.

"Wait!"

He stopped and looked over his shoulder.

"I'll do anything." She shoved her treasures back into the leather pouch and cleared another step, only an arm's length away from him now. "I'll give you anything."

Arioch looked away, keeping his features neutral as his creature growled from somewhere behind her. He let the moment drag, knowing she'd squirm for him before his eyes found hers once again. Damn, if she wasn't tempting... He wanted to see what it looked like when she truly begged, and imagined it would be so fucking pretty. The thought stroked a sadistic part of him as he watched the raw emotions threading her delicate features–so bright and pure, so absolutely ready to be corrupted. It was sweet, the naivety in it all, that she didn't consider him to be the monster behind the shadows.

"You don't know what you're offering." His voice was lower than he'd intended, his accent pulling at his words.

She swallowed.

"I just... I just need a favor." Her jaw clenched, and she dropped the leather pouch onto the rock next to her, loose coins scattering across the ground. She was losing blood fast, he could see her eyes glazing.

"You'll give me anything?" he asked, his voice thick.

Her lips parted, and for a moment, she considered. The seconds dragged long enough for Arioch to coax the Varcolac in further, a vicious growl sounding from within the black mass. She squeaked, closing the distance between them, her hands grabbing onto his shirt as if she might try to crawl inside it and hide. He could feel her knuckles brushing against his chest through the fabric, her forearm against his abdomen, her body so close that the air between them simmered. The shadows under his skin slithered–they wanted to touch, and he did too. So he wrapped an arm around her waist, his fingers fanning out over her ribcage. She was frighteningly small and cold … cold like the dead. And for a brief second, he wondered what it might take to warm her.

"Answer," he growled.

He was not patient, not after he'd watched her run for so long.

"Anything." she said finally. His lip curled.

"A soul bargain," he said calmly, relishing the shock on her face.

"No," she whispered, her eyes widening, "anything else… I…"

"I don't want anything else from you," he said, toying with the end of her braid.

She looked at him in disbelief, as if he'd just snuffed out the last hope she had.

"Go on." He tilted his head slightly, waiting for her to deny him, for her to take her chances with the Varcolac. He was curious to see if she was smart enough to realize that the only route that would result in freedom for her would be death. Turning back meant facing whatever she was running from, and agreeing to his terms meant giving herself to him.

"It's hungry," he drawled lazily, nodding towards the monster, "and who am I to deny it its well-earned prey?"

Something fierce flashed in her eyes.

Interesting.

"My soul …" she said hesitantly, tasting the words on her tongue, "in exchange for…"

"Anything you like," Arioch murmured, wrapping her braid around his fist once, twice.

She swallowed, something unnamed tearing at her features, something dark and conflicted.

He pulled on the white strands of her knotted hair, tilting her chin towards him as she grit her teeth in a deliciously defiant way.

"Yes, *your soul* ... or you can take your chances with what lies beyond the shroud." Cold indifference laced his features while fire sparked under his skin.

"Asylum," her words were frigid, just like her eyes as she stared up at him, the fear he'd seen moments ago tucked safely behind contempt, "and the promise of safety."

He ran his tongue along the bottom of his teeth. "You'll be safe."

Tsk tsk tsk, little goddess. You have to be specific, or you'll give me all the power...

"Is that all?" He raised an eyebrow, waiting for her to stipulate a time frame, knowing that if she didn't, he'd get to choose for her.

She swallowed, sparing his Varcolac one last look, before she gave the barest of nods.

"Use your words. Tell me your soul is mine," he growled watching a thin line twitch between her eyebrows, full of anger and spite.

"My soul is yours," she managed through clenched teeth, while ice frosted the edges of her irises.

He tightened his hold on her braid, tipping her head back until her neck was bare and straining. Her eyes stared past him with cold resignation, refusing to meet his gaze, which made the challenge even sweeter. He didn't need her eyes, just her mouth—even though some fucked up part of him wanted both, wanted her to watch exactly what he did to her.

Her nostrils flared as Arioch unraveled the braid from his knuckles and slid his hand over her jaw, the pressure of her hair still imprinted on his skin. She was close enough for her to share his exhale, and when she did, he felt something writhe from a place past his bones, a place that would have held a soul if he'd had one. It thrummed against the silver strings of fate that were woven into his very being, a feeling that reared its head every time he took a soul.

He bit past it, the discomfort of it, because when those cold eyes ignored him like that, he couldn't entirely focus on anything else. The resolve was so bright in her gaze, that it made him want to find out what it took to break it.

Her soul was his.

His.

The shadows under his skin simmered with excitement as he leaned in closer. This wasn't part of the process, but he couldn't resist, leaning the bridge of his nose against hers and sliding his tongue over her bottom lip slowly. She went rigid in his arms as he tasted her down to her cells.

Achlys and honey.

He breathed her in, wondering what a privileged Keloseros runaway had locked away inside herself that made her taste like death's flower and the Gods' nectar.

"I've always wondered what a Dioscuri tastes like," he murmured, tugging her closer.

He slid his thumb over her bottom lip, parting it slowly, before touching his mouth to hers. A noise escaped her, a soft kind of whimper that made him want to tease other sounds from her.

He couldn't help the hand he slipped into her hair as he lingered.

Lingered for too long, closing his teeth around her bottom lip, *just a taste*, as he pulled her into his mouth and ran his tongue over her.

She stayed still, her heartbeat bruising her ribs. Each torturous beat sent a pulse up through his fingers and down his body, while a heavy heat settled in everywhere he didn't fucking want it.

Move away from this.

He pulled her closer instead. And to his surprise, she melted against him, the hand she had on his shirt tightening. She took his air like it was a life force, her breathing shallow as her lips started to move. He let her kiss him back, soft and timid, every part of his mind imagining how that mouth would feel on the rest of his body as he felt the wet glide of her tongue.

Hot.

Wet.

A fucking headache waiting to happen.

The last of his thoughts slipped from him as their tongues slid across each other in languid, lazy strokes. It was honey and ash, fire and flowers, everything good and bad rolled into one delicious mixture. Until, suddenly, something sharp cut through the haze. Arioch hissed as her teeth clamped down hard, breaking his skin in a hot flash of pain.

He tightened his grip on her hair until she groaned and let go of his lip, chest heaving, and mouth stained with his blood. Arioch clenched his teeth, tasting metal on his tongue, an intoxicating brand of anger and something more sinister twisting around his neck. He stared down at the Dioscuri, her eyes blazing with cold fire that he imagined would blister skin if exposed to it for too long.

Good girl.

The thought grated across his mind unintentionally. She wasn't going down without a fight, and Arioch found a smile tugging at his bleeding lip in approval.

This is going to be fun.

"Gods help me," she whispered doing her best to hold back the trembles.

Flames licked at Arioch's skin, something angry and cracked brewing inside his chest as he heard the plea for divine intervention. He scraped his teeth along his bottom lip, reining in the control that once again threatened to tear itself from his grasp.

"I'm the closest thing you'll find to a God down here," he growled before dropping her to her feet, anticipation coiling every part of him. He grabbed ahold of her hair and her mouth opened with the pain, just enough for him to draw her into a bruising kiss.

He could feel the shadows coaxing her soul, calling to it, whispering to it... separating it from the very fabric of her being. She choked, fighting for air, fighting for the thing that he was stealing, as one quickly became two. She writhed against him as the first drops of her soul breached her throat, grasping his chest for support as she endured inch by inch of the discomfort. It only took only moments for the bright essence to spill across his tongue, lacing itself into his very being. A shudder ran through them both as her soul shifted through her body and flowed against his lips, cold and harsh, like peppermint.

Fuck, she tasted right.

His body lit up as she settled into his pull, her soul dripping down the back of his throat and into his bones. He felt it move through him, leaving a line of ice behind as it shifted from his neck to his shoulders and down onto his right forearm, finally settling in just below the crook of his elbow.

He broke apart from her, his vision flickering slightly as her tired body slumped in his arms. Her soul was burning into him, so much brighter than any Nephilim's soul ever had. She was still fighting, even now.

He looked down at his arm to find a glyph there, a flame perched on a crescent moon, the soft white outline of it standing out against his dark ink. His jaw clenched as her essence wove itself into every fiber of his being, interlacing itself in his shadows and replacing that hollow ache that came from living with the lack of a soul.

He ran his tongue across his bottom lip, catching every last bit of her taste with one glaring thought that started a slow pulse against his temples.

Death's flower doesn't belong in the outside world. It belongs in mine.

3

Chapter

Aheia

Aheia woke up gasping, the air stinging her throat with a familiar taste. It was clean, but the type that wrenched her insides and reminded her of what a room smelled like after blood and guts had been scrubbed from its floors using harsh chemicals. The taste coated her mouth, making her tongue feel heavy as her chest constricted, a familiar vise that preceded stifling panic. She peeled her eyelids back, looking around the room while nauseating air refused to fill her lungs.

No.

She shot up, her hands grabbing the white sheets that were pulled taut across her body like someone had tried to make the bed while she was still sleeping. They caged her legs down like the very threads were vexed over the disruption of her body against them.

Her gaze fell onto a familiar painting that hung across the room above a familiar white desk that stood next to a familiar gold-trimmed door. The eyes of the Mithra—stroked into existence by a brush that held thickly pigmented oils—were staring her down, venom in their gaze. Like they were irritated at the fact they had to stare at her day in and day out.

No, it can't be.

Aheia reached into her mind, finding memories of shadows and teeth, memories of the tall Avarice, of the pain in her leg.

"This can't be," she whispered to herself, tightening her grip on the fabric tucked around her body, just as echoing steps shattered the silence around her.

Clack. Clack. Clack.

She'd heard that sound many times over, and each time it coaxed fear from the place she tried to hide it. Aheia knew those footsteps like she knew the smell in the air, and the sheets bunched in her fingers. She was back in Keloseros.

The door to her room opened with its unforgettable creak.

Why does the door creak? With all of the ornate gold detailing, why does the door creak?

Her vision started swimming with the effort it took to inhale, as she watched the light from the hall throw a long, thin column across the bed, splitting her down the middle. She scrambled back like the phantom touch of the light would somehow strip her armor and spill her secrets if she let it touch her.

"Aheia, dear." Ophion bled into the room—his wings ducking through the doorway, dressed in all white—with a smile Aheia knew well.

Upon first look, he seemed harmless with his gray hair, neatly trimmed beard, and clean lines. But she'd known him too long, knew that smile covered up the blood that followed his footsteps. His blue eyes sent cold, prickling needles around her neck; the color was too similar to hers, even though genetics had nothing to do with it.

"Good. You're awake."

The Malek was followed by two Dioscuri guards—both clean-shaven, with short hair to match—that looked as if they were born of the same mold, vacant expressions on their faces. They were light creatures, just as Aheia was, though their powers, just as hers, were useless inside of the walls of Ophion's house. He'd put wards into place long before Aheia was born, neutralizing the space. It would have leveled the playing field, she supposed—kept him from caressing her mind within these walls—if he didn't own the board and pieces on it.

"What do you want?" Her voice wavered, and she cursed herself for it.

Don't let him see you like this.

"Watch your tone," Ophion snapped, "is that any way to speak to your father?" he crooned, a sadistic smile spreading over his face.

The Malek had married Andromeda, a Dioscuri, because of the ties it would fasten between their two races, but Aheia was not a product of that union. Ophion wasn't her father, not by blood, and every time he insinuated otherwise she felt a pang of anger in her chest.

If she'd been his daughter, she would have had wings like the children he had with his other wives. If she'd been his daughter, maybe

Aheia's life wouldn't have been consumed by the cold and dark things that snaked through her veins. If she'd been his daughter, maybe he wouldn't have hurt her.

And on days where she lost her will, lost that spark she desperately clung to in hopes of feeling warmth, she found herself wishing she was his daughter. Because then she would have never known a life quite like this.

But her real father was dead, and Aheia had no inkling of who he was. Sometimes she wondered if he could have helped her understand herself. She could have asked him questions; found out if he, too, felt cold; if he, too, felt darkness in his blood that dug into his chest with sharp talons. Maybe his people had left him too, maybe that was another rotten thing that lived inside of them both–a thing so broken and heavy that others couldn't bear it.

Aheia was used to others leaving. Everyone always left. And for some reason, pretending it was something buried deep in her genetics made it feel less like her fault.

"There have been reports ..." Ophion continued, his smile widening. The expression twisted his conventionally handsome features into something unnerving. "You've been seen in the Southern territories again, Aheia. You know you're not allowed to be there."

Her blood froze.

This can't be. It's not real. It's not real. It's not real.

It had to be a memory because she remembered this exact conversation, recalled how he'd visited her after she'd snuck out in hopes of a distraction, thinking she'd been so careful.

"You were seen with one of those lowlife Fae rebels."

Fuck, fuck, fuck.

She was pulled back into her old self, the one who hadn't run across the red sands, the one who hadn't killed to stay alive, the one who had barely survived.

"It makes us look bad."

She had been careful, making sure she was aware of her surroundings, even as she snuck off with nameless bodies and lost herself in the darkness for a few hours. But not careful enough, it seemed.

"I'm sure your informants are mistaken," she said, her voice trembling slightly.

He noticed.

"Do you think so?" he laughed, nails on a chalkboard. "Let's not pretend. You know exactly what you're doing, Aheia, and I'm tired of it. Maybe it's time for a few more days in the glass."

She choked on her next breath, her heart hurtling blood through her like there wasn't enough there to keep her alive.

"No."

It was the ghost of a whisper.

"You need to learn your place." He inclined his chin, looking down his nose at her while he motioned to his guards. They started to move closer, their expressions unbothered. The urge to scream for Kal reared its head, followed closely by shame because there was nothing he could do, and she knew that. Kal–her personal guard that spent the better part of each day with her–had been her only friend here, the only Dioscuri that made her feel like less of a burden. He'd helped her, listened to her, seen her break down completely— he was the only one who felt like family after her mother's passing. But he couldn't be around at night, and even if he was, there was nothing he could do to stop this.

"I can't have you making this family look bad."

Ophion said the word 'family' like a curse, before shooting the Dioscuri a final look. At his signal, the guards went for her–one grabbing her ankle and dragging her across the bed, the other winding cold, rigid confines around her wrists. She whimpered at the way the metal bit into her, writhed against her restraints–even though she knew there was no hope for escape–and ground her teeth down so hard her head started aching. She fought with the fear and urgency of a caged animal, even though she knew it was futile, kicking out and hitting one of the Dioscuri in the shin. He hissed, slapping her across the cheek, the pain hot and fast on her skin.

"Not the face," Ophion said lazily.

She groaned as they fastened the restraints around the bedpost and tightened them until her temple was pressed against the white stone, forcing her to face her *father*.

His grin became serpentine as his left hand toyed with the gold chain on his wrist and his wings twitched. He always fidgeted in these moments, like he wanted to dole out the punishments himself but held back.

The suits behind her shifted.

She heard the fabric moving before she felt the hand on her shoulders prying down her dress to expose her back. Aheia knew what came next because she'd lived this story before, lived it many times. They always came in the night, healed most of the evidence–save for times Ophion wanted her to remember–and then left her broken but pristine come sunrise.

The first lash always left her gasping for air. The pain was sharp, slicing against her back each time the leather met her skin. She tried to prepare herself, tried to brace for it, but Ophion had instructed them to vary their speeds and strengths so that she couldn't anticipate them. The more she fought, the longer their sessions ran. Aheia clamped down her jaw as her eyes burned at the pain, her mind begging for a distraction.

That's when Ophion stepped closer. She refused to make a sound, wouldn't give him what he wanted, as silent tears ran down her face and sweat pearled on her skin.

"So stubborn, *kóri*," he sneered, burying his hand inside his jacket. He pulled a knife from the folds of the suit and balanced it in front of her. The gold showed the reflection of her own blue eyes wide against the blade, unable to hide her fear as he scraped it down her cheek. "Let's see what we can do to ingrain the rules in your pretty little head."

No. No. This isn't right.

Ophion had never gotten involved before, not like this. Her breathing was ragged as he disappeared from view. Aheia pulled on her restraints until her wrists were raw.

No, no, no.

She couldn't breathe, couldn't speak, couldn't think.

And then, she felt the blade digging into the already open wound on her back, and she screamed.

4

Chapter

Aheia

"Wake up." Aheia's lungs flooded with hot air as she gulped and gasped, her throat dry and tight. Nausea squeezed her stomach so hard she tasted the bile in her mouth moments later, forcing her onto her side to avoid throwing up on herself. The vomit burned her sinuses and splattered across a slick, dark surface, the sound of it echoing around her.

Her vision was slow and blurred, like she couldn't entirely rid her eyes of a haze as she rubbed the back of her hand across her mouth, the lingering sour taste churning her stomach.

"Fuck," she murmured in between heaves.

"I'm not cleaning that," an unfamiliar voice said.

"Fuck off, Lúc." An answering growl she didn't recognize either.

Aheia blinked away the dryness to find herself staring at a Nephilim she'd never met, his black shirt soaked in her vomit. Her eyes trailed the ruined fabric up to his face, catching the hints of ink up his neck and along his jawline. It almost blended with his dark skin tone and made his amber eyes stand out uncomfortably bright. His gaze felt intrusive, like he could see every thought passing through her mind, a stern expression carved into his straight features as he furrowed his brows.

"I ruined your shirt," she said wearily, her mind still trying to separate the memory of Ophion from the reality in front of her.

"Your priorities are wildly skewed." His voice was calm as he helped her lay back against a soft, velvety cushion, a callused hand at the nape of her neck.

Aheia's eyes stayed trained on him, watching his every move until a flicker just behind his head caught her eye. She craned her chin to find small orbs lining the dark ceiling overhead that reminded her of dying stars. Each one was its own supernova, collapsing in on itself, consuming and rolling into a void before replacing its edges with new colors that threw a kaleidoscope of light onto the room below.

It refracted across dark marble walls that were etched in intricate detail, gold veins running through them and bleeding down onto the floor. The space itself was big, lined with alcoves broken up by thick, tall columns that were covered with flowers. Aheia thought she recognized the delicate black flora from a book she'd read in Keloseros. If she was right, then these were Achlys, or more aptly named "the flower of the dead". The smell of them was intoxicating and sharp, almost spicy and it mingled with small wisps of incense smoke that rolled off censors hanging around the room. Each one was dark gold and held an intricate design, no two the same. There were jewel-toned couches and chairs that stood against the black marble floor on heavy gold feet that matched gold tables that accompanied every cluster of furniture.

Aheia took a jarring breath, letting her body settle back into the realization that the nightmare she'd suffered was just that: a nightmare. She wasn't in Keloseros. She was... in Aljira.

Her gaze lifted back to the Nephilim in front of her slowly, a strand of dark, braided hair falling into his amber eyes as he wiped a hand on his shirt–dirt, and sweat rubbing off on the fabric.

Her dirt. Her sweat.

Her stomach churned as flashes of hot, red sands filled her vision and pressed into the soles of her feet; she felt how the kernels had burned the cuts on her hands, the blood warm and sticky, the Varcolac's teeth...

She gasped, sitting up in a panic, her fingers flying to her legs in search of the long, bloody gashes she remembered.

She found nothing. No wounds.

No scars.

No evidence of the pain that felt ingrained in her memory.

She opened her mouth intending to ask if the demon had healed her, but as soon as she did, another wave of nausea pulled her under. Aheia braced herself against the burnt orange cushion beneath her and rubbed the heel of her palm into her eyes, feeling a new pain gathering at her temple. It dug into her mind and slithered down her spine, twisting and curling itself into her gut until she was doubling over in discomfort, her whole body throbbing.

Breathing started to feel impossible as her chest constricted like there was a vise being tightened around her ever so slowly. Her eyes started burning as she felt the hollow pressure spread from her chest to her limbs, like a physical reaction to a new emotion that hit her mind in one brutal burst. Sadness.

She shook her head, loose tears falling down her cheek as a familiar lump lodged itself in her throat as if she had just witnessed a great loss, or someone had died even. That's how brutally her heart wept, and the worst part was that she couldn't originate the feeling, didn't understand why. At least, not until the Nephilim in front of her moved from view, and she was left staring at arrogant and irate, ash gray eyes, dark curls, and pensive shoulders. The Avarice from the border was leaning against the back of a wide, green chair that faced a tall fireplace, daggers still slung across his chest, black sleeves rolled up over his forearms. The sight of him pulled Aheia's sadness deeper like her very bones wanted to consume it, the invisible vise tightening once more around her chest. She gasped, clutching at the fabric over her heart.

This was wrong. Something was wrong.

"You'll get used to it, *Ruhí*," a shadowed smirk tugged at one side of his lips, "your soul needs some time to settle."

And as if on command, her body gave another hollow echo that vibrated through every fiber of her. The realization clawed its way through the tightness in her chest and settled between her ribs in a punishing loudness that wouldn't let her ignore it. Her reality came crashing down around her, as she stared at him, remembering his lips, the pain she'd felt as he pulled her soul from her body, the panic in her veins.

It was longing—that's what Aheia felt. Something inside of her was missing, and her heart was mourning.

"You feel good on me." His voice was black velvet cut by sharp knives, his thumb skirting the edge of a white glyph on his forearm.

My soul.

She stared, her lips parted, mesmerized by the bright outline as his tan, fingers caressed the skin just outside of it, silver rings glinting against the orbs shining above. Her body jolted forwards, her hands clamping down on the cushion underneath her as an unwelcome spark ran down her spine. She dug her nails in so tight that her knuckles became white, fighting against the way her body responded to his attentions, hot, wet air pushing from between her lips. Her teeth clamped down hard, grinding against each other in an effort to hold onto the sadness and anger that started to slip from her as he replaced it with something else entirely.

"I shouldn't have..." she choked, her breath hitching. Another swipe across the soft white outline had her rubbing her thighs together, shame gripping the back of her neck as an ache settled between her legs.

What have I done? she thought, battling between the realization of her actions and the glaringly obvious. She'd been so tired, so afraid—she'd been dying; she had given up her soul with little to no bargaining. She hadn't asked any questions, hadn't resisted—not how she should have.

What is wrong with me?

"No, you shouldn't have." His tone was sharp and irritated.

"Am I dead?" she rasped.

Another swipe, a heavy weight settling in the pit of her stomach.

"That's ... a complicated question."

"Who are you?" she asked through gritted teeth, melting further and further into the couch beneath her.

"Even more complicated."

"Are those the only words you know?" she snapped, seizing a moment of strength and forcing herself to shaky legs before she'd drown in the cushion.

He gave her a dark chuckle, the sound of it shaking her insides as if it had somehow seeped into her skin as the embers in his eyes flared, promising a fire that would burn her.

Mistake.

"Careful."

It was that word that pulled her mind from the madness he was pushing her towards and spiraled threads of cold ice through her body. She'd heard that warning before, over and over again in Keloseros, and it was the anger at that simple command that had her closing the distance between herself and the Avarice. "Or what?"

Mistake.

"Or I'll have to take your mouth, too," he said calmly, though she thought she saw that fire flare in the depths of his eyes as he moved his hands onto the back of the chair he was leaning against. He was a picture of bored arrogance, though Aheia knew it would be foolish to think that the facade he gave her now was anything but a mask that hid the darkness, the blood, the shadows he possessed.

She took a shaky breath, hating how he noted it, hated how it betrayed the strength she tried to portray. But the aftereffects of his touch were still fading, mingling and mixing with the sadness that hurtled back, the two conflicting feelings rolling into each other, cresting and breaking like a wave until she couldn't tell which was which. She was furious–furious with him for possessing her soul, furious with herself for giving him what he wanted, furious with her mother for dying, furious with Ophion for killing her. She wanted to scream, wanted to scratch and claw and hurt, because she was in pain, and she needed someone else to feel it with her.

"*Skotá.*" The insult they used for Nephilim in *Gjóssa*, the Mithra language, felt hot on her tongue as she imagined doing so much more than curse.

The Avarice in front of her took her in slowly, cracking his neck and rolling his shoulders like the word hadn't affected him in the slightest. His eyes, however, suggested otherwise burning through her with an intensity she'd only seen on the bright pyres they burned on holy days to honor Aether.

She swallowed.

Mistake.

"You're angry," he said, the voice of a predator. Then before she could move out of his way, he shot his hand towards her, winding his fingers around her throat until she choked. "It's sweet."

His tone dripped down her body like warm and thick honey, wrapping her in hot need for more of the sound. It felt good, being this close to him, too fucking good. But it wasn't *her* that needed him close like she needed air to breathe; it was the bargain between them, the piece of her he held in his grasp.

It felt like her soul was calling to her and would do anything to be back inside of her body. *Anything.*

She curled her fingers into her palm until the feel of her nails distracted her from the ache pulsing between her legs. The effort of this shook her arms, but it was worth the pain cutting through the confusion in her mind like a knife, letting her glimpse whispers of reality. Unfortunately, her reality wasn't any more enticing than the lie building around her, though the feelings that bordered the pleasure her soul forced into her mind were easier to digest, because they made sense. The disgust she could handle. The anger she could handle. Disdain she could handle. Whatever had been forced between them with their bargain, she couldn't.

Her eyes filled with tears as she looked anywhere but his, that gaze too heavy. She wasn't used to weighted gazes, to stares that were anything but shallow. The room held no answers as she looked around, one Nephilim leaning against the wall with a blood-curdling grin on his face, the one wearing her vomit lounging in one of the tall wingback chairs. What would they do if she screamed, if she tried to run, if she fought? And it felt like she should, even though she had no idea what she'd do after. It wasn't like she could escape, nor was she here against her will, which somehow made it all worse, propelling self-deprecating thoughts through the fragile landscape of her mind.

"Go ahead and scream, *Your Grace*," the Avarice said as if he'd read her thoughts, a low and angry rasp as he leaned in close and squeezed his hand. "They'll enjoy it just as much as me."

Your Grace. No. No. No.

"You know who I am," she managed, small navy circles dancing around her vision as breathing became almost impossible.

"Yes, *Aheia*, I know who you are. It seems that I have the advantage since your careless words can only mean you have no idea who you're dealing with," he continued. "No one speaks to me like that in *my realm*." He bared his teeth, a breath away from her. "Not if they value their life."

My realm.

The realization settled into her bones.

His realm.

Her lips parted.

She had thought him a guard, someone who watched the border. But he was the furthest thing from.

He was *Alshaytan*.

She'd heard about him from secondhand stories. Her blood chilled as she met the fire in his eyes and the singular thought wrapped around her throat alongside his hand.

You gave your soul to Arioch.

Her knowledge was light, but what she did know was that he was Ophion's equivalent in Aljira, that he was the gatekeeper of Gehenna, and he was oftentimes referred to by mortals as *Mithrek Morta*.

The fact that she was staring up at Alshaytan should have scared her. She braced herself for the feeling that would dry her throat and jump start her pulse against her ribs, but all she was met with in the now-hollow space next to her heart was anger and loss.

"Your mistake is assuming the threat of pain scares me," she ground out, the familiar darkness in her veins coating her skin as she spoke.

The silence between them was charged, his grip on her neck tightening for a moment before he spoke with eyes black as the onyx of the border.

"Disrespect me again."

It was a challenge.

"Respect is earned," she gasped, her toes barely touching the floor.

"Not when you're in my home, begging for asylum."

"I will never beg for you," she growled.

He grinned like he knew a secret she could never understand. "You will if you want to stay, Ruhí."

"We had a deal."

"I held up my end. I promised you asylum and safety from my Varcolac, but the amount of time I allow is in my hands."

My Varcolac.

Fuck, of course. If he was Alshaytan, the monster that had chased her through the Borderlands was his, directed by him, corralling her right into his waiting arms, as he pretended not to care less about if she handed over her soul.

Gods, this is fucked.

He'd hurt her.

He'd *really fucking* hurt her.

And that wasn't the part that confused her but rather why the hel he had bothered. She didn't understand why he'd gone to the lengths he had. Why pursue her like that when she was already running towards Aljira on her own accord? Was it to toy with her, simply because he could? To hand her over to Ophion and get whatever reward she was sure he'd already offered anyone who would bring her back?

"Gamsió, skotá." Fuck you.

His eyes lit with a hidden smile that didn't reach his lips. "Filthy fucking mouth, Ruhí."

"Don't call me that," she spat, without knowing what it meant. "That's not my name."

"You're in no position to make demands," he said, finally letting go of her neck, her body crumbling, her legs weak as she gasped for air, her fingers caressing her sore throat.

"What does a brat from Keloseros have to do for the kind of attention you're commanding? Why are they offering such a high price for that pretty little body?" He leaned back against the chair, crossing his arms.

"Are you going to turn me in?" she managed, pushing at her emotions until she could fold them into the dark corners of her chest, trying her best to negate the panic that was starting to prickle cold heat across the back of her neck.

"That depends on you."

Hope slipped between her fingers and dripped onto the floor. "Ask me nicely, Ruhí ... I've seen your claws, and I'm not sure I care to have them digging into my back for the entirety of your stay." His lip tilted into a smirk on one side. "Let's see how sweet you can be."

"You're disgusting," she spat. "You sent your monsters after me, just to pretend that asylum here would require a price when all you had to do was give me some time."

The words rolled from her lips quickly and coated her skin like armor. She brought up her hands and shoved at his chest, fury fraying her reasoning. He didn't budge, his face cold and indifferent while her entire body lit up at the contact.

"You knew what was on the line when you crossed over into my territory. Don't act naïve, it doesn't suit you." He ran his thumb over his lower lip, the implications simmering between them like something hot and tangible. "I'm not like the Čist you're used to, Ruhí. That pretty face won't get you what you want here ... and it certainly won't get you anything from me. You're lucky I offered you a deal, instead of taking that life of yours into Gehenna itself, or sending you back into Lyria, which seems to be a fate that scares you more than death ... more than me."

Aheia's eyes flickered to the soft white outline on his forearm, and she couldn't do anything but watch as he caressed the edge of it with his thumb, her body tensing. Her mark looked so small and insignificant against his dark skin, a small crescent married to a flame that was surrounded by the dark inky shadows painted on his arms.

She swallowed, the warmth rolling through her, battling the ice that his words teased from the darkness, frost burn at its worst.

"I'm the thing standing between you and whatever you're running from. If you want to take your chances, fine." He clenched his teeth and directed his next words at the Nephilim behind her. "Lúc, take her back to the barrier."

Aheia whipped her head towards the other demons, watching the one who'd been leaning against the wall push himself away with his foot.

No. Fuck.

Her lips parted as Arioch passed her, his body brushing against hers, little pangs of lightning prickling between them.

"Wait!" She gripped onto his shirt, the fabric warm against her cold skin. "You can't–you have my soul…" Her body wanted to pull him close, while her mind wanted to lash her hand across his cheek.

"I can't?" He tilted his chin looking down at her with a force that had her knees weakening.

She swallowed, the air thinning quickly, "Gods … you're–" she hesitated.

He narrowed his eyes. "Finish the sentence. Tell me more about myself, *little goddess*."

She took a moment, letting the silence simmer between them.

You're horrible.

You're fucked up.

You're a monster.

But instead, she chose her words carefully, the type of sentiment that hid wicked undertones in a proper shell. "You're everything they said you'd be."

She stood her ground as his gaze dragged itself down her body and rested on the fingers she was curling into his shirt.

"One day," he hissed, pulling her hand away as if it disgusted him.

"One month."

"One week." Arioch grabbed her braid and pulled her head back until pain tugged at the base of her neck. "No more."

Aheia clenched her teeth, feeling his words burning into her body like their bargain had written itself on her skin in fire. "And one more thing," he said with another tug that pulled a whimper from her lips. "You know my name. Use it."

Then, he walked out, addressing the bile-soaked Nephilim as Shiron, who promptly followed him; each step he put between them forcing the pull on her chest to surge until a heavy, empty feeling replaced it.

5

Chapter

Aheia

Aheia had to focus to bring her breathing down, didn't know how to still the tears welling up in her eyes as Arioch left, the need to follow him cutting her to her core.

She wanted to claw at his face, but in the same breath wanted to lick across those tattoos on his arms. Her mind was divided, torn between needing to run as far from him as she could and feeling like she might suffocate with each step he put between them.

That's why the tears rolled down her cheeks, why she trembled where she stood, why her skin felt too tight. Her heart was mourning. It had lost the thing that wrapped around it, kept it safe, kept it alive. It was searching, and Aheia couldn't seem to tell it that there was no use.

She wiped her hand across her face, smearing the tears into the dirt that crusted her skin, and turned to find Lúc standing, his elbow leaning against the back of a chair, still grinning, a black blade now in hand.

Aheia ground her teeth until her jaw hurt, focusing on the physical pain because it distracted her from the hollow echo in her chest. That was her usual game–scars on her skin were easier to handle than the gashes inside of her.

"Come on then, princess." Lúc tilted his head slowly, twisting the dagger on the pad of his hand, some of the black, wild hair he had pulled back into a leather strap falling into his thin almond-shaped eyes. His gaze was black, so dark that there was no discerning between the pupil and the iris, yet more expressive than anything she'd seen in the easily dissected Mithra blue eyes. The color matched the ink that swirled around his arms and neck, and onto the side of his jaw and ear on the right side of his body. Glyphs in *Lujha*, the Nephilim language, lined the column of his throat on the left while dark animal claws were painted on the right. They caressed the edge of his jaw, long lines gracing the side of his face and across his ear as if whatever creature was on his skin below the black fabric of his shirt was tearing him open.

His teeth flashed at her as he watched her staring brazenly at the silver he wore in his ears and around his neck, clearly noting how she clenched and unclenched her hands, his eyes darting from her left fist to her right.

"Where?" Her voice was weak and strained as she pushed the words through her teeth, putting as much ice into her stare as she could muster. It didn't matter how small she felt; she'd pretend. She'd pretend that–for once–she wasn't.

He flashed her another grin but didn't answer, his eyes dancing with amusement before he gave her a slow once over, tongue resting in the corner of his mouth, the wide side of his blade sliding across his knuckles repeatedly.

Aheia furrowed her brows, noticing the faint lines on his fingers. "Are you a shifter?" The question escaped her before she could rein it in, a forwardness that, had she let it slip when she was in Keloseros, might have gotten her in trouble. But she swallowed the habits of her upbringing and held tight onto the way she behaved when she escaped into the southern territories and spent time with the rebels instead. She would not shrink back here, no matter how much the demon in front of her unsettled her. He had to be a shifter, and Aheia ventured the guess that whatever animal was living in the art on his body, was what he turned into. Her eyes dropped to his knuckles, to the white thin lines just above, and wondered if his claws would be as black as his fingernails.

"So many questions, princess." Lúc cocked an eyebrow before jerking his head towards the door. "Go."

But she didn't move, just waited for him to lead the way, and even though the defiance was little, it was enough to ratchet her confidence slightly. Lúc rolled his eyes before he left her behind, stepping into the hallway on his right and muttering something in his language under his breath. Aheia kept her strides fast to match his long ones, her eyes drawn to the black bead of blood that welled up on the pad of his finger where the blade of his dagger was perched. She bit the inside of her mouth, imagining the phantom pain of metal piercing her own skin, but when she looked up at his face, she didn't see any discomfort in those dark thin eyes that were trained ahead. They made their way past closed doors and stone statues, Lúc twirling the knife every so often. Aheia counted the rotations. *One, two, three* turns, a slow trickle of blood dripping onto the floor like it was nothing. She envisaged he was no stranger to blood, that it coated his skin frequently, that it slicked back his hair or painted his mouth as he grinned. He looked like the type who used his teeth to fight and like maybe, just maybe, the blood called to him and he responded with relish.

Aheia's gaze was drawn to the paintings hung between the marble slabs, all of them saturated with rich colors that told a story one had to coax from their depths. They were different from the ones Ophion had hung in his house, oil-painted females and males, all of them pasty-skinned, in neatly orchestrated scenes. They were emotionless, whereas the paintings Aheia now roamed her eyes over were anything but. The colors themselves seemed to evoke more feeling than the people in the Mithra paintings ever had. She supposed it was because they told of their history in a clinical way that she never thought would be possible for a painting. If she closed her eyes now, she could picture them: the four gold-lined canvases that linked Ophion's dining room— each one depicting a different moment in time.

She remembered many nights spent sitting at the table, the aroma of bland food steaming around her as she stared at the mural overhead. Thick paint curled itself around the gold chandeliers holding bursts of Dioscuri *Brite magyck*, a slow flicker across the shadowed faces above. It depicted the Malek, angelic verities with thick, white wings that were perched just above the Dioscuri, Aheia's people; the creatures that held light at their fingertips just as she once had. When history talked of Mithra, it spoke of those two species, the most powerful of the Brite beings that lived in Keloseros: The Malek in seats of power and the Dioscuri in the role of the courtiers and enforcers. It rarely spoke of the Fae, the Nymphs, the Shifters, nor any of the other beings that lived throughout the cities and Callay Forests, even though many had given their lives in the early years when the power dynamics had been established.

The Malek spun a narrative that portrayed themselves and the Dioscuri as the highest form, the purest descendants from Aether and Theia, the Old Brite Gods, while any other creature was simply a product of breeding with mortals eons ago. Aheia thought it was bullshit.

But it didn't matter what she thought, nor what most females in Keloseros thought, because they were not meant to think. Though she'd caught glimpses of a different way of life, now and again, amongst younger Dioscuri. She'd often snuck out of Ophion's house after her mother's death, into the southern territories in an effort to distract herself from her own life. What she'd found were exciting new minds, Nymphs, and Fae and Shifters all of which dreamt of a different life.

And for a brief moment, whenever she lost herself in that company, she could see it too. But then she was pulled back to that house, and the way her mind opened was forced shut tight by the gilded cage around her.

It had been those people that had her daydreaming while she was kneeling in the pews of the church at the center of Keloseros, taking in the dry sermon and pretending to pray when instead she wanted to scream, wanted to tell them how jaded she thought their interpretations of old texts were. And they were just that, interpretations. So, she supposed she could be wrong just as easily. Though the segregation that the hands of the High Mithra, the ruling class, forced on those they saw as lesser, couldn't have been the Gods' intentions. It would take a cruel deity to create beings simply for the purpose of existing in poverty and pain. She had to believe that if the Gods were real, another thing she struggled to believe, that they would have wanted a peaceful life for all their creations. That was not what the Malek wanted, and the Dioscuri followed their lead, most of them simply happy to live their cushy lives at the center of the city's elite, while others suffered on the outskirts.

"What are those orbs called?" Aheia asked Lúc, watching the little stars that lined the ceiling of the hallway. In Keloseros they lit the cities using Dioscuri magyck, another reason the Malek had decided to favor them, but this—this was different. Aheia's Brite magyck had always been stark, a light that could blind and burn while this was soft and colorful, like it was pulled directly from the galaxy outside, a hum emanating from it, just soft enough that she caught it between footsteps.

Lúc followed her gaze and lifted his eyebrow. "We call it Solas. It's—" he tapped the blade against his knuckles sifting through his words, "it's energy."

"Where does it come from?" she asked.

"I didn't think you'd be this talkative," he said scrubbing his face.

"I'm hungover as fuck, do you mind?"

"That doesn't seem like it should be my problem," she said, keeping her features neutral.

Lúc shot her a look that statement deserved and continued on silently, winding through different hallways until the interior around them started to change from sleek, black marble to rough, beige stone. It was as if they'd entered into a different world, their new surroundings reminding Aheia of ruins she'd encountered in Lyria on her journey. She half expected to see vaulted ceilings and stained-glass windows but found nothing of the sort as they stepped into a foyer. The room had eight tall walls assembled in a circle, a big fireplace across the way, a boarded-up door to her left, and a grand double staircase on her right. She took in the old furniture around them—cold, hard surfaces covered in dust.

Dust in Aljira, she noted, feeling absurd for thinking that was out of place.

The fireplace appeared as if it hadn't been lit in years, black stains running up the outside where the flames had licked towards the ceiling. Next to it stood an old cart holding empty glass decanters covered in more dust, surrounded by chairs and tables and looking just as forgotten. Lúc walked across the space without explanation, heading towards the stairs that led to a second story. She followed him up the steps and down another hallway, the light orbs dwindling the further they walked until they eventually disappeared. Their sudden absence left them in the dark until they passed into a narrow hallway bordered by windows on either side. The scene Aheia saw when she looked outside stopped her in her tracks.

This isn't possible.

She gaped, looking out over a dark sky peppered with stars and muted swirls of blue and purple that threaded themselves through different constellations. Her gaze traced the twinkling stars down until it caught on a skyline filled with lights and tall buildings—shooting up from the ground in rigid, clean lines—just as dark as the black border.

It was a city that spanned too far for her eyes to follow from her spot at the window, bordered by a wide, iridescent river that separated the buildings from the compound. It seemed so wide that it rivaled a lake, the brightness of it glowing like the water had millions of fireflies trapped within.

Aheia's heart was beating in her throat as she leaned against the glass and looked down at the waves crashing against the black stone below while the water tore on with a fury, like it had somewhere important to be. Her lips parted as she watched, her mind reeling.

She had heard stories of Aljira, but they had been filled with fire, brimstone, and screams—a crumbling city in the middle of darkness, swallowed by flames. But this ... this was something she hadn't imagined in her wildest dreams.

"This isn't real." She felt her head shake while her eyes were stuck on the scene in front of her.

"No, of course, it couldn't be," Lúc scoffed. "Not when your kind have painted such a pretty picture of us monsters and our city."

She shot him a look and caught the tail end of his grim expression, which was quickly replaced by that same smile he wore earlier.

She raised her eyebrow before returning to the sky outside. It was so placid, so calm ... *It can't be real.*

"Do the days look the same as the night?" she asked.

The Shifter exhaled pointedly like he was bored of her line of questioning and nodded tightly.

"How can you tell when you're supposed to sleep?"

He leaned in slowly, grin widening. "I get tired."

She glared, realizing that obtaining any information at all would be a fight. "Why am I here?" she asked, crossing her arms as a chill threaded up her spine.

"A question I should be asking you, no?" Lúc asked.

Her brows furrowed. "Why am I *here*?" she repeated, gesturing to the hallway and running her hand down the old stone, such a stark contrast from the clean, black marble. "This place is different."

"That's not an answer for me to give," he said simply.

Do all of them have that stare? she wondered. It was a look of undivided attention. She wasn't used to being heard, much less paid attention to.

"What is this place?" she gestured towards the city. "This can't be..."

"It's Aljira, princess." Lúc grinned, all of his teeth showing as he flipped the knife in his hand. "Not what you expected?" He leaned against the stone between the windows. "Don't believe the truths told to you by the light. The brightness you're used to casts the most vicious of shadows." Aheia mulled over his words as she followed him.

Nothing here was what she expected.

6

Chapter

Aheia

The hallway Lúc led her down was a dead end, one shabby door breaking up the stone. The Shifter left her in front of it without another word and sauntered back where he'd come from, still twirling his dagger. Aheia stepped inside, closed the door, and leaned her back against it, exhaling everything she'd been holding onto since she woke up in Aljira.

Gods, she still couldn't believe it. She'd made it. Her chest ached as she slid to the floor, the darkness that lived inside of her pulsing through her veins. She was used to its presence, and it wasn't the dark or even the broken parts of her that brought forth her fear. It was the frigid cold she seemed to carry in the marrow of her bones, ice that was worsening every day, stinging deeper as the years drifted past her. It terrified her, feeling her heart freeze more and more with each bruise and every broken command. It had driven her to search for ways to warm herself. It's what pushed her into precarious situations, what had her slipping into dark alleys with nameless bodies, what made her hold her fingers over open flames for a split second too long. But none of it worked, each failed vice leaving her a little colder, and a little more burnt.

The cold always seemed to find her. It found her when she slid across the floor, her dress soaked in her mother's blood, her hands so stiff that she thought her fingers might fracture if she moved them. It found her when she fought to break out of the glass cage that Ophion had forced her into as a corrective measure, her arms threatening to crack up to her elbows. It found her when she stabbed Iaonnis.

That day haunted her more than the rest. It had been the day that the cold had folded its frigid grasp around her chest and squeezed, her memory failing when she tried to recall anything past the ceremony in Ophion's chambers. It was all a fog in her mind. She didn't know how she'd come into possession of the knife, how she'd overpowered the boorish brute in front of her, nor how she'd sank the blade through his sternum.

Aheia's mind snagged on the memory, and her hands shook but she tried to take comfort in the silence as it held her in its palm. For the first time she wasn't running, wasn't listening for footsteps, wasn't looking over her shoulder, and it was overwhelming. The absence of urgency left her enveloped by exhaustion, her body feeling boneless as she let her head rest against the door. There had always been a part of her that was on guard, her life in Keloseros preparing her subconsciously for her run through Lyria. The way she'd listened for Ophion's footsteps in the night had been traded for the way she listened for the hunters, the hooves, the dogs. She'd avoided the Lycans, the wolves that walked in mortal skin, and the *Helren*, who survived off blood. She'd avoided the creatures that lived in the dark forest; she'd skirted certain death over and over again just to run towards it in the end.

She let a long breath slide from her lips, trailing her gaze from the rough stone ceiling down towards a large, black bed that stood in the center—just a simple mattress on dark wood. There were no colorful orbs here, and the only light that lit up the space was shining in from the tall windows lining the far wall. The rest of the room held a small desk in the corner and an old wardrobe, the walls rough and beige like the rest of this wing. Her eyes drifted across the windows, and she watched the galaxies swirling around each other in hypnotizing movements.

The view was not what she'd expected, but not a lot in Aljira was. Even the Nephilim seemed almost civilized when she'd been taught the opposite.

She supposed Arioch wasn't what she'd expected either. From the stories she'd heard, she knew he'd killed his father in cold blood to take over as Alshaytan. Arioch had given Ophion problems ever since he had stepped into power she'd heard as much through closed doors and late-night meetings, but beyond that, her knowledge was fuzzy. She knew nothing more of his family or his motivations, only that she had given him her soul in return for... not nearly enough time. She knew she should have outlined her terms *before* he took her soul, but she had been so tired, so frightened, so drained. Her brain hadn't felt in her control, and something inside of her was ready to beg for any semblance of peace.

Seven days was nothing. *Nothing*. And the voice inside her made sure to tell her exactly how stupid and weak she was for her lack of foresight.

Aheia got up on shaky legs and walked over to the wall of windows, curling herself onto the cushion that rested under it. Her eyes drifted over the landscape below, her breathing shallow. The iridescent river she'd seen from the hallway was running its course on this side of the compound, diving over the edge of a tall waterfall that appeared to plummet into a void, the spray clouding up around the edge, blocking the bottom from sight.

The water reminded her of the one beautiful place in Keloseros, the only place that Ophion hadn't been able to ruin for her: the lakes nestled against the white trees of the Callay Forest.

It was a white reflecting pool said to have been created by Theia, that sparkled if the sun hit it just right. The energy surrounding the peaceful waters was a well-hidden secret; it could slow an erratic heartbeat, or calm tight lungs when the anxiety became stifling. Andromeda had taken her there from a young age and told her to touch the water when she felt cold, when she felt sad, that it would always be their place, no matter what happened around them.

Aheia went back even after her mother was gone, spending countless hours of her life tucked against a tree trunk, toes dipped into the cool liquid while reading her books. She preferred to be alone there, but occasionally she'd dragged Kal out to the spot. He was always pushing the boundaries of Ophion's rules with her and reassuring her that she was strong enough to weather the difficulties she faced within the house. The memories turned dark quickly as the lake in her mind was replaced with the vision of her chamber and Kal prying her from Iaonnis' body, bloody knife in hand, a maniacal laugh on her lips. Without him, she may never have escaped Keloseros.

She curled her fingers around her legs and let herself fall apart for a moment—just a moment—as she brought herself back into the present. Eventually, she'd need to lace herself back up to face what was waiting for her outside of this room, but the darkness in her veins pushed her down and whispered wicked things into her ear about how she'd likely signed Kal's death warrant with her actions.

Tears fell onto her forearms, her chest squeezing uncomfortably. It pulled her mind towards Arioch and her soul on his arm. Her stomach fell, her body prickling with the memory of his hands on her skin, the way he had tasted on her tongue, and how he'd grinned when she was hurting. Aheia tried to focus on the sinister parts of their interactions, but no matter how hard she tried to hold onto her anger, something hot and heady slid down her body. She shook her head as if it would rid her of the ache building between her thighs, a hot betrayal and proof that her body wanted his touch, wanted him close. Her mind wanted the same except it was so she could slit his throat instead. Because the way he was able to make her feel when his fingers ghosted across her soul on his skin made her furious.

Would she always feel like this? Would she feel him like this even after she left his realm?

Pull yourself together. You don't want him like that, she repeated to herself like a mantra as she rose from her spot, opening up the wardrobe across the room and sifting through dark fabrics. The garments were oversized, the same shirts she'd seen Arioch, Lúc, and Shiron wearing, and it made her consider whose room this might be. She resumed her search, pulled out an arbitrary piece of clothing that seemed comfortable enough, and headed through the side door to her right.

She stepped into a large, dark washroom and leaned her hands against the rough, stone vanity on her left, taking in a long breath before raising her eyes to her reflection. The shadows thrown onto her skin made her features look hollow and broken, her face smeared with red sand, her hair knotted into a nest, and the faint scars on her arms and hands pink against her pale complexion.

They'd healed her.

Why heal me when the wounds were created on purpose?

She shook her head, feeling the phantom pain in her legs as she tugged her dress off, never wanting to see it again. It had been one of her favorites, one of the most comfortable dresses she owned, but now it held bad memories within the threads. She shivered seeing herself in the mirror–bare, save for a small holster at her leg.

An empty holster.

The white-hilted dagger—fuck, it had been pretty—had fallen from her grasp days ago. She remembered the exact moment she lost it, fighting against one of the smaller wolves that populated the Black Forest. She'd kept the leather as a reminder, or at least, that's what she'd tell anyone who asked. Because the truth of it was that she enjoyed the sharp way that pain in her leg provided clarity when she tugged the holster past capacity

Aheia undid the buckle, hissing as she peeled away the leather, her skin stinging with an angry, red imprint. The pain felt good. It was real. It pulled her mind from her life for a simple few moments.

She swallowed, taking a long breath, the air still heavy and wrong, like it was fighting her.

"I don't know what to do," she whispered the words into the empty room, staring down at the holster in her hands. She hadn't meant to say it out loud, but the thought had worked its way into her tight chest. "Gods, I wish you were here." Her eyes met her reflection in the mirror for just a moment, pretending the flash of blue was her mother's. "I don't know how to do this."

She felt so alone and so helpless. Aljira had been her goal for a long time, but it had felt incredibly final in her mind–so much so, that she hadn't let herself think about what came after. Now that she was here it didn't feel like she'd hoped it would.

Seven days and then what, Aheia?

She dropped the leather strap to the floor and rubbed the heels of her palms into her eyes until she saw colorful splotches burst against the darkness.

Her brain felt like a jumbled mess, her thoughts straying from the issue at hand. It was like she wouldn't let herself consider her next moves, like her very self was working against her in this.

Why won't you let me think?

Focus. Focus. Focus.

She pulled her hands away and blinked, trying to sort through the voice in her head.

I'm hungry.

Where did the energy go?

Why is it so dark here?

I'm really hungry.

Aheia grit her teeth, giving herself one last look in the mirror. "Tomorrow. I'll think tomorrow."

Her reflection stared her down with doubt in her eyes, but then there was always doubt, always insecurity, always a nagging voice in the back of her mind that questioned every decision.

It was exhausting.

She'd consider her options tomorrow, but for now, she'd try to shut off her brain as much as she could. Aheia stepped into a larger shadowed cavern nestled between what seemed to be a tub and the window, one that looked like a more archaic version of something she'd used in Keloseros. If she was right, there would be some sort of knob she could use to summon water from the ceiling. Aheia padded into the darkness, letting her fingers drift over the rough stone as a guide, thinking about how much easier this would have been if she'd looked for a light source.

But she didn't want to see right now. It was all too much, and if she kept the darkness wrapped around her, she could pretend it was simply one of her dreams.

Her fingers found purchase on slick metal, pushing and pulling until it finally gave way. From somewhere in the darkness above, a soft drizzle of cold water hit her skin. She gave it a moment before stretching out her hand and feeling for the water. It was a thin trickle, enough that within moments her palm collected a small pool, but not enough to clean the sand from her body. She returned to the wall and twisted the knob harder, hearing the splatter on the floor become louder, and the water hotter as droplets landed on her leg. She waited and tested the temperature, stepping underneath the spray when it finally felt warm enough. Her lips parted on a moan and stayed that way as the water ran down her skin.

It burned.

It had been days since her last real washing, and the dirt seemed to have become part of her, only loosening when she used her nails to scrape it off. Aheia felt her way across the other wall to see if she could find anything to clean herself with, using what little light the stars provided. Her fingers discovered a small alcove that held stacked glass containers, which she knocked over clumsily reaching inside. She caught one of them, before it fell onto the floor, and opened the top, smelling a deeply fragrant aroma. She leaned in too close, the tip of her nose dipping into a cold gel, and inhaled a scent of clove and cinnamon.

Aheia wasn't entirely sure if it was soap, but she imagined it was better than nothing as she scooped some out. The consistency of it was cold and glossy but it started to foam as she worked it into a quick lather between her hands and rubbed it over her skin, the smell of it imprinting itself on her body. Her hair was more complicated, and it took her a while to unknot it and get her fingers through the long white strands, pain pinching at her skull with every tug.

After she was satisfied, she turned off the water and stepped into the room, feeling the cold air against her wet skin, and squinted around for a towel, but didn't really care when she came up short.

Wet cold feels the same as dry cold, she thought as she grabbed the shirt she'd found in the wardrobe and pulled it over her head. Then, she left the washroom and let herself sink into the soft silkiness of the bed, not caring that her hair was still sopping wet and dripping water across the satin. She'd felt so incredibly tired, so exhausted, but now that she lay in a bed much too big for her, surrounded by the quiet, she felt awake. She stuffed a couple of pillows around her body and hugged one of them, her gaze drifting to the bedside table.

Sktotá.

The pouch she'd dropped at the border was perched there. Arioch had given it back, in what felt like a taunt disguised as a kind gesture. She pushed the pillows aside and got onto her knees, grabbing ahold of the pouch and loosening it roughly.

The sight of the crystals and gold coins nestled amongst the leather only made it all worse. She'd counted on these to be enough to buy her some time, but instead, they were useless. Her fingers pulled one of the blue stones free, her chest tightening at the sight. It was one of her mother's jewels, the only thing of her that she had left.

Useless.

A tear sprang free, a slow trickle of sorrow amongst the irritation and she lost herself in a moment of anger, throwing the bag to the floor. The contents scattered across the rough stone, her fingers shaking as she held onto the blue crystal.

When the warmth of the anger ebbed, she was left with nothing but the hollow pain in her chest, a cold, broken pain, that pulled her back against the mattress and held her down with unrelenting claws.

7

Chapter

Arioch

Arioch leaned back in his chair, balancing a dark glass that held liquor older than him, in hopes of clouding his mind. He was on edge, more so than usual now that he carried Aheia's soul on his arm. It was fucking intense, the slight little outline burning into his skin like she was fighting her very existence on his body and amongst his shadows. He'd never had a Mithra, and fuck if it wasn't the opposite of what he'd expected.

He was sitting at his desk, trying to focus on the large map that divided Aljira into its territories, but his shadows wouldn't let him stay on task. They seemed to be just as intrigued with the little goddess, keeping up an annoying barrage of whispers in his mind, wanting to feel her pale skin on their tendrils.

He exhaled roughly and flexed his fingers, watching her soul move across his tendons, the distance from her almost worse than the proximity. No one had ever responded to his touch on their outline quite as she had, and it had been almost amusing how she'd tried to hide it behind her anger. The memory of it made his already swollen cock twitch in his leathers. He'd been hard ever since she pushed back, ever since he caught a glimpse of something dark swirling around those bright blue irises suggesting a wealth of secrets she seemed to fight to keep hidden. It went past the fire she spit his way when he toyed with her, something rooted much deeper. He knew because he recognized it, saw those kinds of shadows in the eyes of his demons, and once again he thought that she didn't seem very Mithra at all.

Arioch rolled his shoulders at the glaring reminder of her biology.

It should have deterred him, the fact that she was one of *them*, but somehow it made all of this so much sweeter. He had no plans of turning her in to the Čist, but the idea of ruining her for whatever they had planned coiled the anticipation at the base of his spine tighter nonetheless.

Fuck, he wanted to wrap his hands in that long white hair and force her to her knees in front of him while those angry eyes showed him just how much she hated the idea.

Arioch grabbed a small wooden box that was perched at the edge of his desk, pulling out one of his pre-rolled inhalants and sliding it between his teeth before lighting it. He took a long drag, the smell of Achlys drifting around him as the smoke burned his lungs and relaxed his muscles.

"Fuck," he muttered, sliding the heel of his palm down the seam of his leather, the friction winding his pleasure higher. He was hoping the smoke might help loosen some of the tension in his body though he had a glaring suspicion that it wouldn't. He glanced down at the white glyph, and it was all it took for his cock to pulse. Fuck, the thought alone... He blew out the smoke, his mind buzzing with a new haze when irritation cut through it with a sharp blade.

"For fucks sake." He ground his teeth together, massaging the head of his cock through the thick leather.

It wasn't enough, not nearly.

He bit down on the end of the inhalant and dragged in a long breath, holding it until his lungs screamed and his shadows settled slightly while visions of Aheia intruded behind his eyelids. She was straining in the grasp of his hand, pupils blown out, pink lips parted, and struggling for air while he massaged her neck.

He stroked down the length of his shaft to the thought of her, lust wrapping its hand around his throat as he forced the smoke to stay in his lungs past the point of comfort, until his vision started to border with dark spots. They danced around her pale face while she stared up at him, eyes wide with the realization of how badly this bond would affect her, how completely she belonged to him while she was seated under his skin.

He'd show her, *fuck*, he'd show her.

And with that thought, he exhaled the smoke, his lungs fighting for air, the tension inside of him so tight that he'd break with another stroke. But he forced his hand away from his cock and onto the edge of the marble desk while he raked his fingers through his loose curls, trying to collect himself.

She hadn't been afraid of him, which was either brave or foolish. No, he hadn't seen fear until he mentioned releasing her to the border. He'd find that fear again, and figure out exactly who held it. Her poor mind already struggled with the bond, and with what she was hiding, it wouldn't take much bending before he imagined she would snap beautifully for him.

But he wanted to be the one to do it.

And from what he'd seen, he hadn't been the only monster she'd encountered during her journey. He'd carried her home from the border after she passed out, her head lolling against his chest, thick white hair sticking to her cuts and abrasions that he didn't have a hand in. He felt anger at the thought that anyone but him had had their hands or claws on her. But the emotion wasn't his own, and he knew it was the bond that had his teeth grinding against each other with restraint.

Her soul burned into him at the thought and his shadows pulled, trying to coax him in her direction, slipping around his feet with the promise of a quick trip to her room.

No.

His eyes skimmed the map across the wall, as he stood from his chair needing to busy his mind with anything but the little goddess just rooms away from him. Looking at the territories of his realm did the fucking trick, the equivalent of being showered in cold water.

He thought about Sahren, his father, and the Siada that lorded over different fractions of Aljira, their names scribbled roughly across each territory. The map showed the cities cleaved by faint black lines, the division of each piece of land decided centuries ago. Most of the Siada had been picked long ago, their families passing rule down their lineage, and under his father's reign, they had held much more power than any one Nephilim should. When Arioch changed the laws in Aljira, many of them banded together against him, which made his life a fucking nightmare. Because while Arioch was Alshaytan, he still needed the majority of the Siada to support him to remain in the seat of power. And since he wasn't the only Avarice in Aljira, though his kind was rare, he wasn't the realm's only option as reigning sovereign.

"Arioch," Shiron's voice cut across his thoughts, the Leviathan leaning against the far wall palming his devotional beads. It was a habit for him just as the blades were a habit for Lúc.

"Aylee brought home a stray," he said, his amber gaze stern.

Arioch quirked his eyebrow, pulling the inhalant from between his lips, red smoke curling over his cheeks and into his eyes. "Did she now?"

"Lúc is raring to handle it, but I figured you'd want to hear what this one has to say first."

"I'm sure," Arioch said, giving the map in front of him one last look, before following Shiron from the room.

They stepped through Arioch's shadows to emerge in one of the side rooms of the compound; there were far too many, most of them standing empty only used for shit like this.

Emryn–her black curls fastened at the nape of her neck, wearing her own set of leathers, sleek wings tucked in tight behind her–was sitting next to a female Nephilim. Her red hair was wild and tangled around her shoulders, her green eyes puffy and rimmed in exhaustion. Her tears dripped onto a dirty, beige dress that looked more like a sack, while bruises littered her arms, and dirt crusted her feet.

Lúc was standing at the back of a bound Leviathan, holding his favorite blade underneath the demon's chin.

"Ral," Lúc tutted, before leaning into his ear. "You make sure to look him in the eyes, *ghabiun*, we wouldn't want him to think you were disrespecting him now, would we?"

The Leviathan growled, his dark, dirty hair falling into his eyes. Arioch didn't know him, but the ink at the side of his neck suggested he was one of Bassam's men, which in turn meant he belonged to one of the Nephilim that lived in Siraj's territory.

Fucking great.

Siraj was a Gods' damned thorn in Arioch's side.

"Of course not, because if you did, I'd have to put this pretty blade of mine to good use, and only one of us is excited by that idea," Lúc continued, running his nose up the length of the demon's neck. The grin on his face made him look every bit the jaguar that he kept concealed behind his demonic form.

Arioch slid his eyes down the struggling Leviathan's dirty appearance, and then to the female cowering next to Emryn, her eyes looking anywhere but in his direction.

"What happened?"

"Aylee caught them running through the streets. The girl was screaming for help and nearly naked. But it's Azalam," Emryn scoffed, "so she's lucky Aylee was coming out of Lynx. You know no one else would have fucking stepped in." A disgusted expression pulled at her features.

Arioch rolled his shoulders, anger curling his insides. The southern Azalam territory was on the outskirts of Aljira, and it felt like it was every other day that the Nephilim he had patrolling the streets were coming to him with news of *Nerium*, the drugs that Arioch had long outlawed, or the blood Trade.

"That's a fucking *lie*," Ral said, spitting on the floor while he eyed the female next to Emryn.

"Excuse *the fuck* out of me," Lúc snapped, kicking the demon in the back of his legs forcing him to his knees. "You don't speak unless you're asked a question."

Arioch turned his back to them and crossed the room, crouching down in front of the red-headed female.

She shrugged back into the couch, her breathing erratic as she wrung her hands in her lap, fear plain on her face. Her lips trembled as she watched Arioch reach for her hand and smooth out her fingers, dissecting the bruises on her knuckles.

"Tell me what happened," he said, his voice low and soft.

She gasped slightly, her eyes wide as she looked at him. "I can't." She shook her head, fresh tears falling down her cheek. "Pl–please don't kill me."

Arioch met her gaze, massaging the back of her palm with his thumb. "You're safe here."

"*Safe?*" Her eyes flared, and for a brief moment, that light green turned into a simmering emerald, her entire face shifting from fear to rage. It looked like from one second to the next she'd become a completely different demon. "You're a monster."

He let his stare drop for a moment. "One whose patience is wearing thin," his voice stayed measured. "It seems you have a pick of monsters." He threw a look over his shoulder to Ral who was still glowering their way. "Choose wisely."

When he returned his attention to her, the dark emerald had once again been replaced by something lighter, and her features softened. He furrowed his brows at the quick change.

Interesting.

"I can't go back," she said, her voice so quiet he barely heard.

"You won't."

She seemed to weigh her options for a moment, focusing on their joined hands and then on him, her words hurried as she spoke. "We couldn't pay Bassam's tithe. He—" Her breath hitched, fingers tightening around his. "He's been forcing some of the Nephilim he thinks would serve well into the blood trade." Her expression shattered completely as she struggled to finish. "I got away but there's more of us, he's been increasing tithes and it's nearly impossible for some to pay."

Arioch clenched his jaw, the anger spearing him until he had to work to keep his shadows in check.

"She's fucking *lying*, Arioch. She's just a delusional whore," Ral spit from behind him.

The female had told him everything he needed to know. It wasn't a far reach to think Bassam was pulling that type of shit. As one of Siraj's favorites, he liked to push his liberties.

"See to her, will you?" Arioch said to Emryn, squeezing the female's hand before he dropped it and gathered his shadows behind him. They built a wall between the two sides of the room so that Ral was cut off from the others before Arioch summoned some more at his fingertips and willed them around Ral's limbs suspending him in mid-air.

"You think you can address me like that?" Arioch raised his eyebrow, unclasping one of his daggers and crossing the room while Lúc stepped back from the floating body grinning. He had half a mind to let the Shifter tear into Ral, but he needed to work off some of the misplaced energy Aheia was generating underneath his skin. Ral's chest was heaving, his arms yanking at the restraints, his eyes glistening with provocation.

Arioch smiled, grabbing ahold of the demon's cheeks, forcing his mouth open before sliding the flat edge of his blade over his tongue. He kept it there for a moment, just long enough for fear to bleed into Ral's features, replacing some of that self-righteous fire. Arioch's heart was beating hard, his hand itching to cut, but he waited, letting time drag enough for the demon to question his next move. That's when he dug his blade inside and sliced across the back of his mouth, severing the thick meat of his tongue.

His shadows were pulling the gurgling Leviathan in front of him taut, each limb stretched to its limit as the Ral's mouth filled to the brim with blood and trailed down the sides of his face. He didn't even get a chance to scream, before Arioch tore his tongue from its home and dangled it in front of the demon, seeing the reflection of it in the tears that were blurring those dark irises.

"There," Arioch said, the calm in his voice covering the rhythm of his heart. He threw the slab of flesh onto the ground, the sound of it hitting stone filling the space like a physical presence, heavy and consuming.

He stared down at his hands, distaste pulling at his features. "That's better." He wiped the blade clean against his leathers crudely. "Your voice was grating on my nerves."

His shadows retracted in the next moment, letting the body fall to the floor, the demon convulsing, blood splattering thick and hot across his leather boots. Arioch crouched down, closing his hand over the horror-struck mouth until his palm patched his open orifice like a seal, and the oxygen the demon was fighting for was cut off completely. "I hope you don't survive this," he spat, before letting him fall against the floor, Ral's eyes fluttering with the blood loss.

Crack.

The sound reverberated through Arioch's bones, and stroked down his spine, urging him to finish the job. He wanted to suffocate him, to cut into him further for taking his name into that dirty fucking mouth, but he locked the urge down, rising to his feet and holstering his dagger.

"Take care of this," he said, cracking his neck, watching one of his newer guards rush over, a slight waver in his movements. He shot a look at Shiron and saw him note it as well, giving Arioch a tight nod. Hesitation would not do. And if that demon–now drenched in blood, clamoring to get the body off the floor–wanted to stick around, he'd need to learn that quickly.

"Bring in Bassam," Arioch said, turning to Lúc. "Siraj will need to be there too."

The shifter nodded, his eyes glued to the blood on the floor, a familiar glint there as Arioch's shadows raked across his muscles.

He didn't feel any relief. It wasn't enough.

It wasn't fucking enough.

8

Chapter

Aheia

Aheia was writhing underneath his touch, feeling the soft hand glide over her breasts and down her abdomen. His lips were gentle and tentative on hers while she tried her best to hold back everything she wanted, but couldn't bring herself to ask for. Her hands shook as she struggled to keep them steady, the pace of his body so slow it was almost unbearable. She felt so cold, colder than she ever had, and the Dioscuri courtier on top of her was doing nothing to help warm her with his sweet, feather-light attentions. She became frustrated as her fingers curled into his shirt, urging him further, faster, harder. But he didn't comply.

She tipped her chin up in exasperation and clenched her teeth, burying the back of her head in the mattress as her mind slipped into her own fantasies, trying her best to focus on the Dioscuri's touch. But she felt nothing–no sparks, no fire—nothing. It was the way her limbs hurt with the cold, how it slithered up her arms and into her chest, that made it clear this would be the last time—because this was not what she needed.

He was trailing kisses down her body, but she was barely registering his movements as she grasped onto the dark need that lived in the hidden parts of her mind, the thing that wanted him to hold tighter, bite harder, and bruise her skin. She pretended the soft hands that spread her thighs were rough and calloused, imagining that they were searing as they trailed over her legs. It almost felt real.

She threw her forearm across her eyes, blocking out all the light as she pretended some more, breathing into it until she could feel the scratch of nails against her thighs. The pain made her whimper, feeding the ache between her legs, his breathing slightly uneven as the hands that gripped her became punishing. She arched her back off the bed, burying her hands in the soft cotton sheets. Except these weren't cotton.

Her eyes flew open, expecting to see her bedroom–the ornate frames, the white furniture–but instead found herself wrapped in darkness. After letting her vision adjust, she was able to see soft outlines, slivers of amber light breaking up the shadows that curled around her now, fingers twisted in dark silk sheets.

"I knew you'd be perfect." Arioch's voice was a low rasp.

Aheia gasped, his heavy arm draped across her abdomen, caging her back against the mattress, as hot prickles slid down her spine. He was laying between her legs, his chest forcing apart her thighs, the warmth between them bringing a red tinge across her cheeks. It was almost unbearable, having him so close—every fiber of her being screaming for him, and every rational thought getting kicked out amidst the longing she felt in her bones.

"No, where's …" she trailed off, as her surroundings became hazy, and her movements slowed. She was slipping, everything was slipping, as Arioch bowed his head, his curls falling across her cold skin. Her soul on his arm brushed against her stomach, and it burned through her in the most intoxicating way. His touch twisted her nerves into tight little knots that made her body stretch and strain, so taut it felt like she might be torn clean in two if he stopped what he was doing.

Arioch squeezed her hip before sliding his tongue across her right thigh, a line of fire following the wet glide against her skin. She writhed underneath his hold as he nipped her, soft and then hard, the feel of his teeth sending jolts of pain and pleasure through her body. He trailed kisses up the inside of her legs, his free hand curving around to squeeze her ass.

She arched into him, trying to urge him closer, get him where she needed him most. But he pulled away, his arm pushing down harder against her stomach.

"Tsk, tsk, tsk. Don't be greedy, *little goddess*," he chided, "you'll get just as much as I want to give you."

His grin was feral, it would have sent anger through her if—if her thoughts had been coherent. In this moment, she understood nothing but the longing in her chest, nothing but the ache between her thighs or the warmth he could offer.

Aheia twisted and turned, trying to find the friction she needed, until suddenly the heat pressing into her body vanished. She was left cold and aching, the air around her shifting as if she'd gone from a room filled with candles to a dark, forgotten hallway. It was hard to tell if she was awake or asleep, but a part of her hoped for the latter because if she was awake, then she'd have to face the reality that she had dreamed about Arioch between her legs and *liked* it.

Liked it a lot.

Not just that, but wanted to beg him for more, and burned for everything he had to give. She pressed her eyes shut tighter, feeling the discomfort in the pit of her stomach.

You don't want him.

The words made her chest constrict in need, need for her soul—to have them both near again because if they were, she could feel whole.

A frustrated groan left her lips as her limbs pulled at the sheets that seemed to want to suffocate her as punishment. She tried to hold onto her sanity, but it was far too late for that. She'd submerged herself into something thick and oily, something she couldn't brush off her skin, something that pulled too hard and whispered too sweetly.

The relief she needed was physical, but it was what it would offer her mentally that made her fingers clench to keep from touching herself. It was torturous. She needed the quiet, and unfortunately, her mind didn't often afford her that. It tended to reel both while she was asleep and awake, leaving her wholly exhausted. She'd tried to find many different remedies, but the most effective one had been sex in all its different shapes and sizes. It was the only thing that seemed to keep the cold inside of her at bay, even if it was just for a short period of time.

Many different creatures had tried to warm her, though most of them had proved underwhelming and fell short as they satisfied their own needs. She supposed they'd thought her a delicate flower, but they were all wrong. The thing that would let her escape lived nowhere near delicate. She wanted something more raw than anyone had been able to provide, though the dream version of Alshaytan had done a fucking great job of trying. His calloused hands had been the perfect measure of rough and unbridled, and it was those hands she imagined on her skin now. She pictured them finding their way down her torso, her thighs, up the hem of her dress, and between her legs, until she couldn't remember the heartless words he dealt in.

His words didn't matter—not in this moment—only his hands, and the memory of his lips in a rough, sweeping kiss near the Aljiran border that had made her forget her own name. It had taken all the strength she had to bite down on his lip and try to regain some of the control that she'd lost just before he stole her soul. She rubbed her palms over her breasts, tweaking her hard nipples between the pads of her fingers until it hurt, until she arched, her thighs rubbing together with the need for any type of friction. She bit her lip, sliding one hand lower and sneaking underneath the soft fabric of her shirt to slide her fingers over the apex of her thighs.

Gods, she was soaked.

She was wet over the thought of *him*.

Embarrassment burned so bright she imagined her skin was glowing, but it didn't stop her from stroking her clit, and letting a moan slip past her lips as images of his black curls brushing over her abdomen clouded her vision once more.

You can hate yourself for this tomorrow.

The satin sheets twisted around her waist in a tightening grip as she rolled her hips against her fingers, feeling every part of her coil with hot, heavy longing. It was spiraling out of her control, pulling and pushing her until sweat beaded on her forehead, her arousal dripping onto the mattress and her fingers becoming rushed and uncoordinated. Her lips parted, the thick air filling her lungs—but acting like it didn't want to be there, trying to escape as soon as she sucked it into her mouth in short gasps. Unintelligible words fell from her while she chased her orgasm, winding herself higher and higher, giving in to the thoughts of what might have happened. Of how he might have had his fingers inside of her, how he might have stretched her around his cock, how his teeth might have felt buried in her neck as his shadows wrapped around her throat. She groaned, spreading her legs wider as she pushed two fingers inside of herself, grinding her clit down on the heel of her palm. Sparks shot behind her eyelids, just as a violent tug spurred within her chest.

She nearly jumped out of her skin, a sliver of ice running through her as she searched the darkness of her room. For a long, torturous moment, there was nothing but silence, accompanied only by her ragged breathing and a frantic heartbeat loud in her ears. She had been so close to coming that her body hurt, physically felt like a coil that was wound beyond its limits, everything inside of her locking up in that tight place, her muscles screaming as she met those dark, angry, gray eyes.

She yelped, her free hand fisting in the sheets as she watched Arioch bleed from his shadows, one hand in his pocket, the other rubbing along the side of his jaw.

His gaze jolted something inside of her, like lightning that threaded through the very fabric of her being. He tilted his head to the side, his eyes moving down her body slowly as he advanced towards her in predatory strides.

The room suddenly felt tight, like the presence of his shadows had cut down its size, the air so heavy that breathing had become impossible.

Arioch looked away, running his thumb across his bottom lip, while the other hand remained in his pocket. "Are you finished?" he drawled, cocking his eyebrow.

Aheia felt the cold heat brush over her cheeks, tingeing them pink with shame. She wasn't shy, but something about his dismissive tone made her pray the bed would swallow her whole.

"Why are you here?" she asked, her voice edged by frustration as she made to move her hand somewhere safer, the silk hanging onto her fingers in betrayal.

He chuckled, a low and vibrating sound that stroked down the center of her body. "You said my name." The corner of his lip twitched, but his expression stayed measured.

"No, I didn't."

Fuck, had she?

"It was such a sweet little moan, Ruhí. Pray tell, what were you thinking about?" He tipped his chin, moving his hand to his right arm.

She was convinced she was a deep red now. "Get out."

"Try it again. A little more conviction this time." The amusement on his face banded something hot and angry around her neck. "Tell me to leave again, and I will."

Get out. Get the fuck out.

The words got stuck in her throat as Arioch swiped his thumb over his forearm, her body buzzing like it had when he touched her soul the first time.

"I'm waiting," Arioch purred a definite smile now caressing his lips while Aheia's heart felt like it was trying to break free and run away.

"Stop," she growled.

He took a step closer, his thumb continuing a slow circle across her glyph that made her fight against the urge to arch into every phantom touch he was giving her. *Gods*, he was in her bones, like he'd reached inside of her and rearranged everything to his liking.

"'No', and 'stop', don't have a place between us," he said, his voice an octave lower. "If you want me to stop what I'm doing, you'll use the word *honey*, do you understand?"

Her body was aching so badly that her thoughts felt like an inconvenience. She nodded, her jaw tight with irritation.

"Say it for me."

"Honey," she ground out as her nostrils flared.

"Good girl."

The praise ignited little bursts of pleasure throughout her body, the tension between them palpable, as he stared at her with eyes banded in bright embers that matched the heat of the cruel smile playing on his lips.

"What now, little goddess?" he asked, arching an eyebrow. "Don't you want to come?"

"Yes," Aheia said before her brain could force her to protest.

"You know what to do then," Arioch rasped, his eyes slipping down her body.

She was suspended between desperation and defiance, need and anger, and it pulled at her, fraying her edges and dividing her in two.

Arioch's eyes turned dark and feral at her hesitation. "Don't make me ask again, Ruhí."

"Or what?" she asked, still frozen in place.

"You lose the pleasure of my company." Arioch rested his tongue against the right corner of his mouth. "Or maybe I'm wrong about you, and this situation is too depraved for your pure and innocent Mithra nature."

Presumptuous fucking bastard.

She bit her lip so hard she tasted blood, a string of curses welling up on her tongue as she felt the challenge of his words.

"Let me bite that lip for you," he said, his right hand twitching.

Gods, help me say no to this.

"Never," she managed, running her tongue over the pain. Something bright and delighted sparking in the pit of her stomach as he watched.

"Just like you'll never get on your knees for me?"

"Just like that, *Skotá*," she said, untangling her fingers from the satin she had hidden them in.

"Filthy mouth," he said, watching her move her hand back between her legs, gripping at her inner thigh as a last form of protest. But it seemed her body couldn't care less about the realities her brain was trying to remind her of.

She flicked her tongue across her bottom lip, trembling under the weight of his gaze as her fingers slid down her center, a moan building in her throat. She couldn't help the arch of her back, the way her eyes fluttered shut in an effort to shove the thoughts of shame and embarrassment to a distant corner of the room as her fingers circled her clit. Nothing seemed to matter anymore. Nothing but relieving the pressure in the pit of her stomach.

"Eyes open," Arioch growled, his voice closer than before.

Aheia obeyed, sucking in a sharp breath, as she watched him lean over her. His hand braced against the mattress next to her that dipped down under his weight, her head sliding against the hot skin of his arm.

"How long has it been, hmm?" he whispered, his eyes roaming, and drinking in every little movement she made.

She couldn't find the words to answer, only offering up shallow breaths and a half-lidded stare as she touched herself, and imagined it was him. Arioch shifted forward, sending Aheia's heart into a gallop, his lips grazing her ear as he continued. "How long since someone has made you come until you begged them to stop?"

She whimpered, feeling the rough glide of his palm on her throat and his fingers around her neck. "That long, huh?" he hummed against her cheek before nipping at her ear lobe. "Is that why you're such a fucking brat?"

She ground her teeth, putting as much ice into her stare as she could find amongst the fire that was roaring through her. But he didn't even seem to notice.

"How do you like to be touched, little goddess?" Arioch moved his lips to her jaw, massaging her pulse point with his thumb. "Sweet? Soft?"

His grip became feather-light, barely there, a whisper that wasn't nearly enough. She groaned, her fingers faltering as she pressed herself into his hand like her body had a mind of its own. She'd lost all of her reservations somewhere along the way, needing the pressure of his touch, *craving* it. Arioch lifted his head, a deviant smile playing on his lips.

"No, you've never been sweet or soft, have you?"

Aheia barely managed to shake her head as she slid two fingers inside of herself and curled them, the heel of her palm stimulating her clit. Arioch's breathing felt ragged against her skin, a dark sound of approval laced into his voice.

"Tell me what you want, Ruhí."

"Touch me," she said, a faint voice at the back of her mind chastising her for it.

"No," he said, his words almost strained.

She rode through the sting of his refusal by sliding a third finger inside, needing so much more than she could provide herself in that moment.

"I can feel you squirming on my skin, and I'm not sure how much longer I can fucking take it, Ruhí. Come for me."

"I'm not coming for *you*," she groaned, the lie pouring from her lips.

"Does it make you mad? That you're undone over *my* words?" he growled, ignoring her.

"Fuck you."

"Hmmm, maybe if you ask nicely," he rasped, massaging her throat, slightly tightening his hold. "You'd fucking thank me for it too, *Aheia*."

The way he purred her name broke her, the sound of it dark and decadent, like a secret that shouldn't be spoken about in public. She arched against him, moving her fingers faster, so damn close to the edge, needing more, needing things she couldn't ask him. *Wouldn't* ask him. She shook her head because her words would betray her once again if she opened her mouth but he seemed to understand nonetheless, tightening his grip on her throat.

"Let go for me."

"Fuck, *Ari*."

His grip closed so tight she felt a vacuum against her ears, her vision rimmed by darkness at the edges, light spots dancing across her mind as the orgasm washed over her. It felt like something inside of her had cracked, leaking bright, pulsing fire into every inch of her body as her release rushed through her. It was a riptide pulling her under, waves crashing on her head until she was gasping for air, and for the first time since her arrival, she felt hot.

"*Gods,*" she whispered, the dark sheets clinging to the sweat that pearled on her skin as she let herself relax back into the mattress, her hands wet and trembling.

"They had nothing to do with it," Arioch said, something agitated lacing his words as he loosened his grip.

The walls of the room felt like they might press in further and suffocate her in a tight square if Aheia moved a single muscle. She pulled her fingers from between her legs and buried them in the sheets next to her, the pain from her split lip finally rearing its head. She hadn't cared earlier, but now it stung. And so did her ego. Reality took over in one sobering sweep and the air in the room seemed to have trickled out from underneath the door, leaving nothing but prickling anticipation in its wake. She'd offered up too much, without needing much coaxing, *again*. Acted like he was a glass of water after days in the desert. Except, now it felt like she'd swallowed gulps from the sea instead, a hollow, sinking feeling pulling at her chest like there was a hand pushing her firmly into the mattress.

Hel.

His breathing matched hers as he sat back enough for her to see his eyes. His stare was heavy and hot–she couldn't handle the weight of it, so she focused her gaze on the silk that now felt more suffocating than comfortable. Arioch reached across and pulled the hand she'd buried in the sheets free. She tried to yank it away, but before she could, he leaned in and wrapped his lips around her fingers. She almost choked, feeling the slow, hot glide of his tongue as he tasted her, grazing her skin with his teeth, his eyes never leaving hers. The air stilled in her lungs as he sucked, the sensation of it sending a line of fire down her spine before he pulled her fingers free, trailing them with his tongue.

"So sweet, Ruhí. At least, one part of you is," he purred, his jaw tightening a fraction before he swiped his tongue over his bottom lip.

"Why did you come here?" she asked, her breathing too shaky, her chest too heavy, and the ache in her body dulled, but not gone.

"Lapse in judgment." His words were clipped as he shrugged; they shouldn't have bothered her, but they did.

"*Leave.*" Venom dripped from her in hopes of ruffling him, cracking that marble shell, of leveling the playing field in *some way*.

No cracks. No ruffles.

Just cold indifference.

"There's that conviction." He gave a grin that didn't reach his eyes before he stepped back into his shadows and left her surrounded by her own, in a room whose temperature had turned frosty.

9
Chapter

Aheia

S hh, sweet girl." Her voice felt like a warm embrace. "Here."
Andromeda took Aheia's fingers between her palms and rubbed
them softly, the friction doing little to negate the biting cold coursing
through her.

"It hurts, *mamá*, I don't know what to do." Tears streamed down
Aheia's face, the white marble hard on her knees. She'd tried to hide
under blankets in the darkest part of her room, but there seemed to
be no hiding from the light.

"I know, dearling, I know." Her mother pulled her hands to her lips
and kissed her knuckles, those blue eyes deep and sad.

"He heard my thoughts. He heard my thoughts, I didn't mean to
think it, I–I forgot where I was for a second," she sobbed, her gaze
stuck to the dark bruise that was starting to heal on her mother's
cheek, its edges turning yellow. "You told me, you told me to be on
guard outside of the house, and I–I couldn't help it. I'm so sorry, it's
my fault, it's all my fault. He's going to hurt you again."

Fuck. He should be hurting me instead. Me, not her.

"No. Hey," Andromeda said sliding closer, wrapping one slender
arm around her daughter's shoulders, pinning Aheia's cold hands between their bodies. "None of this is your fault."

"But he–he'll hurt you, and it's because of me," Aheia cried, the tears
dripping onto her white cotton dress. "I thought about our conversation last night and he ... He *heard*."

"Look at me, *pajdí*." Andromeda tipped Aheia's chin, wiping the tears from her eyes. "This–" She took Aheia's fingers and slid them over
the bruise on her cheek. "This is nothing. This, I can survive easily."

Aheia looked away, feeling the way the battered skin beat against her touch, like Andromeda's very heart was jumping against her fingers.

"But this," she continued, dropping Aheia's hand and cupping her cheek instead, "I can't survive this look. Be strong for me. It's temporary, ok? All of this is temporary."

Aheia's eyes snapped to hers. "It's not, this is our life."

"*Andromeda!*" Ophion's voice echoed through the cracked door to Aheia's room.

"Hide," her mother said quickly, pulling away, but Aheia held onto her, panic gripping her chest and twisting tight.

"No." Her eyes were wide and alarmed.

"*Aheia,*" her mother hissed under her breath, prying Aheia's hands from her and yanking her onto her feet behind her, pulling her towards the ornate doors of her closet. "Don't come out, no matter what you hear. Do you understand?"

Aheia shook her head, strands of her hair sticking to her wet skin as she gulped down air. "No. *No.* mamá, please, don't go to him." Aheia tried to hold onto the door, but her mother pushed her back, the weight of her shoulder against her sternum forcing broken coughs from her lips. Aheia stumbled, her hands flying back to catch herself against the array of white clothes that lined the closet, hangers clattering with the impact.

"Hide. I will come to get you when it's safe."

"No." Aheia tried to lunge for the door, but Andromeda slammed it. *No.*

No.

No.

She fumbled with the knob, the gold cutting into her hands as she tried to wrench it open.

"Stop. Aheia, stop," an answering hiss came from the other side.

"You can't make this decision for me," she cried. "I can't let you take the beatings for something I did, *please.*"

For something I thought.

"It'll be ok," Andromeda's voice wavered. "None of this is your fault."

The ice coiled Aheia, tightening her grip around the knob until she felt her skin break under the ornate design, unable to move.

"No, no, no, no," she repeated it over and over again, trying to will herself to move without luck. "Mamá."

She heard scraping on the other side of the door and then felt vibrations against the wood, followed by a heavy *thunk*.

"Mamá, don't. Please, let me out," she cried, her voice so broken she didn't know if Andromeda could hear it.

"I will. I will, *pajdí*."

"Andromeda." Ophion's voice was muffled, but it shot ice down Aheia's spine and fear into her stomach, turning it to lead.

"I'm coming!" Andromeda shouted and then in a low voice, "It's temporary, dearling."

Aheia shook her head frantically, willing her shoulders to move, the door rattling but not giving in to her.

Then she heard retreating footsteps across the marble and the door to her room shutting.

Aheia bit her lip so hard that she tasted blood, flashes of her mother's bruised skin filling her mind. There had been so many bruises, so many healed bones, so much blood.

No.

No.

No.

"It's my fault. It's my fault. It's my fault."

Aheia couldn't do anything but stand there, frozen to the spot, her heart beating in her throat, the sound of its rhythm in her chest filling the silence around her until it was replaced by the familiar screams she'd heard before.

"*No!*"

She sat up in a panic, coming face to face with Lúc who was standing over her, his brows furrowed.

"Relax, princess, I'm not into necrophilia," he scoffed as if she had inconvenienced him before tossing her a white piece of fabric. She turned it over in her hands, a stark contrast to the sheets.

"Let's go," he said, shrugging.

"Where?" she asked, feeling fresh tears on her skin, her breathing still slightly shallow.

But he didn't answer, just busied himself clasping and unclasping the small piece of leather that held one of his black knives against his chest.

Aheia bit down on the urge to reach for it and drive that pretty blade hilt-deep into his shoulder. "I can get dressed by myself," she said sharply, watching his hand pull free the knife and play with the blade.

It looked like a subconscious action, like it was the most normal thing in the world.

"But where's the fun in that?" He threw her a cocky smile.

Irritating, but not threatening.

She exhaled pointedly through her nose, the silence stretching.

"Fine, but hurry. I'm fucking hungry. You've slept through most of the day, and I haven't eaten since this morning." Lúc gave her one last narrow-eyed glance before he stalked across the room and closed the door behind him.

"*Skotá*," she mumbled the insult for what felt like the tenth time since she entered the realm. It didn't seem to bother the Nephilim as much as she'd hoped, but every time she let it slip across her lips, it felt like another piece of armor was being added to her pale skin.

She gathered herself–or tried to–as she threw the silk that had clung to her so tightly last night away from her body.

Fuck, fuck, fuck. Aheia cradled her head in her hands, her bare feet meeting the cold, rough floor below. She'd been so fucking *stupid*. She could still feel Arioch's hand around her throat, still hear his filthy words against the shell of her ear, pebbling her skin. She'd given in, with barely any fight, and for what? To get herself off and let him watch?

"What the fuck are you doing?" she chastised herself as she rose on shaky legs and padded across the room, the white piece of fabric hanging limply at her side.

When she glanced out the window, the sky was still dark, and her groggy mind struggled to grasp the fact that it was, in fact, a new day. Her chest still felt hollow, worse even, like it was sore and healing at a glacial pace. The further Arioch seemed to venture, the tauter–almost expectant–her body became. The nearer he was the more she wanted to... well...

She grit her teeth.

Focus.

She looked at the mirror across from her and dropped the fabric, the reflection of her eyes turning her stomach.

They were *her* eyes. Andromeda. It had been years, and still... The recognition of them lived in the shadows that followed her around, forcing her to see not her reflection, but her mother's lifeless and blood-splattered gaze in place of her own. It always took her several moments to shake the chill and the memory that haunted her sleepless nights, but when she finally did, it was just Aheia gripping the counter, staring so intently back that she almost faltered.

She swallowed.

She's gone. She's gone. She's gone.

Aheia peeled her bruised fingers from the edge of the sink and cradled them to her chest for a moment, trying to push all her broken pieces back into place. When she gathered herself enough, she turned on the faucet in front of her and let cold water run through her fingers. It turned hot quickly, and she waited for it to hurt before she splashed it on her face, clearing the rest of the fog from her mind. She looked back at the reflection that seemed to be judging her, laying out all of her flaws in front of her, and plucking at them like they were strings on an instrument.

And, fuck, if she knew how to play.

Her chest felt just as bruised as her fingers when she looked over the shadows that cut apart her fair features—the white of her eyelashes, droplets of water falling onto the black fabric covering her skin, the hollows of her cheeks, the outline of her throat. She looked like a ghost, and she supposed she was—just a whisper of someone much better, much stronger–someone who belonged somewhere. She exhaled slowly, ignoring the melancholy tune that her reflection started to play in the mirror, and tried to tame her unruly, white hair instead. She'd had it short for a while, but only until Ophion had talked about liking it that way. Then, she'd let it grow and vowed to never cut it again.

It would have been nice to have it short in moments like this though, a simple style that wasn't so heavy on her head, a length she could pull back without having to use multiple straps of fabric to support its weight. Alas, she stood there, raking her fingers through the silky, white tresses, piling them on top of her head. She didn't have any way to secure it, but it was long enough that when she bunched it and wove it through itself, it would stay put well enough—at least for now. Once she had her hair out of the way, she slid her hand down the side of her neck, feeling her pulse in an unsteady rhythm against her fingers, the faint ghost of a bruise building there.

What is wrong with you?

Last night rushed back in a fury that made her cheeks heat. It was as if she couldn't control her hands, her breathing, her heart–none of it. Even before Arioch showed up with his tight grip, she'd thought about him, dreamt about him. And she liked it.

Wanted it. Wanted *more*.

Her exhale was shaky as she tried to focus on anything but the cold heat that gripped her neck.

It wasn't just his touch, was it? the voice crooned in the back of her mind, sending memories of coarse and coaxing words that had pushed her right into oblivion. *You liked that too, remember?*

She shoved the nagging reminder to the side and bent over to pick up the white fabric, unraveling it from itself. A dress. A white dress. She hadn't seen anything white here. Not in the closets, not in the halls, not on the Nephilim.

Why was he giving her white? Was he taunting her? Was this a joke? Was he parading her around like his prized prisoner?

You're here of your own free will, she thought, the words grating across her mind, unwanted.

You have nowhere else. You have nothing else. No one else.

The reality of it frosted over her edges. She had six days. Six days, which she couldn't see past ...

I won't go back. No matter what that may mean.

The thought didn't feel like her own, but even so, the words felt easy. There was no doubt in her mind. This would be her last stop before joining her mother on the other side. Because there was nothing else for her in this lifetime. She sure as hel wasn't going to let the Mithra touch her again, control her again, all for power and politics.

No.

Ophion had taken her mother, her childhood, whatever semblance of happiness she'd created for herself. He wouldn't ever get his hands on her again and the realization of it shouldn't have felt as peaceful as it did.

Six days.

Aheia pulled off her shirt and slid on the dress. It smelled clean and fresh, like washed linen, the fabric soft against her skin. It was snug, but comfortable, made of something silky and light. She slipped the straps over her arms, the hem of it coming down to mid-thigh, simple, not what she expected. There were no harnesses, no metal clasps, no over-the-top cutouts. It was just ... a dress.

She exhaled slowly, steadying the tremble in her breath. "*Boríte nare kánete.*" You can do this.

Her reflection seemed to doubt it as she left the room and met the

Shifter in the hallway.

Lúc was leaning against the opposite wall, arms crossed, expression annoyed. It seemed to be a character trait all of the Nephilim she'd met here shared. When she closed the door behind her, he gave her a short once-over, something glinting in those dark eyes before inclining his chin down the hallway. They walked in silence for a while, their footsteps against marble the only sound.

"It helps to smile," he said suddenly, his face pensive like he was deep in thought.

"I don't smile," she replied, something rivaling disgust creeping over her shoulders and staring up at her. She hated when people took the liberties to tell her what to do, especially males. She couldn't stand it, and if she'd had the light at her fingers, she would have knocked the cocky bastard back on his ass. But instead, she kept her weapons cloaked between her words, leaving her tongue sharp and her sentiments short.

"Aren't you supposed to be all happy and sunshine?" he prodded.

"Only in good company," she threw back at him as they rounded the corner, another stretch of hallway separating them from what she remembered as the foyer.

"Feisty little thing," he mumbled, "considering you *want* to be here."

"I don't want to be here," she said, and it was only half a lie.

She *needed* to be here.

"Sure," he replied and then continued as though nothing had happened. "I hate this wing," more to himself than to her. "I don't know why he put you here. He never puts anyone here."

"Why?" she asked but he ignored her again, pushing his tongue against a silver lip ring that he hadn't worn last she saw him.

"What meal is this?" she asked instead as they cleared the second hallway.

"It's somewhere between morning and evening. Whatever you call that in your world," Lúc answered, keeping his gaze ahead.

Less than six days.

They continued until the silence became threaded with voices and the corridor gave way to another foyer–slick, black marble with gold veins running through it. The space was large and open, rooms without doors branching off at four points, and staircases leading to a second floor dividing them. Laughter and chatter floated around them, another thing she hadn't expected. Screaming, maybe, but not laughter.

Lúc led them through the foyer, and off to the side through an archway that opened into a large... atrium?

Aheia's lips parted in amazement as she took in the view in front of her. They stood on the threshold of a vast, open space that was all windows, with galaxies and stars peppered into the background. There was no horizon, only sky, reminding her of open nights when she'd laid on her back against cold sands in otherwise hot deserts, gazing up at the stars and wondering if the Gods ever heard her prayers.

The windows were broken up by fragrant black flowers that she recognized as Achlys, winding themselves up the room, covering every inch in petals, only disrupted by the wall to her right. It seemed to be built right into a mountain, the jagged rock contrasted the delicate beauty of the flora and the straight, clean lines of the rest of the architecture. She let her eyes gaze across the rough stone, watching trickles of water run through the crevasses until they dripped into large, gold basins anchored against the black marble floor, like a natural fountain. Several Nephilim were perched on the edge of the gold bowls talking animatedly, some holding books, some holding chalices, and some throwing small silver coins into the basins.

The books they held seemed to be from multiple nondescript stacks leaning against the walls, broken up by plush, maroon couches, and tables with intricate, gold designs. Her eyes drifted up and across the domed ceiling of the structure, drawing little patterns over the fractured glass that reminded her of a large spider web, chandeliers hanging at various lengths from thin strings. She watched as small orbs of energy bounced and danced behind crystal votives, refracting the light in a kaleidoscope of colors onto the scene below.

The air was thick with incense that smelled of dried flowers and herbs and mingled with the scents of the foods piled high on the various tables. The Nephilim sitting around them were leaning against each other and talking, laughing, throwing insults and jokes across the room, both in the mortal language that both races shared and in their own.

The chairs were replaced by dark, thick pillows resting underneath the gold tables topped with ornate candles. There were all kinds of Nephilim around the room, some regular Leviathans, some Shifters that had their claws on display, some *Syraphem*, their wings tucked tightly behind them, while yet more nondescript dark creatures were seated amongst them. Aheia couldn't help but stare as she stepped across the threshold and into the lion's den.

10

Chapter

Aheia

Lúc led her through the tables, the conversation around them slowly being stifled by their presence. The marble was cold on her feet, and the air in the room was hot against her skin, creating the most delirious combination of sensations. Lúc shifted through the Nephilim around him, commanding stiff attention from some, and grins and whispers from others, all of which made Aheia consider his place with Alshaytan.

Her chest made sure she was well aware of Arioch's presence before her gaze found him at the other end of the atrium, almost forcing her to stumble when her eyes landed on him, sitting next to Shiron and a Syraphem that had dark skin and her tall wings tucked in tight behind her back.

There was nothing special about the table; it wasn't set at the head of the room, and it wasn't any bigger than the others. She would have been able to pick it from its counterparts just about as well as she could discern between ice and frozen water. And somehow *that* was the detail that gave her the most pause.

In Keloseros, the hierarchy of a room spoke to rank and tradition. The Mithra sat at long, straight tables, with clear organization, the head of each household perched at their appointed spots. The order of power flowed down through dinner etiquette and underlined class like it did at gatherings and meetings. But here... there appeared to be no rhyme or reason.

Arioch was facing Shiron, who was gesturing as he spoke while Alshaytan listened and smiled. It even seemed to reach his eyes, which were more placid than angry. He was sitting cross-legged on one of the dark cushions, a flowing black shirt hanging over his shoulders loosely, sleeves rolled just above his elbows.

Heat crept up the back of her neck, and she prayed to anyone who could possibly hear her in this realm that she wouldn't blush as her mind wandered to what had happened between them last night. She remembered the deviance woven into his features, the rough grip of his hand on her throat, the words he spun around her neck before pulling so tight that she couldn't think straight. It hurt–it would never not hurt— the fact that she couldn't control herself around him, her feelings dictated by a small, shiny glyph on his skin.

He must have felt her too, because those tranquil eyes turned to her, calling on a familiar storm as their gazes met across the room. She clenched her teeth and straightened her shoulders, hiding her features behind one of the masks she spent years cultivating for uncomfortable social commitments and political dinners. Her expression suggested bored elegance while a slight, non-threatening smirk concealed that all she wanted to do was run.

Lúc stepped ahead of her, swiping a piece of fruit from a neighboring table, and narrowly avoiding a hand that swatted after him. Heads turned after them as they passed, and Aheia became increasingly nervous, her heart picking up its pace. She had to work hard to keep her hands from fisting in the fabric at her sides, a nervous tick she hadn't quite shaken from her younger years. But it became hard to keep those fingers steady when she was the brightest thing in the room, a slow trickle of white paint running down a moody canvas.

They were only breaths away now, Lúc leaving her to seat himself next to Shiron and the Syraphem, as Aheia stopped in her tracks. Her chest begged her to get closer, and her mind fractured at the thought.

"Sit," Arioch said finally, tipping his chin towards one of the cushions next to him. His words were clipped, the command in his voice threading its way through her chest in a way that made standing her ground harder than she cared to admit.

Arioch picked up a red berry from his plate as the seconds slipped over the marble behind them, his eyes never leaving hers while he waited. Then, after the silence had stretched into something uncomfortably grating, he swept his tongue along the bottom of his teeth, and she caught frustration creasing his features.

"You'll sit or you'll kneel." His voice was passive, though she caught the faintest of glimmers in those dark eyes.

"Not much of a choice, is there?" she asked, a cold edge woven into her words.

"Choice? don't use words you don't understand," he drawled. "Everything you do here, and everything you've already done, has been of your free will, *Your Grace*." The statement was suggestively laced with everything she desperately wanted to forget.

"The title," she said, her voice wavering. "I don't use my title." She hated it. It reminded her of the family she was forced into, of brittle smiles, and blood dripping onto white floors.

He gave a tight nod and reached for one of the oranges perched on a mountain of exotic fruits in front of him, dismissing her wordlessly. Suddenly, whether she sat or not didn't seem to matter to him in the least. And it was the broken need for approval, that she'd never been quite able to shake from her screwed-up mind that pulled her onto the cushion in front of her. Her hands folded out of habit, and she spoke her realization before she could consider her words.

"You don't pray before you eat?" They had never touched a morsel of food before thanking Aether back in Keloseros.

Lúc snorted, loading up his plate.

"What makes you think we haven't already?" Arioch pulled a dagger from his chest harness, balancing the black tip on the table next to her.

She gave Lúc a pointed look, who'd started digging into his eggs while filling up his chalice with an orange liquid. Then, she made another mental note that joined the rest.

They do not pray before they eat.

"You can't just drag me out of bed," she said, changing course, her words floating further and further from her control as the irritation banded tighter.

"You seem to think that don't you, Ruhí?" The corner of his mouth twitched as if he wanted to smile. "Did I drag her out of bed?" he asked, and even though his eyes were trained on her, the words were directed across the table.

"No dragging of any sort," Lúc said through bites of some dark and charred meat.

"No, just stalking and staring," she bit out, fumbling for words strong enough to protect herself with.

Arioch narrowed his eyes for a split second and threw Lúc a scorching look. The Shifter shrugged, though his calm demeanor seemed to shrug along with him.

"*Ghabiun*," the Syraphem said, rolling her eyes, before giving Aheia a quick once over and returning to her food.

"Fuck off, Emryn," Lúc shot at her, biting at his lip ring before he raised his chalice to his mouth and drank.

When Arioch's gaze returned to Aheia after a long minute, his expression was back to arrogant boredom.

He scored the orange he was holding at the top. "Go on then, say your prayers," he rasped, "if you must."

Aheia shot him a scornful look before letting her eyes drift over all the food piled high in front of her. She hadn't had a real meal in ... longer than she could remember. And it smelled so good, that it made her mouth water and stomach rumble. She might not have bothered to pray, but now that it felt like a challenge, she bowed her head and mumbled a few words in her language. They felt heavy on her tongue as she continued the tradition she was raised in with an empty heart. The words were almost as hollow as the echo in her chest when she thought of how difficult it was to hold faith after so much hardship.

They've never helped you before, Aheia ... And you've never believed in the words, the voice in her mind tutted, turning its back. She'd been exploring her own beliefs for a long time now, having lost her faith along with her mother, and while she didn't know how to feel about the Old Gods and all the lore connected with them, holding onto the idea that there was a bigger picture, some pre-planned destiny gave her solace. Though, she didn't believe the words fell on big ears in the sky, but rather that just maybe, the universe would hear her instead. So, when she spoke her prayers it was to the universe, to the only thing that had ever proven its presence to her.

When she finished and looked up, she found the attention of the table on her, all of them looking varying degrees of bewildered. It almost made her smile. She never imagined Nephilim being so ... normal.

"That's enough," Arioch said with a gruff edge, jolting the others from their daze. Aheia flashed him a look bordering on thankful until he continued. "We have our own traditions. Thanking the Gods for food that our own people worked hard for is not one of them."

Surprise curled around her. She didn't disagree with that thought.

She looked at the other Nephilim, all of whom had turned back to their food, wondering what the rest of them must have thought about her.

"Have I struck a nerve?" She tilted her head at Arioch, and reached for a bright red apple, pressing its waxy skin to her lips in an ambitious bite before setting it back down.

"*U tebya umy roht,*" Arioch rumbled, leaving her flipping through the sparse words of theirs that she understood without any luck. "I'll give you that."

He ran his tongue over the black blade he'd used on the orange before setting it down next to the plate near her hand.

"Since you think that you can say, and do, whatever you like here, let me make the rules very fucking clear. You're welcome to explore." He pulled a jar of honey towards his plate, focusing his attention on the gold liquid in front of him. "As long as one of my guards is with you, that is. A female, if that would make you more comfortable." He popped open the top before returning his stare to her. "Stay out of the way when there's business because most Nephilim won't appreciate one of your kind staying in our world, let alone here. And lastly," he ran his tongue over his bottom lip, "those fingers of yours have been busy... no more of that."

Her lips parted. *Did he just–*

"Not without permission, Ruhí."

She locked down the sound that welled up in her throat and threatened to spill from her lips as she felt everyone's eyes shift to her once more. Aheia leaned forward, and as if it made a difference, as if somehow whispering could make this conversation more private, she lowered her voice.

"You're psychotic."

An approving hum left his lips as he tore apart the blood orange he'd scored at the seam, dark red juice dripping down his hand.

"You're in no position to disobey." He tipped his chin slightly, giving her a heated once over. "There are rules here. You follow them."

"Or what?" she replied.

There was an uneasy shifting around the table, and she couldn't help but glance at Lúc, and then Shiron, both of them suddenly finding their chalices incredibly interesting. Meanwhile, Emryn was leaning her arm against the table, chin perched on her palm, drinking in every word.

"Try me and find out," he growled, fixing her with those eyes. "In my home, when you say my name, I know about it."

He dipped the small, golden spoon into the honey before drizzling it across the piece of dark red orange he'd carved out. She swallowed, watching him, as the conversation around them slowly drifted into the background.

"That means," he picked up the piece of fruit, juice, and honey dripping from his fingers and onto the table as he brought it to her lips. "Open your mouth." She hesitated, but his eyes suggested less patience than before. So, she did as she was told, and wrapped her lips around his fingers. A delicious burst of sweetness followed by a slight bite spread across her tongue as she tasted the softness of the fruit. His eyes were fixed on her mouth, something simmering in between the threads of gray, as he trailed his fingers from her lips down and around her chin in a tight grip.

"When you're stretching yourself around those pretty little fingers pretending they're mine, I'll know about it."

She choked as a trickle of orange dribbled down the corner of her mouth. It hurt to swallow the piece of fruit, like she'd inhaled it and now felt the juice in her nose. She pressed her eyes shut, the sweetness turning sour as she forced it down her throat. When she opened them again, Arioch was licking honey from the side of his hand, amusement breaking up the anger in his eyes.

"So sweet, don't you think?" His words were innocent enough, except that they made her fantasize about her own fingers in his mouth instead.

"So sweet ... at least one part of you is."

She grit her teeth, clearing her throat against the sting of citrus that now ran along the back of her throat and into her sinuses. At least the discomfort had distracted her from the embarrassment that flushed her cheeks, from the feeling of being much too visible in her white dress, much too exposed. She focused on the anger that bubbled up inside of her, coaxing the darkness from underneath her skin.

The expression Arioch wore on his face twisted her insides, a look that suggested she was a wounded animal rather than a Mithra. She hated it. It grated on that darkest part of her, propelling the sanity she grasped for so desperately just out of reach. She was gone, so far gone that it wasn't quite her that reached for the knife in front of her, not quite her that threw herself at Alshaytan with the blade. Because if it had been her, she would've restrained herself, would've known the attempt was dangerous.

Her vision was bordered by angry pulsing bursts of light as she clawed after him, his hand catching her uncoordinated wrists in a tight grip, the black blade only inches from his neck.

She was shaking, her anger ebbing and flowing, crashing and rolling, pulling her under. Everything was bright–too bright—she couldn't breathe, couldn't see, couldn't think.

"Aheia." Arioch's voice was sharp enough to pull her attention from his throat, snapping her eyes to his. She felt pinned by his stare, even as she heard shifting behind her, even as she saw tendrils of darkness sweeping into her line of sight.

"What now, Ruhí? What if I let you get that knife on me?" he rasped, his expression apathetic.

"You want to find out?" she pushed out between her teeth, her heart racing.

Arioch slid his other arm around her waist and pulled her in tighter, her chest pushed up against his while she knelt between his legs, the knife suspended between them. His eyes danced, like she'd given him exactly what he wanted when he leaned down slightly, his hand wrapping around her throat before pulling her and the blade closer.

"Show me." Arioch was still grinning like he was daring her to do something he didn't think she was capable of.

He let go of her wrist so she could push the knife flush against his skin and the air stilled when she did, the room going silent. Aheia didn't have to look to know that every pair of eyes were on them, that there must have been guards around them, that he could have had her thrown in chains if he wanted to.

"Come on."

His voice dropped an octave, his accent pulling at those words, as he swept his tongue over the inside of his mouth and let it rest in the corner. It was like he read her every thought–and challenged them–as they drifted into her mind.

Aheia snarled, pushing harder, relishing the hiss that escaped from between his teeth when blood followed the blade. She watched the black line trickle down his skin and onto his shirt, feeling the overwhelming urge to do it again, wanting to hear him make another sound.

"Don't hurt yourself." His voice was husky and thick against her skin.

"You're the one at knifepoint." She nicked him again, teasing a growl from between his lips.

HELFYRE

"Do you think I would be if I didn't want to be?"

11

Chapter

Arioch

She grit her teeth, her eyes resolute in the way she stared at him, those light blue irises filling with something dark, like ink eating up porous paper. She was shaking, slight enough that no one would have noticed it, but he felt the tremor of the blade on his skin. Her eyes were wide and frantic like she couldn't decide what to do, like she didn't understand how she'd gotten here. In that moment she looked both like she wanted to tear out his throat with her teeth, and like she might start crying.

"Not many have made it this far and kept their lives," he rasped.

"You can't kill me," she said, her demeanor changing with her words, her shoulders stiffening and her jaw tensing. It was like whatever indecisiveness she'd encountered had let go of her, leaving behind a Siren that would take pleasure in seeing him bleed.

He swallowed a smirk, his cock thickening in his leathers at the cold storm that raged in her eyes. "Killing you isn't quite what I had in mind." He slid his hand onto her lower back, keeping her close when she went rigid, her breath hitching slightly.

"Don't do that," she said, her voice a low hiss.

"What am I doing?" he asked. She clenched her jaw, her angry eyes avoiding his, while her soul burned into his arm.

"If you're going to hurt me you'd better look me in the fucking eyes when you do it."

Her gaze snapped back to his, her lip twitching, and her knuckles brushing against his collarbone as she readjusted. "Sick fascination with my eye contact."

Witty fucking mouth.

He liked that.

"It's only good manners." He said, his fingers fanning out over her skin. *Ah fuck.* She felt good pressed against him. Too fucking good. It took a lot of gods damned restraint not to slip his hand down her ass and find out exactly-

"Why did you have me herded towards your border?" she said suddenly, cutting off his thoughts, like she'd realized that this may be the only time she could coax the truth from him. Little did she know that lying took energy he had no plan on expending.

"Because I wanted to," he said, curious to see exactly what she was capable of. So he pushed her further. "Because I wanted to know what death sounded like on the lips of something so bright and pure. And fuck, those sounds you made–they were so Gods damn pretty, Aheia, when my monster bit down on your leg. I can't wait to hear that whimper again." It was a coarse lie that lived between shards of truth.

She scoffed, something like disbelief curling her features. "You're–"

"A demon, little goddess. That's the word you're looking for," he said quietly, his lips inches from hers, "with no obligation to you past what we agreed on."

Then, just as she looked like she had opted for flaying him open, she pulled the knife from his neck instead, and drove it into the apple she'd dropped onto the table, the wood crunching underneath the blade.

"Shame," Arioch said, feeling the sting of disappointment in the back of his mind. He'd expected more after everything he'd seen, everything he'd heard. But whatever had crept into her eyes moments ago was gone now. She turned her head, avoiding his gaze once again, a red flush spreading across the bridge of her nose.

He let himself follow her pink skin, the tint disappearing below the neckline of her white dress. She was still kneeling between his legs, the proximity of her making him ache for more of what she'd given him last night. The thought alone made his cock twitch, and he knew she felt it when she heard a small gasp pass between her parted lips.

"You're sick," she hissed, reddening further.

Her hips slid against his leathers as she squirmed, the white hair she'd had stacked on top of her head falling into loose curls around her face. Arioch narrowed his eyes looking at her for a moment, truly looking at her.

She was beautiful, but she was ghostly. The fabric of her dress hugged her thin frame, showing off just how malnourished she was, the white blending with her complexion, almost making her look sick. He'd picked white because he'd supposed it was what a Mithra would want. But it didn't look right.

Her eyes looked unfocused now as she stared past him, like from one second to the next he'd lost his grasp on her, though she'd never been closer to him physically.

What the fuck is going on in that mind?

He held onto her a little longer, because moving his arm felt impossible. Her soul begged him not to, his shadows begged him not to, and whatever piece of himself was left in between those two forces didn't particularly want to either.

He felt the blood, wet on the nape of his neck, and focused on the pain instead of her when he finally let go. Aheia sank back on her heels, blinking up at him, her eyes glazing over slightly before she gathered herself and sat back on her cushion.

"Eat," Arioch said lazily, scooping out a generous helping of rice and dropping it onto her plate.

She ignored him, toying with the edge of her dress. "No."

"You sure like that word."

"And you sure don't seem to understand its meaning."

He leaned in pointedly, close enough to brush her arm with his.

"Are you done?" He snatched one of the halves of the apple she'd split apart and took a bite. "Eat."

Aheia looked as if she was weighing her options, ultimately reaching for the other half with a sour expression on her face. She took a bite, and just for a moment, Arioch saw her features smooth. She was hungry, and the only reason she wasn't eating was because he was asking her to.

That wouldn't do. Not at all.

He waited until she finished it, cleaning off everything, and leaving behind the thin core.

Good. Not enough, but better.

She sat back, her eyes lingering on the food in front of her for a moment. "Am I free to leave, or do I have to fight for that as well?"

"You're free to leave," he echoed, picking from his plate without so much as a glance in her direction.

He heard her move and fought to keep his gaze off of her until he knew she'd disappeared through the doors to the atrium, his chest physically relaxing with the distance. Then he shot Emryn a look.

"Take some fucking food with you, and make sure she eats it."

The Syraphem returned an irritated glance but kept her thoughts to herself as she flourished her hand and made a few pieces of meat disappear into thin air before following the Dioscuri from the room.

She's not your concern.

Arioch rolled his shoulders and swiped his finger over the wound at his neck.

"Have we heard from the Mithra?" Arioch asked Shiron, picking up the blade Aheia had mutilated the apple with, wiping it against his black napkin.

The Leviathan shook his head. "Nothing. The hunters after her were Fae, and they have no way to glimmer back into the realm from the Neutral Lands. It will take them at least a day to make it to the nearest Mithra vortex."

The Neutral Lands made certain types of magyck impossible to use, similar to how certain Mithra couldn't summon their gifts in Aljira, nor the Nephilim in Keloseros. The rules of nature varied depending on the species and the race. For instance, Shifters could still take their forms and Heretics could still practice certain magyck. Brite and Dark magyck, just as light and shadows however seemed atmospherically challenged. It was due to how the energies of the world clashed with their genetics. Both races had their own vortexes, ways to re-enter Keloseros and Aljira, each of them hidden and only accessible to natives of the realms.

"I'd imagine they'll try to use her presence here to their advantage," Lúc said, his eyes focused across the room on Tariq, a tall Leviathan with black horns that was leaning against a dark column, reading. "If we know anything about Ophion, we know he has a flair for the dramatic."

Arioch repositioned on his cushion, his body uncomfortably aware of the distance Aheia was putting between them. "She can't stay hidden here; the Siada will hear of her arrival if they haven't already. If Ophion thinks he can catch us off guard, he's wrong. She'll need to make an appearance in Aljira soon, and it needs to be on our terms," he said.

"Arioch." Kar's soft voice drifted in from behind him, the green-haired empath stepping into view moments later. Kar was one of the Nephilim that stayed at the compound, the sweetest Leviathan he'd ever encountered with the most vicious teeth he'd ever seen when provoked. She worked closely with Emryn, especially with the Nephilim that needed in-depth emotional work done. "Mazikeen sent word. She needs to speak to you."

12

Chapter

Aheia

Aheia's stomach growled as she left the atrium, the anger doing nothing to satiate her hunger. She should have eaten more, but she couldn't stay, not in that room, and not with him. There were too many eyes on them, and with every argument–even when the words had felt just and right on her tongue–she seemed to lose small pieces of her securities. It was like Arioch plucked them away and tucked them in his back pocket without the slightest effort.

She was almost back to her room, stepping across the black marble threshold and onto the rough beige rock that divided the compound in two when the Syraphem from her table showed up on her heels.

"That was dramatic," she said, and Aheia remembered Lúc calling her Emryn.

Aheia shrugged off her presence and continued up the stairs, her footsteps echoed by the Syraphem.

"I am not a child. I don't need supervision." For fucks sake, she was 28 years old in mortal years, though time moved differently in both realms, which meant their lives stretched and days felt longer.

"Neither of us wants to be here," Emryn replied behind her, before thrusting a fistful of something dried and brown into her field of view. "It's hardly a choice, Dioscuri. Now, eat."

Aheia stilled at the top of the stairs and grabbed the meat, looking over the demon in front of her. She had dark brown hair and lashes to match and wore the same leathers Arioch and the other males did. Her skin was adorned with tattoos, which seemed to be a pattern with the Nephilim, at least the ones Aheia had encountered so far. Some of Emryn's Lujha glyphs looked similar to Lúc's, which made Aheia wonder what they meant.

Aheia took a tentative bite and almost moaned, the taste of piquant spices and smoke cutting through the sour anxiety that had spread across her tongue. Aheia's lips parted as she watched Emryn graze her own thigh, pulling the fabric of her dress to the side, catching a glimpse of a long, slender dagger inked onto her tan leg, with intricate designs bordering its shape. Emryn curled her fingers against her skin, and suddenly, like she had reached into the ink and pulled the dagger from its home, she now held a knife as real as the meat that was still on Aheia's tongue. It glinted in her hand, light flicking off the blade as she brought it up and carved into the side of an apple that she pulled from thin air. Aheia stared at the spot on her thigh, now daggerless, and then at Emryn's face, who looked bored as she peeled back a piece of the fruit.

"Magyck." She shrugged. "You know, refusing to eat only hurts you, not him," she said matter-of-factly in between bites.

"Can all Syraphem–"

"No." She sauntered past Aheia in the direction of her room. "Then what are you?"

"I thought your kind were supposed to be polite or something," Emryn threw over her shoulder. "It's rude to ask."

"Politeness doesn't keep you alive, does it?" Aheia caught up to her and kept pace as Emryn glanced down at her and once she had seemingly decided that she wouldn't be offended, she answered. "I'm a *Shadow Heretic*," Emryn said, twirling the knife as they passed by the first set of windows.

"Syraphem can be Heretics?" They had Brites in Keloseros, but most of them were near mortal, the bloodlines having been kept "pure" by Malek standards.

"Anyone can be a Heretic. My mother was a Shadow Heretic, my father ..." she hesitated, her straight features hardening. "He's Syraphem." The words sounded acidic.

"Your mother, she's–"

"Dead."

"And your father?"

"Should be."

"I understand that."

"I don't care."

Aheia let the insult roll through her, watching Emryn's wings tighten a fraction behind her. The topic sparked tension all around them in cold bursts, and Aheia chose to loosen her grip when the anger reared its head, changing the subject instead. "You sit at Alshaytan's table. Do you hold status?" Females were not allowed to hold positions of power in Keloseros.

The Syraphem narrowed her eyes, and a slow smile spread across her lips as she trailed the wet dagger over the rock in front of her. "What do you know about our race?"

Aheia tilted her head, leaning her back against the cold window. *Cold*, it was cold outside.

Every bit of knowledge on the tip of her tongue suddenly felt judgmental and generalized. Since she'd gotten here, absolutely nothing had been as she was told nor as she expected it to be. Now, staring back at the Nephilim in front of her, it felt that any and all words would be wrong, no matter how carefully she chose them.

"I've heard that you're creatures of darkness." She watched Emryn's blade as she continued the scraping pattern on the wall. "You thrive in chaos, and you worship the Dark Gods." She stopped there, tucking all of the nastier pieces of information away.

"So, you know nothing then?" Emryn raised her eyebrow. "Though I suppose thriving in chaos is close to describing any of us." She dropped the knife to her side and pressed it against her thigh until it melded back into black ink, looking permanent, and immovable, like it had never left her skin.

"Enlighten me," Aheia said, crossing her arms and straightening her back.

"It would take too long to do such a thing." Emryn's expression held a condescending undertone as she crossed her arms, mirroring Aheia. "But I imagine what I've heard about females in Keloseros is true. That you live to serve, that your purpose is to breed?"

Aheia opened her mouth to speak, but her words strangled her.

"For all our diversity as a race," Emryn continued, "one thing has been consistent throughout the shifting beliefs, the religious quarrels, the magyck: the lore has always favored females, we all *came* from a female when 'Amm created us. We serve the same way males do, we fight, we carve, and we have our place here." Her words held pride and something that edged defensiveness. "We've sworn our allegiance, but we are not objects, not like females are objects in your world. Those of us who serve, do it of our own free will." Her eyes drifted to the window and took on a faraway look. "It wasn't always like that. Life was much harder for us all during Sahren's reign. Arioch has changed that for us, but there was heavy fallout. What you've walked in on is … complicated."

"Meaning?"

"There's a delicate balance here, and you threaten it," she said, her words as sharp as the dagger she'd held moments ago. And suddenly the reason Emryn seemed to hate her very presence made sense. So, Aheia kept the rest of her questions locked away, doubting the Syraphem would deign to answer them anyways as they finished their trip down the old hallway.

Once they made it through past the long line of windows, Aheia tried one last thing.

"What does Ruhí mean?" she asked.

The Syraphem looked over her shoulder, dark eyes dancing with humor. "Not a chance."

When they made it to her door, Emryn reached behind her back and, similarly to the apple, came back with something she had no room to carry on her body. It was a book, leather-bound, with a gold spine.

"I'm hoping this will keep you out of trouble," she said, narrowing her eyes, an expression that was quick and calculated. "I don't have time to follow you around."

"I'd rather you didn't." Aheia took the book and fanned through some of the old pages. There were notes in the margins and some drawings at the bottom of winged creatures, swords, and fire. "This is yours?'

"Yeah, so don't ruin it; it's my only copy."

"Why are you giving me this?"

"You look like you need to escape our world for a little while. You should understand most of it, though it slips into a couple of different languages." Her expression softened for just a moment before her hard exterior wrapped back around her lean frame. "But hurt the book and I hurt you." She tapped the side of her thigh before walking back down the way they came from.

Aheia curled up on the window bench in her room and stared at the book in front of her. She was restless, her mind stumbling over itself, taking in everything she'd learned and seen in the last day.

"What are you doing?" she whispered to herself, for what felt like the millionth time. The longer she sat the less she felt in control, and the more she felt an urgency trickle into her veins. Her days were already dwindling, and time seemed to become even less tangible than before.

You need to figure out your next moves. What's next? What comes after Aljira?

"That's the trouble isn't it?" she answered herself, leaning her head against the cool glass of the window. She couldn't quite see past Aljira.

What if you find a way to stay?

She bit the inside of her cheek. There was no direct law against a Mithra living in the Dark realm, though it was unheard of. She'd have to get Arioch's blessing, but from the way he acted, her presence was a nuisance—merely an opportunity to toy with something new. She imagined her place here would not be well-received, and once again she would become a burden.

"More trouble than she's worth."

She exhaled slowly and opened the book, leafing through a couple of pages, feeling the sinking feeling of self-doubt pull her into the cushion beneath her.

A Nephilim would never help a Mithra ... well, not without something in return.

And she had nothing else to offer.

13

Chapter

Arioch

Arioch stepped across the cracked ground of the unmarked cave, an uneasy feeling in his chest. He always felt some semblance of reverence when he approached Gehenna, but today felt different, though nothing around him seemed out of place.

The cave stretched tall and wide in front of him, the same as thousands of others that lay just below Aljira in a dizzying maze, designed purposefully to both keep unwanted visitors out and hold in the things that were trapped behind Gehenna's walls. The mortals often spoke of this place, but in their stories they molded Aljira and Gehenna into one beast, using the term hel in reference to either. Meanwhile, Aljira was simply a victim of geography.

But the misconception went past mere naming. The mortals had created their own lore for his race out of fear, one that spoke of cities lit with flames, filled with decomposing bodies, clouded with souls. It didn't help that eons ago the Malek descended into Lyria, and preached their own version of history to anyone who would listen. They had painted themselves as the gatekeepers to some higher power, while they framed the Nephilim and all they stood for as unholy and against the Gods' will.

Arioch looked at the bare cave walls, the ones that the mortals pictured being devoured by flames. Gehenna was far from the helscape they imagined. But for all the things Gehenna wasn't, it was dark and dingy, hiding sadness and death in its shadows. The same shadows thrummed in Arioch's veins, the kind that all Avarice were born with, the ones that the goddess 'Amm had spun around them. He felt the tendrils slither underneath his skin as he made his way across the barren landscape, pulling and coaxing him closer to their home, the place where so much of the Calmani magyck rested. The pressure was coiling around him as he felt the volatile energy below his feet—the same essence he had learned to tap into to power Aljira with the help of his Heretics, allowing them to move away from fire to light their homes and towards Solas instead.

The Gods who had created Gehenna had long since abandoned them and in their absence, the Nephilim and the Mithra pretended they were their equals, though their magyck was nothing close to the Calmani that the original four carried at their claw tips.

The Malek had quickly taken point among the Mithra in Keloseros and created a strict hierarchy that saw five of their old family bloodlines in charge with one *epísmos* that was elected among them.

Arioch knew it was far too easy for the reigning sovereigns of both realms to imagine themselves as deities, had seen it with his father, and saw it now in Ophion. Arioch was under no illusion; none of them were Gods. They were the unfortunate bastards that shouldered the consequences of someone else's immortal boredom.

His own role as Alshaytan was all but forced upon him. It shouldn't have been him, it should have been his brother Kazim—he was the eldest.

Arioch flexed his hand at the memory of his family.

Even after all these years it still wound hot talons into his middle that squeezed until he couldn't breathe, a concoction of pain and guilt and loss that he hadn't been able to drown out no matter how hard he tried. He never wanted to be Alshaytan, hadn't expected it, and would give it up in a heartbeat if it meant he could barter for Kazim's life. It didn't matter that his brother might not have done the same for him, didn't matter that they'd hated one another for most of their childhood, didn't matter that they grappled over their father's approval without regard for one another. None of it changed the fact that Arioch had screamed and fought when the Mithra killed Kazim. It hadn't changed the fact that he'd almost stripped himself bare trying to stop it.

No.

And it never would.

Arioch gritted his teeth at the memory, his insides squeezing tight until his breathing became labored.

The Malek, the Dioscuri—all Mithra Čist, could rot for all he was concerned, and that would have been reason enough not to hand Aheia over. It also should have been his motivation to hate her—but he couldn't quite seem to convince himself. There was something fractured about her, something dark that he saw in those broken moments when she seemed to lose control—right before she plastered that practiced, placid look back into place. He couldn't hate her because he couldn't assign the blame of an entire race to one being. Nor would his body allow it, not when her soul begged him to return to her, to stay close. None of that stopped him from hating himself just a little bit more for what felt like a betrayal to his kind, though, especially when he replayed last night in his mind.

The voice that was whispering about his morality and what he should or *shouldn't* be or do was weak, pushed to the side by his shadows, his wants, his desire to watch Aheia squirm for him again. And more than that, his drive to figure out her dirty little secrets in the process.

He had questions, even though some of the words hadn't fully formed in his mind, as he stepped towards *Nahr Alnufus*, the River of Souls. He gazed down into the stagnant water at his feet, bodies floating by while the surface stayed serene. This was one of many resting places for dead souls, one of the hundreds of rivers just like it, each of them fabled to reach deeper than Lyria's core. The souls suspended there were mere whispers–an echo of a life lived, dripping from the walls with each death and collecting in the river. They were as alive as the rock that cracked underneath Arioch's boots. It wasn't how the mortals described in the stories, either. They'd had some notion of an "other side" that would greet them in death. But the souls and the bodies were pulled from each other once the life drained from them completely and settled in separate resting places within Gehenna; the bodies hidden away in deep caverns while their souls floated in large rings for eternity, lifeless and gray, their eyes expression-less—all the same.

He hated those eyes.

They seemed to see past all of the shadows he'd built up inside of his chest, that he'd used to bolster the marred insides he hid away from everyone in his life, making sure to keep even the closest Nephilim at arm's length. Their lifeless eyes seemed to laugh, even though such a thing was impossible.

The entrance to Gehenna lay across the water, hidden in the cave wall that would part for him once he approached. Arioch stepped onto the iridescent surface of the water that carried him on an invisible barrier, dark wisps of smoke curling underneath his feet, as he made his way to the other bank. He didn't have to look when he felt a shift in the air next to him to know Mazikeen had glided to his side, the embers woven into her dark skin singeing the barrier with each footstep.

They moved wordlessly, an action that was more muscle memory than anything, the same movement repeated thousands of times through the years, crossing the dead together. There'd never been anyone else, and there never would be. He wouldn't allow that. The burden they shared was theirs alone, and he would do everything in his power to keep it that way.

Maz seemed to be made for the dead.

The Djynn had lived thousands of lives, rolling through time like it was a mere annoyance to her. She had been bound to him for what felt like eons, even though, in reality, it had been substantially shorter. She was an Ifrit, a Djynn that similar to Nephilim and Mithra Heretics, carried magyck at her fingertips, though hers was much more dangerous. Her story was harrowing, and she didn't often speak of it—he didn't push her to either. They both kept their shadows and their darkness close, like the things that lurked in ominous whispers and broken mirrors, just out of sight.

He shot her a look as they cleared Nahr Alnufus, catching the outlines of red ink that graced her wrists. That magyck was what kept her bound to this body, to this form, and had appeared the moment he'd accepted the offering of her life. She'd promised him her allegiance and had kept her word, serving as one of his closest and most loyal subjects. Maz had striking, dark eyes, almost black, and wore gold jewelry in her nose and ears that he'd never seen her without—the only parts of her past that she carried with her. Sometimes when he looked at her, he saw whatever slithered under her skin, barely contained in her current form. She was a force of nature even now but unbound, she consumed it.

The ground shifted when they approached as if Gehenna felt them near. The rock wall repositioned, loose stones ricocheting off the ground, and the dark and jagged corners rolling to the side, leaving behind a crack wide enough for two. It ran up and along the ceiling, so tall that it was almost impossible to discern where it ended, breaking apart low-hanging stalactites that would fuse back together as soon as they passed the border.

"Unimpressive," she said in a deep, sultry voice. "I somehow thought a Dioscuri would be ... shiny."

"Not in this realm, Mazikeen. She's all but mortal here. What did you need from me?"

"Are you sure?" The Ifrit furrowed her brows, her long black dress dripping onto the floor like onyx oil that never seemed to let go of her body. She was almost as tall as him in this form, which was small compared to what she was unleashed. The usual fire that sizzled across her hair was reduced to soft embers lighting up around her neck as her frustration flared. He knew if he spared a glance, he'd see her dark irises banded by orange sparks, her skin prickling with the same tiny embers that trailed her hair. The fire blazed when her emotions got the best of her, even though she liked to pretend she had none. Arioch knew better, and it was just as well.

"Why do you ask?"

"Something's wrong." Mazikeen shook her head, her expression pensive.

"Wrong?"

"There was a disruption. The city suffered a short outage, so quick it wouldn't have been obvious to anyone, a simple hiccup in Solas. But I felt it here; it came from the cage."

"That's not possible."

"And yet it happened," she said in a bored drawl. "Cracks have formed before, but the timing seems too strange."

"You're talking about the Mithra?" Arioch's pulse jumped.

"Yes. I fear there are more layers to this than you think, Alshaytan. Let me question her. I can make quick work of it if you let me use a knife."

"No touching, Maz," Arioch growled as the shadows slithered beneath his skin. He was calling to his Varcolac that appeared moments later, its tendrils curling around his legs in acknowledgment. He'd only seen his creature a handful of times when it peeled back the smoke of its own accord. It was large, not quite a dog, not quite a wolf, with tall ears, a heavy snout with protruding teeth, and eyes that spoke of lifetimes lived. It could go from being a vicious monster to a docile pet in mere moments, and on occasion, he considered naming it. Maz ran one of her long dark fingers through the tendrils, teasing a growl from their depths as they trekked into Gehenna together.

14

Chapter

Arioch

The creation of Gehenna itself was a thing of legends that varied depending on the source. While stories disagreed on the specifics, all of them converged across one singular piece of information—that it was first created for Manāt and the dead that had littered Lyria at his hands.

The history of the Old Gods had been transcribed by different oracles across time, and told of Aljira's creation, how it was pulled into existence by 'Amm—the Dark Goddess that kept herself wrapped in stars and soft shadows—who created the Nephilim race out of loneliness shortly after. The life in 'Amm's realm attracted both Theia and Aether, the two Brite Gods who interwove their Calmani magyck into a desolate part of the world, pulling Keloseros from the barren rock. The realm lived in perpetual light and became home to the Mithra, the Brite Gods' children.

Lyria wasn't completely empty at the time of the Gods' arrival. A few cities were strewn across the continents, populated by immortals that had learned to live in the harsh environments with perpetual darkness around them, save for whatever light was cast by planets that skirted their orbit. And while the other Gods were attracted by life, the cold and hungry existence in Lyria was what attracted Manāt, the most vicious of the Deities.

He was a blight that the world never completely recovered from, taking up a dangerous fascination with the immortals that lived in the cities and developing a thirst for creation. Manāt wanted his own race just as the other Gods had their Mithra and Nephilim; children that would worship him and live their lives just as hungrily as he did. That was how the Kaymaat came into existence, Demi Gods that inherited Manāt's power of creation and darkness.

The Demi Gods were ravenous, hunting down the immortals to satiate their need for energies to stay alive. They sliced through the once endless lives that populated Lyria and forced them into short and broken existences, which for a while, seemed to be enough.

But it wasn't the same once death became part of their world. The energy of the now mortals ceasing to satisfy the Kaymaat's urges, they soon turned to the children of the other Gods They broke down both borders to spread death among Keloseros and Aljira, Manāt's same immortal boredom thrumming through their veins as they doused the realms in blood.

They were more dangerous not only because of their intense Calmani born magyck, but because they, unlike the other races, kept their power when entering each realm.

The other Gods knew they couldn't let Manāt and the Kaymaat continue, not if they wanted to remain on this planet. So, 'Amm and Theia banded together, forging a cage built with Brite and Dark Calmani that could hold Manāt and his children inside. They tricked him, a ruse that forced 'Amm to give her life, the last parts of her floating into the sky and melding with the moon.

The sub-realm would become a resting place for those dead souls that Manāt and the Kaymaat had claimed. While the remaining Gods couldn't eradicate death, because it was hidden in the shadows that had splintered across millions of moments, they could promise that the dead would find their rightful spot in Gehenna after their passing. They created the *Wraiths*, ghostly creatures that collected the bodies from the face of the world and brought them back to Gehenna, ensuring their peace there.

Lyria dealt with the fallout at the hands of the Kaymaat long after the Demi Gods were imprisoned with their father. They'd played with creation for years before their downfall, molding children of their own: the Djynn, the Helren, and many more, all of them powerful, all of them dangerous, and all of them thrown into the world without care.

Arioch accepted the existence of the Old Gods, though they had never seemed to hear his prayers in the past. He'd resigned himself to acknowledging them only when he felt his shadows baring their teeth. He wasn't quite himself when they seized control, and some days it took all of his concentration to hold them back. Because despite everything he believed about himself, the shadows were evil. They thirsted for violence, even as he tried his best to keep his mind level.

His powers slithered and pulled as he stepped down the tall, winding staircase that would lead him into Gehenna's depths, the darkness around him giving way to soft, gray obscurity. It was almost like being swallowed by storm clouds, bursts of red and amber lightning flashing around him in nondescript patterns. There was no railing here, and when he looked over the edge, there was no indication of an end; only charred, black stairs that disappeared into the smoke below. It would take him days to climb to the bottom—or at least, that's how it felt—the urgency of his own shadows growing with every step. He became blood-thirsty, and angrier, as the seconds stretched into minutes, and the minutes turned into hours. He wanted to hurt, wanted to fight, wanted to cause pain, but the needs weren't all his own. They were coming from his shadows and the way the energy spoke to them so close to the cage that imprisoned Manāt.

Down here, he couldn't separate himself like he was used to, couldn't seem to find the line that divided him from *them*.

Arioch ground his teeth as he cleared the last step, his chest pulsing, and his skin taut. He was standing on a narrow walkway, suspended in the void, that led across an invisible barrier, the first line of defense of the cage that loomed underneath him. He inhaled slowly, his shadows stuttering off his shoulders like they always did, guiding him into the haze that made sight almost impossible. The prison itself had been built by Brite and Dark, the specifics of which had gotten lost over time with the exception of one detail that had set up the entirety of the Nephilim political system. It was that the Avarice were the only species that could touch the guarded walls and mend them, should cracks form along the barrier. They were the only ones who possessed shadows at their fingertips. It was why Avarice had a history of being Alshaytan. The magyck came at a price, as it did with most creatures. For Arioch and his kind, it meant the lack of a soul in place of those dark smoky tendrils. It was poetic, in a fucked up and twisted way; not possessing a soul, yet craving another's.

He came to the end of the walkway and looked down,

complete darkness meeting his gaze, broken only by wayward flashes of amber light above his head. He imagined it was what standing in the eye of a hurricane might feel like, a storm brewing around him while the center was calm. He held his hand over the invisible cage below, feeling a new heat running up his entire arm as he closed his eyes. His shadows wandered, and he watched them disappear on the back of his closed eyelids, the tendrils slipping from them and diving deep into the void below, slithering along the slick wall that encased Manāt and his children to check for any irregularities. They caressed the ancient symbols that were etched into the air, the second line of defense, and it sent fire through his blood, forcing him to his knees. Every time he let the shadows taste the old magyck, it took everything he had to stay on the edge of that ledge, not to follow them over, to answer the siren call that was bigger than him, sung by a God who was tired of being confined.

He grit his teeth, feeling his powers spreading thin and encasing the entire surface, bit by bit until he thought he might tear apart at the seams. A laugh ripped itself from his chest, the pain splitting his insides and twisting his gut. The sound was manic as it echoed around him, wild and detached.

Arioch dug his nails into the edge of the walkway, the rough stone cutting into the pads of his fingers as he checked the last of the wards before his shadows came rushing towards him when he called, forcing him back in a slow crawl. The magyck was holding strong, and he could feel the dust of it under his skin, no cracks, no fractures, nothing out of place.

He wondered if Maz had imagined the shift. Though that seemed about as likely as the shift itself.

He put distance between himself and the cage, finding his way back to the staircase, the magyck burning like acid when his powers slithered back from the depths.

He fought to rise to his feet, his heart pumping so hard he felt it in his throat as he took the first step up the staircase. His muscles resisted, forcing him back down into a crawl, his shadows rebelling just as much as he clawed himself higher. It was as if every fiber inside of him fought to both stay and leave, threatening to split him in two. It took clearing multiple landings for the pressure to lessen, for the desire to light a fire that would consume his entire realm to ebb from his mind.

Rising to the top felt like hours, but there he could finally breathe, sitting on the edge and cradling his forehead in his hands. It was moments like these in which he wished he could give it all back, wished he was insignificant.

He let himself feel it for another heartbeat before locking the feeling away tightly and meeting back up with Maz at the entrance of Gehenna.

15

Chapter

Aheia

She'd slept. For the first time, her mind was quiet and free from the intrusion of her past. Sleep pulled her under in such a thick wave that when she woke it took her a breathless moment to figure out where she was.

The sky outside of her window looked the same as it had when she'd drifted from consciousness, which left her searching for any indicator that might tell her what time of day it was. She found it sitting outside of her door, a tray piled high with food.

It looked similar to what she'd seen in the atrium before: a variety of meats, rice, and fruit, as well as a carved blood orange that was drizzled in honey in the center of the tray. She felt a blush creep into her cheeks, the flush spread through her body, her mind forcing the memories of Arioch and his hands ahead of her rational thoughts. Her stomach turned to lead, and the hunger she felt at the smell of the food transformed into something needy and aching that had her leaning against the doorway, her legs unsteady. After taking a moment to gather herself, she reached for the scroll tucked underneath the black plate and unraveled it. There, in thick, inky letters, she read:

Don't forget to pray before you eat this morning, little goddess.

Her brow furrowed and her heart pounded in her ears as anxiety coursed through her.

Morning.

An entire day had come and gone, wasted on sleeping and reading. She'd let herself decompress, but now there was a new immediacy in her mind. Time was quickly dwindling, and though she didn't have a plan, she found her feet carrying her down the stone hallway that led towards the old foyer. Her pulse was thrumming in time with her footsteps as her mind reeled.

Pretend that staying in Aljira is not an option. What would you do then?

Her steps grew more frantic.

Maybe go west.

She'd considered the Badlands, where the Djynn were rumored to live, knew they dealt in wish-fulfillment of their own, but her knowledge of the beings was more lore than fact.

There is no guarantee in the west, she said to herself, her thoughts guiding her down the steps and past the fireplace in the foyer.

If you don't go west, you are stuck. If you go east, you'll run around the fucking world and right back to where you started and you have no means of breaching through to any of the parallels.

She hurried down a long hallway, identical to the one outside of her room. Here, though, the waves were breaking against the glass, the iridescent water rolling and swirling like it was chasing her along.

You'll die staying in Lyria. You can't hide from them forever. And then like a knife across her skin, *You'll die either way... or worse.*

The thought pushed ice down her spine, so cold her fingers ached, the sweat that beaded on the back of her neck doing nothing to warm her. She picked up her pace, her feet scraping against the rough rock underfoot, eyes trained on the end of the hallway and two tall double doors backlit by a dark night sky. Her fingers fumbled with the gold knobs, opening the doors and stumbling out onto an open balcony, a chilled wind whipping around her, caressing her cheeks and tangling her hair.

The water was roaring on both sides of her, framing the balcony that was made of old stone just as the rest of this wing was, tumbling past her into a dark void below. She stepped forward, grasping onto the black, metal railing, rocking forward slightly to look over the edge.

She couldn't see the bottom, and she wondered if she jumped, how long she'd fall before she was swallowed by whatever lingered below.

A thought ...

"Watch out." The voice made her teeter on the edge, gripping the rail harder.

She looked over her shoulder, finding Shiron leaning against the tall door behind her, his arms crossed over the blades on his chest.

Her eyes caught on the dark beads he wore around his neck, and she thought she recognized them. They looked similar to the devotion beads the Mithra wore.

"Where's the fun in that?"

"Staying alive," he said, unamused.

"Overrated, I think," Aheia said. She'd meant it to be light-hearted, but it came out thick and sad. "Life is…" she looked down into the void, tiptoeing to the railing, "fleeting, for mortals. For us, it's just … pain," she murmured the last word to herself as she caught some of the warm spray on her face.

She heard shifting behind her, and then Shiron leaned onto the railing next to her.

"You believe in the Gods?" he asked. "You prayed yesterday."

Aheia gave him a long sideways look before returning to the void below.

"I don't know; I've never felt their presence. The Gods have never responded, never seemed to hear me before. Meanwhile, there's Mithra in charge pretending to be just as powerful, and expecting similar treatment," she scoffed. "All I know is that for all the prayer I see in this world, the poor become poorer, and conflict amongst us thickens each day."

She waited a couple of moments, studying the Leviathan next to her before continuing. "That's not the answer you were looking for. Do you believe?"

It took Shiron equally as long to answer.

"Yes," he said, more to himself than to Aheia. "I've seen too much. I have to believe there's a purpose to it all. I know of their presence in this world–Aljira and Gehenna are proof of their power–but I choose to direct my own decisions rather than to wonder about what some higher power might do in my circumstance."

Aheia considered him for a moment. "I think kismet and purpose can be separate from the Gods. My mother used to tell me that the universe's energy was around long before the physical rock we live on. Powers and destinies were doled out, planted in fate, centuries before the Gods appeared to make Lyria their playground."

"Then what do you believe happens after death?" Shiron asked his expression hard.

"Nothing," Aheia said.

"Nothing?"

"I think we just disappear, dust in the wind, forgotten, or bodies in Gehenna, I suppose, but still dead. It's not like we live on down there, right? It's just a resting place." She knew how bitter it sounded. "Why remember us? What makes us so special?"

Shiron leaned his elbows onto the railing. "You don't want to be remembered?"

"Most of the people who have remembered me in the past were people I'd much prefer forgot me instead." Aheia stared over the railing until her eyes started playing tricks on her as the spray of the water morphed into small shapes.

The thought of Mithra and Gehenna sparked another question that had been working its way through her mind. "Why do they call Arioch *Mithrek Morta?*" she asked. It suggested something along the lines of angel of death, but at the same time, tied the word to the Mithra, not to the Nephilim.

Shiron's lip twitched. "The mortals think everything in existence had to originate as pure and just. They would never accept the fact that Nephilim were created at the hands of 'Amm because they believe us all monsters. They think that our race was born out of sin, or devolvement–that something horrible had to happen to taint our good moralities early on." He shook his head. "Fallen Mithra."

Aheia's brows furrowed at the information. "The mortals believe that Nephilim were once Mithra?"

"Something along those lines," Shiron said, shrugging off the subject. "Do I need to worry about you jumping over the edge?" He shot her a look. "I've never wanted offspring. I don't enjoy being responsible for other people, and you're making me remember exactly why it grates on my nerves."

"No," Aheia said, and she meant it.

Shiron pushed back on the railing. "It would hurt. It would really hurt," he said, underlining his point. "Go back to your room, Aheia. I'd escort you, but I have somewhere to be."

"The beads," she said as he disappeared from view, "are they prayer beads?"

Shiron halted with his back turned. "Yes." And with that, he left, the doors swinging shut behind him.

Aheia had gotten lost in the beauty of the world outside, letting herself drift off amongst the stars as she wondered what the different constellations might be called. She'd learned as much as she could from books out of Ophion's personal library, and conversations with some of the more radical minds in the southern territories. It was said that the stars dictated as much of their lives as the sun cycle did, explaining different beings' personalities depending on the month and time of their birth. There was also loose speculation about how the moon could affect someone's behavior, something about tides and body composition. She wondered if the stars and the moon that were ever-present worked differently here as she stepped back into the hallway, her eyes on the galaxy outside.

When Aheia turned, she yelped, facing unwavering darkness as the door snapped shut behind her. Her eyes met long, sharp, familiar teeth, and suffocating shadows that swallowed the surrounding hallway. She stumbled back against the door, making herself as small as she could as her heart rammed itself into her ribs, as she remembered those same teeth digging into her skin just outside the border.

There was nowhere for her to go, no escape from the balcony, and she had a feeling that doors wouldn't hold a creature like this, just as the border magyck had melted around it, the resistance of it a mere idea.

The only thing she could think was to try and pass it, keeping her bargain close in her mind, knowing she'd be safe here... Though the Varcolac didn't make her feel particularly so as she squeezed her way past its massive body, the creature's teeth following her as it turned its head. By now, she knew the beast well, knew its game. At least she did out in Lyria. Here the rules were different.

It was meant to protect the realm, and Aheia got an overwhelming feeling that it hadn't decided if she posed a threat or not. Her heartbeat sped up, and so did her feet. She was running again, and the Varcolac followed, matching her pace.

Gods.

She flew through the foyer before skirting across the new, black marble, down empty hallways, casting back the occasional glance even though she didn't need to. Aheia knew it was still there; she could hear it, could see the shadows coiling. It hadn't made a move to attack her, only followed in unnerving proximity.

Her feet slipped on the slick floor, sending her to her knees before she scrambled up again, bruised, but moving for the nearest door. It was locked, so she continued down the line, trying each of them, none of them budging.

"Why the fuck does anyone need this many doors?" she groaned, pushing against another, proving to be just as immovable as the rest. The shadows curled up her legs and she shrieked at the touch. It felt like mist.

She kicked it off, backing away from the creature slowly, the mass convulsing in front of her like a rolling cloud until her back hit the wall. Her fingers fumbled with the fabric of her dress as she slid along it, and was met by yet another door. Closing her eyes, she pressed back, the dark handle dipping down under the pressure of her palm. Not expecting it to give way, she fell back onto her hands when the door swung open, leaving her a scattered mess on the floor.

16

Chapter

Aheia

Aheia whirled around, climbing to her feet clumsily, her white hair spilling across her face as if trying to hide her from the room.

"She knows how to make an entrance."

Her eyes rose to find herself in the middle of a scene that drained the blood from every part of her body. Lúc was standing at the center of the dark room, hands covered in blood, one of them clenched in the dark gray shirt of a demon Aheia didn't know. His face was so split apart that she wouldn't have recognized him if she *had* known him. Shiron's hands were just as messy, although his clothes were somehow still perfect, his face calm and measured. The only evidence that he had just beaten the Leviathan in front of him to a pulp was the mess across his knuckles and the drops of blood on his face.

Her chest constricted, nearly pulling her clean off her feet for the second time as she met Arioch's burning gray eyes. He was standing across the room, leaning against the wall, his posture relaxed, and his arms crossed over his chest while his features suggested pure rage.

She swallowed, her gaze drifting to Emryn who walked towards her, her wings flaring for a moment, her expression exasperated as she grabbed Aheia's shoulder. "It's like you're trying to get hurt," the Syraphem hissed.

"*Sho byaal hon.*" A Nephilim standing to the left of Arioch said, his face twisted up in disgust as he took her in. "Her kind isn't welcome."

Arioch shifted against the wall, his gaze never leaving Aheia's. "Let's not get hung up on whose kind is welcome, Siraj, when your own cousin is standing on the brink of exile."

Emryn looked at Arioch, and he gave her a quick nod at which the Syraphem dropped her hand from Aheia but stayed close, crossing her arms.

"Respectfully, what the *fuck*, Alshaytan," a blonde Nephilim next to Siraj said, his black horns short and peeking out from his hair. He wore a dark gray suit, same as Siraj, with clean lines and as far as Aheia could tell, no weapons.

Arioch pushed off the wall, rolling his shoulders. "What's that adage, Eros?" He stepped closer to the mess of dead and bloodied Nephilim in the center of the room and let his gaze drift over the bodies while Lúc looked at him with a feral glint in his eye. "If you have to add the term *respectfully*, then there's a chance you'll ruin my fucking mood."

The blonde scoffed but Siraj put a hand on his shoulder. "Alshaytan–"

"Her presence with us isn't a point of discussion," Arioch cut him off. "However, what exactly we should do with Bassam is."

"Enough. They've learned their lesson," Siraj said, following Arioch into the center of the room, his eyes continuously flicking to Aheia as if he was assuring himself of her presence.

Arioch's calm exterior seemed to waver when he looked at the demon. "*They* have, Siraj," he nodded towards the bodies, "*he* has not."

At his words, a Nephilim that had been standing in one of the darker parts of the room emerged from the shadows, her blonde hair short, gold jewelry glinting in her nose and ears, her blue eyes piercing. She grabbed ahold of a Nephilim that was cowering near Eros. Then, she dragged him over to where Shiron was readjusting his devotional beads and Lúc stood grinning, trailing his tongue across his bloody knuckles.

Aheia shivered.

"*Please*, I was only conducting social maintenance," the demon Aheia guessed must have been Bassam said, struggling in the short blonde's hold.

"Maintenance..." Arioch narrowed his eyes, drawing out the word like he was tasting it as he said it. "You think you're qualified for such a task?"

"They couldn't pay the tithe, Arioch. They–"

"What did you just call him?" Lúc snapped.

Bassam shrugged back as Arioch shook his head, picking an invisible speck of lint from his shirt. "Remind me what authority you think you possess?"

"I, well … It's … This is my …" Bassam's eyes flashed to Siraj who stared him into the ground, his arms crossed.

"Your … *what?*" Arioch sounded bored as he inspected the Nephilim. "Nothing here is yours. You think you have power?" He quirked an eyebrow, while Aheia could do nothing but watch. "Show me. Persuade our dear Aylee to let go of you, or maybe you'd like to try your hand at stopping Lúc from ripping your insides out."

Bassam struggled in Aylee's hold once again, but this time it was halfhearted, something sinking in his eyes.

"Please, I only–"

"You forced females into the *blood trade*," Arioch said the words like they were a curse and Aheia thought she could see a fine line of fury bisecting his stony exterior. "For failing to pay a tithe that is not law."

Bassam only swallowed, his eyes darting to Siraj again, who looked like the whole situation tasted wrong. And it did; it tasted so wrong it was hard for Aheia to keep her composure.

She wanted to wash out her mouth with something, anything, that would take out the sour sting.

Forcing females into the blood trade.

"I'll give you anything," Bassam pleaded finally, forfeiting the last of his resistance.

I'll give you anything. It's what she'd said to Arioch the night she flung herself into his realm. They were words she'd never get back, words that were no longer hers because she hadn't just given him anything; she'd given him *everything*. And that reminder lingered across from her, standing tall, features now plainly twisted up in anger.

"Siraj," Arioch said, turning his back to Aheia. "I need your agreement."

Aheia caught Eros sneering at her from behind Siraj, that smile making him look like a reptile.

"I'm not defending him, Alshaytan, but he has a family," Siraj's voice dropped in a familiar way. It almost sounded like he expected the statement alone to excuse Bassam's action.

"Yes!" Bassam struggled against Aylee's hold, his eyes darting around the Nephilim. "I have a daughter, I could give you my daughter."

Silence followed as the words expanded in the room like a tangible thing.

I could give you my daughter.

Aheia's heart jumped against her ribs. And Siraj's eyes flashed to the ceiling so quickly she almost missed it. He looked irritated.

"She's beautiful, just like her mother, and she'll serve you well." Hurried, scared, cowardly words.

"You'd sell your daughter? To *Alshaytan*?" Aheia breathed, the Nephilim standing with Siraj turning their attention to her.

"Asmaht, Mithra," one of Siraj's people hissed at her, his eyes dark and angry. She met his stare with strength, hanging onto the anger that Bassam was conjuring.

"You don't address her," Emryn snapped but the demon that had spoken didn't take his eyes off Aheia.

"She should not be here," the Nephilim continued, his face twisting in distaste. "It's wrong."

"Siraj, control your younglings," Arioch drawled, crossing his arms.

"It's wrong!" The demon shouted, spit flying from his mouth.

Aheia saw him move. It was so quick. She could barely follow his actions as he crossed the room, his gray clothing a blur, a knife poised in his hand. He lunged for Aheia, just as she recoiled, her arm flying up to brace against the impact, her heart jumping in her chest. She'd readied herself for the feel of metal, for a blade that would slice her skin, but it never came, a soft drift of air brushing across her cheek. Aheia's eyes widened at the shadows that had spread through the room, whipping around the Nephilim like a storm, and at its center, Arioch. He had his hand wrapped around the blade that had been meant for her, holding the knife inches from her face. It was cutting into him deep, black, blood dripping from his palm and onto the floor.

She watched as he tore the knife from the demon by the blade and grabbed the hilt with his uninjured hand before driving it deep into the offender's neck.

The air around them seemed to still with the shadows, everyone's breath drawn as they watched the Nephilim sag to his knees, the blood pooling at Aheia's feet.

A vicious growl broke from Arioch's chest, and from the corner of her eye, Aheia saw Lúc's long claws drawn out over his knuckles. They were sharp and black, and when she looked into his eyes, they'd changed to a deep purple. He blinked slowly, canines pushing past his lips.

"*Hal ant malnunje*," Siraj barked, his eyes blazing. "You do not move without my permission, *ever*."

The Nephilim around the room stepped back, anger plain on their faces, their hands on their weapons.

"Alshaytan, you have my apologies," Siraj said, but Arioch's eyes were busy sliding across Aheia's features like he was looking for something in her face while his injured hand clenched at his side. Her heart squeezed in her chest, and it felt like it was crooning for him as she let herself realize that he'd saved her life.

"Thank you," she whispered, feeling a wave of warm gratitude wash over her.

"Don't take it personally." The corner of his mouth twitched while his eyes stayed stoic, and he tapped her glyph on his arm.

Right.

It felt so real–the emotion. But of course, it wasn't, it was her soul. She clenched her jaw, the warm prickle that was spreading through her intensifying when Arioch reached for her and pulled her against his chest, addressing Siraj like nothing at all had happened, his voice bored and arrogant. Aheia didn't hear their exchange, her gaze trained on the floor in front of her. She could feel her soul burning against her through the fabric of his clothes, the hollow in her chest worsening. Her eyes were starting to fill with tears she didn't want as she focused on the blood, on the bodies, on anything that would give her an escape from the pain in her chest. It was like standing with the ghost of a lover who'd been killed by the enemy–a need and yearning that felt like what she imagined the blade of that dagger would have if the demon had succeeded to stab her with it.

"Are you going to be strong, or are you going to let them see this?" Aheia jumped in his hold. He was speaking against the shell of her ear, his voice a soft rasp, low enough for only her to hear, while he stroked his thumb over her pulse point in a slow rhythm.

She swallowed over and over again, trying to calm down her heart, the tears threatening to fall only worsening as Arioch leaned his chin onto her head. She inhaled deeply watching him motion to a Leviathan that had been standing in the darkness of the room, his large stature a commanding presence. He had two horns winding across the top of his head, bordered by black curls that were pulled back at the nape of his neck, his eyes as dark as Lúc's. He was holding onto some silver machine that gleamed in the light, a long needle exposed on one end and a dark liquid held by a glass receptacle on the other.

"I think I want to leave you alive for now," Arioch said, leaning his chin on top of Aheia's head as he pulled her out of the way so that the tall Leviathan with the horns could take their spot in front of Bassam. "But I'll leave you with a reminder."

"No, *please*, Siraj, please!" Bassam struggled in Aylee's hold, black blood dripping from the wound at his neck.

"Do me a favor, give Bassam a unique design–don't forget something special for those eyes," Arioch said to the horned Leviathan.

"No–you can't," Bassam cried.

"Don't worry, Tariq's time is precious. He'll work fast," Arioch said as Tariq readjusted the gleaming metal contraption he was holding so that it started to buzz.

"You're dismissed," Arioch said to Siraj. "Keep your men in line." It was a warning that took up the room and hung heavy among them.

17

Chapter

Aheia

Arioch gathered his shadows around them and Aheia gasped as he pushed her through, holding her breath like she'd been submerged in water. It felt odd and warm, and if she hadn't been so manic, it might have even felt tranquil. But when she stumbled out the other side of the darkness, Arioch's hand still wrapped tightly around her neck, she was anything but calm.

A scream tore from her lips, her hands flying to his chest and burying themselves in the fabric of his shirt, her feet perched on the edge of the railing that lined the balcony in the old wing of the compound. He was holding onto her by the neck, this grip the only barrier between her and certain death as the wind whipped through her hair. She fought to get closer, weaving on the tip of her toes, feeling her heels dip slightly while she struggled to stay on the metal, the iridescent river water gurgling and rushing past from both sides.

"What the *hel* are you doing?" she shouted over the sound of the roaring water, her eyes locked tightly on the void below.

"Careful with that sharp tongue of yours, little goddess," Arioch growled.

"Let me *go*," she hissed, her mind still heavy with what had just happened. It almost felt like she'd woken up, her brain slow and pulsing. Arioch narrowed his eyes, loosening his hold on her slightly, forcing her to tighten her grip on his shirt. If he dropped her, she wouldn't be strong enough to hold onto the flimsy fabric.

"Stop." It was a whimper, and it was so Gods damned weak that a tear escaped her.

Stop. She chastised herself, *not here, not with him.*

Arioch's eyes seemed to soften a fraction until he spoke, and his words dragged razors across her skin. "*Stop?*" he chuckled. "Come on now, you know better."

She shook her head, her toes starting to hurt with the effort of holding herself on the edge of the railing. "*You're insane.*" It came out more of a squeak than she'd intended.

Her stomach fell to her feet as she peered over the edge, the abyss below pulling at her vision. She felt her heart beating in her throat, and the longer they stood like that, the faster her pulse raced. There was panic in her veins, and it had her breathless, but in the same instance, she felt tight anticipation curling her middle.

What the fuck is wrong with you. You should be afraid. Be afraid.

"Do you think I'll let you fall?" Arioch purred, and she almost jumped. Alshaytan had leaned in while she was focused on certain death below, the rasp in his voice stroking across her insides.

She swallowed, turning her head towards him, his lips inches from hers when he brought his other hand to the side of her jaw, and ran it down to the nape of her neck. Every touch was a Gods damned spark that fed the flame in the pit of her stomach. "Your pulse is racing," he said, his lips brushing hers as he spoke. "But it's not fear is it?"

For all the wind surrounding them, none of it seemed to want to touch her lungs. "Why are you doing this? Is this supposed to be punishment Because I interrupted you?" Her words were shaky, and she hated herself for it.

"If I was punishing you," he said, "you'd know."

The slow flame in her middle roared, and she bit back a whimper. It was torture ... and it sure fucking *felt* like punishment. But she'd try to hide it, wouldn't give him that power.

"Do you think I'm a monster?" he asked, moving his mouth to her neck and grazing his teeth over her skin.

She nodded wordlessly and for a moment he stilled. Then she felt his teeth, a bite that was strong enough to force a sharp inhale between her lips.

His tongue chased away the sting, hitting that spot below her ear that had her back arching into him slightly. "Yet you're not afraid of me." He bit her again, harder this time and she hissed, leaning into his mouth to try and lessen the sting.

"No."

And it wasn't a lie. She couldn't fully bring herself to fear any of it, not with the bond and bargain looming at her back.

"That's something we should remedy, little goddess. It's just good survival instincts to fear a predator who's above you in the food chain."

Her jaw clamped shut at his words, a protest stuck in her throat as her mind throttled her with images of Arioch *devouring* her and leaving nothing behind.

Holy shit.

Her wants and needs were clashing against each other in a dizzying rhythm, unwelcome thoughts filling her brain until she couldn't differentiate herself from what her soul demanded.

"I've seen you afraid–saw it at the border and when I threatened to send you back," he said, slackening his hold further. "Someone in Keloseros holds your fear in the palm of their hand and milks it from you when they squeeze. There's a look there, your eyes seem to freeze, your lips part, your breath hitches. It's too sweet to be dedicated to anyone else."

Her heart jumped as his arm became less of a presence and more of a suggestion.

"However, I don't see that now. You should be terrified— dangling that fragile life of yours over certain death, but you're not. You should have been terrified in that room, but instead, you stood your ground. So, tell me what makes a creature that doesn't fear death run with such resolution?"

She had nowhere to go. He'd thrust her into another cage, one without bars, forcing her words when all she wanted was to say quiet. But when she thought about what she was afraid of, she found a semblance of strength and met his gaze with every last ounce of it.

"Fear of life."

And the words were true. Death was nothing compared to the life she faced if she got dragged back to Keloseros.

Arioch's eyes narrowed, as he slipped his hand from her body completely, leaving her on her tiptoes, grasping onto his neck for dear life.

"*Gods,*" she squirmed, "why are you doing this?"

"Do you want to die?" He tilted his chin, dissecting her face like he was cataloging each reaction.

She swallowed, her breathing erratic as shook her head no.

"You're lying." His eyes sparked.

"You don't know anything about me."

Arioch's lip quirked before he leaned down. "Don't I? Isn't that what makes you so angry, little goddess? The fact that you can't hide from me like you hide from the rest?" One of his hands slid up her back, featherlight, not enough to offer resistance, but enough to pebble her skin. His eyes flashed down to her glyph on his arm. "I know more about you than anyone right now. You can't pretend, can't wear those vain, pretty masks and fool me."

Not with your soul on my body. He didn't need to finish the thought but the knowing glint in his eyes confirmed it.

Aheia averted her gaze, embarrassment slithering up her spine in little pricks of ice, but Arioch cupped her jaw and forced her chin up, his hold punishing.

"Don't," he tsked, sliding his thumb across her lips and parting them, the blood on his wounded hand cold against her skin. "Life is too long for shame, Ruhí. You are what you are, and you like what you like."

The bond hummed between them, vibrating through every inch of her as her mind took control of her words.

"And what do you like?" she whispered before she could rein the words back in.

Fuck. She *really* hadn't meant to ask that.

The side of his mouth twitched. "Do you want to find out?"

She shook her head in another lie. But it wasn't her that wanted to know, not really. At least, that's what she told herself in a dizzying mantra—it was the confounding way she ached to be whole again, to get herself back.

"What happens if I break our bargain?" she asked, eyes slipping towards the river roaring past the railing.

Don't do it.

Arioch raised an eyebrow.

Don't do it.

She felt his touch lingering on her jaw.

Don't do it.

Aheia sucked in a breath, and before the rational part of her could get the upper hand back, she slipped her hands free, letting herself drop.

The air *whooshed* from her lungs for the millisecond she'd moved before Arioch's strong arms wound around her middle, pulling her against him roughly. She lit up like someone had thrown oil on a roaring pyre, a rush snaking through her like she hadn't felt in a long time. It was reckless and maddening and *distracting*. She let him haul her close, both of his arms wrapped tightly around her, and she could have sworn she felt him laugh. But when she finally looked up, chest heaving, eyes bright, his face was unreadable.

"Gives new weight to the phrase trust fall," Aheia breathed, her hands landing on his thick muscles.

He just stared at her for a moment before shaking his head. "Don't ever make that mistake."

"What?"

"Trusting me."

Of course, she didn't trust him. And she supposed that was the truth that she shoved to the side until she couldn't see it among the dark thoughts that lived inside of her. He might have dropped her. She might have died. And death might have been easier.

She sucked her bottom lip between her teeth, fishing for something that could rescue her from whatever they'd sunken into together like a life raft.

"You're bleeding," she said, clearing her throat.

"I bleed all the time," he said, his voice rough. She met his gaze.

Dark.

Scorching.

Consuming.

Of course, he bled. Because he wore his knives on his chest, and she imagined he fought his own battles and carried scars on his skin that told the tale. He wasn't like Ophion who had other males do his dirty work, not when it really came down to it.

Aheia kept his gaze as she peeled his injured hand from her body and flexed his fingers apart. The gash was long across the center of his palm, and it would scar if he didn't get it healed. "Isn't this just a scratch to someone like you?" She exhaled slowly, breathing out some of the tension that had rattled her, prodding the wound on his hand again, as the challenge lingered in her words. His eyes picked her apart, stripped her down, and melted her armor like it was nothing. She'd never seen a color so cold be so burning hot.

"Let me fix it," she said. She'd learned how to stitch up wounds earlier than she should have had to.

"No," he said slowly, pulling his hand from her grasp. But she held on, her nails digging into his skin.

"Let me do it."

Let me hurt you, and then hear you thank me for it.

Without warning, he pulled her from the railing and set her down on shaky legs, his eyes burning into her like he might have seen a glimpse of her thoughts. Aheia watched him leave her standing in the middle of the cold balcony, his warmth evaporating while he walked to the opposite wall and sat down on a ledge next to the tall doors. He watched her stand there, his eyes caressing every part of her, deep in thought, before he extended his hand and crooked two fingers, motioning her closer. Aheia crossed the space without hesitation and sat down next to him, her hands in her lap, her heart in her throat.

"Violence from beautiful creatures," he said, flourishing his hand and retrieving a needle and thread from somewhere inside his shadows. Then he leaned over, just as he dropped the two things in her small hands, his lips brushing the shell of her ear, "is one of the things I like."

18

Chapter

Arioch

There were too many unanswered questions floating between them, and the more time he spent with her, the more were added to the stack. Seven days–he'd given her one week–because that was his magyck number. He usually lost interest in his playthings not long after that.

But this, this was intriguing, she was intriguing.

It seemed that death didn't scare her, which meant that wasn't what she faced in Keloseros. The thought wound his curiosity tighter, as he pulled back from her side, watching her eyes shoot to the needle and thread now sitting on her palm.

His little pet's lack of self-preservation hadn't been the thing that caught him off guard, not after the last couple of days, but he hadn't anticipated the death wish she seemed to have. She'd let go of him while he dangled her off a balcony, her eyes bright and pupils wide with excitement. And after all of that, she'd asked to stitch his skin. His skin. How the fuck did a bratty royal from the light realm know how to suture a wound?

He locked that question away for later and lay the back of his injured hand on her thigh. She jumped slightly, her legs clamping together as his knuckles depressed her skin and skimmed her dress higher.

So nervous.

He liked her nervous. It made her soul burn just a little brighter, the pain of it shooting right to his cock.

Fuck, she looked so soft and pliable, so absolutely Gods damned *edible*. And it made him consider exactly what he wanted from her. He could kill her eventually, truly fuck with the Malek–since it seemed that getting her back was important enough to have her chased through Lyria. If he killed her he'd quiet the inevitable questions of his people and take a stance against Keloseros while he imagined it would swing the support amongst the Nephilim back in his favor.

Or... or he could spread her legs and see just how far he could push the bond between them. Power came with both, and so would the beautiful little sounds and sweet, loud screams he could tease from those pink lips.

Arioch skimmed his knuckles higher, just to see her squirm, watching how her skin pebbled beneath his touch, her breathing shallow, her hands fumbling with the needle and thread she was clamping down on now.

You could fuck her out here and nobody would hear her scream.

His cock thickened in his leathers, pulsing against his seams painfully as she parted her lips, the tip of her tongue darting out while her eyes glazed over with concentration. *Hel*, he wanted to find out how that tongue felt on the rest of his body, suck it into his mouth until she couldn't breathe, see it wrap around his length.

He bit down on a groan, as images of her forced onto her hands and knees against the rough ground in front of him flooded his mind, tightening the tension at the base of his spine until he had to hold on to his restraint with both fucking hands. It would be so easy to grab that fragile little neck and push her down, to nudge her thighs apart and rip that stupid, flimsy white dress off of her. Her pale skin would scratch horribly, her blood painting the stone, and he would feel her pain on his arm as he stretched her cunt around his cock, until she couldn't *speak*—until that insolent mouth could do nothing but fight for air.

But then he remembered exactly where they were, and it locked his desires down tight. The first time he fucked her wouldn't be in his father's old wing. Disgust curled into his middle, the anger flaring inside of him at the old memories that were tucked into the old foyer just beyond the door to the old balcony.

"You wanted to stitch," he rasped, "go on then."

Her eyes snapped up to his like she'd been shaken from a trance, her breathing uneven, and he thought he saw a flicker of something there, but she reigned it in quickly, retreating into herself.

That won't do ...

He cracked his neck, the tension rolling through him, his shadows strumming along his muscles like they wanted to tear him open to get to the little Mithra sitting next to him. Arioch leaned in closer, snaking his free arm around her and pulling her onto his lap, giving them enough space to drive him crazy and to let her protest.

"What the *fuck*," she whined, grabbing onto the arm pressed into her chest. She shifted in his lap, brushing against his groin as she straightened on his leg.

"Better stop squirming. I can't promise I'll hold back if you keep rubbing your ass against me like that."

She stiffened. "I'm just trying to steady myself." The words sounded shaky on her lips.

"Let me help you," he smirked, moving his hands onto her abdomen, and pulling her body back against his until they were flush with each other. She whimpered, her back arching slightly, her hips rubbing over his cock as she gripped onto his bloody hand for support. He groaned, at the feel of her, sliding his hand from her abdomen onto her thigh and resting it against her cold skin. "Now that we're all *adjusted* ..." He skimmed his chin across the top of her head and brought his wounded hand up in front of her.

Aheia pressed her legs together and curled her fingers into the delicate fabric that covered her lap, staining it black. She was stiff, perched on his thighs, her cold and his warmth creating something dizzying. Her hair spilled down her back, pooling between them, so damn long, he just wanted to wrap his knuckles in it and pull. So much to play with...

He was waiting for her disapproval, for her to fight him, preparing his words for when she did. But nothing followed except more silence. After moments that slithered into minutes, she started to relax, leaning back against him one vertebra at a time. She unraveled some of the string and started threading the needle-like she had done it a hundred times before.

She showed no hesitation when she knotted the end of the string and lowered his hand, nor when she sunk the needle into one end of his palm was almost mechanical. It stung, but nothing he wasn't used to.

"Good," he said, against her temple, watching her carefully, the approval escaping him before he could rein it back. He shouldn't want to reward her, not when she was one of *them*, but when she rocked her hips back against his length because of his words, the need to talk her onto a new ledge imprinted itself onto his mind.

Aheia likes praise. Just like she liked the thrill of a near-death experience. He could work with that ...

Fuck, he wanted those legs draped across his shoulders, to feel her squeeze—

"Do you *want* me to hurt you? Stay still," she hissed.

Yes.

"Keep going," he said, tipping his chin towards his palm, desperately needing a distraction from the hum that their bond forced through his body.

Aheia rolled her shoulders like she was trying to loosen the tension between them just as much as he was trying to drive it higher. This was *torture*, and no part of him minded. She continued her work, placing tight, little sutures along the seam of his wound, her movements quick and precise, his blood coating the tips of her fingers and her knuckles as she tugged on the dark string. He clenched his jaw, drawing a slow figure eight against the inside of her thigh, relishing the way her legs flinched under his attention.

"Almost done," she said, a slight tremble in her voice, the needle slipping in the blood and stabbing him just deep enough to truly hurt.

"*Ow*," Arioch growled into her ear, making her jump in his hold.

He slid his hand up her leg, fingers brushing against the hem of her already short dress, inches shy of where her thigh met her hip. His shadows were rolling off of him in a wave, curling themselves around her slowly, and stroking down her legs. She sucked in a breath like she was being submerged in water when they caressed her skin, wrapping themselves around her ankles.

"It's just me," he said, against her ear.

"Is that supposed to calm me?" She swallowed, pulling the needle from his palm with shaky hands.

"Calm? No," he chuckled.

Aheia watched the tendrils flatten over her limbs, drawing a pattern across her skin that looked a lot like Arioch's tattoos. He watched her eyes trail them slowly, before she switched the subject, hesitation tingeing her voice. "I–" she exhaled slowly and looked down at her hands. "Is there a way to stay? After this bargain is over?"

His lip curled. "Why would I want you to stay?"

"I didn't ask about what you wanted ..." she said slowly, a quiet edge working its way into her words.

"It should be the only question in your mind, *little goddess* ..." he said, squeezing her thigh. "What I *want* is the only thing that matters if you're interested in staying here past our bargain."

Aheia gripped his wounded palm tight in a rush of anger, her nails digging into his flesh, a sharp sting shooting up his arm.

She wanted to hurt him, and he was inclined to let her try her hand at it some more because fuck if it didn't feel good.

"You're insane," she hissed for the millionth time.

"The sane can't survive in this world, *Aheia*," he chuckled.

She sunk her nails into him further, and he had to work to stifle the groan that vibrated his chest. Instead, he leaned in close, his lips brushing against the shell of her ear, his eyes on her fingers digging into his wound. "That's not a deterrent."

He watched her neck bob as she swallowed, her breathing uneven. "Which of the two gets you off?" She angled her head slightly. "Receiving pain or forcing it onto others?"

He couldn't help but grin at her anger, the cold fury circling her irises–it was beautiful. "I don't plan on carving obedience from you, little goddess, though there is a part of me that thinks you'd enjoy the pain I have to give."

"I don't want any of what you have to offer," she said, her gaze sliding to his.

"Then I think we're done here, no?" He started to move, but her grip tightened on his palm.

"Let me finish."

"Suggestive of you." He nudged her head straight ahead so that he could run his teeth over that spot just below her ear.

"It's not," she ground out, leaning into his mouth like she hadn't just lashed him down with her words.

Arioch brushed his thumb over her thigh before widening his seat, forcing her legs apart with his. Her dress rose higher, bunching up around her hips, his hand sliding up further, only inches from the apex of her thigh.

"Then *finish*, Aheia. I know you know how," he growled, thinking about the fact that she wasn't wearing anything underneath the dress. *An oversight ...*

"*Fine*," she said, gripping the needle between her fingers before she returned her attention to his hand, and he returned his to the way she was pressed into him, every part of him rigid against her soft curves.

When she pricked him deeper than necessary he barely noticed, creeping his fingers higher on her leg.

"Stop," she said, her voice hoarse. He met her heavy, half-lidded gaze, the ice in her stare more like pooled water, her breathing shallow, her lips parted.

"You know the word, little goddess, and stop is *not* it." He massaged his thumb against the inside of her thigh, feeling her warmth on his fingers. "Seems you're not cold everywhere." He grit his teeth giving her time to tell him no in earnest, allowing her the opportunity to end what was happening between them. But she didn't, even as she fixed him with an angry stare, and he didn't care to hold onto his control any longer.

He closed the distance between them, cupping her center, hearing her gasp at the contact. *Hel*, she was wet, the evidence of everything she'd tried to hide coating his palm.

"Fuck," he rasped against her ear, "perfect little goddess, soaking through your dress on my lap." The words were anything but controlled as she leaned her head against the scruff of his beard.

"It's just ..." she panted, grinding against the heel of his palm, "m-my soul,"

"Mhmm. Your *soul* likes this," he growled, circling her clit with his thumb. She bucked her hips, the needle falling from her hand as she grabbed onto his arm for support, her legs nudging apart further to give him better access.

"No–fuck."

Arioch didn't let her finish the thought before he slipped his finger inside of her in one thorough stroke. Holy fuck, she was swollen. He groaned, leaning his forehead against the back of her head, his gaze coasting over her spine and along the curve of her ass pushed firmly against his cock. She moaned, her body locking down so tight that he had to move slowly, grinding the heel of his palm against her clit as he slid his wounded hand onto her waist, holding her in place.

"Gods," she whimpered, her voice trembling as he started a torturously slow pace, curling his finger inside of her until he found the spot that had her sucking in a sharp breath, her eyelids fluttering.

He clicked his tongue. "I'm the only *God* you should be concerning yourself with while my fingers are inside of you." The idea of her begging anyone but *him* made him fucking feral.

"You're no more than my captor," she pushed out between her teeth as he thrust inside of her again, speeding up his pace.

"It's fascinating how you keep trying to spin my charity to your liking," he said. "I am not your captor. I am doing you a *favor*. You're here of your free will and I am getting tired of reminding you." He added another finger, driving her towards yet another edge he wasn't planning on letting her fall from. His hand on her waist moved to tip her chin until her back was bowing and she was looking up at him, the crown of her head pressed into his chest. "You hold power but choose to discard it, simply because it's easier to play the victim."

Aheia's lips parted.

"Playing the victim in my realm will get you eaten alive, and I'll fucking enjoy it."

Her eyes widened, her hips rolling against Arioch's hand, something furious and bright fringing the blue. "Fuck you," she hissed.

"Ask me one more time," he said, pushing his cock up against her ass, the pleasure she promised so Gods damned maddening.

Her jaw tightened, the anger coiling into her features as she took what he had to give, ate it up like she was fucking starving, her moans almost enough to make him come in his leathers like a youngling.

She shook her head against his chest, clamping one of her hands down on his thigh so hard he felt her nails, her other grasping the fabric of her dress that was now bunched up around her waist, pulling it taut over her stiff nipples. Arioch's mouth watered, wanting to bite and suck, but he couldn't quite get there at this angle, and he enjoyed the view too much to move her.

"Get up on your knees," he groaned, lifting her so that she could straddle his lap while she faced the open balcony.

She obeyed, *thank fuck*, and raised herself, her temple now level with his chin, his fingers buried deep inside of her. "So good at following instructions when there's a reward in it for you, hmm? I wonder what you'd do for me if I used my tongue instead."

"Ari—*hel*, I'm so close," she cried, riding his hand harder, her movements becoming quick.

The way she said his name, gave him a nickname, blinded him. He almost let her come right then and there. But not now, not here. His hand stilled, her cunt tight and pulsing around him, a soft whimper escaping her as he went rigid.

"Not tonight." His words held a dark edge. "You broke the rules."

She almost cried as he pulled his fingers away, cold air rushing between her legs.

"No." Her legs gave out and she fell back against his lap as he pulled her dress into place, while he brought the hand he'd had inside of her to his lips. He cleaned off his fingers, his arm bracketing her throat as he did, forcing her gaze onto his mouth while he licked off her arousal.

"My home, my rules, little goddess."

"You can't do this," she mewled, yanking against his hand in an effort to free herself.

"Don't fight too hard, or you'll make me think you actually want this." He smiled, an easy, arrogant look. "And don't try to finish yourself off either. I'll make this ache feel so much worse."

She wriggled, her ass moving back against him, and sweet lords if it didn't stroke him just the right way. "We have an event tonight, and you'll attend it with me."

"No," she ground out between her teeth.

"It wasn't a question."

"I'm not going with you," she hissed.

"You will if you want to stay," he said, his eyes dancing.

"You can't dangle me like this." She grasped onto his leg, her own quivering. "I–" Arioch leaned closer, forcing her chin towards him with his bloody hand, leaving a print on her pale skin.

"I'll do what I please. I'll dangle you, tie you up, show you off, and then break you, and you'll thank me with those pretty lips of yours for anything and everything I give you."

"Better males have tried," she spat, pulling her chin from his grip.

He laughed. "Better males?"

He stood without warning, sending her toppling to the ground without the darkness to hold her back. "You expect me to care about your affection?"

Her bloody palm slipped against the stone, and she looked up at him with a cold fury. He straightened his sleeves and shot her one last look.

"Be ready for tonight," he ordered.

"I don't have anything to wear," she huffed.

He turned, only offering her a quick smirk before he left her behind and disappeared through his shadows.

19

Chapter

Aheia

Aheia was seething, her body wound so tight that she thought it might tear apart at the seams as she climbed the steps towards her room. She felt high-strung thanks to the combination of not eating and the way Arioch had edged her moments ago. She needed to be by herself, to breathe through this, but when she opened the door to her room she found she already had company.

"Oh Gods, there you are!" A bright and excited voice met her, coming from a Nephilim who was standing at the foot of her bed, clutching something eye-catchingly sparkly.

She was beautiful, with green, corded hair reaching past her waist, pale skin that was adorned with so much ink Aheia could barely discern it, and wearing a black dress that was covered in gold jewelry. Her emerald green eyes stood out from dark charcoal paint surrounding them, dainty tattoos curling across the bridge of her nose.

"Oh–" Aheia shook her head. "I wasn't expecting–"

"I should have waited outside, but I was told you'd be here to look over the choices." Her eyes lit up so much that Aheia wondered what the brightness was covering. "When you weren't, I figured I would lay it all out for you instead."

"Is this for tonight?" Aheia asked, stepping closer and running her hands over the exquisite fabrics in front of her.

"Yes."

Aheia furrowed her brows. "How long have you been here?"

"A while."

He was planning this all along...

"What's your name?" Aheia asked.

"Karyme, but please never call me that—I'll think you must positively hate me. Kar is fine."

Aheia inhaled slowly, the tightness in her skin loosening slightly. Unfortunately, with the calm came a slow panic. She had no idea what to expect from tonight, didn't know what Arioch wanted from her, why he was bringing her—well, she supposed she knew that. Something about making a statement, but the implications of that worried her beyond anything else.

"You look pale." The Nephilim tilted her head, dark green hair falling into her eyes as her brows furrowed.

"I'm always pale," Aheia said, letting the door shut behind her and sitting on the edge of the bed.

"Yea—and to that point, why the fuck did he put you in white... white is not your color, my love."

Aheia's eyes widened slightly at the lilt in her tone, and how cavalierly she was talking. It had been a long time since she'd spoken to anyone who didn't hold a dark edge.

"What are you?" Aheia asked, a soft laugh accompanying her words.

The Nephilim shrugged her shoulders, the gold jewelry hanging across her body clinking slightly. "I ammm..." She tapped her finger to her chin in contemplation. "I am divine energy, I am in love with colors, and I am the most important thing in this world." She winked. "But I get the feeling that's not what you meant." She sat next to Aheia and took her hand, grasping it tightly. Something about the Nephilim made the gesture feel so seamless and comfortable, like they'd known each other for years. "I'm a Leviathan but I'm also an empath, and that anxiety of yours is giving me shivers."

Aheia shook her head. "I—"

"No, don't worry." Kar clapped her hand around Aheia's reassuringly. "You'll look great."

"That's not exactly what I'm anxious about," Aheia said, closing her eyes for a split second. When she opened them, Kar was looking at her, eyes serious, like she'd discarded her sweetness for a split second.

"Lions aren't afraid of wolves," she said. The strength in her voice made Aheia wonder about how many wolves the empath had faced in her lifetime.

"And what of other lions?" Aheia asked.

"If you're with Arioch, there are no other lions." She smiled slowly, narrowing her eyes. "Ooh, now that is a whole other emotion." Her smile widened and she bit her bottom lip dissecting Aheia's face slowly. "Careful with all of those feelings."

"He has my soul. I can't control it," Aheia said, slight irritation tugging at her.

"Hmhmm." The Leviathan grinned, a glint in her eyes. "Alright, go wash up. But first–Gods, it's dark in here."

She padded over to the door and ran her hand down the side of the wall. Her fingers were searching, and when she found what she was looking for she traced a pattern over the stone. That's when, from seemingly nowhere, flames blossomed around the outline of the ceiling. Aheia yelped, it wasn't energy, it was fire.

"Ok, you need to show me what you did." Aheia grinned, feeling the warmth travel through the air.

Kar held out her hand and when Aheia met her, she dragged her fingers down the wall. "Feel that?"

There was a line in between the stones that felt warm and soft, and underneath her fingers she saw, a slight discoloration– easily missed. The flames roared as she moved her hand down further and dimmed when she went the other direction.

Aheia shook her head in disbelief, before finding the same mechanism in the washroom. When the fire roared there, she could finally see her surroundings clearly. She walked over to the water alcove and stood in front of the jars she had blindly rifled through a night ago. They were filled with different soaps and fragrances, all of them hand labeled. The one she'd used the other night was black and held the name of spices she didn't recognize.

Aheia made quick work of washing herself, this time finding a plush towel underneath the vanity to wrap around herself. When she stepped back into the bedroom it was like the sun had exploded. Her jaw dropped, looking around to find fine silks, laces, and tulles strewn across the furniture.

Kar was standing at the foot of the bed staring at each dress like it owed her eyrid, her brows hard and furrowed. "No, that won't work." She grabbed the satin and threw it over her shoulder. "I'm sorry. You're beautiful, but you're not right." She was talking to the dresses like they were alive, and it made Aheia smile.

"Sit," Kar said to Aheia without looking at her, eyes glued to the sparkly gold in front of her.

Aheia did, walking across the room, sitting behind the small desk in the corner, and finding a stack of gold receptacles that held different powders laid out.

"Ok." Kar clapped her hands together before she pulled up a chair and sat in front of Aheia, sliding two tattooed fingers under her chin and tipping it up lightly. Her eyes turned analytical and calculating. "You're so beautiful."

Aheia didn't know how to take the compliment, never quite knew what to say. It didn't help that most of the times anyone had called her that before it had been a means to an end. They wanted something from her.

"Ooh, another nerve." Kar dropped her hand and slid a couple of the powders in front of her. "Sorry, my love."

She unscrewed one of the gold tins and picked up a nearby brush, swirling it in something that looked like dark charcoal.

"White dresses... demure, demure, demure. You're not demure." It was almost like Kar was talking to herself again, but then she looked up at Aheia and her eyes sparkled. "I can feel that fury inside of you." She leaned in, and tapped the brush on the edge of the receptacle, discarding the excess. "Let's pull some of that out of your features."

Aheia nodded, feeling a little too vulnerable. She couldn't decide if she was relieved about the fact that even if she tried to wear a mask in front of Kar, the Leviathan would be able to see through her, or if it worried her. The empath skimmed the brush over Aheia's eyelids, then when she was satisfied, continued to coat her lashes in dark charcoal, some of it dusting on her cheeks. She outlined her cheekbones in a dark color and said, "To give you an edge."

She finished off what she was doing and painted Aheia's lips with a nude color that smelled like Achlys, the flower she'd seen in Arioch's atrium. By the time Kar had finished her face, her hair had dried under the soft flames above their heads. She wove Aheia's bright mane back over the top of her head in a thick and almost messy braid, loose strands framing her face, with gold loops clipped into the right side, in a straight line that made her look like she had her scalp pierced. The rest of her hair hung down her back, the braid ending at the top of her head.

Then the empath walked over to the bed and picked up the glimmering, golden dress, and handed it to Aheia. "I'll let you get dressed—I think this will really make them think twice before making comments about your Mithra blood." She grinned, and Aheia's heart pounded.

For once Kar didn't comment on it as she grabbed the threads and walked into the washroom with them.

Gods, the dress was heavy, each thread made up of individual gold crystals. It took her a moment to understand, but she ultimately slipped it over her body, the sheer fabric part of it covering her chest and hips, the strings woven around her like a spider web. She slid the last straps into place and tried to fasten the back, but it was lined with small clasps that she couldn't get on her own. She was grumbling, only having found homes for two of the hooks, but in a mismatched array that left gaping holes in between the fabric, when Kar opened the door.

"You should have called. Let me." She undid the hooks and realigned them. "For all its beauty... it's, um, complicated." Kar looked at Aheia with a wicked expression on her face before refocusing on her back.

It was the first time Aheia had let herself look, truly look, at her own reflection today. The first time that she didn't double-take, didn't imagine her mother's eyes. For the first time in a long time, they were hers. The gold of the dress glimmered in the firelight, almost like someone had plucked the stars from the sky and laced them around her, leaving thin cutouts around her waist and her hip. There were slits of her skin showing around her stomach and chest, just enough modest coverage where it was needed, ending in soft drips down her legs. It was like the waterfall outside of her window, the front shorter and the back dragging across the floor. Her eyes looked striking behind the black charcoal. She looked... like a lion.

"There." Kar leaned her chin on Aheia's shoulder and grabbed onto her hips, squeezing reassuringly. "Striking. Alright–oh, I almost forgot." She slipped from the washroom.

Aheia picked up the train of her dress and gave herself one last look. Her reflection stared her down, holding all of her own reservations, and she decided that's where she'd leave them— with the girl in the mirror.

Then she followed Kar, who was rustling through a dark leather bag that was perched on the bed. She looked at Aheia. "Sorry–for all the colors and swirls in this brain–it's disorganized." And then she nodded to the floor. "Put on those shoes, they'll help with your height."

Aheia sat on the edge of the mattress and pulled on the gold, strappy heels, wrapping the laces up her calf and securing them.

"Here it is. He would have been irritated if I forgot this." Kar slid to the ground in front of Aheia. "May I?" She held out her right hand and when Aheia stretched out her leg she picked up a golden dagger from the floor. It was dark like honey, and slender, sheathed in a simple leather band.

"What—?"

a long time, they were hers. The gold of the dress glimmered in the firelight, almost like someone had plucked the stars from the sky and laced them around her, leaving thin cutouts around her waist and her hip. There were slits of her skin showing around her stomach and chest, just enough modest coverage where it was needed, ending in soft drips down her legs. It was like the waterfall outside of her window, the front shorter and the back dragging across the floor. Her eyes looked striking behind the black charcoal. She looked... like a lion.

"There." Kar leaned her chin on Aheia's shoulder and grabbed onto her hips, squeezing reassuringly. "Striking. Alright—oh, I almost forgot." She slipped from the washroom.

Aheia picked up the train of her dress and gave herself one last look. Her reflection stared her down, holding all of her own reservations, and she decided that's where she'd leave them— with the girl in the mirror.

Then she followed Kar, who was rustling through a dark leather bag that was perched on the bed. She looked at Aheia. "Sorry—for all the colors and swirls in this brain—it's disorganized." And then she nodded to the floor. "Put on those shoes, they'll help with your height."

Aheia sat on the edge of the mattress and pulled on the gold, strappy heels, wrapping the laces up her calf and securing them.

"Here it is. He would have been irritated if I forgot this." Kar slid to the ground in front of Aheia. "May I?" She held out her right hand and when Aheia stretched out her leg she picked up a golden dagger from the floor. It was dark like honey, and slender, sheathed in a simple leather band.

"What—?"

Kar smiled and undid the holster just to secure it around her thigh, readjusting the dagger so it sat on the outside of her leg. "You're not really fully dressed without a weapon, at least not here."

"He told you to give me a dagger?"

"He did." Kar stroked her thumb across Aheia's thigh in another gesture that should have made her uncomfortable, but didn't. "Alright,

I'm late myself." She got up and grabbed the bag off the bed, leaving the discarded fabrics and receptacles behind. "Keep that chin high. Don't let those wolves intimidate you."

Aheia opened her mouth and closed it, unable to find the words. She wanted the Leviathan to stay, wanted to learn more about her, but before she could get those thoughts untangled from the ones that still grappled with the fact that Arioch had given her a dagger, Kar disappeared into the hallway.

Her fingers brushed against the warm metal, and she could see herself reflected.

Lions aren't afraid of wolves.

20

Chapter

Arioch

Arioch rubbed the heel of his palm into his chest, feeling the dull ache of Aheia, even across the city, though the separation made it slightly more manageable. He fucked up on that balcony... he'd edged her but fuck, he was just as worked up as she was, and hadn't let himself find relief before heading into Aljira.

He didn't tend to be early to these meetings, but he needed to get out of the compound and put some distance between them. He'd shadowed into the top floor of the old citadel that stood in the middle of the city, like a large spider at the center of its web. He took a seat at the round onyx table, the only modern touch in the otherwise antique-stoned room, and waited for the others to arrive. This was not where he held official meetings, but that was not the point of tonight. He wanted to get this over with. Just the thought of having to discuss the topic made his skin itch, because he didn't care what any of them had to say about it. There was no way to please them all, and in this one reality they lived in there were too many outlooks. The situation was as it stood, and it wouldn't change—*couldn't* change—not with her soul present on his skin. So, this was superfluous. And it would put him in a mood because he *knew* he would get pushback, at least from half of them.

There were a lot of fragile minds to juggle, and no part of him wanted to do it now, not when he was still straining against his pants, the fabric much less restrictive than the leathers. It had taken everything inside of him to walk away from Aheia earlier, and then not to slip into her room while she was getting ready. The only thing that had held him back was knowing Kar was in there with her. He supposed that's why he'd sent her. That and knowing Kar would tap into how she felt better than he did.

Not that he cared.

His shadows flared slightly at the sentiment.

The Siada started showing up one by one until eleven of them were seated together with Hashem, the Syraphem, and Siraj missing. Arioch had no intention of waiting.

"This meeting is last minute," Rami, one of the Leviathans, noted, leaning back in his chair, dark hair tousled. "Word came with the invitation to tonight's event."

Arioch's patience was already wearing thin. "You were no afterthought, Rami, I assure you."

"Is it true, a Dioscuri?" Malika asked, leaning onto her forearms, a glint in her dark, red eyes. She was a Leviathan that held territory in the northern region, and if he had to compare her to any of his own, it would be Lúc. They wore similar smiles.

"I hear she's more than that. What angle are you playing here, Alshaytan?" Taher cut her off. The Leviathan held territory in the western parts, near Azalam, and took pleasure in grating on Arioch's nerves.

"Don't worry about my angle," Arioch said with a sideways glance at the Avarice, Ali, whose shadows were slowly curling around his body. "This meeting was a formality. All you need to know is that she's here and that she is my guest."

"*She's Mithra.*"

"Is she?" Arioch asked plainly, cutting Hani off. The Leviathan furrowed their blonde brows and leaned back in their chair, playing with the glass in front of them.

"A Mithra would never show hospitality to a Nephilim if the roles were reversed," Taher said, his dark red hair falling into those green eyes as he spoke.

"We are not Mithra," Arioch said simply. "Nor is the decision yours, Taher."

"We have a voice here," Rami spoke up, his eyes contemplative.

"You do, but this is not a debate." Arioch leaned back in his chair and draped his arm across the back.

"How long does she stay?" Kamaria spoke up, her gray wings fluttering slightly. She'd been one of the newer Siada and received sideways glances from the others around the table.

"That depends on her," Arioch said, taking a sip of his liquor. "This will cause conflict," Farah, the Shifter, said, her dark, long braids slung into a swirl at the back of her neck. She was striking, with bright blue eyes that contrasted her dark skin, one of the newest Siada. Arioch had gotten more push back about her addition than any of the others, because she was a Shifter, and Shifters were still not accepted like other Nephilim were.

It was disgusting.

"It might," Arioch said carefully. "But the conflict has been alive for decades."

Just as Taher opened his mouth, the door to the room opened and Siraj walked through, his gray hair slicked back, eyes irritated.

"I apologize," Siraj grumbled, trailed by Hashem, whose wings were tucked tightly behind his back. They took a seat next to Hani. "We were delayed."

Arioch's jaw tensed. "I can see that. I trust it was life or death."

Hashem's expression soured. "Of course. What have we missed?"

Arioch hated repeating himself, so he didn't. "As I was trying to say. This meeting was just a brief pulse check, nothing more." He kept his words emotionless.

"Have you heard about the Mithra?" Hani bridged, sending a furtive glance Siraj's way.

"Yes..." And then he furrowed his brows. Arioch didn't like the look in his eyes.

"I won't stand for this," Hashem decreed, straightening in his seat, his wings flaring. "This makes us look *weak*."

"And whose opinions are you concerned with?" Arioch cocked an eyebrow.

"If the Mithra think–"

"The *Mithra* won't be the ones tearing down your border if you continue to stand against me," Arioch snapped, his shadows flaring as the room buzzed with chaotic energy, the Siada straightening in their chairs.

Tear him apart
Rip out his feathers
String him up outside of the citadel

Arioch's shadows whispered viciously, the words converging and overlapping until they were nothing but a rough hum against his ears.

"Is that a threat?" Hashem's grip on the arms of his chair tightened until his knuckles were white.

"It might be a threat if I didn't own you. I'll excuse that slip this once."

"Hashem," Farah snapped, her claws extending over the dark surface of the table, the sound of the scratch slithering through the room. "Enough."

"Shut your mouth, *Shifter*," Hashem said, standing with such force that his chair fell back against the floor. Siraj's eyes narrowed at the Syraphem as he leaned forward against the table. "I'll be damned if I let a *dreske* like you speak to me like you hold any authority."

Arioch leaned back in his chair lazily, the anger coiling him tighter. He wouldn't give Hashem the satisfaction. His eyes drifted over Farah, who looked feral.

"Hash," Salman, a Leviathan from the northern territory, hissed, "step down."

Arioch stood slowly, his shadows sliding from his shoulders and across the floor, painting the stone black. "You worry about looking weak, Hashem." He stepped closer so that he was toe to toe with the Syraphem. "You don't need my help with that."

Siraj stood, clapping his hand on Hashem's shoulder, his eyes contemplative as they looked at Alshaytan. "There's a time, and it's not now."

Hashem's jaw worked tirelessly to no doubt hold back exactly what he thought, shooting a glance at Siraj. "This would have never happened during Sahren's reign," Hashem spat. "This is a *disgrace*."

"Make no mistake," Arioch growled, "*no one* is asking you to stay in your position. You'd do me a favor if you gave it up, really. You can take up residence in the slums of your territory with your family instead. I like that way of life for you."

He could have been more forceful, but Hashem was boastful. The Syraphem was all talk and no action and loved throwing his weight around. He'd been on the warpath ever since Arioch denied his offer of marriage to his daughter and then gave her asylum. He shouldn't have done it. It was a surefire way to pull the Siada's wrath, but he couldn't shake the look he'd seen in her eyes when she begged him to decline wordlessly, the fear bright on her features. Arioch was more concerned with the Leviathan at his back than with the Syraphem. Siraj made his moves in silence and covered his tracks, keeping his tongue in check and having others do his dirty work. He had Hashem in his back pocket and Arioch was sure it was a tactic, a way to distract him. But that wouldn't work; he wasn't his father.

Hashem's nostrils flared, and his mouth opened and closed like a Gods damned fish before he huffed and turned on his heel, storming from the room.

Siraj shook his head, sitting back down.

"Listen." Arioch didn't want to be here anymore. "This meeting was simply because I wanted you to know about Aheia from me before you saw her tonight. That's all," he said, fixing his sleeves. The Siada shuffled back in their chairs to stand with him. "Enjoy yourselves." He nodded at them and wasted no time leaving the room.

21

Chapter

Emryn

Emryn wasn't nervous often. But nonetheless, she stood outside Aheia's room in the old wing, tapping her red, strappy heels, trying to calm the churning in her stomach. Irritation was easier, so she sank her claws into it and let herself feel that instead. She could be irritated because she had to attend tonight's event. She could be irritated because she had to see her father. And even more specifically, she could direct her irritation, because without Aheia this whole thing wouldn't be happening.

Gods.

Gods above.

And she wasn't responding to her knocking.

Emryn flexed her wings. They felt extra heavy tonight. She didn't usually notice them, or at least not their weight. They were a natural extension of herself, but with her family looming so close, and the threat of being forced into that old life as the daughter of a Siada, they felt fucking heavy. She had to actively remember to pick them off the ground, so they weren't dragging, a habit she fell into when she became... nervous.

Fuck.

She knocked again and crossed her arms, the light and silky material of her dress feeling suffocating.

I don't want to go.

I don't want to do this.

It had been moons–twelve to be exact–since she'd seen Hashem, her father, and many more on top of that since she ran from her home and turned up on Arioch's doorstep.

Alshaytan knew this would be hard for her.

But he'd trusted her, had given her so much responsibility. She figured this might have been a new test–to see if she'd falter.

She wouldn't.

She never faltered, not since she'd stepped into this compound.

She held her own here, carved out her space amongst the other Nephilim, rose through ranks, and started training many of the demons that were part of Arioch's forces, alongside Shiron. She meant something here. Had found her own type of family here, not blood, but covenant. And that was more important–she reminded herself over and over again.

The blood of the covenant you chose over the water of the womb you were born from.

She almost grinned to herself. No one used the saying correctly–most thought it meant the opposite.

Emryn knocked again, and this time the door swung open. A new wave of irritation hit her at the sight of Aheia.

We wouldn't be having this Gods damned event if it wasn't for you.

Her mind wouldn't let it go even as she stepped back and took a breath.

"Sorry," Aheia said slowly, clearly seeing the apprehension on Emryn's face. "I was reading."

The statement loosened something in Emryn's chest, just slightly, just enough to let her relax a fraction.

She offered her a tight-lipped nod, motioned, and started down the hallway, hearing Aheia trail her, the dress that Kar had picked dragging across the marble in a soft swoop. It was beautiful. She was beautiful. Breathtaking really, and Emryn wondered if that was what held Arioch's attention, or if it was simply because he enjoyed riling everyone he came in contact with.

That's not it. Her mind chimed in, and she knew it was right. She'd seen it in his actions, the way he made sure Aheia ate, the way he'd sent Kar to talk to her and feel out her emotions, the softness that most people might have missed but she recognized because he'd shown it to her as well. Not in a sexual context, but in an almost reassuring way. She'd missed it at first, too, had been so on guard that she questioned every single gesture.

Emryn always wondered how it worked for others. She'd never fallen in and out of lust like Lúc, and Arioch, and Shiron–well she wasn't sure about him. He kept to himself, and was quiet about his movements most of the time, but she'd seen him now and then with another Nephilim. She wasn't like that–had never been attracted to another like that, not that quickly at least. It took a lot for her to feel that way.

"Keep up," Emryn said, her tone holding a cold edge as she saw Aheia pick up the train of her dress from the corner of her eye.

Ugh.

I wouldn't have to see my father if it wasn't for you. She couldn't break away from it, couldn't loosen the hold her mind had on the statement, and it wound her wings tight on her back.

Her father hadn't liked the fact that she fought against the marriage proposal they'd extended to Arioch, even though he had made it clear that he had no intention of accepting. Alshaytan took one look at her face, a frightened little thing, white as a sheet, holding her stomach's contents in her mouth, and shook his head. She imagined he'd seen the terror in her eyes and while he'd feigned a cold calm exterior with the Siada, he'd made it a point to step through his shadows and into her room the same evening nonetheless. She didn't know what had pulled him back, what had made him feel like he owed her any explanation–he didn't. But still, he told her his mind that night, how his denial had nothing to do with her and that if she needed someplace safe, the compound was open to her.

She still didn't know why Arioch had bothered.

Her father assumed that it had been her fault–that Emryn simply wasn't chaste or pious enough–that Alshaytan must have been able to tell that she was no good. Of course, it was her fault in his eyes–it would always be her fault. Just as when she wanted to read instead of attending the events they held, just as when she was late to their sermons because instead of dropping to her knees for a figure in the sky she wanted to learn how to fight.

It was always her fault.

And the denied marriage proposal had been the last straw for her father.

He was going to beat the life she didn't want into her.

But it hadn't just been her father's last straw, it had been Emryn's. She'd barely survived his ministrations, but with the last bit of strength she'd had in her she dragged herself out of her room and towards freedom. She didn't remember much of it, had jumped from one of the windows in the dining hall and almost killed herself flying to Arioch's compound. Then somehow she'd clawed herself inside on bloody knees and broken fingers, her wings gathering cuts dragging over the rocks outside.

The memories were vivid in her mind, and she could see herself in a bloody heap against the marble floor, just inside the foyer that she now walked through with Aheia.

Fuck, this trip down memory lane was not helping her.

"Didn't think I'd see you tonight, *traveske*." Tariq flanked her left side and threw a look over his shoulder at Aheia. The term of endearment floated between them, something like a kitten. Emryn had hated when he called her that after they first met, so of course, Tariq had made a note and used it as often as he could.

"I couldn't leave you hanging, who else would make sure you don't devour Lúc?" She looked over at him and gave him a rare smile, one she held for people she cared for, only. Tariq's loose curls were pulled back around his horns and bunched at the nape of his neck, his clothing black and formal, made of thick fabrics. He was handsome, she supposed, but he was also something of a cousin to her, in her heart.

"The Shifter can handle himself just fine," he said, a wicked glint sparkling in his eyes. "I'm more worried about you, little one." He wound his arm around her neck, pinching her hair.

"Fuck off, Tariq." She threw her shoulder into him as they entered a new hallway, tight and dark, that led to a winding staircase on the side of the Atrium. He looked over his shoulder again, and so did Emryn. Aheia looked mildly irritated, but the discomfort that shone in her blue eyes was strong enough to push out the cold anger.

"Say the word and I'll rip his throat out," Tariq rumbled in her ear, and she knew he was talking about Hashem.

"I can handle it," she said, shrugging from his hold.

"Oh, but wouldn't it be fun to watch me handle it for you instead," Tariq purred, giving her a wicked smile.

"Arioch would skin you and force me to keep you alive for the process." She rolled her eyes, her fingers sliding over the tattoo on her thigh briefly, another nervous tick. She could feel the magyck there, thrumming against the pads of her fingers, and it reassured her.

"Kinky," Tariq said, winking at her before hurrying down the spiral staircase ahead of Emryn and Aheia.

"Where are we going?" Aheia asked, taking his space next to Emryn.

"The city," she said simply, descending into the dark room that held one of the vortexes underground. Tariq had already bled through the swirling magyck when Aheia and Emryn made it to the bottom, the vortex taking up an entire wall. It looked just like the border, dark and alive. Aheia's eyes widened as she took in the sight.

"The city?" She raised her eyebrow.

"Yeah, it's a vortex." Emryn was too irritated to elaborate. She'd understand soon enough. "Go on."

She tipped her chin towards the wall, but the Dioscuri stood her ground, something nervous slithering through her features.

Emryn rolled her eyes and took a hold of her forearm before dragging her into the vortex herself.

22

Chapter

Aheia

Aheia walked through the vortex, the magyck dripping over her skin like warm water. It caressed every part of her like it wanted to reassure her, as her fingers trembled. Faint memories of the fire she'd encountered at the border stole the air from her lungs until she realized there would be no pain. She held her breath anyway, feeling the tug on her arm, and didn't let it go until Emryn pulled her out the other side. Her eyes narrowed, the light here was much lower, and she needed a minute to adjust. They'd emerged in a dark room, the energy dull against the ceiling emitting just enough to light up the few dark couches and gold furniture.

Then the traitorous hum in her chest lit up her skin, the familiar feel of her soul wrapping itself around her and pulling in all directions.

Gods, get a grip. Her breathing quickly became labored, and she could feel herself slipping like she was standing on the edge of something unnamed. Her exhale was rough as she tried to fight the panic, turning her head–feeling his presence without having to see him.

She grasped at her throat while cold shards of ice slithered up her spine at the thought of being near Arioch again, feeling her soul so close and wanting him so badly when she knew nothing about him.

Nothing, but... that he held her life in his palm and enjoyed toying with it on a whim, that he had chased her with the Varcolac for his own sadistic amusement, that he got some sort of joy out of seeing her squirm, and that when he touched her none of it seemed to matter.

She turned on her heel, her chest constricting so violently that the air in her lungs whooshed from her body, her hands flying to her heart in an effort to catch it, as she came face to face with those dark gray eyes.

Fuck, he looks delicious.

She bit her lip, doing nothing to scold herself this time. She felt strung out; she needed his touch, and it infuriated her. Arioch's eyes narrowed at the edges, his expression calm except for those irises – the embers simmering with a familiar anger that lived beneath the ash. He was wearing black dress clothes, complete with a leather strap that held his daggers, silver rings gracing each hand, and hair pulled back with a couple of loose curls framing his face.

He was standing across the room with Lúc, Shiron, and Kar, a thick cloud of red smoke buzzing around them, an inhalant between his teeth. She'd smoked something like it before, but it wasn't the red kind – it had been white and meant for her anxiety. Another thing she would have been lashed for if Ophion found out.

Emryn dropped her arm, and joined the other Nephilim with Tariq, leaning into Shiron who whispered something into her ear before passing her his inhalant. She seemed to visibly relax at whatever he'd whispered to her, and across the way Aheia noticed Kar's shoulders sinking slightly. It made her wonder how much the empath was forced to feel, and if it was as much as she thought, how in the hel she was so sweet.

Aheia felt incredibly out of place, the discomfort settling into her stomach like a heavy weight. She didn't know how she fit, once again, couldn't curl her edges enough to make herself blend, and that realization coaxed her anxiety back with a vengeance. She swallowed, unsure of what her next steps were supposed to be, while everyone around her seemed to know without a doubt, and waited for her to walk the laid-out line.

There was a world between them and Aheia had no idea how to cross it. She felt like she'd drown in the murky confusion underneath her feet before she could reach the Nephilim. So, she stood, tried to hold herself a little taller, tried not to let the way Arioch's eyes roamed her skin affect her, and tried not to clench her fists. But it was no use, her soul on his arm made it impossible for her to lock herself into place, a slow flame building at the base of her spine. She never thought there would be a time when she didn't want the warmth, but here in this moment, so Gods damned displayed, she held onto her ice with both hands.

It seemed like an eternity before anyone moved before anyone spoke, and when they did, the tension cracked at both ends. Tariq sidled up next to Lúc, his expression serious, his eyes hard, and Lúc's lips parted at the simple action of Tariq's shoulder brushing against his. Kar murmured something to Shiron who had his hand on her shoulder, and he smiled–smiled. She hadn't seen the demon smile since she got here...

It wasn't until Arioch moved that she felt she could dislodge her shoes from the old, coarse rock, that now felt like they were being devoured by quicksand instead. Alshaytan crossed the room slowly, his hand pulling the inhalant from his lips, smoke curling around his mouth in a slow exhale, those striking eyes heated and dark.

Every step ratcheted her anticipation higher. She didn't quite know what she was supposed to be here. But she supposed she'd never known what to be in Keloseros either–never fit their mold, despite how the Malek cut off bits and pieces of her to try and make her fit.

"Come here," Arioch rasped, holding out his hand.

The simple command slithered its way down her body and raised the hair on the back of her neck, as resistance built itself into Aheia's chest. But she pushed past it, sliding her fingers into his healing palm, feeling the stitches underneath her hand that reminded her of what had happened earlier that day–how it had felt. It threw her heart into a sprint, and she hoped to the Gods he couldn't tell. Though when he rotated her wrist and slipped his index finger onto her pulse point, she knew he saw everything. He saw past what little parts of herself she'd tried to pull together in front of him to hide, and something about that allowed her to drop her mask altogether.

She was tired. She was exhausted. And holding on to her facade was draining.

His eyes dissected her as he pulled her closer, his free hand caressing her jaw in slow, lazy strokes.

"Open your mouth," he said, his voice husky.

Aheia sucked her bottom lip in between her teeth, indecision rolling through her, but Arioch's thumb pulled it loose roughly, the pad of his finger lingering against it. "Careful biting your lip like that, little goddess. I'm scraping by on restraint right now."

She inhaled sharply, the heat in the pit of her stomach flaring. "Is that supposed to be a compliment?"

"It can be whatever you like." The edge of his mouth curled. "But don't make the mistake of taking the sentiment lightly." Then his smile dropped, eyes black. "Open your mouth."

Aheia did and his hand slipped back to where her jaw met her neck. "More."

And again, she did.

He massaged her skin, soothing the ache in her jaw slightly.

"We'll have to work on that range, won't we?" His lips quirked again, and the smile played in his eyes.

Aheia watched as he pulled back his hand and plucked the inhalant from between his lips after taking a long drag. Then he threw it to the side and pulled her closer, tipping her chin. She stumbled across the ground, her hands flying to his chest as he leaned in and touched her lips with his, letting the red smoke flow into her open mouth. She jumped, the thick smoke lighting up against her tongue, her throat fighting it for a moment before she felt the buzz creep into her mind. She relaxed slightly, the concoction of what tasted like different florals swirling down into her lungs, Arioch's lips leaving prickles of energy where they touched hers. Her eyes widened when he pulled back, tipping her mouth shut with two fingers, and then resting them on her lips.

"Hold it for me," he said, his voice husky, looking down at her through thick lashes.

The smoke was invasive but warm, she could feel it sinking into her slowly, her mind dipped in a comfortable haze that had her chest loosening ever so slightly. He kept his fingers in place past the point of comfort, and when she went to exhale he wouldn't let her.

Her eyes widened and his smile grew. "Is that all it takes?" He leaned in, brushing his nose against her temple as her lungs strained. "To make you choke?"

She coughed, her lungs screaming, the smoke stinging her nose as she gulped down air, her hands tight in his shirt. Arioch chuckled, winding an arm around her waist, his fingers sliding down the small of her back slowly, while his other hand rested on her shoulder.

"What the *fuck*," she hissed in between coughs, blinking away tears.

"How do you feel?" he whispered against the shell of her ear.

She stilled, talking in slow, full breaths. She felt... good. She felt calm, even. Her thoughts were hazy, but they were her own, her body relaxed even after the coughing fit. And for some reason, the lack of discomfort was the most grating thing, because her mind told her that she didn't deserve to be at ease.

"Why are you bringing me here? What does tonight mean?" She pulled back slightly, needing to find space between them.

"Because you're staying here, and everyone needs to know who you belong to." His eyes flashed. "It puts a claim on you... that safety you were begging for comes with a price."

"My soul wasn't enough?" She cocked her eyebrow, anger gripping her chest.

His lip twitched like he wanted to smile, his eyes dropping to his right forearm, and she cursed her body for responding to just a simple look.

"Your soul buys you entrance here. Safety comes with a show of power. Tonight, you'll act your part."

"And what part is that?" Her brows furrowed.

"*Mine.*" He caught one of her long, white strands between his fingers. "No one touches what's mine."

She pushed his hand away. "I'm not yours."

He hummed, the corner of his mouth pulling into a deviant smirk. "Mind, body, and soul, Ruhí."

The anger burrowed deeper, the ice in her veins flaring. "Interesting," he continued, tilting his chin slightly, his eyes scouring hers. "What?" she hissed.

"You look like you want to tear my throat out with your teeth."

"I do," she growled.

"And any other time I'd let you try, little goddess. But tonight, we play. Everything depends on it. Do you understand?"

"Spell it out for me, Alshaytan."

"Stand by me, play my game, be the pet they expect." She narrowed her eyes. "You're sadistic."

"Yes," he said, grinning, "but that's not what this is. This is you carving out your place in a world that you don't belong in–a world that would see you swallowed whole, and torn apart just for what you are."

Don't. This is weakness. Her mind offered, while her body acted like it might let him drag her through his darkness until her soul was stained and became a smudgy gray.

"Do you understand?" he repeated, his words clipped.

"Yes," she pushed past her teeth, a slow pressure building at her temples.

He pulled back enough to watch her eyes, and then his gaze slipped further and he mumbled something in Lujha that she couldn't make out.

"What?"

"The knife looks good on you," he whispered, followed by the soft stroke of his fingers against the outside of her thigh. "Keep it with you, always. Use it on anyone who dares to put their hands on you, use it on me if you feel unsafe."

She gaped and thanked the Gods it was dark. "Careful, or I'll mistake this for kindness, Alshaytan," she said, a little too breathless to muster the bite she intended.

Arioch chuckled and the sound vibrated through her as her hands clenched the fabric of his shirt. This was too much, she was all but shaking, needed more, needed less. Her mind was tearing itself apart and just when she thought she'd crack, his teeth pinched the skin at the nape of her neck. The pain slithered down her body and drove between her legs, mingling with the need to have him touch more of her.

"I can't let you break just yet, otherwise I'll have nothing left to play with," he said, sliding his tongue against her skin, right over the bite mark, to chase away the sting.

Aheia leaned into his lips for a moment before pulling away and flattening her dress. "Kar will kill you if you ruin her hard work," she said, her voice shaky.

"She's right." Kar's voice floated around them as the others gathered at the far wall that swirled with the same magyck they'd stepped through to reach this room.

Aheia met Shiron's gaze, strong and silent, and wondered what those eyes had seen to make him so rigid. And then Lúc's, bright and alive, playing with a challenge at all times, even when no one had brought one forth. Next to him stood Tariq, who she barely knew. She considered how they talked around Arioch, how relaxed they seemed, and wanted to know more about their roles here—especially Kar and Emryn. They clearly all *mattered*, and it reminded her that she didn't.

Arioch curled his fingers against the back of her neck and led her to the group of Nephilim, Aheia's nerves giving way to something else.

Lions aren't afraid of wolves.

That's the role she'd play tonight. Because if she wasn't a lion, then she'd be a lamb when she'd promised herself she wouldn't be.

"Show me that *helfyre* tonight, little goddess. But more importantly, show *them*," he said.

She watched her dulled reflection in the magyck ahead. The gold dress was glimmering on her body, and something in her blue eyes seemed to match. It was bright, and she caught it when she tilted her head, holding back the urge to reach out and caress her own skin. She didn't look like herself, or maybe she did. Maybe she'd never looked more like herself than at this very moment. But what did fever dream Aheia know of any of those things?

The Nephilim started to walk through the wall, and Arioch's fingers stroked over her exposed skin for a moment, almost sweetly, almost intimate—but she realized it was only to get her attention when she met his eyes in the reflection.

She watched him lean into her counterpart, felt his breath on her neck, watched his strong jaw and the tattoos that reached across the edge of his throat as he spoke to her, to them.

"You look mesmerizing."

Her reflection smiled but she didn't feel it on her lips.

"But please do remember that while you're here no one else touches you." And then, with an expression that had her searching for her own morality, he continued. "I don't want to hurt any of my own, but I will, and their blood will be on your hands."

She wanted to protest, felt the words bubbling up in her throat, but before she could speak he nudged her forward and into the wall.

23

Chapter

Aheia

Arioch's Nephilim walked in front of them, Kar's arm looped through Emryn's, Tariq ahead, and Shiron and Lúc just behind. They made their way through the crowd of Nephilim packed into a large, open room. The music was loud here, and it hugged her just like the red smoke that floated around them. In Keloseros they had slow and traditional music, played on stringed instruments, and sometimes someone sang. But it was never very happy or upbeat. They were tragic stories, odysseys of years past when the plagues swept Lyria, and of Nephilim and their conflict with the Mithra. She supposed this wasn't exactly happy, but it felt heavy just like the abstract paintings in Arioch's hallways had. There was emotion there being conveyed in a way that Aheia didn't quite understand, vibrating through her very bones.

Her heart was racing, but she kept her strides measured, hiding everything that might have betrayed her—the shake of her fingers, the momentary increase in her breathing, those nerves at the back of her mind. The defense mechanisms that threatened to pull her into old habits wouldn't help her here, not tonight. She needed to be different, be a *lion*, not the lamb she'd had to play in Kelosersos. If she muted herself here the way she'd been forced to around the Mithra, then she feared she might lose her voice completely.

Aheia let her gaze drift over the bodies in front of her, the throng thinning around them as the stares fell her way. She swallowed, keeping her chin high, pretending like she'd done this a million times, as Nephilim parted and bowed their heads when they passed. Arioch's hand drifted up her spine slowly, her soul brushing against her shoulder when he cupped the back of her neck and squeezed slightly. She shot him a look and saw him already staring at her, his other hand tucked casually in his pocket. The fire that banded his eyes burned into her, and she inclined her chin further, leaning into his arm slightly as he stroked up her vertebrae with his thumb.

It felt monumental, commanding this much attention, and the version of herself that lived in the light would have shrunk away. But it was impossible to shrink when Arioch stood behind her with such strength. If she truly was his toy, his pet, his *thing*, she should have felt lesser. But when she looked up at him, and those eyes burned watching her and only her, she felt seen and fucking powerful instead.

The whispers rose around them with Arioch's shadows as they crossed the room, making their way towards a large gold basin. It stood in the middle of the space, right where the domed ceiling peaked, covered in a beautiful frieze that depicted what Aheia assumed was some moment in history for the Nephilim. The paints were dark and saturated, threaded with gold that bled down towards the walls and onto the columns that lined the room. There were no windows here, the smoke and shadows filling the space and obscuring the light thrown from the Solas orbs above.

Aheia watched as Emryn slid her hand over the rim of the basin, the others scattering around it, standing just shy of the crowd that had formed in a large circle.

"What is this?" Aheia asked quietly enough for only Arioch to hear.

"Water," he said, taking her hand and leading her closer. It had an iridescent glow to it, just like water in the river that passed by the compound.

"Water is sacred," he continued, slowly pulling her arm forwards and dipping their joined hands into the liquid. "It can save a life, just as it can take a life." He washed her fingers with his, and as he did, the crowd around them shifted. She let her gaze break away from Arioch's face for a moment, finding a myriad of expressions staring back—most of them surprised, some of them angry, others contemplative and intrigued. Something inside of her suggested their reactions weren't just about her presence, but about his actions as well.

"The Nephilim believe that the Rivers were created when 'Amm lost her life, her own eternal tears."

Aheia lifted her eyes to his, the light of the water illuminating the dark gray. "The Nephilim? Not you?"

His jaw tensed as he pulled back her hands, the warm water dripping off of their fingers and across the marble floor.

The whispers became louder, as his shadows curled up her ankles, his eyes narrowing like he was about to answer. Aheia caught a couple of words floating past her *Mithra, she's glowing*, and *can't be*, but it was disgusting that stopped her in her tracks. Or rather, stopped Arioch in his. His head snapped to a short Nephilim on their right, who was wearing a sneer until he met Alshaytan's eyes.

"It must be hard to speak up when you're surrounded by so many demons," Arioch said, his voice a low timbre, his eyes flashing to Lúc who was already moving, pulling the Nephilim from the crowd by his neck.

"I–" the small male spluttered as Lúc threw him towards Arioch, who wound an arm around his small frame, pulling him into his side like he was telling a friend a secret.

"Now that you have a platform," he said, loud enough for everyone to hear, "repeat what you said."

"It's n-not worth repeating," he stuttered, dark eyes darting from Aheia to the crowd behind her.

"I'll tell you what," Arioch growled, kicking the back of the demon's knees, making him fall against the rough ground while keeping a tight grip on the back of his neck so that he stayed upright. "You apologize, and *if* Aheia decides she can find it in her pretty heart to forgive you, we'll stop." He wet his bottom lip, his shadows climbing around the Nephilim's throat slowly, a wild glint in his eyes. "I'll stop when *she* tells me to."

"No–*please*, I didn't mean–" But Arioch's shadows bent him by the throat until he was taut, his hands wrenched behind his back, his words cut off by new little tendrils snaking their way into the Nephilim's mouth. He coughed and fought, his blue eyes bulging, pleading silently with Aheia, who could do nothing but stare. It felt like an out-of-body experience, and for a moment she lost her voice, and worse, the handle on herself. For a fractal of time, she felt a hot trickle of volatile energy run through her chest and wanted to see the demon dead. But she couldn't, couldn't, couldn't. She grit her teeth, and stepped towards Arioch, reaching for his forearm. Her fingers fanned out over the ink there, his muscles flexing and warping the shape of the shadow tendrils. He met her gaze, and he looked different, murderous, callous. It shouldn't have sent excitement through her veins. But it did.

"I'm satisfied," she said slowly, curling her hand into the crook of his arm until he broke the contact with his shadows and wound his hand around her waist, the other still outstretched, tendrils dripping from the Nephilim's mouth as he fought for air.

He let her slip her hand into his hair, something she'd wanted to do for a long time, even if it was mostly to pull and make it hurt, standing on her toes to diminish some of the height he had on her. He leaned in when she pulled on his curls, and let her brush her mouth against his once, twice, and a third time before running her tongue along his bottom lip.

A sound of approval vibrated through him, worsening the ache between her thighs and it was a betrayal—she knew that—but once again, she didn't care. Her brain tried to keep this interaction fake, but her body didn't seem to care, urging her further, deeper, more... She was too tired to care, too exhausted, and giving herself over to the need that was heavy in the pit of her stomach sounded so sweet.

He gave her his full attention then, the hand around her waist moving to her hip and tightening until it became punishing, exactly what she wanted despite herself. She stayed there against his lips, still and waiting. It made her feel powerful, having Alshaytan at her fingertips, with the reins in her hands. She moved to grip the base of his neck so she could pull him closer and kiss his lips. It was soft and delirious, and something jolted between them the moment she slipped her tongue into his mouth.

It tasted like him. So much him.

Her head tipped, needing more, needing so much more. And he gave it to her, taking their kiss in a new direction. It was the type of kiss that was reserved for moments in dark hallways and between silk sheets, but they didn't have that privacy. Instead, they had an audience, and that seemed to feed the pleasure winding between them. She moaned as he pulled her closer, his cock pushing into her soft stomach, his fingers squeezing and kneading her while he bent her back enough to tower over her again. He was like a wave that was threatening to pull her under, and it made her fear that she might never come up for air once he did.

He broke away, running his nose up the side of her neck, his breath hot and prickling. "So sweet."

While the words were innocent enough, she knew better. The way he said them suggested anything but–sounding so fucking dirty.

"It's for them, not you," she said quietly enough for only him to hear.

"Then why does it feel like all mine?" he murmured into her ear as she tilted her head to see the Nephilim Arioch had been strangling, still bound by shadows.

"Let him go, please." She looked up at Arioch through her lashes, sucking her bottom lip in between her teeth, drawing his gaze down to her mouth.

"Very well." He rested his chin against her temple, and slipped his shadows away, letting the demon fall to his hands and knees, his palms pressed against the ground inches away from Aheia's feet.

"Thank you, fuck, *thank you*. I'm sorry," he rasped.

Arioch slipped behind Aheia, pulling her body against his chest, and wrapped his muscular forearm around her waist before leaning into her ear. "Do you like that, *little goddess*? Having my people on their knees in front of you?" The heat flared through her so bright the ice in her chest started melting.

Be who you need to be. She thought, pulling her features into cold indifference while she raised her leg and wedged the front of her high heel underneath the pleading Nephilim's throat, jerking up his chin.

"I've had a lot of people on their knees for me, *majte*, this... is less fun." She used the term of endearment that loosely meant "honey" in her language, watching Arioch's lip twitch before he broke out into a low chuckle, his hand squeezing her hip in approval.

"You all should know better," Emryn sing-songed, shifting the attention to herself. Many of the Nephilim averted their gaze. "He'll make you pay if he catches you talking about his new pet."

Tariq brushed past them, grabbing ahold of the Nephilim still on his knees in front of Aheia and wrenched him into the crowd, as Lúc watched with a hungry glint in his eyes.

"I know the Mithra's presence is controversial, but she is mine, and I hope you'll all be on your best behavior around her." She saw a devious smile crossing his features as chuckles raked the crowd. "There are no expectations of you tonight, only that you enjoy yourselves," he said, and the expressions she saw on the surrounding Nephilim's faces, even though he had nearly killed one of their own, were reverent, and bright. "Take advantage of it, little heathens."

Cheers sounded and the throng of demons started shifting, some stepping near and washing their hands, others leaving the center of the room for some of the shadowed alcoves that held dark furniture. Meanwhile, Arioch leaned into Aheia's side. "Where do you hide *this*?" he asked.

"Hide what?" Her voice was barely above a whisper as he lifted her body from the floor. She squeaked, instinctively wrapping her legs around him. "*Hey!*"

He slid his tongue along his bottom lip like he might try to take a bite from her throat. "*You.*"

She wound her arms around his neck and played with the ends of his hair, telling herself once again that it was for everyone around them—not for him, nor for herself.

"You think you know anything about me?" she asked. "Having my soul doesn't give you that privilege, Alshaytan."

His lip twitched, and his eyes drew down to her mouth. "Are you telling me, or yourself?"

Aheia held his gaze, even though she wanted to avert it with every fiber of her being. And it wasn't because he was right, but because she was wrong. She was so fucking wrong. Her chest ached for him, and so did her body, and the bargain felt stronger than ever, pulsing and hungry. Words had run out now. They'd walked into an alley surrounded by brick walls too high to climb, and there was nothing left. She knew that, she saw that, but it didn't matter. Tonight wasn't about words, tonight wasn't about truth. Tonight was blind. She'd follow her desires for once, and ignore the way her mind reprimanded her.

"It's just a game," she breathed, her eyes glued to his lips as he sat back against a deep emerald couch.

It needed to be just a game. Hope had no space here. Because if she found hope amongst the burning shards of whatever dangerous thing that was lit between them, she'd break once it was ripped from her grasp... because he was a demon, and he had her soul. Nothing would ever be clear, nothing would ever stay neutral, and with four ... almost three ... days of freedom left, her life narrowed to a pinhole in front of her.

"Does it matter?" He cocked an eyebrow, amusement dancing in those dark eyes of his.

She shook her head, readjusting on his lap, her knees barely touching the cushions on either side of his hips. "You're presumptuous, thinking I want this."

He hummed in agreement before pulling her closer, the stubble of his beard scraping across her cheek as he leaned into her ear. "Am I?" She inhaled sharply, but he cut off her protest. "Your mind may not want this, little goddess... but if that's so, you should remind your body of the same."

"My body doesn't want you any more than my mind." Aheia struggled to keep her voice calm.

Liar.

"A fact?" She felt his fingers trail a soft outline down her spine.

"Mhmm..." She couldn't quite find the words.

No.

"You're making a Gods damned mess on my lap, little goddess." She drew in a breath as he nuzzled her neck. "And the filthier I talk to you, the harder you're grinding yourself against my cock."

It took all she had not to close the distance between them as he massaged her bare skin, the ice he'd melted from her chest pooling in between her legs and turning into something painful and throbbing.

Fuck.

"It doesn't mean anything," she groaned.

"It doesn't have to mean something for you to enjoy it." She hated that he was right.

"What do you want, Aheia?"

Aheia hesitated for a moment, before she reached for his arm, staring down at the white outline of herself. It was mesmerizing, and when she touched it, her body felt it. But it wasn't the same. It felt comfortable, familiar. However, it did not affect her like Arioch's touch did, no matter how many times she brushed her fingers over his tan skin.

"To know why it feels like you're running your Gods damned hands between my legs when you touch my soul."

"Because some part of you wants me to."

Aheia watched him move his left hand, hovering it just above her glyph, the mere proximity of his fingers making her squirm slightly. "I didn't want that when you did it the first time, right after you took my soul ... and it still felt that way."

He raised an eyebrow. "Didn't? But you do now?"

She shook her head slowly. Another lie. Her eyes followed his fingers, watched them caress the skin just outside of the white and it affected her so badly she lost control of her voice, a soft whimper escaping her.

"Fuck," he rasped, his nostrils flaring as he repeated the motion. "Did you finish yourself off today?"

She steadied herself against his chest, her hands looking for purchase in his shirt. "N-No."

"Good girl," he whispered before straightening in his seat, and grasping at the back of her knees, pulling her closer. She ground her teeth as he wound both arms around her waist before returning his touch to her soul, his cock pressing between her thighs at the same time.

It felt like he was stroking down her center, like he was sliding his fingers over her clit in slow, tantalizing circles, without ever moving his hands from behind her back.

"I don't know how to do this," she moaned.

"You don't have to do anything," he whispered, his own voice corded with restraint.

"This isn't fair, I can't–I–" Her thoughts drifted further and further until she felt them slip from her grasp completely.

"Part of me wishes you'd made yourself come," he said, talking over her, his pace picking up slightly, "because then I'd have an excuse to make you hurt the way I want to."

She whimpered, sliding her hands from his chest and digging her nails into the side of his neck. "What would you have done?"

His eyes snapped up to hers, embers blazing. "Next time I'll watch you fuck yourself, over and over again until you're so tender that it *hurts*." He bared his teeth, his arms tightening around her. "I want to see you flush like that all over, I want to see you in pain, Aheia, and then I want to fuck you until you can't speak–until your legs give out and you're fucking raw, until you shatter so completely you're not sure you can pick up the pieces without my help."

"*Gods*," she gasped, chasing an orgasm that was just out of reach.

"And so fucking help me," he said, moving both of his hands to her hips instead, the loss of him more punishing than the grip that would leave bruises. "If you take their names into your mouth again while it's me between your thighs, I'll fill every one of your holes with shadows until you can't breathe, let alone speak."

It wouldn't take his shadows to render her breathless, not when his words forced their way down her throat so entirely.

Her knuckles were white with the strain of hanging onto him, the pressure at the base of her spine coiled tight enough that it threatened to shatter her.

A wave of anger at the denied pleasure washed through her. She growled leaning into the nape of his neck and sinking her teeth into his skin until she tasted blood welling up in her mouth.

"*Fuck*, Aheia," he groaned, his cock twitching against her core as she tensed her jaw, the taste of his blood lighting up her nerve endings. It was sweet and hot and heady and it seeped into her body like it wanted to become a part of her. It set the fire inside of her roaring, and the intensity of it frightened her. She pulled back, her breathing erratic, his blood hot on her lips, her eyes wide. She hadn't meant ...

"I–" She touched her lip, her fingers painting black, her eyes drawn to the black outline of her bite on his skin. "Why do you taste like that?"

"Demon blood can affect certain creatures in different ways," he said, his chest heaving, his hair looking slightly disheveled. "No need to starve, tell me what you're hungry for."

Aheia grit her teeth, as the orgasm she'd been chasing ebbed slowly. "Who are you to feed me all the things you think I lack?" His blood was rushing through her, mingling with the red smoke to pull her into a frenzy. She leaned in close, unable to stop herself from sucking his lower lip into her mouth while his hands pressed tightly against the small of her back to diminish any space between them.

24

Chapter

Aheia

Alshaytan." The voice barely registered as Aheia slipped her hand onto Arioch's abdomen, feeling his muscles flex beneath her touch while his lips devoured her own. It was a bruising kiss, one that would leave her black and blue in more ways than one.

It wasn't until Arioch pulled away that she registered her surroundings, watching his eyes black as night, his features furious, staring over her shoulder.

"Not. Now," he said, his voice that of a predator.

"You cut our meeting short, Alshaytan, I have a few things to discuss," the familiar voice said, and when Aheia looked over her shoulder, she saw Siraj standing in front of them, hands clasped behind his back. He gave her a long look, the kind that felt almost appraising.

"If you're particularly attached to your eyes, I suggest you keep them off of what's mine," Arioch said, his voice sharp.

"Of course," Siraj said, holding up his hands.

"Bad fucking timing," Arioch shot back, his words razor sharp.

"It won't take long," the Nephilim said.

"I'm listening."

"Not in front of ... it—"

"*It?*" Arioch's voice cut him off at the knees while his hand slipped back onto Aheia's thigh and squeezed reassuringly.

"She is Mithra. A Dioscuri," Siraj said slowly, as if it would explain everything.

"She's none of your concern," Arioch said. "This is your last warning."

Siraj narrowed his eyes but said nothing as he waited.

Aheia slipped her hand onto Arioch's biceps and squeezed. "Don't go."

He looked down at her, embers in his eyes flaring. "You're tempting, so fucking tempting, Aheia, but I have to take care of this."

"You don't … not now, *Ari*." She pulled herself against his lips. "Our game isn't over."

She watched the vein at his temple pulse, and his pupils threatened to abolish the rest of the gray as they expanded into a void, a vortex that pulled her in closer, closer, closer.

"Be good." He almost smiled. Then he slipped her from his lap, leaving her seated in the middle of the green couch. "Or don't. I much prefer the prospect of punishing your bad behavior."

Aheia's irritation flared, mixing with the still abating orgasm and whatever high she was on due to the demon blood. She watched Arioch motion to Lúc, who looked equally angry as he stood from a couch a little ways away and readjusted the front of his pants, leaving Tariq behind with a beautiful, dark-skinned Nephilim with long pink hair clinging to his side. Shiron followed the two and before they disappeared into the throng of Nephilim ahead, Arioch turned back for one last look that had her questioning every piece of her morality.

She became eerily aware of herself now that he was putting distance between them. Her chest became hollow like it always did, but the feeling was cut by whatever mind-altering substances were coursing through her.

"It would be nice to get through one of these things without a fucking scene," Emryn scoffed, appearing from between a couple of dancing Nephilim and sitting down on the other end of the couch.

"Where's the fun in that?" Tariq purred, slipping his hand onto the waist of the pink-haired female, who giggled in his embrace.

Aheia didn't know what to say, didn't know what she could say.

She groaned, cradling her face in her palms. She'd all but come on his lap in public, let him strum her like a Gods damned instrument—and he had known exactly which strings to pluck to make her sound for him. And then he'd left. It didn't matter how irrational it was, but that infuriated her.

He left.

"Your father sends his regrets." A new voice cut through the music playing around them and Aheia dropped her hands, finding Eros leaning against a nearby column. He was talking to Emryn just as Kar melted from a crowd on her left, her skin pearling with sweat, her face lit up with a smile. That was until her eyes found Emryn. Aheia watched her frown and shudder, her shoulder rolling slightly before she took a long drink from the glass in her hand and sat next to Aheia on the couch, giving her a quick smile before focusing back on Eros.

"I doubt it," Emryn snarked, crossing her arms.

"Said he misses you." Eros pushed off the column and stalked closer, his face rivaling that of a snake about to throttle a mouse.

"Fuck off, Eros," The Syraphem snapped, her wings adjusting against her back.

Eros only laughed, circling closer until his eyes landed on Aheia.

"It's a *pleasure* to meet you," he said, holding his hand out to Aheia.

Kar bristled slightly next to her as Eros waited for Aheia to move. She placed her hand in his and he bowed, his hair falling into his face as he kissed her knuckles.

"This is fascinating," he said, his lips curling into a sour smile.

"You've met her, now leave," Emryn said before forcing a saccharine and entirely fake smile onto her lips and giving its full force to Eros, "*respectfully.*"

"Oh come on, our first Mithra in a long time–this is a special night." Eros' grin spread wider as he looked at the Syraphem.

"Alshaytan won't be happy about this," Tariq said, leaning back against the couch, his legs stretched out lazily.

"She can't speak for herself?" Eros lifted a brow and it made him look slimy.

"*She* can," Aheia interrupted, straightening her shoulders. "And if you would like to speak with her, you may want to address her, not them."

Eros' eyes narrowed, a sparkle shining from their depths.

"Do you have a real question for me? Or do you simply like to hear yourself speak?" Aheia tilted her head, folding her hands in her lap.

"Such bold words, even without Alshaytan to protect you." Eros took a step closer and she could physically feel the other Nephilim shifting around her.

"I wasn't aware that I needed protection here." She furrowed her brows.

Eros chuckled. "We all need protection. Isn't that why you're in Al-jira? Because your kind is chasing you down?" He tilted his head to match her, his tone coaxing. "Why *is* that?"

"Eros," Tariq snapped, and his voice held a dark command. "You may wait until Alshaytan is back if you insist on this boring line of questioning, but until then, you'll leave the Mithra alone."

Aheia eyed him, the irritation already in her chest winding its way into her middle. "I don't need any help in the matter."

"It's not help," Tariq said, barely acknowledging her existence, his eyes on Eros. "You know how he feels about his property."

Aheia's jaw dropped, the irritation evaporating into blazing anger.

Property.

Fuck no.

She turned to address Tariq but before she could, Kar grasped ahold of her hand and pulled her onto her feet. "Let's dance." Her eyes darted from her to Eros. "Come on dearling, let's not waste that precious time of yours."

Aheia glowered after Eros, but let Kar drag her into the writhing bodies in front of them.

"Eros is built for confrontation," Kar said, leading her between the Nephilim.

"I don't belong to Arioch, I'm not an object," Aheia said, but the words felt useless on her tongue, especially considering that tonight she *did* belong to him. At least in public.

Kar frowned, "I'm sorry about the situation you're in," she said, holding up the glass in her hand. "Drink this. I'll be back, I need to make sure Emryn doesn't try to tear Eros' throat out because Tariq will watch and laugh instead of intervening."

Aheia shot back the sweet drink, whatever liquor was in it mixing with the blood and smoke and lack of soul in her system. It was delirious and made her mind slow and hazy as she danced, the music and bodies winding around her tightly. Kar never returned, or if she did Aheia didn't notice. The need for the demon who'd left her on that couch was flaring in the depths of her stomach, so hot that she couldn't focus on anything but as she let the Nephilim move her to a foreign rhythm. She had to pretend to be Arioch's for his people. She had to pretend not to want him for her own sanity. It was tearing her apart inside and took over her mind, reordering her thoughts until she couldn't imagine another moment without Arioch even as she reminded herself weakly that he'd left.

He'd left.

They all always left, didn't they?

And it didn't matter that it was merely for a moment nor that she had no grounds for the anger. He owed her nothing, in fact, he'd given her space, which was something she'd thought she'd wanted. The emotions that twisted themself around the ache in her body once again weren't hers, not entirely. And that thought disappeared as quickly as it crossed her mind like it was running from the feeling circulating through her, leaving her angry and aching and alone, surrounded by Nephilim.

The music was intoxicating as it mixed with the very real push and pull of the crowd; the nameless faces, hands on her body, limbs and hips pressed into her as they lost themselves in a sort of oblivion she'd never experienced. The more time passed, the harder fighting the pull of her soul became, and it was something in how the red smoke and blood played with each other in her veins that had her leaning into the creature behind her. She needed Arioch, but whatever Nephilim had his hands on her waist at the moment would do for a distraction; in this case, a dark-skinned demon with gray eyes...

They reminded her of Arioch's.

But they were wrong, too light, like clouds after a passing storm.

The demon slipped his hands from her waist and around the small of her back, pulling her closer, and despite herself, she let it happen. Arioch had left her, so what did it matter. She wasn't his property in earnest so what did it matter. She needed this... So, what did it matter?

Aheia let her head fall back, her skin prickling cold, a frustrated groan leaving her lips while sweat pearled at the back of her neck. It was a strain, holding herself together, not to tear through the crowd and find her soul. She slid her fingers over the soft fabrics the Nephilim in front of her wore, barely registering them underneath the cold that was frosting her nails.

The world in front of her felt fractured, the smoke and the incense pressing on her senses until she blurred together with the others. There were hands—on her arms, on her legs, on her throat, stroking and caressing in a way that had her tingling as reality slipped out of her grasp completely. It was like an out-of-body experience, pushing her to chase something that was just out of reach.

She looked into the cloud-gray eyes in front of her, just different enough, not his.

Not his eyes, Aheia.

She reminded herself as the gray morphed and twisted into the color she needed, flashes of Arioch replacing the Nephilim that was dancing with her. She saw Alshaytan's smirk, his dark curls, his tattoos, and when he pulled her against his mouth she didn't stop him. An unfamiliar spice lit up her tongue, an unfamiliar body pressed into her, a kiss she didn't know on her lips, and it shattered everything. Panic broke out across the back of her neck in hot pinpricks.

Mistake.

It rang in her ears, but she couldn't seem to turn away. The foreign slide of a tongue interrupted her thoughts, followed by teeth on her neck and nails grazing her arm. She felt weightless, gave in to the bodies that were pressing in on her, and felt her mind slip further and further from her grasp until all at once, the pressure from all sides vanished.

Aheia stumbled and her chest wrenched tight, the air escaping her lungs. Her eyes searched frantically, her hand clawing at the fabric of her dress in search of relief, except when she found Arioch's dark gaze it seemed to get so much worse.

He was standing a few feet away, everything about him a line of rigid anger.

She watched the shadows stuttering off his shoulders, a wall of gray drawn around them with Nephilim suspended in the curling shadows. It was like they had stepped into the eye of a hurricane, everything but the two of them suspended in mid-air.

"What..." Her words felt like cotton on her tongue, like she was slipping from a slow trance.

"You kissed him." Not a question.

She bit her bottom lip, everything inside of her wanting to cower away from his burning gaze. He looked like he'd tasted something unpleasant and held it on his tongue, his jaw working overtime to hold onto the control she saw peeling from his body.

Arioch moved, closing the space between them before she could offer a defense, his fingers digging into the back of her neck. She whimpered, her hands grabbing ahold of his shirt as his other hand found its way onto her jaw.

"You're angry," she said, grasping for words in the blank space of her mind.

Her head felt fragile in his hold like he could crush her without any effort if he wanted to. And he looked like he wanted to.

"You like skirting the line, little goddess ... go against every rule I have, every order ... Yes, I'm fucking angry."

"It's more than that," she said, fear tingeing the heat that gripped her throat.

"Is it?" He tilted his head, shadows creeping across the floor and caressing the bottom of her feet as his eyes darkened. He hauled her face so close she had to stand on the tips of her toes, her calves straining as much as her neck.

"You shouldn't have done that," he growled.

"Please," she choked, "no."

He leaned in, biting her bottom lip, his tongue sliding against her sensitive skin. Something animalistic broke from his chest, his eyes burning through her.

"I can fucking taste him, Aheia."

She watched his expression change as he spoke. For the second time since she'd met him, she saw a fine crack in his façade as his features betrayed his emotions.

"Fix it," she whimpered, her voice as chaotic as she felt. She buried her fingers into his shirt. "Replace him."

Arioch tightened his grip, a volatile smile on his lips. "I don't reward messy behavior." He nipped at her bottom lip, hard enough for her to squeal, dragging it out between his teeth until it hurt. "These lips are mine." He curled his fingers into her windpipe and squeezed. "If you taste anyone else ..."

Tighter.

Tighter.

Too tight.

You're pathetic, a small inner voice crooned as she felt the heat pressing in around her, something molten slipping down her spine, *trauma-induced glutton for punishment ... Fuck.*

The walls of shadows around them melted slowly, releasing some of the demons and the surrounding Nephilim who were all craning, whispers sliding into the dark space that had held them. A pair of tendrils dragged *Gray Suit* into view, forcing him to his knees. The Leviathan on the ground was offering hurried apologies, his clothing askew, but Arioch paid no attention, his gaze pinning Aheia in place.

Then she felt it. His shadows. They rolled up her legs, a very real caress against her skin as her eyes widened, darting from the crowd behind him, back to Arioch, his tendrils touching her in too many places.

"Do I scare you?" he asked, his right hand tightening on her jaw and his shadows moving with it. The tendrils caressed her waist and moved higher until they had a firm hold on her throat, replacing his hand, tipping back her head. She writhed, trying to test her limits, but they held her rigid, another few forcing her wrists behind her back until he had her trussed up with no space to move.

"Yes," she breathed, fear and excitement melded with each other.

"Not enough it seems." He took a step back, admiring his work as his shadows tightened, her shoulders screaming out against the angle. "You undermine my authority at every turn, Aheia," he said, stroking two tattooed fingers down her windpipe. "You think you can bend others to your will ..."

She squirmed, his words turning harsh under the heat of his gaze. "But that pleasure is reserved for me." The shadows that had a hold on her legs gripped so tight that a broken sound worked its way up her throat. "Let's see how much bending you can take." He nipped her ear with his teeth as the pressure against her legs edged pain.

She grit her teeth, her mind on the audience beyond the darkness, as the warm amber light started trickling through tapering tendrils. Their surroundings became loud, the incense stronger, conversations happening beyond them in hurried tones.

The Leviathan next to her was just out of view, and she could only see him from the corner of her eye as Arioch's shadows worked their way up the gray fabric of his suit. He was mumbling apologies that went unheard as Arioch stepped back, his eyes the shade of black that one found between burning embers, dark and hungry.

He twirled his fingers until she felt the shadows at her back spread around her ribcage, slipping through the gold strings of her dress, and across her skin. They rubbed across her breasts and wound around her nipples so hard that she flexed her fingers and yanked against her restraints. Arioch slowed his movements, keeping her taut as he forced the tendrils lower, compelling new shadows up her legs, slithering higher and teasing the apex of her thighs in slow, tortuous swipes. Embarrassment held her tighter than the shadows in that moment.

"If you come before he chokes, he can live," Arioch said without warning, soft splutters growing louder from the demon at her side. "If not, well ..."

"Don't," she whispered as her hips rolled into the friction, the pleasure swallowing her mind whole.

"Ask me nicely." His lips pulled into a soft smirk.

"Please, don't."

"That doesn't sound very sincere," he said, lessening the pressure between her legs.

"No, no, p-please. Don't kill him." It was frantic and broken. "You made me do this, Aheia. I told you, made it very clear. If he dies, his blood is on your hands," Arioch said, returning his shadows.

Her knees buckled, and she fell into the dark hold as the tendrils slipped past the satin between her legs, licking across her heated core. She cried out when she felt them inside of her, biting down on her lip, remembering the demons watching and the one choking at her side. She felt tears in her eyes as she toppled towards the edge, full of pain and pleasure, sadness and shame.

Arioch stepped closer, just a breath away, as the gurgles next to her grew louder.

"How badly do you want him to live?" he grit through clenched teeth, his shadows twisting inside of her, his nose sliding against her temple.

"I don't want him," she cried, completely overstimulated. It hurt. It was too much.

"No?" His fingers found her throat, and he squeezed, his shadows giving way to him.

All she managed was a feverish head shake as her legs quivered, fire running down the length of her spine, feeling like there was nothing left, nothing that belonged to her anymore.

"What do you want, then?"

It was like she floated from her body entirely, watching herself slur the next word, the one that he teased from the depth of her chest. Her lips didn't move and yet they did, her mind was blank but it decided for her. She couldn't feel the truth or the lie as she spoke it.

"You." It was strangled, quiet enough for the words to stay between them. She'd contradicted herself so many times, that she'd lost the way home.

"You can't have me," he said almost dryly, just above a whisper, and then leaning into her ear, he growled, "but you *are* mine." She couldn't reach for any new words, stars taking over her vision. Her body shook as it found its release, a muffled cry breaking past her lips when Arioch slid his hand over her mouth, flexing her fingers against the shadows that were pressing into her skin. He stroked her through it, slowing his movements as she came down, sadness replacing pleasure as his words found her conscious mind. It was depraved how they had fed into her orgasm and then dipped her in darkness the moment she could truly hear them.

He pulled his shadows back, her legs giving out as she fell to her knees, the floor unrelenting. He didn't move to help her, just readjusted his shirt, closing his eyes for a split second. There was a soft thud that pulled at her attention and she whimpered, curling her shaking fingers around her throat. Gray Suit was laying next to her, dead eyes looking up as shadows dripped from his open mouth.

25

Chapter

Arioch

The tension in Arioch's body was so tight that he had to work to pull his shadows from Aheia.

The little Mithra on all fours had fucked with his mind and he hadn't quite expected it. He wanted to keep her down, grab her neck and push her into the rock for what she'd done, the fury in his veins bright and hot. His shadows were stirring, raking over his muscles, begging him to let them slip back around that tight, little body of hers, a violent pulse of need leaving him rigid. His dick was straining against the waistband of his pants and the fact that he was so Gods damned hard made him even angrier.

Those sounds she made were so fucking delicious, he wanted to hear them again and again. But he'd forced them from her in public and now everyone knew–knew his sounds.

She was under his Gods damned skin, and he hated her for it. He wanted to make her hurt for that, but in the same breath he wanted her to like it, wanted her to ask for more, and it made everything too complicated.

Nothing was mutually exclusive anymore.

Aheia pushed back onto her feet, her breathing out of control, her eyes drifting over the dead body next to her, tears still fresh on her face, the dark makeup staining her cheeks. His fingers itched to rub it into her skin, and then smear it so much worse, imagining those pink lips wrapped around his cock until she cried.

"Arioch." Shiron appeared at his side, leaning into his ear. "The Mithra–they've sent emissaries. They're on their way now."

Fucking timing.

"We'll meet upstairs," Arioch said, still pulling himself together as Aheia fixed the tendrils of her hair that had been pulled loose, her pale skin flushed.

"They found you fast," he said to her, his voice like sandpaper as he raked his hands through his hair.

Aheia froze, every part of her stilling until–for a moment–she looked like a statue. Those blue eyes of hers widened, her pupils dilating, her lips parting. Her soft features changed, real fear tingeing her for the first time since he'd threatened her with the border, a tremor working its way into her hands. She tried to force the expression behind one of her masks, but it was messy and easy to pick apart. There was no hiding what she felt, not from him. It was as if her disguise was askew, deep cracks running through her exterior.

But it wasn't what she tried to hide from him that strung the vise on his chest tighter. It was the fact that he didn't like seeing the fear in her eyes. In fact, he hated it, when he should have enjoyed it.

Fuck.

"Better practice those sweet words of yours." He knew the only thing stronger than her fear would be her anger, so he chose his words carefully and spun them in a way he knew would distract her. "While I decide on what to do with you."

"What?" she snapped, a slight bite returning to her tone. "We have a bargain."

He grinned, the type of grin he knew would boil her blood.

"How you'll appear with me is another story ..." He tilted his head slowly. "Will you be bound and gagged at my feet, or will you be standing strong at my side?"

Her jaw clenched the fear frosting over into something vicious as he continued. "You're in luck. I don't tend to tie up females unless they ask me nicely." Like he hadn't just restrained her with his magyck.

"I'll never ask for that from *you*," she hissed.

He wet his bottom lip, watching as some of Lúc's Nephilim dragged the dead body from next to her across the floor. He knew Ophion would send someone, but fuck if they didn't have a knack for shit timing. Lúc came up behind Aheia and unwound a couple of white strands from the beads on her dress.

"Why do you have so much fucking hair?" Lúc murmured, his eyes glued to her back as he worked.

"Because males like you have told me they liked it short," she snapped, venom dripping from every word.

Arioch's jaw wound so tight it felt like his teeth might crack. "You flatter yourself." Lúc grinned, a glint in his eyes. He gave her a simmering look, before bumping her shoulder with his softly as he disappeared into the crowd.

"Follow him," Arioch said curtly.

Aheia glowered.

She was angry.

Good.

Aheia was standing against the adjacent wall, her arms crossed over her chest, staring at the floor. He couldn't quite read her at that moment, and her soul didn't clear things up for him. She'd been silent since they left the crowd of Nephilim behind, but at least the fear hadn't returned, not quite. She looked anxious, but it was being pushed around by the anger at his actions.

Lúc was sitting next to Emryn in one of the chairs that lined the wall, his feet crossed over her lap as he pulled an inhalant from his pocket and lit it. The silence was becoming grating and loud, like the anxious energy, wanted to make itself known amongst them. He let his eyes drift to Aylee who was holding a drink between her red painted fingers, the snake tattoo on her wrist winding itself up her arm and disappearing under the black satin of the dress that clung to her curves. He hadn't let Kar in the room because he knew this would be too much for her, and Tariq was handling shit downstairs with Shiron. He didn't expect violence, but if it came to it he had no doubt Aylee, Emryn, himself, and Lúc could handle it.

The door to the room opened, and Aheia's eyes snapped up, arms hugging herself a little tighter as two Mithra entered. Disgust curled itself into Arioch's middle, as he stepped closer to Aheia, her body shuddering slightly at the proximity. He watched her closely, how her eyes dissected each of them: one tall with white hair and the second with blonde curls, both of them with bright blue eyes and clean pressed suits.

Aheia fisted the material at her sides, her gaze trained on the blonde Mithra, whose features were a little too soft for Arioch's liking. She was staring at him, her expression softening, something new threading her expression, something that made her soul burn into his arm.

"Kal, *my Gods*," she said, her voice close to a squeal as she ran across the room and jumped around the Dioscuri's neck. Arioch dug his hands into his pockets, locking down the urge to send his shadows after her.

"You're ok, you're alive." Her words were muffled against the fabric of his suit as he hugged her close, his fingers burying themselves in her hair.

Fuck no.

"*Me?*" the blonde said pulling her back, those fucking fingers still in her hair. "You're alive."

"Your confidence in me is overwhelming," she laughed, and Arioch realized that he'd never heard her laugh before.

It was beautiful.

He stepped closer, pulling the Mithra's attention towards him, and it was then that Aheia seemed to let herself focus on the other Dioscuri in the room. Arioch saw her jaw clench, something sobering sweeping her features.

"Kal, why are you here?" she asked. "Why are you here?" Her voice cracked slightly, urgency taking over her words.

The Dioscuri looked down at her, his smile fading slowly.

"Why are you here?" she asked again, letting go of him and taking a couple of steps back. "Why are you wearing a *suit?*"

Kal's stare hardened and he looked at the Dioscuri next to him who betrayed nothing in his features.

"We're here on orders," Kal spoke, his eyes not once leaving Aheia's.

"And what does your *fearless leader* want?" Arioch snapped his fingers, finally pulling the blonde's attention.

"You have something that belongs to him." His gaze slipped back to Aheia who stepped away further until her back hit Arioch's chest. She jumped, but she didn't pull away, her posture relaxing slightly.

"Ahh..." Arioch smiled, the feral type of grin that no one would mistake for happiness. "And he's sent his little messengers to collect? It must not be very important if he didn't deign to grace us with his presence." He slipped his hand onto the back of Aheia's neck.

"He wanted to keep things civil," the irrelevant emissary spoke up, but Arioch kept his eyes on Kal.

"Keep things civil?" he scoffed. "That would be a first."

"He hopes for a bright future between Keloseros and Aljira."

Bright future.

Arioch shifted his attention to the little goddess in his arms and leaned into her temple, massaging the side of her throat with his thumb. Her pulse was quick, too quick for comfort.

"No," Arioch said and that simple, quick word had her leaning into him further. Gods, he hated how *good* this felt.

"You haven't heard what we have to say." Kal took a step forward and the other Mithra shot him a look.

"I'm not interested. Ophion's little daughter is here of her own free will." Arioch slipped his hand from her neck onto her throat and the other onto her hip, keeping his touch light. He'd bruised her with his shadows, he knew she was going to feel sore for a while.

"She does not *belong* to you," Kal said, emotion threading his words.

"*Everything* in this realm belongs to me ... including those precious lives of yours." His voice held a predatory edge.

"You have no claim on her." Kal took another step, and his mask peeled from his features in frail rolls.

"Does that one speak, or is he just decoration?" Lúc piped up pointing one of his knives at the white-haired Dioscuri next to Kal.

"They're all just decoration," Aylee murmured, finishing her drink and setting it onto the floor next to her.

Arioch leaned down and wound his arms around Aheia. "Would you give me a hand," he purred into her ear, delighting in the shiver she gave as he lifted his arm to her chest. She looked up at him, slowly slipping her fingers onto the fabric of his shirt, and trailing it up. She was shaking against him as she tugged at the material, her eyes glazing over slightly, like maybe she wanted to cry.

"More of a claim than you do," Arioch said, flexing his forearm so that her soul was on full display.

"*Pantydmaos Theos*," Kal hissed at Aheia, fists clenched at his sides like it took all of his strength to hold back. "What did you *do*?" His voice was akin to an adult scolding a child and it coaxed Arioch's shadows from his shoulders slowly.

"The only thing I could do." Aheia found her voice, and it was shaky, but it wasn't weak. Kal's eyes softened and it wrenched Arioch's irritation higher. "Aheia, please ... don't be stupid." His gaze dipped to the floor momentarily. "Come back... everything will be ok."

26

Chapter

Aheia

Kal... Gods, no. Aheia's heart was doing something that felt a lot like it was cracking.

"He's lying, that's not something he can promise you," Arioch chided softly in her ear as she watched Kal's features twist with anger, his eyes darting to where Arioch's hands rested. She saw the distaste there, that he didn't like how Alshaytan was touching her, and speaking to her. But what made everything murky and uncomfortable was that Aheia *did*, needed it even. Because Kal was here, and he was wearing a suit. How much time had it taken for Kal to truly swear fealty to Ophion? What had Ophion promised him in exchange?

"You're working for him," she said looking at his clothing. Kal didn't ever wear a suit, had refused even as her guard, to wear anything but the comfortable, white threads she'd seen on his body. He'd told her that suits meant conformity. The Mithra next to him looked at him with confusion while Kal shifted uncomfortably, his eyes darting towards the ceiling momentarily, his hand running through his shaggy, blonde hair.

"This thing you've started ... is complicated."

This thing I started.

The ice in her body flared.

"You're joking," her voice wavered, not with weakness but with anger. "What are you trying to say?"

He exhaled pointedly, and Arioch leaned his chin against the top of her head like he was content to let this play out.

"After what you did, did you really think you could evade him completely? *Angeloj—*"

"*Don't*," she hissed at the pet name. It felt like an insult now. Arioch stilled, his body growing rigid behind her.

"Don't you *dare*," she growled, twisting her hand into the crystals at her waist. All she wanted to do was rub her fingers together, to summon the light that had left her... but she knew she couldn't, had lost it forever.

"Aheia ..."

"After what *I* did?" Her breathing became heavy and angry, and the air burned.

"You killed Iaonnis."

The words floated through the room and spread like a poisonous gas. Everything seemed to slow for one torturous moment, and her ears felt a slight ringing as visions of blood and disparity threatened to strangle her.

"Isn't this getting intriguing," Arioch said, a lilt in his voice.

The trickle of cold that had started in her chest spread through her body in a violent wave, freezing her fingertips. It hurt, hurt enough to pull her back into her mind. She was shaking, but it wasn't fear, not anger ... it was something intangible.

"I had no choice," she said, her voice not her own. "There's always a choice."

Anger poured off of the Dioscuri, but it wasn't any match for the cold fury that now tore at her.

"You told me to run, Kal," she growled.

"It doesn't matter now," he said, his exterior becoming hard before he looked at Arioch. "We simply request you give us back what's ours."

What's ours.

"You're being repetitive," Arioch mumbled. "You didn't follow protocol, and you know it." His voice turned commanding. "It gives me the right to slaughter each of you." He stroked his fingers against her neck, and she could feel the tightness there, like his shadows were still pressing in, even now. "It's convoluted... all of this, isn't it?" She got the feeling he was speaking to her, not the room.

"You'll start a war if you try to kill us. I thought you were smarter than that," Kal hissed.

She breathed slowly, following the rise and fall of Arioch's chest behind her, her next words aimed at Kal. "You think I made a mistake?"

The Dioscuri hesitated, fumbling with the jacket of his suit before he finally answered. "You know what he is."

"I know what you are," she said, snapping her eyes back to Kal. "Though I thought you were different."

"Your anger runs deep, Mithra. This is loaded," Arioch said to Kal, a deviant grin in his voice. He toyed with some of the crystals on her dress. "This is personal for you."

He turned his attention to Aheia, and his voice dropped an octave. "Friends? Family? More?"

"Friends, I thought," Aheia said quietly, the sadness overtaking the manic anger for a split second.

"Ahh, so not blood ... " His words became cold when he readjusted and threw them at Kal. "But while she thinks of you like that, you think about what it feels like to fuck her."

Kal hissed, his eyes finally meeting Arioch's.

"Not all bright and pious, your kind ... are they?" Arioch said pensively, massaging her skin as a new wave of ice rolled through her, paired with embarrassment.

"She doesn't belong here," Kal pushed out between clenched teeth, his cultivated facade laying in ribbons on the floor. "Oh? Where does she belong? With you?"

Aheia's breath caught.

"Yes. She belongs with us," Kal said, though it wasn't what he'd asked. She didn't need to hear the answer to know he'd asked the right question.

"What did Ophion offer you? Her?" Arioch prodded. "If you play the hero and bring her back like a good soldier, he'll let you have your turn with her? After all, it is a suicide mission, you showing up here without invitation, you have to have known that ..."

Kal's eyes flattened. "No. It's not–" He stumbled over his words a little too quickly, a little too guiltily, and she knew that Arioch had leaned into the correct pressure point.

"She'd be happy," Kal spluttered. Aheia's eyes widened.

"Before or after they torture her raw? Before or after you force her into something she has no interest in?"

"It's better than *this*," he hissed, his arms going wide in a dramatic gesture. "She loves me." And then to her, "Aheia, I know you love me. It's why I did all those things. Aheia—remember all of the times we escaped the house? I could provide you with a good life..." He faltered, trying to find the right words while nausea churned Aheia's stomach.

Has he lost his fucking mind?

Another arrangement she would never be asked about, another instance in which her choice would have been taken from her.

"She loves you?" Arioch's lip twitched. "You think you're on her mind when she's in my bed?" Aheia faltered but bit down on the need to fight against the lie no matter how slim the margin to truth was.

"You're lying," he pushed out, taking another step, the other Dioscuri grabbing onto his arm.

"Maybe," Arioch grinned, "or maybe I know exactly what this pretty little goddess tastes like."

Kal wrenched his arm out of the other Mithra's grip so hard, that Aheia thought he must've strained something.

"You've wasted a trip," Aheia said, working to keep the tremor from her voice while she felt like she could jump from her skin at any moment. She clenched her fists against the pain in her head. It felt like it was splitting open down her spine. She grit her teeth, but there was no holding back what worked inside of her, as her fingers burned like she had submerged them in icy water for hours.

"Lock it down, Ruhí," Arioch whispered into her ear. But she couldn't hold it and didn't know what she was trying to control. She cried out in agony as shadows whipped around her until she was submerged in darkness while she split apart, bright, hot ice tearing her skin from her body.

27

Chapter

Aheia

Aheia's mind was screaming, visions of her past melding toge-ther with nightmares she'd endured in the last years, the blood of her mother, the blood on her hands, the blood on her soul that would never scrub clean. She was engulfed in darkness, and it was stifling, suffocating, and cold. She moved, realizing she was laying down somewhere, only because there was no weight on her feet, and pressure at her back. She got up, stumbling and clawing at her sur-roundings.

"Let me out!" she screamed, her voice so hoarse it barely made a noise.

"*Ahid*, Ruhí." Arioch's words drifted around her in a deep whisper, his hands sliding over her skin, and down to her wrists restraining them.

"Let me go," she groaned.

"You need to calm down," he said, his breath floating across her neck, her chest screaming in pain. This was different. It wasn't the need she was used to, nor the attraction she felt—it was like he'd cra-cked open her sternum and slid his fingers down her beating heart.

She gasped like a fish on land, the pain throttling the sounds from her throat.

"What did you do to me?" she cried, tears hot on her cheeks.

"Kept you from tearing yourself apart," he said, as she felt warmth against her back, the feel of daggers sheathed in leather against his chest, hard lines that met with hers as she struggled.

"How is this possible?" She was still fighting. She feared if she stop-ped she'd break down completely. So, she kicked out against him, bruising her wrists and trying to get away from him.

"It's not," he whispered, his hold loosening.

She wrenched again and this time, he let her go.

She screamed... screamed for all the loss, her life, the self that she felt slipping away the longer she was displaced. She screamed for the way she wasn't happy even when she was, for the way she was losing a grip on herself, for how the ice took over her body, and for the lack of control.

"*Kahlee.*" It was faint and staticky, like a word mumbled from a different room. It was a word she thought she'd heard before, though she couldn't pin down the moment. It lived in her mind just out of reach, like something spotted from the corner of your eye. She cried, clawing at her skin, her dress—everything feeling too tight.

The whisper sounded again, and she felt it tug on her body, like every fiber of hers was being pulled into the void in front of her.

"*Khalee.*"

"I don't understand," she rasped, crawling forward despite the pain and sinking further into the deep, inky blackness in front of her.

"*Come find me.*" It was a cracked whisper that made every single hair on her body stand on end.

"No." She clamored back, the darkness becoming so complete in front of her that it looked like a black hole.

"AHEIA!" Hands gripped at her shoulders and pulled.

She fell back before doubling over on herself, the pain flaring.

Is this death? Is this dying?

"Ruhí, come back to me." It was Arioch's voice, Arioch's hands—his arms, his body pressed into her back. She felt him against every part of her, felt her soul against her abdomen as he cradled her close.

The pain seemed to break, just as she thought she couldn't take any more of it, like an ebbing tide, rolling back and forth across her until eventually, she could breathe again.

"What was that?" she gasped against the sobs that still racked her.

"Where did you go?" Arioch asked calmly, his scent wrapping around her.

"What?"

He didn't respond, and silence slinked around them while he held her. It felt like hours passed, though it could have only been moments before she calmed slowly, her breathing finding a new pace. Her body was still thrumming, like she was a raw nerve.

Aheia had to focus to relax into Arioch's hold, letting him pull her off of the floor until she was sitting, her back to his chest. She felt a softness that she had never before felt, a safety she had always wanted. Maybe that was just as naive—to believe what he offered was safety.

But she supposed that those who were hand-fed safety would never need to learn to lick it from blades as she did. It might cut her open, but somehow she'd take that over all her other options. So instead of running, this time she leaned into the darkness. She let it envelop her as she breathed through the pain of it, until her lungs were so full there was nowhere else the air could go.

"That's it, Ruhí," Arioch stroked across her hair slowly, "come back."

"My body hurts," she murmured as her eyes became heavy. He didn't seem to be breathing.

"I know."

It was the last thing that she registered before she drifted, further and further from consciousness, the darkness behind her eyes the same as the darkness surrounding them. All the while, Arioch just stroked her hair and murmured things in his language in her ear. She caught some of them, but couldn't be sure of their meaning.

28

Chapter

Arioch

H*el.*
What the fuck.

What had just happened still seemed unreal. He didn't fully understand what he'd witnessed, had felt like a spectator when his shadows tore from his body and enveloped Aheia. He found her screaming, tearing at her dress, crying like someone was physically ripping her apart, a shock wave of energy rolling off her body and throwing him back.

He'd grappled his way closer, gotten his arms around her before she disappeared, drifting out of view and into a darkness he couldn't see past. And then she'd reappeared suddenly, like his own shadows had been shielding her from him.

Arioch was staring down at Aheia's body lying limp against the floor. The stone was slightly cratered around her, thin, tapering, spider-web cracks running outward from her like she'd fallen from the sky and broken the ground.

Lúc, Emryn, and Aylee had been thrown back just like the Mithra, all of them trying to get to their feet, the air still ringing with residual energy. Lúc drew his weapon and Aylee looked ready to fight, her nails poised.

"*Taelma?*" Orders, Lúc asked his voice unwavering. Arioch ground his teeth. This complicated things further. But it also made them infinitely more interesting.

He crouched down next to her body, the gold threads of her dress in a disarray. He'd learned that she was running because she'd murdered a Mithra, at least that's what they claimed. But after what he'd just witnessed, he knew that murder was simply their cover. Ophion didn't care about murder. It harrowed the Malek about as much as it did Arioch, both of them desensitized to it in the roles they held. He'd pursued Aheia far too furiously for something like the death of another Malek. Arioch knew Ophion was greedy, and the amount of eyrid he was offering for what they claimed was the reason for her chase was too big.

What are you, little goddess?

He rubbed his chin absentmindedly, letting his gaze drift over her soft features.

They seemed to shift in the back of his mind from something vulnerable and small to something with teeth, and it made his chest tighten. There was more to this, there had to be... and he'd find out what.

"Ophion will compensate you. He'll make returning her worth your while," Kal said finally, his breathing slightly uneven as he looked down at Aheia.

Interesting.

"What do you know?" Arioch asked, stringing a verbal noose around Kal.

"Nothing." His eyes flared slightly, and in that moment Arioch didn't care if it was a lie or not. He'd enjoy torturing the Mithra even if he didn't end up knowing a single thing.

"Leave *Kal* alive, you know what to do." Arioch smiled, something deranged pulling at his features as his shadows prickled underneath his skin.

Revenge. Revenge. Revenge.

It doesn't matter who they are. They do his bidding. They deserve death.

"No," the other Dioscuri said, "you can't—"

"I can do anything I want," Arioch growled watching Lúc lunge past him and swipe his blade, cutting through the middle of the emissary's throat. The Mithra's blood splattered and landed on Arioch's tongue. He hated the metallic taste.

Aylee was on his heels, grabbing ahold of Kal who was clamoring out of the way as Lúc dug his hands into the dying Dioscuri's chest, a manic look in his eyes.

"You can't do this—they'll come for us!" Kal shouted, fighting against Aylee's hold as she dragged him off.

Everyone loves using "war" as a threat, he smiled at the thought. The problem with it was that he wouldn't mind a war. It was overdue.

His eyes drew down to Aheia. She looked dead, and when he touched her she felt dead. The little goddess was cold as ice, but as he watched, he saw her chest fall and rise. He slipped his arms underneath her soft body and picked her from the crater she had formed.

"Sayyid." Maz's voice was unmistakable.

He turned to find her blazing, her hair more aflame than he'd seen it in decades, her eyes bright orange and wild. She didn't give the carnage behind him a moment of her attention, only stared at Aheia. Her breathing was heavy, quick, and unmeasured, and it unnerved him more than Aheia losing her mind. Maz didn't lose that cold, bored facade of hers. Ever.

"Mazikeen." He felt pulled into ten separate pieces, his shadows slithering underneath his skin. *"Ma hi?" What is she?* Maz took another step, reaching her hand out to Aheia. Her fingers were dark, veins of bright ember running up her arms and just as dangerous as any other part of her.

"Maz." He threaded command into his voice, enough of it to make her blink. He had never tried to control the Ifrit, but he couldn't let her touch the enigma in his arms, not without Aheia contracting third-degree burns. Maz gave the slightest of shakes, her eyes placid. "It's Gehenna," she breathed, her voice thick and then finally meeting his eyes. "Something's wrong."

Arioch's shadows vibrated. "What happened?" he asked.

"Come." She straightened, seemingly regaining some of herself.

Arioch nodded Emryn over and passed Aheia off into her arms softly, her expression pensive and tight. "Check in on her mind." And then when Emryn furrowed her brows, "but be careful in there."

Emryn's eyes flashed to his and her jaw tightened, before giving him a curt nod and pulling Aheia's body from his arms. He watched the Syraphem walk back towards the side of the room and rolled his shoulders trying to ease some of the tension there. But it was no use this time. The further Aheia went, the more the discomfort built, and it made him consider what it would mean for her to leave his realm.

He hadn't expected to feel like this, hadn't anticipated how much she'd affect him, and most of all didn't know what part of this was her soul, and what part of this was her. Because if he lost the glyph on his arm, he had the feeling that she'd leave an echo behind, and that echo would feel frightfully similar to an obsession. He'd thought that before, after he tasted her for the first time, but he'd written it off as the bond that was greater than both of them. Now, he wasn't so sure.

"*Alshaytan.*" Maz's voice snapped him back, and he nodded, hiding his thoughts in the shadows as he followed her.

Maz and Arioch stepped through his shadows, the cold of the darkness soothing against his skin. He hadn't realized how much of him it took to contain Aheia, but now—away from that damned room—he felt drained, sweat beading on the back of his neck.

The shadows stuttered underneath his skin as they always did when they neared Gehenna, and he let them roam from his shoulders when they stepped across the Nahr Alnufus and through the gate, passing by the Calmani glyphs that kept hel safe.

Mazikeen had been speaking to him during their descent, but he'd found it hard to concentrate. She equated what had happened here to the earth shifting below her very feet. They made their way through the secondary gates when he realized she wasn't being metaphorical. They stood on the edge of the staircase, their eyes fixed on a large jagged crack that ran the length of the floor beneath. Maz started speaking quickly and hushed in her language. Prayer.

Mazikeen did not pray.

Arioch's jaw started hurting with the strain he put on it. "Hel…"

He started walking down the stone steps that were suspended in the air without support, kicking his boot against the edge of the crack. "What in all the higher powers…"

"I checked into some of the lower levels before coming to find you—just to make sure everything was contained. The monsters are roaming. I could hear them from the stairwell, more than usual. But there are no cracks or breaks in the Calmani magyck there."

Arioch's mind reeled. Whatever had happened to Aheia was felt by the realm, and it had affected Gehenna …

"This is not right," Maz said, an edge Arioch rarely heard clipping her words. "If this happens again, there's a chance she'll free what's below. She can't be here. You need to get rid of her."

Her words held weight, but there was no way in hel that he would hand her back to the Mithra, at least not before figuring out what she held inside of that little body of hers.

"We need to speak to the Shaytān," Arioch said, his eyes drifting across the cavern to make sure there was nothing else out of place.

"As you wish." Maz's body was taut with irritation. He caught the embers on her neck flaring like they always did when she disagreed with him. He bent over the thin crack, watching soft tendrils of air escape and rustle around him. It was warm, and it had an odd smell, something dark and spicy that he couldn't place. He shook his head and followed Maz across the crack, and down another winding stairway that was hidden against the far wall and appeared when they approached.

Both Brite and Dark had their version of Fates, the Mithra had Moyrai: winged creatures with bleeding and bandaged eyes that could see into time and thought, a thing of legends that stayed wrapped up with enigmatic lore and misdirection. He knew of their existence because just as the Mithra had Moyrai, the Nephilim had the Shayṭān: an oracle that tethered the strings of fate from death. The Shayṭān was reborn every couple of centuries, a poor soul singled out that would carry the burden of becoming the new oracle. Fate could choose anyone it pleased, and would burrow itself into their chest, pulling the creature of choice into madness with visions and predictions. Arioch had only ever been around this oracle, but he knew its time would come to an end eventually. He'd never had to receive incoming Shayṭān but was told by his great-great-grandfather that the new oracle sought out whatever Alshaytan was in charge with an intrinsic pull that was the same one that let the Nephilim discriminate between night and day in Aljira.

As he stepped into their cave the slithers began, low and slow, bouncing off the jagged rock around him. He could only see because the oracle lent him its sight. Down here there was a darkness that fire wouldn't penetrate, and even Maz's embers didn't break through. His vision adjusted, and the familiar feeling of someone else's vantage point slipped into his mind. He saw himself approaching, saw Maz next to him, and saw the cavern walls that were inscribed by ancient Calmani runes.

"There's a shift."

"There's a shift."

"There's a shift."

It spoke as a broken echo.

"Hypocrisy."

"Hypocrisy."

"Hypocrisy."

Arioch felt as unsettled as he always did staring at himself.

"I'm here because ..."

"I know."

"I know."

"I know."

It always knew.

"What is she?" he asked, hearing Maz move next to him.

Silence. And in the silence, he knew they wouldn't answer.

"You don't visit us anymore, Alshaytan, don't bring us the things we crave. Only when it's convenient and you want answers." The echoes became loud, and he saw the cave as one, the focus shifted around marble statues carved into the face of the jagged rock. Four of them, the four original gods. Dark and light married in one space.

"An oversight," he said. He hated it down here. "One I will rectify."

They shifted their focus, moving their gaze from him to Maz and then over the walls, landing on the statues that formed a sort of gazebo around them. They looked out of place, carved from dark slag and bright white sandstone, with soft edges like someone had taken months to unearth them from large blocks of stone. The lighter gods had slight veins of black running through them, and he recognized Theia and Aether. Their hands intertwined in a tight grip, their fingers merging until there was no way of telling where one began and the other ended. Manāt was standing tall, his claws stretched in front of him like he was reaching for something just out of reach, and 'Amm was curled into herself, cradling her chest.

None of the statues seemed flattering. It seemed almost like what the Gods may have looked like in their last moments.

The Shaytān's eyes continued their sweep of the room slowly, seemingly without true direction.

"What is Aheia?" he asked, as the gaze turned back to him, drifting across and sweeping to the left.

"A question without an answer," the oracle crooned, a soft lilt in its disjointed voice.

"How?" he asked, his words clipped.

Silence spread through the cavern, the kind that felt loud.

In a singular voice with no echo, it said, "The outcome won't change. You know. You don't know. Fate has cemented itself, those hot threads inside your chest have been spun for you long before your time."

"Can you tell me anything?"

"Next time, bring me a treat." There was a smile in the voice, and Arioch knew in the way his sight dimmed, that the oracle was pulling away.

29

Chapter

Aheia

Aheia was floating, suspended in darkness as whispers pulled at her from all sides.

She tried to move, tried to run, but couldn't find her legs, couldn't find her limbs—until all at once reality rushed into her mind, and her surroundings crashed back into her field of view, leaving her rattled.

She fought off a splitting headache, pressing the heels of her palms into her temples and gritting her teeth. She blinked, feeling the exhaustion roll off her body.

She was tired, felt heavy—felt like she'd slept for days, and it made her jolt upright in a panic. There was a foreign fabric wrapped around her body–black and soft. The threads smelled of leather and dark spice, and her chest recognized Arioch's scent before she did. It pulled her back into her memories, into every painful moment—every pleasurable moment—of Arioch's shadows and how easily they'd made her come, and how the audience around them fed her need. She remembered how she'd whimpered and, and—oh Gods—how she'd ...

She felt the phantom touch of his magyck move across her skin like it was still there, remembered the feel inside of her like an imprint, and the *fucking shame*.

Gods, it was blazing hot.

She groaned, scrubbing her face before she remembered about the charcoal that Kar had painted her with, and pulled her hands back abruptly. Fuck. Black streaks coated her palm and she figured she looked like an animal with all of the powder smeared on her cheeks.

She yanked back the dark covers, the gold dress she'd been wearing replaced by a dark shirt long enough to hang like a dress, her dagger still holstered at her thigh. Had she been in Keloseros they would have taken that.

Keloseros ...

Kal's visit came rushing back. Kal, in a *suit*.

Aheia couldn't see past the Mithra, didn't remember anything past finding out that Kal wanted to take her back. And then she...

I must have passed out.

She had to have been sleeping, her nightmares had been so vivid that the pain haunted her even now. She'd dreamt that she was dying.

Her legs felt boneless as she eased onto her feet, looking around a room she didn't recognize. The walls were old stone, but different from the rock in her room and held only the bed she was sitting on and a small black chair in the corner.

She swallowed, nerves prickling her neck as she padded across the room and followed the call of the Aljiran sky to one of the windows on the far wall. She pressed her fingers against the glass, her eyes drifting over the landscape outside. It looked like she was in the middle of the city, the tall buildings she'd seen in the background from her window at the compound shooting into the sky in front of her, opaque glass wrapped around them like onyx mirrors. There were Nephilim bustling in and out of establishments and some sort of horseless carriages riding through the street which were made of the same material as the buildings. She parted her lips, watching Syraphem fly through the sky, some landing on the sidewalk below. The city felt just as alive as the rest of the realm did, a realm that was known far and wide for death.

But then maybe not everything was as it seemed at first glance in this world, Aheia thought. Keloseros was said to be peaceful and bright when she knew the dark dealings that were kept out of reach from the sun. It seemed the two realms were more similar than anyone would admit from either side, but in Aljira the darkness was no secret.

Thud.

Aheia whirled around, her back pressing into the cool glass, eyes scanning the dark room. The Solas above was dim and flickering, the shadows from the furniture and dark corners hidden from its light. Aheia's heart started an unsettled thrum in her chest. She hadn't imagined the sound. And it didn't come from outside.

"Ari?" she whispered. But she knew it wasn't him because her soul would have called out.

Then suddenly, the door to the room opened and three Nephilim whom Aheia had never seen before bled into the room.

"Finally found you," drawled the middle demon, who had dark horns and hair to match, his voice dripping like thick oil that stuck to her body.

"What do you want?" Aheia asked, curling her fingers against the window.

"To do what Alshaytan should have done," the Nephilim on his right sneered.

Anxiety shot through her and told her to find a way out of this room. But there was only the door that the three Nephilim were now standing against like a wall of muscle. The fabric of her shirt felt slight at that moment and the blade at her thigh became heavy with importance as her fingers itched for the weapon. She knew that she couldn't grab it yet.

With three of them, she had one shot—if that. She still hadn't recovered from the weeks of running, from the lack of food or the exhaustion, but the very real threat of death edged into her mind as she backed away from the window and towards a darker corner. Corners were a bad plan, she knew that, but the shadows that lived there might give her an advantage.

"Your kind taints everything they touch," the left one spit, and she saw bright white teeth. "Fucking *disgusting*."

"This is a mistake," Aheia said, her voice trembling, the darkness that lived in her veins vibrating.

"*You're* the mistake," the horned Nephilim laughed. "It's time for you to go home."

Home.

No.

She hovered her hand near the dagger, its metal hot against her cold skin. So fucking cold. It was like she might crack with the wrong movement.

"Why are you doing this?" she breathed, her head pulsing.

"We're just righting a wrong," the middle Leviathan threw her a crooked smile that held wicked unspoken intentions.

He stepped closer, pulling his blade from the inside of his jacket, and the others followed, closing in tighter until they were only an arm's length away.

You have to move now!

Aheia grasped at her blade then, pulling it from its sheath and lunging for the closest demon, before he could fully comprehend it. She dug the knife into his shoulder, black blood spluttering from the wound as he screamed, the other two jumping into action. Hands gripped onto her body, trying to pull her off the Nephilim while she held onto the blade like the lifeline it was.

"Mithra *whore*," the demon in front of her spluttered, his knife clattering to the floor as his hands grabbed ahold of her hair and tore so hard she could feel strands ripping from their roots. She yelped, her finger slipping in the black blood that was coating the hilt of her knife, eyes darting towards the door. But before she could think to run, she felt hands on her shoulders and nails digging into her skin. She wrenched the knife back, slicing it through the air behind her clumsily while the demon in front of her picked up the blade he'd dropped.

The hold on Aheia became iron, her free hand restrained behind her back just as her dagger hit its mark. A loud hiss sounded behind her, "Fucking *bitch*,"

She screamed, her knife hand yanked back and twisted so far that she gave in to the pain, dropping her weapon to the floor. She shrieked, kicking and pulling at her shoulders, flashes of her past bleeding into her conscious mind. She saw Ophion stepping closer, taking the spot of the horned Nephilim, she saw the blood pooling on the floor behind him. She saw her mother's lifeless body.

And she whimpered a helpless sound that broke the dam of tears building in her eyes.

"You really think you can escape us?" the Nephilim at her back hissed into her ear.

No.

She twisted and kicked out against him, but the demon in front of her palmed the hilt of his weapon and swung, his knuckles cracking against her cheekbone.

Her head snapped to the side, pain bruising her skin, the metallic flavor of her own blood trickling into her mouth. She spit it onto the floor and grit her teeth.

No. Not like this.

"Now, let's see what your insides look like." The demon in front of her grinned, holding his blade against his collarbone.

Aheia squeezed her eyes shut, her strength fading into the darkness behind her lids. She held her breath, fishing for that acceptance she'd felt before when thinking about death. But she couldn't find it, not when it was being dealt out by the hands of others. The world seemed to disappear, the demons drowned out under the erratic thumping of her heart in her chest. Until suddenly she heard something impossible.

A blood-curdling snarl.

Aheia opened her eyes, her breath caught in her throat when she was met with darkness. Shadow magyck filled the room the light from the Solas and the galaxies outside were snuffed, with soft strips of light shining through where the tendrils tapered. Aheia squinted, sound returning to her ears, the demons cursing and whirling around, their knives drawn.

Another snarl sounded and it was closer this time, the sound standing the hair on Aheia's neck on end as she stared ahead into a spiraling tendril that was moving around itself, like it was trying to draw her in.

The Nephilim looked around frantically, a moment of calm settling in until teeth gnashed through it. The hands and blades that had been constricting her movement were pulled from her body roughly, leaving her stumbling back against the wall, her body melting through the darkness like it was water. Her palms scraped across the rock, catching herself before her head could hit, while screams and shouts filled the room. Blood splattered the side of her face from the depths of the magyck, and she tasted it. Metal and ash, sweet and hot. She wiped her forearm over the wetness on her skin, trying to orient herself. She needed to get to the door, needed to escape—because the danger was alive, and had been traded for something much bigger.

She stumbled along the wall until she hit the bed she'd woken up in. *The door is across the room.*

Aheia swallowed, another scream jolting her into a sprint. She had only made it a few steps past the bed when her feet caught on something soft and heavy and she was sent flying to the floor. A yelp left her lips, her body tense as she braced herself, her hands crashing into the stone. The darkness thinned enough to show her the mangled carcass of a Nephilim, his ribcage torn open, his lungs and innards spilling from his chest and onto the floor. Aheia gagged, demon's black blood coating her skin, and the ends of her hair.

Her lungs filled in short and panicked bursts, wayward thoughts of prayer forcing themselves into her mind but she pushed the thoughts away quickly. Prayer wouldn't do anything for her. It never had.

She listened in the darkness, hearing the screams turn to gurgles, and then nothing, the all-consuming sound of claws scraping against rock the only noise.

It was moving towards her.

Closer.

Closer.

Until she saw long black talons breaking through the thick smoke in front of her. She recognized those talons. The Varcolac edged near, its breath hot and wet on her face as she held onto hers in an effort to stay still.

The creature bled from its shadows while a soft film of smoke clouded its features. Aheia could barely make out its dark, yellow eyes, the long wolf-like snout, and the teeth that dipped past its mouth. It was staring at her, its ears tall and sharp, fur matted with blood that was still dripping from its jowls.

"Please—" Aheia breathed, pushing back slowly.

The Varcolac followed, its head tilting, a soft groan humming from its chest.

She knew it would be futile to run. There was nowhere she could go, so she closed her eyes again, waiting for pain that never came. Instead, she felt a gentle nudge against her temple.

It was ... soft.

Her eyes flew open, finding the creature's face level with hers. The yellow irises were alive, just like the shadows, thin threads of warm honey weaving through the yellow pools, the pupils dilating slightly as they roamed her face.

It might have been stupid of her, but she raised a trembling hand and held it up towards the Varcolac's snout. The creature growled and she stilled, but then it leaned into her palm, its fur coarse against her skin. An exhausted laugh escaped Aheia. It wasn't a sound of joy, but of relief, a broken and breathy sound.

"Thank you," she whispered, before squinting at the slowly returning light. The room took shape again, the tendrils pulling back into themselves, forming into a large black mass, covering the entirety of the creature it was hiding within. The scene in front of Aheia turned her stomach to lead. Two of the Nephilim were unrecognizable, their black blood splattered across the wall, their organs smashed against the floor, while the third was still convulsing in a corner, sputtering his last breaths, and it sounded like his lungs were filling with blood.

She knew the sound.

30

Chapter

Aheia

It wasn't the killing that shook Aheia, nor was it the prospect of death, but the very real possibility of being dragged back to Keloseros. The thought of falling back into her old life unraveled her, and she was left kneeling in a pool of blood, mind groggy, with a dull hum in her chest.

Nephilim died like mortals. Dead eyes, cold bodies.

Yet Aheia was colder. Even without the Varcolac's interference, she would have fought until she couldn't. She would have killed herself on those blades before she let them take her anywhere.

The monster stood behind her snarling, its big, heavy body pressing into her back. A tendril curled around her waist and she felt a soft nudge between her shoulder blades.

"Messy," she murmured, something tired settling into the depths of her bones, pulling the soaked t-shirt into place as best she could before turning her head, seeing dark shadows in her peripheral.

"Thank you."

Her feet moved before her mind could catch up with her actions, turning from the bodies, and leaving the room. She didn't know exactly where she was walking, but she knew shadows followed, knew that her shirt was dripping dark blood onto the floor, and knew her feet were leaving sticky prints behind.

And then as the moments faded and time seemed to slip from her grasp, bodies started drifting into view as she arrived at a tall, old staircase. Her mind picked odd things to focus on, like how the rock was similar to the old stone in her room at Arioch's compound but just different enough. It was lighter, smoother, and it didn't quite feel like rock. Her hand glided down the thick, intricate railing, painting it black. She would have cared in any other instance, pulled her hand back, considered how porous the stone might be and if it would stain. But not now. Now, she'd paint the world around her black. Because she wasn't weak, and wouldn't let any Nephilim think she was.

Her vision focused in the direction her chest was urging her; She could feel the pull, knew she'd find him, and the demons around her didn't matter. But this time he found her first, his eyes simmering, his right fist clenched so hard that the veins on his forearm were protruding. The Nephilim around them made space as he approached her, some vanishing and some running. His gaze was hot and furious and it sent fire down her spine, twisting and curling into her middle until it hurt to look.

Aheia hesitated at the foot of the stairs, standing across from him, a world apart. Two things that should never coexist, a chasm of reasons to hate each other littered between them. But when he curled his fingers and beckoned her forward, the reasons cracked and broke underneath her feet.

"Aheia," Arioch said, his words bridging the space and giving her enough ground to walk on.

His gaze traveled behind her and then off to her right, followed by a slight nod to Lúc and Shiron, who'd been trailing him. The two Nephilim passed her, Lúc giving her a quick wink, Shiron's eyes hard. The Varcolac followed her, she could feel it at her back as she took Arioch's hand and let him lead her back into a corner, where he sat and pulled her down with him, her legs draping between his.

"What happened?" Arioch rasped, putting one of his arms around her waist tightly.

She sighed, the comfort of his embrace giving her lungs space to breathe fully for the first time since the other Nephilim touched her.

"Can I sit here?" she asked quietly, feeling the weight of his arm.

Safety. Safety licked from a black, sharp dagger.

He pulled her back against his chest until her shoulder was nestled against him. She felt him breathe, strong, and measured. But there was something under his skin, she could feel it. Like energy, her soul, or maybe his shadows—she didn't know. It was more than just the forced bond they shared, it felt separate and it echoed within her. The push and pull was becoming hard to discern in the span of very little time. What she wanted and what the bond between them demanded had been clear up until this point, but now they twisted into each other, and it all became... murky.

"How long did I sleep?" She looked up at Arioch, catching the end of him telling Emryn something in Lujha, those eyes a furious void. Emryn ... she hadn't noticed the Syraphem that was standing off to the side, her eyebrows furrowed before she slipped from view again. Aheia gripped the dagger still in her hand and wouldn't give it up, even as blood squeezed from between the leather and her fingers.

"A day."

She leaned into Arioch and rested her temple against the top of his shoulder, breathing him in. Leather, ash, sweet spices.

"I want your shadows, there's too much light in here," she said quietly.

Her words echoed through the room and pushed everyone around them from her mind as she watched the wisps drift from his skin. It looked like he was burning.

The Varcolac laid down at her feet, the large black mass blocking out half the room even in its position on the floor. Aheia smiled into the wild tendrils as Arioch's darkness wrapped itself around both of them. It was so warm, like a cocoon, just him and her and no more migraine-inducing, blinding white light.

"It likes you," Arioch said finally, breaking the soft silence between them.

"It?"

"The Varcolac."

"*Glykó skýs*," she said absentmindedly, seeing little patterns form in the complete darkness against her eyes the longer she stared into nothing.

"I don't know if I would call it a sweet dog," Arioch said, his chest shaking her as he chuckled.

A beautiful sound.

"It ripped the spine from one of your Nephilim like a sweet dog," she said, her voice detached.

The energy between them shifted as she gave him a trickle of new information.

"Are you hurt?" he asked, an edge in his voice.

"It's mostly their blood," Aheia said, feeling it on her skin, cracking when she shifted as it dried against her.

"Their?"

"I think I have a small cut." She didn't want to talk, she didn't want to think—and for once she didn't want his words either. At least not these.

"How many, Aheia?"

"Does it have a name?" she asked, her brain feeling heavy.

"The Varcolac? No." His edge deepened, fringing on the softness of his words.

"You should name your pets," she said, searching for distractions around her. So, she thought about the creature and that if he hadn't named it, she would. Maybe Koutávi. It was something like 'small dog' in her language, and the absurdity of a creature made of smoke and darkness being named something like that made her smile.

"It's not a pet." Arioch's hands found the side of her neck, his thumb stroking over her pulse, featherlight. "Tell me what happened. I need to hear it from you, Ruhí."

She swallowed, leaning into his touch. "I'm covered in blood. It's tight—feels tight."

He went rigid against her, his arm squeezing around her a fraction. "Let's change that," he said, shifting them both and scooping her up in his arms.

She cradled her dagger to her chest and held onto his shirt with her other hand as he stood, wondering how he knew where he was going until they stepped out from behind the darkness. It was eaten up by a low, amber light, soft enough that Aheia only needed a couple of seconds before she adjusted to their new surroundings.

Arioch set her down slowly, running his hands up the sides of her body as he straightened, making sure that the wobble in her legs didn't take her down. Her feet met familiar black marble, but the room was new. She looked around, finding a large tub in the corner, and clean lines of marble dividing up what she now realized was a washroom. She inhaled, feeling his scent wrapped around her. It was stronger here, stronger than anywhere else.

His room.

He'd taken her to his room.

31
Chapter

Aheia

Arioch stepped into the dark corner of the washroom and turned the knob, the water starting to pool and fall from the ceiling as Aheia stood, still holding the knife. He worked quickly, wrapping his hands around her waist and walking them back until both of them were standing underneath the warm spray, fully clothed. His hands brushed her wet hair from her face, his leathers sliding against her legs as he shifted them slightly.

"Tell me what happened," he said, running his hands over her arms.

She swallowed, letting her neck roll back, a slight crack between her bones. "There were three of them. They wanted to take me back, said I didn't belong here ..."

"*Sa'aqum 'Ida Laem tafeal,*" he growled.

"What?" She'd missed half of the words he spoke as she watched the blood drip from her skin.

"Keep going." His breath was hot against her ear.

"I had your dagger, so I stabbed one of them in the shoulder..." she said, glancing at the weapon. A shudder ran through her as flashes of knives and skin covered the shower wall in front of her. "I don't want to talk about this." She squirmed, the cut on her lips pulsing. "Koutávi, she saved me."

Arioch stroked her skin. "She?"

"Your shadow creature–that fire is female," Aheia said. "She."

He hummed. "She." It sounded like agreement. "What did you call her?"

"Koutávi. She should have a name. Without her, they would've..." She trailed off, losing focus as her mind rebelled against the memory.

"I'm going to get rid of them." He murmured, sliding his calloused palms down her legs before hooking his fingers underneath the seam of her shirt, stilling for a moment. "That's all." He nodded at the blood on her skin and tugged the fabric that was doing the bare minimum to cover her higher.

Aheia didn't protest, was too exhausted to even find the desire to. She let him strip off the shirt and throw it to the side with a wet thud, the sound wrapping around them both as cool air brushed against her exposed skin. She was bared to him for the first time, and though he'd had his hands all over her body, this seemed more intimate.

"I'll fix what they did," he said, tilting her chin back, his thumb ghosting across the bottom of her bruised lips. The water dripped from his curls and onto her face while his eyes held her attention, lit embers moving back and forth between the remnants of burnt ash. It spoke to something inside of her, the dark things that she felt snaking through her, the thing that had reared its head when Arioch sliced into the Nephilim who'd tried to attack her a few days ago. The memory of it clouded her mind, and it prickled sharp anticipation through her.

Is that what he'd do to the demon that might have survived Koutávi?

"Our bargain remains—they didn't break that—but I broke my word. They forced my hand the moment they laid theirs on you," he continued, his voice soft. She didn't know how to handle soft, not from him, and it wasn't what she needed. Soft would force her tears, would force her emotions from the stifling box she'd crammed them into. If she opened that clasp, she didn't know if she could ever close it again.

"Stop," she hissed, pulling her chin from his hold and focusing on her hands. Her fingers were caked in the blood that was slowly cracking at the knuckles, remnants of the Nephilim rimming her nails. She didn't know if Arioch and her were still playing, or if their earlier game had ended because there was no need to pretend here between just the two of them, even though no part of her wanted to stop. And that scared the hel out of her. That's why she pushed him away, that's why she looked anywhere but his eyes–because the slow thrum of her soul was reminding her of what this thing between them really was. That didn't diminish the pain as her heart squeezed at the words he was spinning around her with such care, coaxing forth a new sensation–one, she feared, had nothing to do with their bargain.

"Aheia, do you know what happened last night? After the Mithra showed up?" Arioch asked suddenly, his voice pensive.

She furrowed her eyebrows, shaking her head slowly. "I assumed I–" she struggled, "I thought I fainted. I don't know. Please, I don't want to talk."

He met her gaze, and for a torturous moment, he searched. For what, she didn't know. Then when he seemed to realize there was nothing else she could offer him, he slid onto his knees in front of her, still so Gods damned tall, even now.

She didn't fight him. Not when he pulled off the sheath from her leg, not when he lathered his soap over her toes, her ankles, her calves, and not as he trailed his palms up the outside of her hips, his hands focused in their touch. She stared ahead, trying to calm down the urgency she felt in the pit of her stomach under his touch, even as her mind wandered to what he'd done with his shadows. She should have been angry ... maybe she was ... but she didn't care about that either, not now. His shadows between her legs, so Gods damned public, had been a punishment, but if she was truthful she'd give anything for the same treatment in this moment.

She exhaled roughly while Arioch continued scrubbing her body, the suds turning pink from the friction. It seemed to take forever, and the ache in her middle was growing worse with each caress, each squeeze. She bit back a moan, tipping her head back. Gods, she couldn't control it ...

She met his stare and fought to keep her footing as those dark eyes burned her. He was on his knees and she had a distinct feeling he didn't kneel for anyone.

"What does Ruhí mean?" she whispered, looking down at him, steadying herself against his shoulder while his hands stilled against her waist.

"It means ..." he hesitated, something glinting in his eyes, "brat."

"It doesn't." She stepped in between his knees, tipping his chin further until it was resting against her stomach and he was looking up at her for a change. "I don't like when you look at me like this–like I'm frail."

He let her stand over him, the water dripping down her breasts and across his skin, his lashes holding pearls of the liquid. "Natye. Frail? How do you believe I think you're frail when you have my people's blood on your body?" He ran his hand over her waist and further up until his fingers fanned across her ribcage.

"I can see it." She ground out through her teeth. "You look at me like I'm broken."

"We're all broken, Aheia. It's what gives us strength. Only the broken can grow." And again, his words felt soft, like he was using special gloves to handle her, like he was taking care of a ward. It wasn't a side she thought he possessed, nor a side she wanted right now.

"Stop," she hissed again, grabbing ahold of his wrist. "I don't want this, not from you, not like that, not like–" She shook her head, realizing that her loose tongue had almost let Kal's name slip.

She'd swallowed it, but by the way Arioch looked at her, he'd bridged the gap already.

"Like who, *Aheia*?" His voice held a dark warning, his accent thick and coarse now.

"*No one.*" She tried to step away from him, but he held her in place with the hand on her ribcage, and then another on the back of her thigh.

"It better be no one," he growled, "because if you were about to compare me to that blonde Čist emissary..."

"What if I was?" Her heart pounded in her chest. She'd never wanted Kal that way, but she enjoyed what she saw in Arioch's features at the suggestion of it. Her attempts to free herself were met with an ironclad grip as she tried to find space between them; though space was the last thing she wanted. What she did want was the anger she saw flaring in Alshaytan's gray eyes every time she fought against his hold.

"Let me go," she hissed, feeling the heat flush her skin.

"*No.*" The word was sharp, and it echoed around the marble that surrounded them as he traded his hold on her waist for her wrists, pulling her down on top of him so she was forced to straddle his thighs. He wound a heavy arm around her middle while she struggled, her naked body flush with his wet clothing, the laces of his leathers rubbing between her legs. "Is that what he would do? Stop, and apologize?" he spoke the words into her ear.

Gods, this was exactly what she wanted.

"Yes," she gasped, the ache in the pit of her stomach building with each little movement as she chased the friction he offered against her clit.

"Does he make you feel this way?" Arioch asked, his free hand sliding over the curve of her ass. "Can he make you squirm like this?"

She braced herself against his shoulders, pushing as hard as she could, the water raining down on them. "Stop touching me."

Don't.

"Such fucking fire," he ground out looking down between them, the hand on her ass squeezing hard enough to tease a whimper from between her lips. "Such a brat. Come on, tell me one more time and I'll let you go."

"Go to hel," Aheia panted, grinding down onto the seam that kept them apart, pleasure lighting up her spine.

A dark chuckle vibrated through his chest. "Already there."

He had her strung so fucking taut that she feared she might snap in two.

"You looked so fucking beautiful when you came all over my shadows." He softened his fingers and slid his knuckles between her breasts towards her abdomen. "Your soul was burning into me like it wanted to make me pay for leaving you on that couch by yourself," he continued, reaching down and slipping his hand between her legs. Aheia bucked in his hold, feeling the rough pads of his fingers sliding down her center. "My violent little creature—not at all what the Mithra think you are. Does anyone else know this side of you, Ruhí?"

She shook her head, having lost all capability for words when he massaged that sensitive skin just to the side of her clit. He was playing with her again, watching her with those dark eyes, a smile building on his lips every time she tried to readjust, to move him exactly where she needed him. But he wouldn't let her.

"No," he hummed, his breath warming her lips. "You can't control it can you, little goddess? You can't hold onto those masks you hide behind while you're playing with demons."

She whimpered as he bowed his head and bit down on the nape of her neck, the sting of his teeth slinking down her body and meeting his touch between her legs. "This side of you is all mine."

Aheia's mind floated from her grasp when he sank two of his fingers inside of her slowly, while he rubbed the heel of his palm against her clit. She couldn't move, didn't want to try, and losing herself in the pleasure he was offering loosened her tongue.

"If I can't have you, you can't have—fuck." Aheia spasmed, her body clenching around him as he stretched her wide, his teeth sinking into that spot just below her ear.

"Fuck," he rasped, "Gods, you're swollen. Were you this swollen when you fucked yourself that first night, Aheia? When you were thinking of me?"

"No," she lied, her hips rolling against his hand like they had a mind of their own.

"No? You weren't thinking about what it might feel like to have my hands on your body, my fingers inside of you?"

She shook her head again, her teeth clenched tight as she chased her orgasm.

"What it would be like to have a demon fuck you?" He stroked against that sensitive spot inside of her, tight pulses of pleasure curling her toes.

"Ari, I–"

"I can tell you," he growled, letting go of her ass and finding the back of her neck instead, the strokes between her legs becoming hard and fast. "Your sweet little cunt is used to undersized Mithra dick. You'll break if I fuck you."

She choked on her next breath, as he slid a third finger inside of her. "You're so tight," he said, keeping her face close to his. "I can barely move my fucking fingers, Aheia."

Fuck, fuck, fuck.

Her legs were shaking, her eyes fringing with little bursts of light, just as Arioch stopped moving completely.

The smile on his lips turned deviant as he leaned in. "Compare me to that Čist one more fucking time."

32

Chapter

Arioch

The bruise on her lip made him fucking vicious. He wanted blood, he wanted everyone to pay. His shadows and that Gods damned soft voice at the back of his mind agreed with each other for once. There were unanswered questions about last night, so many fucking questions, and it seemed the more answers he uncovered the more uncertainty spun itself around them. But her eyes were unfocused, and she had been pulling back into herself, the glaze that sheathed her gaze—only broken by her anger—made it clear she wouldn't open up any further. And though the anger seemed just another device to shove him away, he preferred that to whatever docile thing was coaxed out before that. It seemed she felt the same way about him, was pushing for his own fury now, her teeth bared, a frustrated whine on her lip as he stilled his fingers inside of her.

"*Fuck*," she hissed in between ragged breaths, a restrained tremble starting in her legs.

"You think I'd let you come after all that?" He furrowed his brows, watching her forehead fall against his chest, her wet hair sticking to her shoulders.

"Please," she whined.

The breathless little whimper drove right between his thighs, pleasure coiling his insides. "Say it again," he growled, holding onto his shadows with everything he had. She wasn't the only one who was failing in her control.

That angry little line between Aheia's eyebrows made an appearance as she peered up at him, opening and closing her mouth. And then with the sweetest tinge of anger, "Please."

Fuck.

He couldn't deny her this—couldn't deny himself this.

Fuck.

"Please what?" He stretched his fingers apart, twisting them inside of her like he wanted to imprint himself into her body.

"*Ah*, please let me come."

He clenched his jaw, his cock pressing into the waistband of his leathers painfully. "And who's making you come?"

She avoided his gaze, knees sliding against his legs with the effort to hold herself up.

"*Who?*" he asked, running his thumb through her folds and across her clit, forcing her body towards an orgasm that was leashed tightly to her next words.

"You," she whispered, her eyes focused anywhere but his.

"Remember that," he said, sliding his fingers from between her legs completely.

"No," she moaned, her eyes wild and pleading.

"Don't worry little goddess, I'll take care of you."

He brought his hand up between them, her arousal sliding down his knuckles as he summoned his shadows and made her watch as the tendrils slithered down between their bodies.

"What are you–Ari, *shit*." Her breathing hitched as his magyck teased her entrance, sliding over her wet core over and over again.

Arioch's shoulders sagged slightly, feeling the pressure release under his muscles as he watched nerves surfacing in her wide gaze.

"What's our word?" he asked.

She squirmed, her thighs quivering, her face flushed when she met his eyes with a half-lidded gaze. "Honey."

"You want this?" he asked.

"Yes."

The word shredded the last of his restraint. His shadows all but moving on their own, pushing inside of her slowly, just an inch, just a taste. She whimpered, her hips stuttering against his magyck greedily.

"More?" he ground out, the lust in his stomach twisting him into knots.

"Yes, Ari, *please*."

Aheia's body arched as he started his shadows at a slow pace that had them sinking a little deeper each time they stroked inside of her. He worked them towards release together, the mere fucking sight of her getting him close to his own, her hips meeting his thrusts in chaotic patterns. Her fingers slid into his hair and tugged so tight he felt strands of it ripping from its roots, sweet, thick words in Gjóssa falling from her lips as she begged him for more. The desperation was fucking delicious. And they shared it. Because he felt like he might burn alive without that cold little creature coming undone on his lap.

"Are you still thinking about that Čist?" Arioch panted as he took his free hand to his leathers and unlaced himself. *Hel*, he wanted to pull his shadows away and bury his cock so deep she'd never quite forget how it felt to have him fuck her.

"No. I'm sorry," she whimpered, her body sagging slightly with exhaustion while her eyes watched him pull himself free. Her lips parted, that cold gaze running over every heated inch of him, something unnamed winding its way into her features.

"No, you're not," he said, as he started to stroke himself, slapping the head of his cock against her abdomen, a bead of pre-come stringing between them. "You knew exactly what you were doing."

She moaned, her arousal dripping from his shadows and onto his legs. "Please."

"Now that I've got you begging you can't stop, hmm?" he growled, sliding the head of his cock against her clit, his knuckles stroking through her wet folds.

"Ugh, *fuck*," she cried, his shadows stretching her to her limits while he coated himself in her arousal.

"You take it so well, little goddess," he groaned, the friction too fucking perfect, too torturous. "*So* fucking well."

She whimpered as his fingers gripped her ass, digging into where he knew he'd bruised her last night. He could see the evidence in light purple splotches—his own fucked up mark. It took everything he possessed not to come for her right then and there.

"I'm close," she whined, her breathing becoming more and more unsteady, her words slowly running into each other as she rolled her hips faster. "Please Ari, please, I–"

He let go of himself and pulled her body against his, his hard length pushed up against his abdomen.

"Take what you need," he growled, holding her up while she rocked her clit against the tip of his cock.

"I can't—I–" Her words were choked out by a moan, her wild eyes lost in his own as she chased her orgasm, the shadows between her legs nearing a punishing pace.

"Come for me," he groaned.

He could feel her, her hips stuttering, her eyes fringed with something dark as she came undone completely, crying out in pleasure; it was all he needed to fall over the edge with her. She convulsed, her body shaking against his as she rode out her release, an animalistic growl tearing itself from the depths of Arioch's chest. He tightened his grip on her ass and leaned his forehead against hers, chest heaving, sweat pearling, and washing away with the water the moment it formed. It was maddening, all of it. He stared down at her, how she had her back arched, his shadows seeping from between her legs, his come on her pale skin.

This wasn't enough, fuck it was far from. He needed so much more, he needed everything she was willing to give him. But this hadn't been about him.

He supported her body, released his shadows, and cradled her to his chest as she went limp in his arms, spasming slightly. He stroked down her spine, his cock still pulsing between them.

This is going to end badly.

"You're being nice," she murmured, as he stepped under the spray of water completely so that he could clean her off. "You don't have to do that, it's not what this is."

He was aware of that, and those words shouldn't have irritated him.

"Keep your mouth shut," he said, trying to contrast the tender touch he gave her.

"Make me," she muttered.

"Aheia," he said with a warning, shifting them so he could get an arm around her shoulders. He saw the red skin of her ass as he readjusted, and it did nothing to loosen the knots she had him in. He walked them from the washroom and set her down on his bed, pulling the dark sheets over her wet, pale skin. Her eyes widened as she watched him.

What are you ...?

The thought circled his mind, had its grip on him, and wouldn't let go. He knew nothing about her, and it seemed the only ones who might were his enemies. He'd question Kal, but he had a feeling that whatever conversation was impending with the Mithra emissary would shift whatever Aheia and he had. He wasn't quite ready for that.

"Rest," he said simply, pulling away from her and taking two shirts from his wardrobe, tossing one towards her. He looked a little too long as she shrugged his threads over her head and scolded himself for it.

That's not what this is.

But fuck if she didn't look–

No.

He shook his head.

He should have taken her to Kazim's room, but he couldn't get himself to head back towards the old wing. Putting her in his brother's old room had been an odd last-minute choice. Her soul had unnerved him, how he felt about her after only a few words had unsettled him, so he put her in a part of the compound he knew would keep him away. The memories that were lining the coarse rock there were suffocating, and though there were good ones peppered in between, the bad ones were so much easier to summon to his mind.

So much horrible shit had happened in that part of the house, the worst of it done by him.

Sadness washed out the lust he felt, leaving behind a cold and hollow pounding in his chest. And he held onto that because he needed it to force himself from the Mithra in his bed.

Arioch shrugged on new leathers and was pulling on his boots when a knock sounded at his door. Aheia was watching him, sitting against the headboard with her knees drawn to her chest, her cheek resting against the back of her hand while she hugged herself.

Shiron was standing outside, his hands covered in blood, his eyes a burning amber.

"There were two," Shiron started, leaning against the opposite side of the hall, while Arioch closed the door behind him and backed up against it. "One of them was ripped to shreds–completely unrecognizable, but the second was still alive–barely. It was one of Eros' men. Lúc and Emryn tortured him–the usual. All they could gather was that Eros has his family. He most likely won't break."

Two?

Arioch's brows drew near. "Aheia said there were three."

"She's sure?" Shiron narrowed his eyes.

Arioch nodded. "It doesn't seem like a detail that would get lost in translation."

Shiron looked down at the floor for a moment. "I'll have some of the guards comb the area. If he got away, he won't have made it far." Then he crossed his arms. "It's a message, Eros wants you to know it was him."

"What he wants is to rally my own against me," Arioch said. "He'll try to frame this in his favor. The death of his men gives him grounds to move against Aheia lawfully. Her actions may have been self-defense, but it's her word against three dead bodies. The word of a Mithra."

"He'll go after her so he can get to you," Shiron continued.

Arioch bared his teeth. This bullshit political conflict was going to be the death of him.

"If I back her, he'll try and convince as many people as he can that I'm delusional." He shook his head. "Where the fuck has Eros been hiding out? He's usually much more present."

"He's been lying low, which worries me," Shiron said. "Tariq and some of the others have been taking turns keeping an eye on the Azalam territories and there hasn't been any loud unrest in a while—which is concerning. Azalam is never quiet."

He knew that Eros was smart and used other Nephilim to do his dirty work so that he could keep his hands clean. But all of that was a distraction of its own. Nothing happened within the southern territories before passing by Siraj's scrutiny. He was the demon standing behind his brother, pulling the strings—he always had been. Eros was just either too stupid to notice or played along happily. After all, Arioch was sure Siraj made it worth his while.

"Do we have anything on Eros? Any proof besides weak association?" Arioch looked at Shiron, who clenched his jaw and shook his head.

"No."

"He's setting traps at every fucking angle." Arioch rolled his shoulders. If they went after Eros now, there would be fallout. Siraj could once again spin it in a way that made it look like Arioch favored the Mithra, which might sway some of the Nephilim whose support for him had been shaky at best. He knew what he'd done when he invited Aheia to stay, but he hadn't expected Siraj to act so quickly.

A mistake he wouldn't be repeating.

"If you kill Eros, Siraj will attempt a revolution," Shiron said. They couldn't go after Eros, but there were alternatives.

"We'll leave his precious brother alone for now." Arioch shot him a vicious grin. "Have you heard from Aylee about the Nerium nests?"

Shiron nodded. "She briefed me this morning. She's located one of them on the outskirts near the dregs in Siraj's territory."

Nerium was a flower, all the drugs in Aljira were made using different flowers, one that would kill a mortal but gave Nephilim a mind-altering high. It was also addictive as fuck, and outlawed.

Arioch nodded. "Have Emryn take some of the Falkri with Aylee and Lúc. Burn it down. All of it, and make sure to string the dead body up in the street."

Shiron narrowed his eyes. "An indirect message."

"You're only doing your duty, keeping the streets clean," Arioch said grimly, while irritation settled into his bones. He wanted to do so much more, so much *worse*, but now was not the time, not yet. "Where's the Leviathan who survived?"

"In the caves."

When he stepped back into his room Aheia was sitting on the edge of the bed, her eyes drawing a line down his body. Whatever dark thing hid in the blue was pure fucking helfyre, the simmering voracity that lived at the core of this world, overwhelming and forceful. She looked feral and demonic, and nothing like the Mithra facade she tried to hide behind.

"Get some rest," Arioch said, catching a tendril of her white hair between his fingers as she shifted her legs, his shirt rising higher on her body when she did. All he wanted was to kneel in front of her and push her thighs wide. He needed to taste her again, needed to split her apart, needed to hear her scream for him.

But he needed to take care of the demon in his caves first, and fuck, would he relish pulling the skin from the fucker's bones. He stepped back, dropping her hair.

"You're leaving." It wasn't a question.

She tipped her head, disappointment plain on her face.

He leaned in, only a breath away from her lips. "Go to bed, Aheia."

She swallowed, her eyes dropping to his mouth before he forced himself away from her, and summoned his shadows into a thick cloud in front of him. He needed to put space between them now because the way his body was lit with need for the bright little thing in his bed was fucking with his mind.

"No." He heard it just as he stepped into his shadows, and then he felt her arms wrap around him tightly. The darkness slithered around them, Aheia clinging to his back like he was a lifeline, her nails digging into his collarbone, her legs squeezing his waist.

Arioch growled, staggering slightly.

"You're not leaving me alone in that bed," she whispered into his ear, her voice deep and sultry.

"Hold on, then." He smiled to himself at the prospect of punishing her for this later. But he liked how she squeezed his middle, how her heels crossed, how her breath felt against his neck.

Fuck, he liked it

33

Chapter

Aylee

Aylee was hanging her legs off of the side of a building, dark, cracked rock cutting into her leathers as she let her eyes drift over Azalam. This part of the territory was on the outskirts of the city, bordered by dark forests that spanned so far they were said to reach the end of the realm, a place no one had gone and returned from. There were creatures that populated the underbrush that came from the old times–before there was any structure in Aljira. The trees looked like a black ocean meeting the sky, much too tranquil for what was believed to live underneath them. It was a stark difference from the city that bled into the darkness. The streets here were cobblestone that looked like they'd been thrown in in mismatched patterns, grout slathered across them in a way that had them sticking up in jagged patches.

The dregs of Azalam were a reminder of Sahren's time in power, a time when a majority of the city had looked like this— looked old. The buildings here were crooked and tall, the windows carved into the side, fire lighting and heating the homes; torches that looked like they were nearly falling off of their metal fastenings, oil dripping into the trash-littered alleys that cut through the cluster of houses in craggy, thin lines. Aylee watched Tariq and Lúc slip around the bottom of the building, Emryn perched on the roof with her, her wings tucked in tight. The younger Falkri recruits had scouted the place, were in position on the ground, and the dead body of the Nephilim who'd attacked the Dioscuri staying with Arioch was in a heap in the middle of the roof. That's why they were here. Aylee didn't care. She would be in the city one way or another, and while it sat wrong with her that it was for a Mithra, she'd gladly help burn down the nest below them. Fire fixed everything. Its ferocity made her skin prickle in excitement, in a nauseating mixture with the distaste she held for the drug-crazed Nephilim that would fall prey to it.

"It's getting worse," Emryn said, her eyes drawing little lines across bodies in the streets. They were Nephilim, out of their minds, eyes turned towards the stars with open mouths and far away gazes. It's what Nerium did to the demons, took them into different worlds in their heads while their bodies rotted. It was a poison that festered and spread until the user couldn't live without it, and would do anything to escape just one more time.

Aylee only nodded, running the silver file she held in her fingers across her nails again. She kept them sharp because she much preferred feeling the blood on her hands than her blades.

"Lúc and Tariq are moving in with the others below," Aylee said over her shoulder, resting her arm against her knee.

"Something feels off," Emryn said, looking up at the stars for a moment. "Something feels..."

"It feels like lightning, right before it strikes." Aylee finished. It had the hairs on the back of her neck standing on end, her skin pebbling in anticipation.

Emryn's eyes slid to hers. "You feel it too?"

Aylee nodded, stashing her file and inspecting her pointed, red nails. "For a couple of days now." She watched their Nephilim break down the front door.

"String him up," Aylee said to one of the Falkri recruits who had been sitting behind her, her hands wrapped tightly around the hilt of a dagger. She nodded to whatever was left of the Nephilim's body and saw a slight scrunch of the recruit's nose. "Now."

"I want to go inside," she said, her eyes bright.

"You have some nerve after last time," Aylee said, her voice threaded with quiet command. "You'll do as you're told."

"Hang him over the side, make it visible. When you're done, go back to the Kaserne," Emryn said, pulling her blades free and stepping onto the edge of the building, her wings spreading and catching the air.

The Nephilim's expression fell, but she got up from her spot and started working on the corpse.

Screams began peppering the air, hoarse and broken, bodies flooding from the decrepit building, falling over each other in an effort to escape whatever was happening inside.

Emryn nodded at Aylee before she dropped out of view on the other side of the roof, her wings disappearing last.

Deep breaths.

Aylee took a moment to suppress the discomfort in her gut. She hated going into nests like this, had known the inside of those walls all too well when she was young. Her past was always threatening her present in these situations, which unfortunately made her really fucking good at her job.

She looked over the side of the building and positioned herself above one of the windows just as a body shattered it and went flying into the street below with a howl. The demon landed on the stone with a heavy crack right before a dark mess of hair appeared from the opening.

Lúc's almond-shaped eyes peered up at her and he grinned, the corners of his mouth painted in blood.

"Come on," he said, his voice a feline purr, giving her a quick wink before disappearing back inside.

Aylee lowered herself over the edge of the building, hooking her hands against the rough stone and suspending herself off the side before she pushed against the wall with enough momentum for her to drop in through the window. Her boots kicked in some of the remaining glass as she landed, a steadying hand pressed against the splintered wood floor.

The commotion was loud—shuffled footsteps flying around her, screams drifting from different poorly lit rooms that were painted in blood and dirt. Flames were already licking up the walls on her right, a broken lantern laying in a puddle of oil, at the center, bordered by dirty mattresses.

Deep breaths.

She straightened up and made her way down the hallway that fed out of the room, the smell of decay, excrement, and smoke billowing around her as she passed the bodies that littered the floor. The dead here had not passed under their hands; no, the dead here had laid in their spots for days.

She ran past the rotting skin and red, splotchy eyes of the corpses, following the screams down rickety stairs just as a dark leather-clad Nephilim tried to push past her.

"Get him!" Tariq growled, a wave of panic-stricken demons pushing into his path.

Aylee hissed, whipping her hand across the Nephilim's face, her nails cutting into his eyes, the blood spurting. He screamed, tripping back, his head cracking against the floor just as Tariq made it across the chaos moments later, his eyes dark. He grabbed onto the screaming Nephilim's shoulder and dragged him off into another room.

"Please, help me, please!" A female with ghostly eyes latched onto Aylee's side, her grip bruising, her fingers crooked.

"Get out!" Aylee yelled, pulling her off and shoving her towards the front of the building and into the sea of bodies.

"No please, please, I need—do you have any more?" The woman whirled around, her expression frantic. "Are you here for more of us?" Her words were shaky, "I just need some more, do you have any? I'm dying." She sobbed, drool pouring from the corner of her mouth as she bared her yellow teeth.

Aylee swallowed her disgust and shoved the woman towards a door that was laying off its hinges, the night sky pouring in from outside.

"Get out if you want to live." She turned her back and made her way to the center of the house, the onslaught of Nephilim slowly thinning. Falkri were pouring oil onto the walls on both sides of her, the flames rolling across the ceiling making it clear that their time was dwindling.

"Are any of your dealers still in the building?!" Emryn's voice rang out.

"No, I swear, they left hours ago, there's no one here." The Nephilim that Aylee had blinded was blubbering while Tariq held his hands bound behind his back, a black blade pressed into his jugular.

"They left! Gods, please have mercy," another cried as Lúc bent his fingers back on themselves until a sickening crunch cut through the roar of the fire.

New screams broke out, Nephilim that had been clinging to the walls were falling over themselves to escape the fire that was starting to roar around them. Aylee looked towards the hallway, the sounds of the room behind her fading out slowly. She watched the last of the bodies scratch and run, tripping across each other. It was like trapping rats in a hot metal bucket and holding a candle to it. They would do anything to escape ... at least the rats that were coherent. The ones so high they couldn't find their reality would burn. It would be a mercy killing.

"Let them burn," Lúc spit in the demon's face.

"Come on!" Aylee yelled. "We need to get out!"

Emryn followed, tucking her wings, the others not far behind as they barreled through the burning structure.

The street was crowded, but none of the four looked back. Their people knew to disperse as soon as they were done, to link back up at the Kaserne afterward. None of them stuck around to watch as the building was consumed by fire. They all knew what it looked like. They'd seen it often.

34
Chapter

Aheia

They emerged from the darkness, surrounded by walls of sand-stone and fire flickering against the ceiling. It looked like they were in a cave, broken up by straight slabs of rock that branched off into different hallways around them. Aheia slid from his back and followed Arioch without asking where he'd brought her. It was desperate the way she wanted to be close, didn't care why or what or where. None of that mattered when they were in such close proximity. They passed by rows of barred alcoves, all of them empty until they arrived at one of the last ones.

"What ..." Aheia stopped in her tracks, her eyes widening as she saw the Nephilim that had attacked her strung up against the far side of the cell. It looked like his arms were dislocated, his head hanging, his breathing short and spastic. He was alive ... barely.

Someone had carved him up, blood crusting his skin, gashes running along his arms and legs, none of which were her or Koutávi's doing. She didn't know how he was still alive, the question circling her mind as she padded inside after Arioch, her hand reaching to rest on his abdomen. It hadn't been a conscious action, but more like she'd been pulled, a fixation that she couldn't quite break. She knew it should have made her feel unsettled, nauseous even, seeing the Nephilim chained to the wall, but all she could find were memories of him pushing his knife against her skin. Arioch leaned down and tucked a strand of hair behind her ear while her eyes were transfixed on the body in front of her. "Go on, little goddess, carve your name from his lips."

Aheia couldn't focus. Her heart was in her throat, a cold prickle spreading across her skin as she stared at the black blood splattered across the cave wall. Fuck, she shouldn't have felt good about seeing the Nephilim like that, because it felt vengeful. The quiet voice of reason couldn't find her in the void she'd sunken into, with the demon at her side leaning into her ear, whispering words that had her melting right in front of him.

Carve your name from his lips.

She only nodded, watching his fingers unclasp a dagger and hold it out to her.

"Talk to me, Aheia," he said, tipping her chin up with the blade, his eyes black.

"No one's ever gotten me a gift quite like this," she said slowly, pulling her bottom lip between her teeth and taking the blade from his hand.

Arioch tensed. "Unwrap it for me." His voice was coarse, rubbing against her skin like kernels of sand.

The need to kill the demon in front of her and the need to fuck the demon at her back was equally enticing as she pressed herself into Arioch's chest and took his hand, slipping it onto her stomach. She wanted to feel every inch of him, wanted the strength he offered while she tried to understand the fixation pulling her towards the violence that lay at her fingertips.

But her mind wouldn't let her linger there as her arm moved of what felt like its own accord and brought the knife to the Nephilim's sternum. His eyes fluttered, but he stayed still, a soft groan breaking from his bloody lips.

Aheia swallowed, her fingers prickling with anticipation as she pushed the blade into his skin and dragged it down the center of his chest. The demon writhed, a broken moan leaving his lips, as she pulled the knife away and watched the black blood dripping from his body.

"He's yours," Arioch said, his hand finding its way onto her hip and squeezing,

She nodded, trailing the blade to his heart. If he had one. The darkness in her veins demanded to know what his ligaments felt like under her touch and what it would be like when they snapped but she couldn't bring herself to give in to that. Her breathing grew shallow as she pushed the knife into his chest and leaned into it, holding onto the hilt with both hands until his bones cracked under the pressure. The Nephilim choked and coughed, blood splattering Aheia's skin as she pushed harder, the blade meeting stone. Sweat was pearling at her forehead when Arioch slid his hand onto her wrist and pulled her back from the body.

"Enough," he murmured.

She didn't feel anything beyond the knowledge that she'd killed him. She wasn't any happier but didn't feel any guiltier either. The demon's blood was streaked across her face from when she'd wiped the sweat from her lip, and when she tasted it her nerve endings fired like little lightning strikes. Her breathing hitched, her body warm and humming, her chest aching while her vision felt slow, like she was catching a glimpse between reality and something much darker.

"You're hard," she whispered.

He chuckled, "I told you I liked violence from beautiful creatures."

"Can I ask you for something then?" She bit the inside of her cheek.

"I'm inclined to give you whatever you want right now," he said, bracketing her throat.

Then let me stay.

The words welled up on her tongue, but she couldn't bring herself to voice them. She was scared that if she did, he would stop and this would end because no matter how much they played into the what-if game, the ending was still set. So, while she had time that was untainted by the impending end of the bargain, she wanted to turn off her brain, for once just feel instead of think. Because she was fucking exhausted.

She would ask to stay. She had to. But not when she felt her arousal dripping down her inner thigh, not when he was finally going to give her what she needed, soul influence or not. It didn't matter, and she didn't want to dissect exactly which part was burning for him, because in a life of cold pressure, she couldn't deny the fire he offered. Not even if it was temporary. She'd burn with him, and she'd enjoy it.

"Fuck me, *majte*," she moaned, pushing her ass back against his throbbing cock, the term of endearment rolling off her tongue before she could reign it in. Maybe he'd think it was a slight. Hopefully, he thought it was a slight.

She waited with bated breath as Arioch stilled behind her, his hand slipping down her throat and across her chest, bunching up the fabric of her shirt and tugging it up over her head. He turned her in his hold, her body rubbing against his in a tortuous slide as the knife slipped from her fingers and clattered to the floor.

She rose up onto her toes and curled her fingers into his hair, clutching so tight that he bared his teeth, and tugged him close until they were only breaths away. His eyes drew across her face like he was cataloging every part while one of his hands rose to grip the back of her neck. The action felt angry, uncoordinated, and almost sloppy. And then he kissed her.

It was bruising and hectic, and it felt like they were two creatures simply lending themselves to something much greater. It was how their respective shadows danced with each other, the way the energy around them sizzled, the way her soul burned, that pulled their kiss into something much darker. His mouth tasted like blood and spices, so Gods damned hot that she thought he might be able to melt any part of her body that he turned its attention to. It felt like he was trying to pull at the frayed strings that hung from her being, like he wanted to see which tug would open her up and spill her across the floor. It was a kiss that became heavy, that demanded answers to questions they hadn't asked each other, while they unraveled one another in a frenzy.

Her teeth pulled at his lower lip, biting down so hard she tasted that delicious black blood just as he pulled her to the floor with him, breaking away only a moment so that he could twist her in his hold and push her down onto all fours.

Aheia slipped, her hand scratching open against the rough stone underneath, and gasped, trying to catch herself before she hit the floor. But Arioch had her, his arm wound around her middle, pulling her back against him while he hovered over her like a prowling lion. She leaned her head back against him, her eyes drifting over the dead demon in front of her when he took the hand she'd injured and brought it to his lips. Her head turned and she watched him slide his thumb over what little blood was sticking to her scratched skin. She hissed, her eyes fluttering shut for a moment as he rubbed the head of his cock against her clit from behind. Then she felt his tongue against her hand and sucked in a sharp breath at the sensation. Her eyes snapped to his, and whatever she saw in his gaze scared the hel out of her. It looked dark and broken, and demonic—so fucking overwhelming, that she shrunk back under the attention. His tongue swiped across her hand again, his cock sliding back and forth along her entrance.

"What the fuck are you?" he whispered, his eyes drawn to the red blood.

"Wha–"

But her words were cut short, replaced by a noise that sounded nothing like her as she felt him push inside of her. She fell against his hold and would have been sent to the floor without his support, her body trying to accommodate the way his width stretched her open around him.

She grit her teeth, pleasure edging pain as her hands dug into the ground. This was a lot, *fuck*, this was a lot. He cursed under his breath, his fingers letting go of her bloody hand and gripping her hip instead, flexing like he was trying to find his restraint between ragged breaths.

"*Ágos ganto*," she cursed, her eyes pressed shut tightly as she fell onto her forearms, the pressure between her legs spreading her so wide she thought he might tear her in two.

Arioch straightened behind her, the sensation of him moving sending small shock waves through her body. A broken gasp escaped her parted lips, her lungs working hard to keep her alive while it felt like she was suffocating. It was something beyond just how they fit, it was more than that, bigger than both of them. The bond between them thrummed, her chest tight, her body so hot that beads of sweat pricked her hairline. The phantom feel of her soul inside of her, even though the glyph was on Arioch's forearm became overwhelming. It brought tears to her eyes, and blurred her vision as emotions she didn't want to involve flooded her heart, emotions she couldn't handle. So, she grit her teeth and rolled her hips against him, even though it hurt. Gods, it hurt, but it felt better than the pain in her mind, the pain in her chest. And the deeper she took him, the more he filled her, the more it fed the hungry ache that made her pulse around him. She could feel his restraint, not just in his actions, but in how it vibrated through her like they were one body, the darkness of his energy seeping into her very skin and winding itself into her middle.

"I think you were fucking made for me, little goddess," he groaned, the rough slide of his callused hand across her lower back urging her on, finding its way between her legs until his fingers were stroking her swollen clit. She cried out, clenching around him, melting into a Gods damn puddle for him, the pleasure pulling rogue words from her lips. She didn't know what she was saying, didn't even quite know which language she had chosen, but she couldn't stop. "This might fucking kill me," he growled, his cock twitching as he rubbed against a spot inside of her that had her arms buckling, and her face pressing into the rough rock underneath her.

35

Chapter

Arioch

uck, her blood had tasted fucking hypnotizing. Maybe it was because she was a Mithra, but he'd never known Mithra to have sweet blood. It imprinted itself on his tongue and mixed with the ecstasy that dripped down her thighs. The need to brand, to claim, to fuck tore at him as he tried to keep his pace slow for her. She was so fucking tight, so Gods damned perfect. He circled her clit over and over, her walls milking him until he had to fight against the urge to ram her into the ground and take what he wanted from her, what he needed from her. He loosened his grip on her ass and pushed the small of her back down so that her chest was pressed into the floor, before bunching up her hair in his other hand and pulling until she was forced to bow back, those blue eyes staring up at him, lips parted in a silent scream. He had no fucking shame. He liked to see her pain, the way it flared in her eyes, the way it coaxed different responses from her. But it had been for her just as much as it had been for him. Because it would be easier to scare her with his darkest parts now than have her uncover them one by one over time.

The thought alone irritated him, fuck, it grated on him and sent him into a delirium because it wasn't something that was supposed to be on his mind, not something he should have even considered. Her comfort was not supposed to matter.

Not now, not ever.

And he supposed that's why he leaned in closer, his teeth nipping at her bottom lip upside down, and he whispered. "That's enough adjusting, I know your pretty cunt can take it."

She whimpered as he squeezed her clit between his fingers, her knees sliding against the blood and the rock when he sunk every inch of his cock into her. Aheia cried out, her teeth digging into her bottom lip as his abdomen hit her ass. It was too much for her, he could feel it, knew it hurt. But he didn't care. Anger pulsed through him in a hot wave, tingeing his intentions until all he could think about was how she had her little hands twisted into the fabric of his being. She was fucking ruining him, and she didn't even know it. So, he'd return the favor, even if it was just physical. He'd make sure that no matter what happened after she left his realm, she'd never be able to think of anyone but him ever again, not in the quiet moments, and not when she had her hands between her legs.

The sound of skin against skin broke the silence of the caves, echoing around the tunnels. He wanted it to reach every corner of this underground maze, wanted to fucking baptize the walls in it, wanted to bottle it and keep it in his nightstand and play it for himself over and over again.

"Ari," she moaned, her gaze fixed on his eyes, tears sliding down her cheeks as his hand bracketed her throat so she was forced to stare at him with those eyes, no hiding, no lying about what she wanted, no bullshit words. Because she couldn't pretend, couldn't pull the lust from her gaze, even when she tried her hardest to deny everything he had to offer her.

"I want–Ari, I—" She was struggling to express her thoughts, and he had trouble hearing them as the pressure around his cock tightened every single muscle in his body, his shadows scratching at his skin for release.

"Tell me," he groaned.

"I want your shadows," she gasped, sucking her bottom lip between her teeth.

Those simple words fucking blinded him. He lost it, lost everything he'd been trying to hold onto. The shadows that had been slowly stuttering from him exploded around them until they were suspended in a void, the cave a faraway thought. The tendrils curled around them, Aheia's hands now grasping onto the tangible dark floor that his powers had replaced the stone with, a low amber light breaking through the darkness around them.

"You look so fucking perfect with my cock inside of you," he growled, underlining his words with an angry thrust before pulling himself from between her legs. His fingers tightened in her hair and yanked her up, turning her body so that she was facing him. The vise of their bond in his chest wrenched tighter as he sat back on his heels and pulled her body on top of his. He'd never had something so cold feel so Gods damned scorching as she settled in on his lap, his length pressing against his stomach. She slid her hands over the inked tendrils that wrapped around his stomach, and over the scars on his chest, not hesitating for a single moment nor asking him about them, thank fuck.

She rose on her knees, towering over him momentarily, her nose brushing his as he repositioned himself, his cock sliding against her dripping, hot entrance. Her lips parted, those blue eyes watching him, taking in every inch of his face, like she was seeing him for the first time as he filled her to the hilt in one slow thrust.

"Fuck, I'll never get used to this," she groaned as he leaned forwards, his forehead dropping to hers.

"Look at me," he rasped, his hand winding around her throat, building pressure slowly, just the way he knew she liked. And she did, keeping her eyes on him while she rode him, her clit grinding down on his abdomen. She was clenching her teeth, a fine line between her eyebrows, like she was angry, sad, and overwhelmed, losing every bit of herself to what was happening between them, though her mind was fighting it. It's what he saw in her because she reflected back exactly how he felt. And for a split second, he thought that just maybe those blue eyes *did* see him, saw all the dark parts, all the fucked up parts, and didn't shrink away. Maybe even enjoyed them.

Only for a split second

This was becoming too intimate, too much for him to handle, and again he pushed her away while he held her close, tightening his grip on her throat until her skin worked up a pink tint, until she was struggling to breathe, until her eyes were rolling back in her head and her eyelids were fluttering shut.

"Keep your eyes on me, little goddess. I want you to know exactly who's making you feel this way." He let go of her throat and slipped his arms around her, letting her take what she needed as he snuck his fingers onto the outline of her soul.

Her gaze snapped to his, a new fire in the depths of that blue, as her body jerked against his, a strangled cry leaving her lips.

"Don't—I—*fuck*." She increased her pace, squeezing him so fucking tight it took everything he had not to come inside of her right then.

"You're going to take this until you're fucking raw," he groaned, his fingers matching her need. "And then I'll come so deep inside of you that I'll always be a part of you."

Her eyes widened at his words, her cunt clenching down so tight he had to jerk his hips harder to get back inside of her.

"No," she moaned, her nails piercing his skin, the pain bursting against his shoulders.

"Yes." He sucked her bottom lip into his mouth and grazed his teeth over it as he teased her soul higher and higher. "And then you're going to fucking beg me for more."

"Stop," she groaned, pushing him away as he tightened his grip. "Please," she gasped, the friction between them building. "It's too much, I can't—"

"You know the word," he growled into her ear. The word that would make this stop. But he had a feeling that's not at all what this was.

She shook her head, her whimpers and moans becoming messy and broken.

"*Let go of me.*" She fought him now, cracking her palm against his cheek, scratching at his neck with those nails. Arioch's lip curled as he restrained her wrists, the blood dripping onto his collarbone. She yanked her arms, and bucked on top of him, trying to free herself from his hold, but instead of giving her space, he pushed her off of his lap and onto the shadowed ground. He pinned her wrists above her head, with only one of his hands and lined himself up against her cunt with the other.

"Give me more of that, I like when you fight," he said, his voice husky as he pushed inside again, his thighs forcing hers further apart.

She whimpered, her back arching as she met his strokes, her eyes screwed shut tight.

"*Eyes open,*" he barked, grabbing onto her thigh so tight that she yelped.

"I don't want to look at you," she said, her voice fraying as she rolled her body against his.

"But you will unless you want me to punish you. And trust me, you don't."

She screamed, a cross between pleasure and frustration. And then she spit in his face. Spit in his fucking face.

He stilled, letting go of her hands, and her eyes narrowed for a moment, something flashing in the deep blue that he couldn't quite discern.

The anger was bubbling inside of him, but it was nothing compared to the need to make her come for him, to make her shatter around him so completely that some of the pieces would be lost. And then he'd replace those with his own, and mold her into the dark, little thing she was meant to be.

"Tap my shoulder if you want me to stop," he rasped, covering her mouth with his palm and letting go of anything gentle that was hiding in his movements before. He drove her into the ground until her teeth were digging into his hand, until she was screaming against his skin, trying to shake her head, meeting his thrusts while her hands gripped his dark curls so tight his scalp sang in pain. He could feel her, she was close, pulsing around him in dangerous intervals. He wasn't going to last much longer, and neither would she.

They both let go of whatever role they'd slipped into, giving themselves into the pleasure unraveling between them. And then her eyes widened and she arched, her head thrown into the shadows as she came, her body straining, her waves of pleasure ripping him over the edge with her. He let go of her mouth, holding himself on shaky arms as she screamed something that sounded a lot like his name. But his ears were ringing, the sound of his blood rushing against his eardrums, his vision fraying at the sides, and hearing anything but the way his heart was thundering in his chest was almost impossible.

When the shadows broke around them and he pulled himself from between her legs, their bodies were nestled against the silky sheets of his bed. Aheia gasped, scrambling before she realized they'd shadowed back into his room and relaxed into his mattress. She was stained in the dead Nephilim's blood, skin slick with sweat, Arioch's come dripping from between her legs and onto the sheets.

He got off the mattress, giving them both a moment, as he stepped into the washroom and picked up a dark, plush towel, catching a glimpse of himself in the mirror. There were three angry red marks on his neck, curls damp with sweat, and random streaks of another demon's blood painted over his ink.

What a fucking sight.

When he stepped back into the room, Aheia was exactly where he'd left her, her eyes trained on the dark ceiling above. He crawled onto the mattress and ran the towel across her skin as she watched, her bottom lip pulled between her teeth, "Talk to me," He said his voice coarse, the sight of his come leaking from inside of her swollen entrance making his dick twitch with need. He wanted more, so much more.

"I shouldn't have..." she started, her gaze slipping down his body. "I shouldn't have liked it. That was fucked up. I–" She shook her head slowly, furrowing her brows.

"But you did," he murmured, kissing the inside of her thigh. She sucked in a breath, her leg twitching slightly.

"Too much." He threw the towel to the side and crawled up her body, seeing a sadness starting to weave its way into her features.

If only you were alone in that. He thought to himself, sliding his fingers against her jaw. Her gaze snapped to his.

"Will you stay?"

"It's my room, Ruhí, where would I go?"

36

Chapter

Aheia

She'd tried to keep her hands to herself, had tried to sleep, but it was fucking impossible when Alshaytan lay next to her, the galaxies lighting up his silhouette. He was staring up at the ceiling, his fingers playing absentmindedly with the ends of her hair, while her gaze drifted across the shadowy ink on his body. It covered so much of him, swirling around his legs, his abdomen, and up his neck like he was being consumed slowly. Her legs were aching, and she couldn't shake how much she liked the feeling as she adjusted between his, her chin resting against his stomach. She let her fingers slide over his thick muscles, watching them tense as she touched, drawing a line from one small scar to another and another.

"Why don't you heal your scars?" she asked, breaking the quiet air between them.

Arioch's eyes stayed glued to the ceiling as he answered. "They're reminders."

"Reminders of what?"

The silence stretched into odd shapes in front of her, until it became strained once again. She didn't always know how to deal with the quiet, especially not around other people, and felt the need to fill it even if she said the wrong thing, even if her words simply polluted the air.

But she held onto her thoughts for a moment, and climbed up his body, sitting on his lap, both of them still naked. She took one of his hands and guided his fingers over her hip. There was no scar there, not one that was visible anyway, but the memory had embedded itself across her bone nonetheless. Arioch's eyes finally shifted, following her hands as she spoke.

"They healed this one." She took a slow breath, calming down the nerves her words conjured. "I was caught sneaking out–I was pretty good about evading Ophion, but one night I wasn't careful enough."

Arioch's jaw clenched, the vein at his temple pulsing and his voice coarse when he finally spoke. "He touched you?"

"His men," she said, forcing a semblance of strength into her voice. "It got worse after Ophion killed my mother... She was a barrier." A heavy lump settled in her throat at the memory.

Don't, Aheia. Focus.

She didn't want to let the memories take her, not now.

Instead, she let go of his hand and fanned her fingers across his ribs, over one especially long scar that ran from his hip bone up the side of his body. "What happened here?"

Arioch watched her for a moment longer, and she was thankful he didn't ask her anything more, though she saw the darkness circling his irises. Something was happening in his mind, but his expression was unreadable.

"Please," she said quietly, the sadness becoming a threatening presence on her shoulders.

He waited another moment, his eyes narrowing slightly before he followed her fingers towards the scar she'd outlined. His gaze lightened for a moment, and she thought she caught his lip twitch when he traced the long jagged line. "Lúc and I almost got spliced fucking around in the parallels."

Aheia gaped. "You've been?!"

The parallels were realities said to exist in jagged lines next to theirs, like planets that were separated by time.

"Almost. We were young, thought we might figure out if the stories were true. If there were other cities beyond the fold. It almost killed us." Arioch readjusted, leaning back against the headboard so that Aheia was sitting up straight.

"Why are you asking me?" He raised an eyebrow, his fingers drifting across her collarbone, over another faint white line.

"You healed my scars..."

"I didn't think you needed any more," he said without hesitation, his fingers sliding down to her arm, zigzagging over the discolored skin that hid her past.

Small pricks of ice peppered the back of her neck.

He noticed those...

No one had noticed those, not in a long time.

"I'm not embarrassed by them." She said slowly, drawing little patterns over her arm, "I'd rather have the scars than the memories. The memories make it hard."

Arioch inhaled slowly, his fingers outlining a soft curved line just below her elbow. Again, so close to her skin tone that it was near impossible to see.

"Ophion was dragging my mother into his room," she said, her fingers following closely behind his. "He'd found out that she was trying to leave him—trying to run." She remembered Andromeda's eyes again, pleading with her, asking her to hide. But she didn't, because she couldn't bear it any longer—couldn't listen to her mother's screams through the walls. "I tried to stop him, and his belt tore open my skin." Her fingers traced the curve again, and this time there was a phantom pain that followed the movement, her eyes drifting off into the stars outside of the window. "I was never strong enough to stop him... And then one day, he ... he ..." It was a strain to remember. "He became tired of me. The burden was too much, I suppose—I secretly think he couldn't stand the way I reminded him of my mother."

Arioch massaged her skin with his thumb. "What happened?"

"I got married."

She felt him go stiff underneath him.

"Iaonnis ... they called him the God of War. In actuality, he was just a brute, who went through wives like they were inanimate objects."

She gripped Arioch's side a little tighter and when she spoke again, "It was more of an ambush really, a quick ceremony in Ophion's chambers, and then a rough shove into my rooms." She shook her head. "I couldn't let that fucking beast touch me. In a fucked up way it felt like an extension of Ophion too—like, if I let Iaonnis touch me, I was giving into everything my mother died for, and ... I don't know how to describe it, but I blacked out completely— I don't remember a single moment after backing away from Iaonnis and towards my bed ..." She cleared her throat, blood and teeth filling her mind. "I just remember flashes. I killed him, but Gods, I don't know *how*. It shouldn't have been possible."

She looked up at Arioch who was watching her, something she couldn't dissect in his eyes. "He was *big*, you type of big, and I don't think I could kill you, even though I might want to."

Arioch was still for a long while, and Aheia simply stared. It was an odd sensation, the lack of emotion when she should have wept for her past. But recounting Iaonnis' death felt factual, like she was simply telling a story about someone else's life, and no matter how tragic it sounded, she felt placid.

"You had every right to kill him." He said finally, voice husky. Her eyes snapped to his.

"What?"

"You showed strength for yourself when you needed it most."

And no matter how much she could feel herself agreeing with him, she couldn't help her words. "I murdered him."

"Ophion murdered him," Arioch said without hesitation. "The moment he decided to force you into his bed."

She didn't know what to say. No one had ever seen it that way and the sentiment made her feel more than she was comfortable admitting.

"Tell me about another," she said, shaking off the discomfort in her shoulders. She drifted the pads of her fingers across a scar just to the left of his heart.

"I got this one from my brother," he said.

"You have a brother?" She hadn't heard about any other family, only Arioch, and Sahren.

"I did."

"What happened?" she asked before she could hold herself back. The question was invasive, and she could see his exterior harden in front of her as their eyes met.

He exhaled slowly, like he was deciding on if he would entertain her question before he finally answered. "Our family was complicated," he said, his voice a low rasp. "Our father wasn't satisfied with the idea that the eldest would take over as Alshaytan. He wanted the strongest. That meant forcing us to fight each other." He pulled her fingers from his chest completely.

"Is that why you're in power? You won?"

His eyes snapped to hers, the vein at his temple pulsing. "No."

"What happened?" Aheia pushed, resting her fingertips on his abdomen, an inability to step away from the subject wound tight into her stomach.

And when he spoke she wished she hadn't. "Your kind."

Fuck. She averted her eyes, biting the inside of her cheek. "A Mithra killed your brother?"

Arioch's jaw clenched, his hands slipping from her skin along with his eyes. "Yes."

"A Mithra killed your brother ..." She mulled over her question. "Why give me a chance? Why take my soul in the first place? Wouldn't it have been easier to just throw me from Aljira? To turn your back? What does my soul give you?"

His gaze was trained just beyond her, eyes hard. "All magyck comes with a price, Dioscuri."

She narrowed her eyes at the sheer calculation of his words. She didn't like the way her race rolled off his tongue. "And what price do you pay for yours?"

His gaze slid back to hers for a moment, but his expression stayed rigid. "The Avarice were given shadows in exchange for something, something every other creature in Lyria possesses."

Aheia's lips parted, her eyes drifting to her glyph on his skin. "A soul."

He nodded slowly, catching a tendril of her hair that was resting against his stomach.

"But it's not yours," she said, and he tugged on the white strands until she had to lean in closer.

"Oh?"

"I mean," she started, swallowing as she watched him gather more of her mane and wrap it around his knuckles. "Does it make a difference? Holding someone else's soul when you're not meant to have one?"

"Soul consumption is a way of life for us. They strengthen the magyck already in our veins. Each soul assimilates into our shadows over time and is eaten by the ink on our bodies."

Aheia's eyes drifted over the tendrils that curled around him. "Is that what will happen to mine? I'll fade away into a memory?"

You'll fade and no one will remember you.

The quiet whisper in her head said while she waited for an answer that never came. And with each unanswered question, his mind was loud when his voice stayed silent.

"You took my soul despite my race," she continued, unable to stop herself now.

"Is there a question?"

"Why?" she asked as he tangled his fingers at the nape of her neck.

"Don't ask about things you don't truly want to hear."

"I want to know."

His hold cinched, forcing her chin up while his other hand grabbed onto the back of her thigh, sliding her flush against his body. Her lips parted feeling him press into her abdomen, her legs a sore reminder of his presence.

"I took your soul because you're one of them," he said, his fingers digging into her thigh, keeping her in place. "Because I knew they wanted you back. I didn't know what you'd done— why they were chasing you—but you seemed important enough to hold onto at the time."

Discomfort coiled her middle while she squirmed in his hold. "Mithra hold their souls in high esteem," he continued, his hand sliding onto the small of her back, forcing her down against his chest. "Taking yours would taint you, maybe even ruin you in Ophion's eyes. And that chance alone would have made it worth it."

Her throat felt tight as she tried to swallow. She supposed that answer should have upset her—would have upset someone whose mind wasn't unconditionally cruel to itself. But she couldn't find much more than a slight tightness in her chest. And once again the bond between them pulled her in closer, the soul on his forearm heated against her as he held her down, sending small pulses that felt a lot like bursts of fire against her skin.

"Is that still what you want? To ruin me for whatever lies past our bargain?" She looked up at him through her eyelashes.

"More than ever," he growled, moving both of his hands onto her ass and sliding her up his chest so they were almost level. A soft gasp left her lips as she felt the head of his cock pressed against her entrance.

Her breathing hitched as she watched his eyes, both of them still in their positions, standing at the edge of something new, something unapologetic.

"Do your worst," she said, sucking her bottom lip in between her teeth, anticipation stealing reason from her grasp.

37

Chapter

Shiron

Shiron was sitting in the Kaserne, their training compound, watching a purple haired Syraphem take down the Leviathan male that had been running his mouth all afternoon.

"Fuck," he exclaimed, peeling his body off of the sweaty mat, glowering at the female who stood over him grinning.

"If you spent half as much time on your footwork as you do complaining about your losses, you might actually have a chance," Shiron said, pulling a towel from around his neck and snapping it at the male on the mat.

"You have a week to improve," he said with a finality that had the Leviathan growling.

"It's easy," the Syraphem smirked, offering him a hand that he ignored.

"It really fucking is." Tariq's voice drifted in from the left side of the ring. He'd just gotten back from Azalam, blood coating his hands and hair, eyes lit with adrenaline. "Your form is lazy as shit." He prowled over to Shiron and leaned his arm on his shoulder which Shiron promptly shrugged off before heading towards a black bench nestled against the proving grounds wall.

"This isn't Theno's dick. Don't come early next time," Tariq said to the male on the mat before joining Shiron on the bench.

"You smell," Shiron drawled, scrunching his nose.

"You don't enjoy the smell of fire and blood?" Tariq leaned his head against the wall, watching the warriors pick up where they'd left off on the mat.

"Not mixed with your sweat," he deadpanned. "How was it?"

"Fucking chaos," Tariq said, his voice dropping. "It's getting worse. Some of those demons had no idea where they were, had lost their minds long before we burnt them down."

Shiron shuddered, fingers absentmindedly drifting across his prayer beads. The drug and the way it had its teeth in so many Nephilim's lives turned his stomach.

"Any leads on that third Nephilim?" Tariq tipped his chin, his eyes trained on the male warrior ahead of them. "*Early*," he barked, pulling the demon's attention long enough for the female to land another blow.

"No," Shiron said contemplatively. He'd tasked a couple of recruits to search the area but it was fruitless.

"I don't think there was a third," Tariq said, adjusting his curls around his black horns. "The Mithra just can't fucking count."

Shiron nodded slowly but didn't answer.

"You saw the other bodies," he continued, getting up from the bench. "There's no way the Varcolac would have left one of them alive enough to walk out of there without a trace ... Maybe the third body was eaten." Tariq's eyes glinted like he enjoyed that idea.

"Unlikely," Shiron said, watching the warriors in front of him.

"I'm leaving for the briefing," Tariq said, heading for the opposite side of the room. "You owe me a drink."

Shiron nodded him off and dropped the towel on the bench next to him.

"Show him what he's doing wrong," he said to the Syraphem just as she drove the male into the mat with her elbow.

Shiron left the room, heading down the hallway that led to the barracks. The last hour had been eaten up by circulating the newer recruits that would move on to fight with Emryn once they had the basics down, but he couldn't quite focus. The energy in the realm had felt stifling, and even prayer and contemplation hadn't loosened the noose around his neck. It felt like something was impending, but he didn't know what, which made preparing for it impossible.

He was planning on checking in on the female they'd pulled from Azalam before he headed back into the compound. The redhead that had yet to give him a name.

He rounded the last corner to find two Leviathans that were fumbling by her door, one grasping onto his neck, blood smearing the floor, and the other dragging his limp leg behind him, pulling on the knob in front of them frantically.

"How did she—"

"No more forks!" the demon on the ground spluttered, throwing the black silverware to the floor with a deafening clatter.

"What in the Gods' name?" Shiron furrowed his brows, approaching the two.

The Nephilim straightened, trying to hold themselves together respectfully as both of them shook with pain. "We brought the girl food and she—" The Leviathan with the neck wound ground out between his teeth.

"She tried to kill us," the other one finished, grasping at the side of his leg.

Shiron gave them both a long, narrow-eyed look before he dismissed them with a nod. "Fix yourselves."

The demons made themselves scarce as he picked up the bloody fork, turning it over in his hand as he entered the room they'd just tumbled out of.

It was so dark he barely saw her outline. The Nephilim was crouched in the corner, food splattered across the floor, her body shaking.

Shiron stayed back, had seen that look many times, knew she had seen him enter, and let her adjust.

"What happened?" It was a meek and strung-out voice, barely loud enough for him to hear.

"You tell me," Shiron said, keeping his words calm and quiet while his hand slid over his devotional beads again, toying with each one in order of how they were constructed for prayer.

The Nephilim stirred, her red hair tousled, those dark horns weaving across the back of her head. She fixed him with a stare that didn't fit her voice—sharp emeralds that cut into him. Her body readjusted against the wall, so she could hug her legs against her chest, resting her chin on her knees.

"I had to defend myself," she said quietly. "They tried to attack me." Her finger reached out and started drawing lazy circles in the food that was spread around her legs.

Apprehension flared at the back of Shiron's neck as he watched her motions, and caught a glint in her eyes that didn't line up with the tone in her voice, nor her actions. She looked poised, her arms shifting in a way that suggested weakness when really, she was ready to fight. Shiron moved in tighter, perching himself on the edge of her cot, turning the bloody fork he still held over in his hands.

"What's your name?" he asked, watching her carefully.

Her eyes flared, the green brightening slightly before they dulled and her expression seemed to fall slightly. "Where's the Syraphem?"

"You haven't answered my question."

The Nephilim's mouth pressed into a hard line. "Are those prayer beads? You do know the Gods don't care about you, don't you?" She tilted her head slowly, predatorily. "They laugh at you."

Shiron flexed his jaw but kept himself calm. "Do you have family?"

"Don't we all?"

He tilted his head to the side as she drew another couple of lines on the floor. "Do you have anywhere to go?" He readjusted the question, watching her still.

She didn't answer, but the silence spoke for her.

"I'll make sure you get some more food," he said, slowly getting to his feet again. This was going to take time—whatever this was. And he didn't have it right now.

"I don't want your food," she hissed, anger flaring.

He nodded slowly, caressing the beads around his throat. The Nephilim's eyes zeroed in on the movement and he saw the vein at her temple pulse. "I want a knife," she said plainly.

"A knife," he echoed, unable to hide his surprise at her request.

"To defend myself with." She shifted back onto her heels, and the way she looked up at him reminded him of a crouching animal. "You don't have to defend yourself here."

"I've heard that so. Many. Times," she snarled, a wicked smile curling her lips. "Why should I trust you?"

"Because I'm the only one here that could provide you with a knife."

She narrowed her eyes at him, something like a hiss breaking free from her chest. "Then I'm fucked, aren't I?" She tilted her head, her breathing quickening. He could almost visibly see her coiling just before she went for him, launching herself off the wall and square into his chest, a feral scream exploding from her lips. He caught her waist, doing his best not to hurt her as her thin frame latched onto his, her teeth sinking into his shoulder.

"Argh!" They fell against the cot, his body sending the flimsy thing flying, the hard marble bruising his shoulder before he could get her underneath him. He pressed her arms to the floor above her as she screeched like a banshee and thrashed, his blood on her lips.

"Stop," he growled, staying light on his toes so that no other part of him was touching her body. The demon below him yanked her wrists free and then threw her head back so violently that it cracked against the marble.

Her body convulsed for a moment, her eyes fluttering against the pain before she kicked out blindly, hitting him in the shin. He hissed, falling to his knee on top of her, while his other leg was still keeping him largely off her body, the pain smarting his bones. She cradled her head, her palms pressed into her temples as she gulped in air.

"Ow, ow, ow." She rolled her head, her eyes becoming frantic, and then suddenly, scared.

She looked like the same animal he'd seen crouching in the corner except now she was frightened, shivering, and confused.

"Oh, Gods, help!" she cried, tears running down her cheeks, her body suddenly so much softer, so much lighter underneath him.

Shiron pulled back immediately, fully aware of his gamble and what he was risking.

The nameless Nephilim scrambled away from him and curled into the corner crying into her knees, shaking.

"Please, *please* don't hurt me again."

Shiron crouched in front of her slowly, holding out his palm being as placating as he could with the wound on his shoulder throbbing.

"I'm not going to hurt you," he said quietly, his voice lower than he'd intended.

Her red-rimmed eyes met his and they were … they weren't hers—not the eyes he had seen mere moments ago. These emeralds were soft and bright, something naive and sweet in their depths.

"What do you want from me? I don't want to do it again, I can't. It's killing me—please," she sobbed against the back of her hand, trying to compose herself.

Shiron sat back on his heels, making himself as small as he could in front of her, his mind snapping back to when he found Emryn on the floor of the compound, mumbling to herself.

"Ok, no more," he said, fighting the sting that built in his chest.

Her frantic eyes snapped to his again. Her lip quivered and suddenly she moved, so quickly he couldn't stop her. The Nephilim wound her arms around him and squeezed hard, burying her face in the nape of his neck. He kept his arms wide with surprise, not touching her, not even as she climbed into his lap and hung on like a child.

What in the Gods' name?

"Thank you." It was a soft whisper. Then she pulled back and she looked up at him. Her eyes slowly ran over his features, in a way that had him wanting to avert his own gaze. "Are you one of Eros' men? He's going to be cross." She looked so fearful at those words.

"Do you know what happened to you?" Shiron asked, easing his palms onto his thighs just behind her, his devotional beads rubbing between them.

"What...?" she breathed, her eyes confused. Then they widened and she started looking around the room, each blink seemingly sobering her more. "Oh no. No no no no no." She fisted the material of his shirt and he hissed as she grazed the wound on his shoulder.

Her eyes were drawn to the blood and her tongue darted across her lower lip which was still painted black.

"Oh NO. Not again, not again, not again." Her breathing was out of hand as she gasped for air, shaking in his lap.

"It's ok," he said quietly, watching her unravel against his chest.

"It's not. You don't understand. You don't understand. Gods help me."

Gods? Did she just pray?

"I'm sorry." She rubbed her mouth. "I didn't mean to hurt–umm." She realized how tight she was holding on to his shirt and pulled her hands back like he'd burned her, rubbing at her tear-filled eyes.

"It's alright," he said, flexing his neck slightly trying out the angle and how much pain it caused.

The Nephilim slipped from his lap and pulled herself onto the cot that was shoved into the other corner of the room at an angle, her eyes glued to the food all over the floor. "Did she..." she mumbled to herself.

"What is going on?" Shiron leaned back against the cot looking up at her from his seat on the floor.

"I don't know what you mean." She smiled, but it shook slightly, another tear rolling down her cheek. She looked manic. He'd seen that before too. He could tell she was working incredibly hard to keep her eyes open, to smile, to pretend that she didn't know when he saw it looping behind that sweet exterior. "Everything is fine, everything is great." She shuddered slightly. "I can clean that wound for you, it looks heinous, where did you get it?"

Shiron narrowed his eyes at her. "An accident," he said slowly. It almost felt like she'd restarted herself, like she'd shuffled through multiple personalities, or maybe tapped into a safety mechanism, an alternate exterior that kept her safe. But this, this was severe. He couldn't quite tell if she was lying when she feigned ignorance about having hurt him, which unsettled him because that was not an issue he usually had.

"I hope it doesn't hurt." The words were sincere, he could tell even though the rest seemed murky.

Shiron stood slowly, her gaze widening as he towered over her. "I'm going to get you some more food, and water. Do you need anything else?"

Her lips parted slightly but she shook her head, watching him cross the room and lock the door as he left.

Who are you and what happened to you?

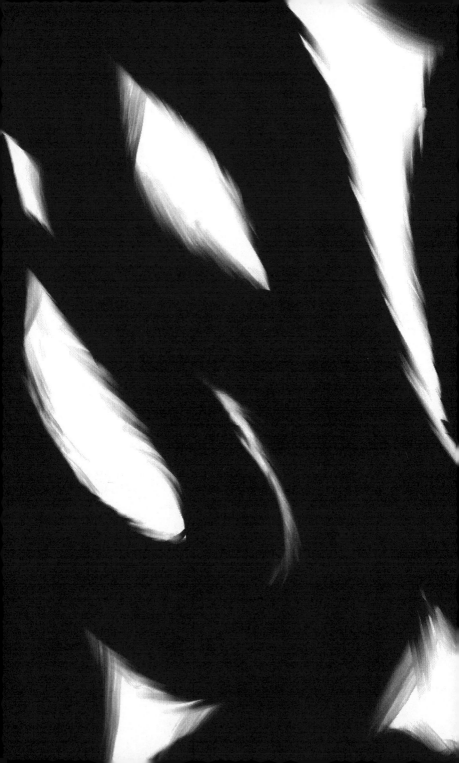

38

Chapter

Arioch

Aheia had fallen asleep on his chest, and he'd lost track of how long he held her like that. It was overwhelming, the need to keep her close, and the thought that he'd never slept with anyone like this wouldn't let go of him. Sleeping felt a lot like kissing, a thing that shouldn't have had a place between them. It was intimate, and so much more convoluting than just fucking was. Though with Aheia, even fucking felt different than it did with the distractions he'd spent his time with in the past. The years after his father's death had been a blur of smoke, liquor, blood, and bodies. Lúc had been the first to join him at this new and confusing court he was building for himself, and they'd spent so much of their time fucking around, abusing their power, ignoring the realm and its needs while they bedded Nephilim together and got lost in red clouds of smoke for longer than he cared to admit. Shiron and Emryn, then Tariq, Kar, and Aylee, all of them different and with fucked up pasts of their own, joined them, and since then their circle had grown further. He trusted them when he didn't trust anyone, and the screwed-up part was that they felt more like family than his blood had. It was a fact that wound guilt into his gut every time he thought about it, not because of Sahren but because of his brother. And he supposed he tried to make up for his shortcomings in the past by treating the few Nephilim he cared for how he should have treated Kazim, even though he knew he didn't owe them anything.

He didn't let himself think about it often, because he fucking hated how tight it wound him, but staring down at the Mithra asleep on top of his chest had him strung tauter than anything had in a long time.

He let himself drift into those parts of his mind, the parts he usually locked down in his shadows, while he watched her and wondered if she dreamt and about what. He wanted to know what that enigmatic mind thought of when she drifted off into sleep—what other horrors hid in her memories.

His chest was humming as he thought about the fact that the little goddess he was cradling hid dark and powerful things within her, things no one understood, including her. It seems that her presence was felt by things older and more dangerous than himself, had affected the very fabric of his realm, and the fact that he couldn't ask her why because she didn't know herself grated on his mind.

His shadows were begging for more of her, his thoughts turning more vicious by the second.

The overwhelming urge to part those sweet thighs and wake her up with his tongue dug itself into his rational mind, made his shadows slither and writhe as he started to reach out for her.

No.

She needed to rest, and he needed to move.

Arioch untangled himself from her limbs slowly, taking care not to wake her as he lay her head down on his pillow and drew the satin up over her shoulders.

He forced himself from her and slipped on some of his leathers, a clean shirt, and his daggers before readjusting his rings and boots and leaving the room. His room was nestled into the new additions to the compound that he'd added after he realized his nightmares wouldn't allow him to stay in any of the existing rooms. It was its own wing, and while the rest of the building saw Nephilim coming in and out of its doors, this was separate and only for him and those close to him. Lúc had his room a floor down, Shiron stayed a floor above, and so did Emryn. Tariq tended to stay on his own and so did Kar, while Aylee was in and out so much that Arioch lost track.

He walked through the dark hallway, the energy above his head humming slightly, and made his way down a winding staircase and into a large, open room. The walls were coarse, dark marble, with a fireplace carved into one, energy dancing in place of a flame. There were orange, velvet chairs strewn in clusters, small gold tables, carts with dark liquors, and boughs of Achlys winding across the wall.

"What the fuck happened to your face?"

Arioch turned to find Lúc sitting in one of the chairs on his right, balancing a black crystal glass on his knee, his leathers unfastened, the ink on his chest that he usually hid on prominent display. He touched the side of his neck, feeling the sting of where Aheia had scratched him and realized his hands were still bloody. They'd fucked and fallen asleep, without much effort to clean themselves up afterward.

Arioch ignored the Shifter, feeling his shadows prickling underneath his skin.

"Should I even ask about what happened the night of the Mithra?" Lúc continued, a blood-thirsty grin returning to his face.

"You shouldn't." Arioch ground his teeth focusing on the black glass decanters across the room.

"You look tense as fuck, Alshaytan."

"I'm always tense."

"Mhmm." Lúc's eyes flashed. "This look has got a very specific name written all over it."

Arioch narrowed his eyes, leaning his forearms on the back of the nearest chair. "Careful."

Lúc stood, setting his drink down. "I thought she might ease some tension, not cause more." He circled closer, his eyes glinting. Arioch knew before he lunged, dodging the Shifter's fist as he threw himself towards his friend. Arioch grabbed ahold of Lúc's wrist and pulled him forward, knocking his shoulder into him and sending him stumbling back.

"You're getting slow."

Lúc bared his teeth, a slow smirk spreading across his lips. "Holding back. Wouldn't want to bruise you. I'll leave that to Aheia."

"Please don't fuck up the furniture." Emryn glided past them, her wings pulled in tight as she wove through the chairs.

Lúc leaned into her with his shoulder as she passed, earning him a shove and an eye roll.

"How did it go in Azalam, anything I need to know about?" Arioch asked.

Emryn shook her head. "No. It was... as expected," her wings shuddered slightly. "It's getting worse. The number of strung out Nephilim in that building ..." Her brows furrowed. "But if Siraj is aware or involved, he's covering his tracks."

Lúc shook his head. "Are you thinking of moving against him?"

"It's overdue," Arioch deadpanned. "I should have moved against him the moment he started telling his people that he'd be the demon to control the devil."

But he hadn't because he'd tried to keep a semblance of peace.

"Hel, you know what I think about all of it." Lúc raised his eyebrow. "Whatever happens, it'll be bloody, but we'll win. We'll fight like demons.".

"Like Gods." Arioch grinned, and then to Emryn, "Where's Shiron?"

"He's checking in on the stray—the one we pulled out of Azalam. The redhead, she's strong but she's having a hard time fighting whatever the fuck went down while she was with Ral's people. I've only talked to her once and she seemed like a ray of sunshine, and then something flipped in her mind. At least that's what it looked like, and she resembled more of a fury than anything." Emryn shook her head, pouring herself a drink.

Arioch watched her expression, sinking into something thoughtful. "You have an idea?"

"I want to offer her a place here. I think that if she survives training she could have potential as a warrior. Shiron doesn't agree, he thinks it'll kill her."

Arioch considered. "What do you think?"

Emryn turned and leaned against the small table, swirling her drink. "She might die either way. This will give her a chance. Her mind feels frail, I can't quite describe it. There's a chance she'll kill herself–possibly other Nephilim if we let her roam free on her own."

Arioch trusted Emryn's judgment, she was tough, but she never omitted the truth or what she believed. She was concise, and made decisions based on logic and fact, whereas Shiron could get caught up in his past. Especially when it came to wounded females and the blood trade.

"Do it," he said, the tension building again in his shoulders. "What's her name?"

Emryn's jaw tensed. "She doesn't have one."

39

Chapter

Aheia

Aheia was dreaming. It had to be a dream. Because when she opened her eyes, she was somewhere foreign, a place she'd never seen before. She appeared to be inside a tall cave, the rock under her feet coarse and cracked and dark, a soft, iridescent glow lighting the space. She blinked, her eyes adjusting to the low lighting that seemed to be shimmering from the ground itself. She saw a long ribbon of water cutting through the black stone, bisecting the room from one end to the other, appearing and then disappearing through large arched openings in the rock face on either side.

It was so *vivid*.

And her mind felt so clear. Usually, her dreams and her nightmares pulled her back and forth, and only when she analyzed it after she woke up did she realize how disjointed it had all been. But this didn't feel that way. This felt incredibly real. Though it couldn't be.

Her heart was steady and so was her breathing, and even though she should have been nervous or anxious, she felt calm. The space around her was silent until it wasn't. Whispers curled around her, and for a moment, she couldn't tell if they were new or if they'd been in her ears the whole time.

Where am I?

She had meant to say it aloud, but her voice seemed to have abandoned her as her lips made soundless movements. The whispers around her increased in frequency and volume, once again with words she didn't understand, from the far end of the cave. It pulled her towards the water, what seemed to be a river, something unsettling raking across her skin. She padded closer, the warmth at the back of her neck spreading down her spine as her toes edged the water.

Her mouth felt dry when she stared into the depth of dead, gray eyes floating in front of her.

Bodies.

The river was full of them.

It should have scared her, but this was a dream and the bodies in front of her weren't corpses. Rather, they were translucent, like they were energy or essence, something almost beautiful in how they shone.

She sank to one knee, balancing her palm on the floor to get a closer look, her gaze catching on the shape of a female that was floating by slowly. Her hair was curling around her in wisps, dark and thick, her eyes gray and unliving just as those of the next body. But there was something about her that caught Aheia's attention, the overwhelming urge to touch the female coaxing her closer.

She reached out slowly, lowering her knuckles towards the iridescent liquid, but just before she was about to dip her skin into the water, her hand hit an invisible barrier. It was like she was separated from the river by the thinnest sheets of glass, and when she pressed her palm against it, it held strong. Her instincts told her to turn away, to find a way out, but something inside of her encouraged her on, made her stand, and extend her leg to test the surface with her toes. It held strong even as she put her weight on it.

Vivid.

She took a couple of steps onto the river, hovering just above it, looking over the females, males, and creatures alike that passed underneath her. The air around her hitched, feathering against her skin like someone was caressing her without a touch, as a slow pain started at her temples the further across the river she made it. She massaged the heels of her hands into her eyes, broken pieces of light bursting against her eyelids as the pain and the whispers grew.

Wake up, Aheia.

Her mind tried to shake itself free of the dream, but when she opened her eyes all she saw were spots of navy dancing over her vision and the same iridescent river underneath her feet. The pain at her temples grew almost unbearable as the barrier she was standing on started to vibrate, tears welling up in her eyes while her vision frayed further, like she'd stared into the sun for minutes on end. Her knees buckled under the now strangling hold of the air on her lungs and she fell forward, her hands shooting out to catch herself. She crashed into the barrier, gray eyes only inches away from her.

And then she saw it. A blink.

It was a youngling, its eyes the same washed-out color. Another blink and a twitch. The body underneath her moved as Aheia ground her teeth against the pain in her head, her focus pulled from the river and onto her hands as they started burning like she was holding them over an open flame. She fell onto her forearms, her body fighting against an invisible hold that dragged her down into the hardness underneath her until suddenly it gave way.

Aheia felt her stomach dip as she fell, splashing into the ice-cold water into a mess of hair and skin. The bodies that had looked so ethereal as she hovered above became real the moment she touched them, not at all as translucent as they appeared. She felt hands on her limbs and nails on her face, as the things around her descended on her and pulled her into the depths of the river. She screamed and kicked, the water filling her lungs as she fought, getting just enough space to break the surface and gulp down some air before a hand on the top of her head shoved her back under. Her eyes burned as the water rushed past her, the slight glow of the surface growing fainter and fainter as gray bodies layered on top of her, dragging her further and further down.

Wake up! Please! Not like this, not like this. No.

Her chest pulsed violently, like it was reaching for the last of her air, her lungs straining as frantic eyes devoured her from all sides. She fought, her fingers tearing at anything they could grab onto, even as they burned.

She choked, her lips parting and water rushing into her mouth, the sensation forcing an inhale from her chest. The water flooded her lungs, and her sinuses burned, the pain in her fingers worsening until suddenly, something inside of herself cracked. She was swallowed by something hot and explosive, drawing her into herself before rolling off of her like a shock wave and boiling the water all around her.

Aheia screamed, but the sound was drowned out. Her body was jerked down even further until she was free-falling, the cold water traded for cold air whipping through her wet hair. Her voice choked up in her throat as the sensation silenced her, and her body slammed against something hard and sharp. She whimpered, the impact squeezing all of the newfound air from her body and bruising with hard jabs against her back.

She coughed and choked, her body burning so badly that moving took every last bit of her strength.

I should have woken up. Falling always wakes me up.

Panic was finally settling into her, her heart racing in her throat, hot prickles of fear bursting against the back of her neck as the ground under her moved with her efforts to propel herself upwards. It was dark, but when she got to her feet, there was enough iridescent light streaming into what seemed to be another cave, for her to realize that she was standing on hills and hills of bones.

Bones.

Nausea gripped her stomach as she looked down at herself, scratches and blood marring her skin, bruises already forming. She looked up to find the river floating overhead, the bodies that had just moments ago tried to drag her under back to their placid state like they hadn't been alive and trying to kill her.

Aheia tried to breathe, but the fear was strung tight around her throat, and the taste of the air made it difficult to calm down. There was a sweet smell that drifted around her. It was wrong, like rotting fruit, thick and syrupy.

The whispers started up again, words she didn't understand, stroking down her spine like a very real touch, just as a noise sounded from somewhere on her right. Aheia's head whipped towards it, and she wished for just a second that she hadn't. Because then she could have pretended, could have pretended like she wasn't watching the hill of bones rattle and move, like there weren't hands clawing their way to the surface. The cave echoed with the sound of falling skeletons, and the sound only grew as from all around Aheia hands started to break up from the ground. She screamed, slipping and falling, her palms scraping, hands grabbing ahold of her ankles as she tried to escape, finding her back against a wall with no way out.

"No," she cried, bodies pulling themselves from between the bones, decomposing bodies with dead eyes and broken skin that were clawing themselves towards her, moaning like they were in pain. They sounded ghostly—something from the depths of nightmares.

Nightmares like this.

"Help!" she screamed, The words bouncing around the room like they were mocking her. "Help, dear Gods!" Tears rolled down her wet cheeks as cold, rotting hands grabbed hold of her limbs. She tried to shrug them off of her, but even if she could escape, there was nowhere she could go. She didn't see an opening, just bones piled high in a clo-sed-off cave, bodies falling over themselves to get to her.

Wake up, please!

She begged herself, her chest constricting violently. "Arioch!" she screamed, hoping that whatever connection they had was deep enough, for him to hear her, dream or not. "Arioch, please help—plea-se! Arioch." Her hands freed themselves from the immediate grasp of two females and found their way to the wall behind her as she clawed at it so hard her fingers bled, just to stay above what was turning to quicksand beneath her.

"Gods, please!" she cried, her voice raspy as the taste of the air im-printed itself on her tongue and made her gag. Sweet, sickly sweet. Sweet like the dead. "Arioch!"

40

Chapter

Arioch

Arioch had spent the next hour sparring with Lúc, his body finally rolling back from the strain his shadows had forced on him. He was bleeding, his lip bruised, his ribs sore, but Lúc didn't look any better.

They collapsed into the velvet chairs, both of them drinking liquor when they should have had water instead.

"What's your endgame?" Lúc asked.

"A loaded question," Arioch said simply.

"Is it?" Lúc grinned, his expression bright. "What happens when Aheia's week is up?"

"We'll see won't we," he said, shooting Lúc a look. The truth was that he wasn't altogether sure. There was a part of him—a loud part—that wanted to keep her here. But it fought with the other side of him that knew the unrest it would spark amongst his people. He didn't give a shit about the conflict it threatened between the realms.

"Fine, be cryptic and fucking broody." Lúc pulled out one of his inhalants and lit it up, exhaling a slow, red cloud. His eyes glazed over slightly as he leaned back, stretching out his legs. "You want a hit, Alshaytan?"

Arioch nodded, but as he reached out, his forearm pulsed. He looked down at Aheia's faint white outline, a cold heat spreading and burning into his skin.

He groaned, wrapping his fingers around his arm. The pain was blinding, fuck, he'd never felt it like this.

It took everything he had to get to his feet.

He stepped through his shadows and when he emerged in his room, the bed was empty, and Aheia was gone. Panic flared bright and hot at the back of his neck. Fuck, how did he keep letting this happen? *FUCK.*

He ground his teeth, feeling the type of helplessness he hadn't experienced since ...

Arioch wrapped himself in his shadows, closing his eyes for a moment to try and calm his breathing and just feel. He was searching for a pull, a pointer, anything that might tell him where she was, but he came up short.

Nothing.

Nothing but the pain.

Until suddenly he heard it, so fucking faint he thought he had imagined it. His name.

He stilled, whispers rising from his back, his shadows coaxing him into their depths, her voice and his name repeating over and over and over again. He let his darkness roam, the tendrils taking control and swallowing him whole, before spitting him back out somewhere deep underneath the surface of Aljira.

Arioch found his footing in the lower caves of Gehenna, stepping through bodies and bones, the cave walls in front of him parting as he ran towards an impossible noise. It sounded like shifting and clattering, and then he heard her scream and it shattered him. He slipped through the death that surrounded him, following the echo of her voice with his arm cradled against his chest, the glyph burning deeper and hotter like it was clawing itself from every cell of his being.

Arioch flared his shadows, dragging them over the dead and stepping over top as he saw Aheia buried under a mountain of rotting bodies, trying to pull herself free from grips that shouldn't exist in the first place. Things down here were dead, stayed dead. He'd never seen anything like this, had never seen them respond to another's presence by resurrecting. His stomach turned to lead as he threw himself forward, grabbing the only part of her he could see, pulling on her forearm, his shadows peeling the dead bodies from her. He tore limbs apart, sickly, sweet ooze dripping from his hands as he managed to get her upper body free.

Her eyes were bright and frantic, fear clouding the blue as she met his gaze. For a moment, she looked like she might try and attack him too, but then she whimpered and threw her arms around his neck, as the bodies around her continued to grapple closer like they wanted to consume every part of the Mithra.

"You heard me," she groaned, her wet body clinging to him as he managed to free one of her legs. She was riddled with scratches and soaked to the bone. He hugged her tighter and managed to pull free completely. They fell back into his shadows and he curled the tendrils around them both like a cocoon, their bodies hitting the now smoky ground, quickly taking them far from Gehenna while she held onto his neck for dear life.

She was crying, her body shaking beneath his hold, her hair knotted back, her shirt ripped. There was blood everywhere.

"Oh Gods," she cried, curling into him. "I thought, I thought it was a dream, but–" she broke off, her voice trembling.

He stroked down her spine, his mind feeling like a faraway thing as the possibilities of what just happened ran through his head.

"Where are we?"

Arioch struggled to find his voice in the darkness. "Lay man almun."

He couldn't wrap his mind around it, didn't know what to tell her, because it made no sense–shouldn't have been possible. The shadows around them tapered and slipped until they fell, meeting the cold hard marble floor of his compound.

"What the *fuck?*" Shiron shot to his feet across the room, and Lúc set down the drink he'd been nursing.

Arioch loosened his hold on Aheia, but hers only tightened, her body still shaking with sobs.

"What happened?" Lúc asked, sliding onto his knees next to her.

"*Argh.*" He grit his teeth and Lúc's eyes widened. Arioch pulled his right arm from her waist, his skin feeling like it was tearing at the seams, right over her soul. He cried out in pain, every part of him taut like his body didn't fit together right.

"Ari, what is it?" Aheia asked through her own panic, her hand shooting to her throat just as the words left her.

"Shi, send Emryn to my room," Arioch choked as Shiron's jaw tensed with understanding. Shiron knew, and Arioch thanked whatever higher power could hear him that the demon didn't ask any more questions before he left the room.

"What is–Arioch..." A broken gasp passed through Aheia's lips before she let go of his chest, clutching her own. She moaned, her body rolling back onto the marble, her back arching as her chin wrenched and her eyes, blown wide with fear, followed his gaze to his arm.

A broken bargain.

The words edged into his mind just as she cried out in pain. "Lúc, fuck, hold her," Arioch choked, as the Shifter went for

Aheia, his hands cradling the back of her head to save her from hitting it back against the marble. She fought against Lúc's hold, and Arioch knew that she had no control over her movements.

He'd seen it before, only a handful of times, all of which had ended in death for the person taking back their soul.

"I'm sorry," he managed, rolling onto his side, shaking so bad that he could barely reach for her, his afflicted arm moving forwards, his fingers curling into a tight fist. Lúc grabbed ahold of Aheia's wrists and held them down just as Arioch grabbed her neck and, with the last of his strength, hauled his lips to hers, a searing pain shooting through him when their mouths touched. He cried out, feeling the glyph on his arm unmerging itself with his skin. The fire spread to his chest as her soul moved through him, racing to its home without regard for the muscles, tendons, and bones in its way. It forced itself up his throat, strangling a cry of pain as it went, pouring back into her mouth in a slow torturous drip. Her body tensed at first touch and then she arched, pressing her chest against Arioch, pulling and drinking until every bit of her essence left his body.

He fell back against the marble, gasping as his lungs adjusted, his skin resettling, and a familiar discomfort returned. The hollow, soulless existence he was used to.

Aheia was panting just as hard, pulling her wrists from Lúc's grasp and cradling her hands close to her chest, shaking with sobs as she hugged herself. Her blue eyes were rimmed red, her wet hair sticking to the cuts on her arms and face, her lips a pale color that blended with the color of her skin. And all of it was his fault. She looked up at him, her brows pulled together tight, sweat pearling on her forehead, wordlessly asking him for something he couldn't give her.

"Get her to Emryn," Arioch said to Lúc, avoiding the way she reached for him, while one of her hands twisted in his shirt still on her body until her knuckles whitened.

"What happened?" she asked, her voice hoarse.

"I didn't keep you safe," he said finally. "You were in Gehenna, and our bargain read that as your death." He gritted his teeth. *I broke our bargain.*

Her eyes drew frantic patterns on the ceiling above her as Lúc got up from his position on the floor, and started sliding his hands underneath her body. But she shrugged away, pushing herself up on her forearms.

"Come on now, princess." Lúc quirked an eyebrow but she kept her eyes fixed on Arioch, something cold and numb threading itself through the light blue.

He recognized it. "You're running on adrenaline," Arioch said, wrapping himself in indifference while his shadows scratched his muscles in rebellion. "But that won't last, and when you come down, those wounds will hurt. Emryn will fix them."

She furrowed her brows, and then she whimpered. It escaped her lips just before she covered her mouth with her palm, cutting off whatever else might have forced its way free. The sound cut into Arioch, cut into the hollow thrum inside of him, and it was worse than her cries. Because it sounded so incredibly lost.

"I should have never–" She slid her hand from her mouth and gripped her neck, then further down, pressing the heel of her palm into her heart. "This is–" The words seemed to drown in the tears that were slipping free and dripping onto the marble, her chest shaking with ragged breaths as she pushed herself into a seated position, her arms hugging her knees. "I don't know how to–" Her chin dipped, finally hiding her face from him.

He couldn't fucking take it, couldn't bear watching her hurt, and on top of that deal with the pain of her loss that was digging into his chest like the blade of a dagger. His muscles ached and his body protested but it didn't matter, nothing mattered for that seemingly infinite moment that was spanning in front of them, but her. And that's why he pushed her away.

"Lúc," he snapped.

The Shifter narrowed his eyes at Arioch for a moment but didn't voice whatever he had poised on his tongue, scooping the Mithra into his arms. She didn't fight him this time, groaning as he moved her.

Arioch kept his eyes ahead even as he felt hers burning into him.

"Focus on the pain. The pain is real, what might have happened–is not," he heard Lúc say as they left the room.

HELFYRE

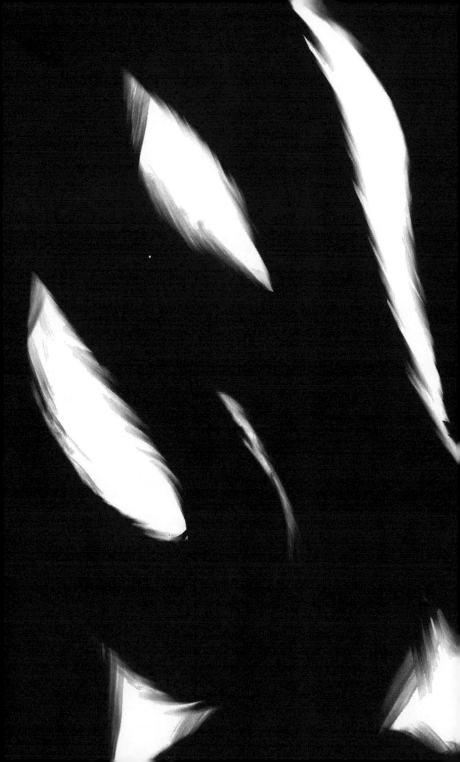

41

Chapter

Arioch

Arioch was still unnerved when he stepped into the caves just be-low the compound, Shiron not far behind as Arioch rounded the corner. They passed a row of ironclad bars lining the far wall, the cells carved into the ground, forming tall alcoves of rough stone. It was down a different hall than where Arioch had brought Aheia, but he was certain her pretty screams had echoed through the entirety of the maze that stretched on down here.

Aylee was resting against the opposite wall, wiping blood from her red claws and onto the dark leathers she was wearing with a dange-rous glint in her eyes. Shiron joined her as Arioch stepped into the cell in front of them. Kal straightened up the moment he saw Arioch. It seemed like he'd discarded that precious exterior he'd held onto when they first met, something rough shining in his blue eyes. His perfect blond curls were messy, and the blood made him look different from the facade that the Mithra were known for. He stood up, slight tre-mors in his shoulders as he fixed his suit.

"Nothing," Arioch started, leaning back against the bars, his hands in his pockets. "No word, no emissaries, no questions about your di-sappearance. It makes one wonder how expendable you are."

Kal's nose twitched slightly, his only reaction besides the intensity of his stare. "If you're going to kill me, please get it over with."

"Don't rush," Arioch said with a chuckle. "Your life will depend on your answers."

"I don't negotiate with demons," Kal growled.

"It's not a negotiation," Arioch murmured, letting his gaze drift down the Dioscuri's suit. He was a fucking mess. "It makes sense, now, why Ophion sent you. It wouldn't matter if you came back, might even make it easier if you didn't—since he promised you something that wasn't his to give."

"What do you want?" Kal hissed, his jaw flexing. "Why does Ophion want her back so bad?"

Kal raised his eyebrows. "Come on, you're not blind. She's not… normal."

Something possessive slithered across Arioch's shoulders.

Normal. For fuck's sake, Mithra are jaded fucks.

"What is she?" he asked, willing the urge to put his hands around Kal's neck back underneath his skin.

Kal scoffed. "An abomination."

Arioch feigned boredom, even though his chest tightened in response to Kal's words like his shadows had heard them.

"Her mother committed adultery early on in her marriage. Aheia's father is—well, was—a Nephilim."

The way he said it made Arioch believe that in Kal's mind, that alone was a sin that could never be forgiven. Which begged the question: why did he want Aheia?

"And?"

"'*And*'?! Her mother not only violated the sanctity of marriage but—-"

"Choose your words carefully," Arioch said, a sharp edge in his voice.

"It's unheard of," Kal said.

Violated the sanctity of their marriage … Arioch almost laughed, while *Ophion has multiple wives.*

"Is that why you betrayed her? Because she's not the pure thing that you've been putting on a pedestal all her life?" Arioch inclined his chin, leaning his head back against the bars of the cell. Part Nephilim … that could make sense, but it didn't explain the effect she'd had, being in Aljira.

"I was the *only* one there for her, and I supported all of her mistakes," Kal snapped, gesturing wildly as if it might explain everything.

"There it is … *Mistakes*." Arioch laughed at the holier-than-thou Dioscuri in front of him. "That's not what support looks like."

The silence spread for a few moments. Then, Arioch asked the question that had been lingering ever since Kal had first brought it up.

"What did you mean when you said that Ophion would make it worth my while?"

Kal smiled and it made Arioch want to beat the blonde's head against the wall until his teeth cracked. "So that's why you're here. To ask her price. You're no better than me."

"No one expects me to be better, Kal. They expect me to be worse," Arioch said calmly.

"Poor girl thinks she's safe with you, doesn't she? Does she know you're here? Does she know you've killed the other emissary and imprisoned me?"

"You're wasting my time." Arioch tipped his chin to the side and addressed the Nephilim behind him. "Finish him off."

He heard the commotion, knew his demons were springing into action and saw it in the flicker of Kal's eyes.

"No—wait." The Dioscuri swallowed, fear plain on his face. "I'll tell you. Then decide."

Arioch nodded and waited.

"You've been blaming the Mithra for something that never happened. You shouldn't believe everything you hear..."

"What?" Arioch's brows furrowed, his body still pulsing, his shadows still tight. He couldn't stay here much longer, couldn't handle this. He needed to disappear into Gehenna, for just a moment, and simmer in the dark. Alone. He could feel the bloodlust creeping in, and paired with the loss of Aheia's soul so completely, he was ready to fight, skin, tear, and break.

"Your brother is alive."

No.

Arioch's shadows exploded from him, his skin screaming in pain as they wrapped around Kal, seeping into his mouth, around his neck, and around every limb until the Dioscuri was choking for air. "How dare you speak of the dead, of *him*?!"

Kal gasped and coughed, the tendrils curling around his eyes. "He's not–dead," he choked out, his face reddening.

Arioch's chest felt hollow, pulling him back into his past, forcing him to remember the good moments he'd had with his family, which was *so much worse* than remembering the bad. It took everything inside of him to pull his shadows back and it hurt, keeping them seated underneath his skin. It was like someone dragged daggers across his arms and back. He steadied himself against the bars, every part of him seizing.

"That's impossible. I saw his body." His bones ached as he watched

Kal splutter, on his knees, trying to catch his breath.

He's lying. Kill him.

The whispers wrapped around his throat and forced themselves into his mind over and over again until he had to grasp onto the iron to hold himself back.

"You saw a body," Kal countered, grasping at his throat, "they made sure he wasn't recognizable."

Shiron passed Arioch and grabbed ahold of Kal's dirty white suit, slamming him into the wall. "That's enough," he hissed through his teeth.

Arioch strained as his shadows escaped him, shuddering off his shoulders in slow increments.

"I'm not—" Shiron's fist landed against Kal's jaw and the Dioscuri's head cracked against the stone while the shadows pulled further and further, Arioch's rage blinding him until all he saw was Kazim's body, charred and burned.

"Not...lying," Kal grunted, blood dripping from his mouth as the shadows grabbed onto his arms and stretched. Shiron let go of the Dioscuri and stepped back as Arioch spread Kal apart until he strained, sending blood splatters across Shiron's face while he fought for air.

"Why?" Arioch rasped, peeling his hands from the bars.

"You played right into his hand," Kal groaned. "They wanted to make you believe that they'd killed him, so you would retaliate and they would have an excuse to eradicate the rest of your family—instead, you took care of Sahren yourself."

"Where is Kazim?" Arioch screamed, crossing the room, slamming the Dioscuri's body back against the wall, his shadows tightening around his limbs.

I don't know," Kal gasped, "but that is his offer. Kazim in exchange for Aheia. He wants to finish something that has been going on entirely too long."

He's lying.

"Do you have proof?"

He's lying.

"Yes."

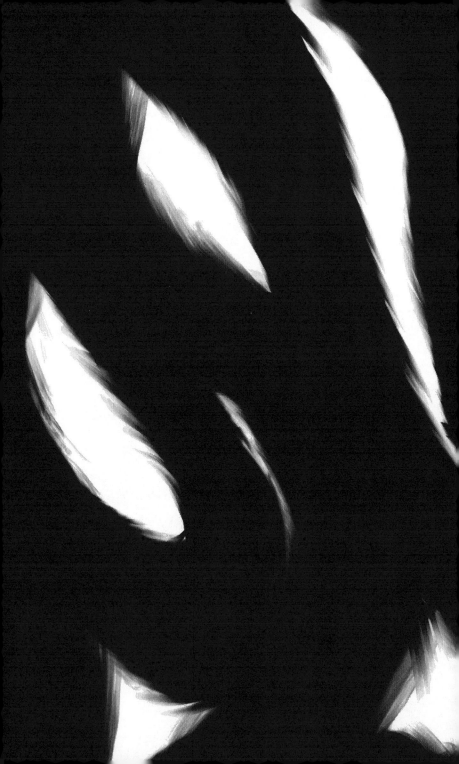

42

Chapter

Lúc

Lúc had slammed back two more glasses of the dark liquor he'd long ago forgotten the name of, in the interest of working himself into a comfortable buzz as he stared down at streaks of Aheia's blood. It was red and thick and something about it had him mesmerized. His head was spinning slightly, the whispers that lived in his mind weaving near unintelligible words around him. He was used to them; the words were why he drank. They were why he couldn't stop losing himself in any Nephilim that showed interest. They were why he got off on pain and blood the same as pleasure. He'd lived with them his entire life, but the vices he chased usually quieted them down, though it seemed liquor wouldn't be enough today.

Thebloodddtrythebloodbloodblooditshotandwarm

It was hushed against his ears, muttered so quickly that all he caught was *blood blood blood*. And how sweet it looked, how comforting... Lúc swayed slightly, kneeling on the floor, and dragged two fingers through the dark, wine-colored liquid. The urge to taste it kicked his brain into overdrive, the need for it weaving itself so deep into him, that it felt like he'd been born with it. Pinpointing his life to this very moment, like the blood glistening on his skin was the only thing that mattered and would ever matter again.

The jaguar inside of him shook the cage that Lúc forced it into like it was begging to be let free. But that wouldn't happen. He didn't like giving in to the beast that lived inside of him, didn't like the way it felt when his claws extended past his knuckles, and the second heart that lived, dead and cold in his chest, sprung to life. So he locked it down and leaned into becoming a different kind of monster, one that he'd created on his own due to his inability to break past the things that had been ingrained in him when he was young: that Shifters were lesser in every way, and that he'd do best not to advertise the affliction he suffered. The thought alone wove acid across his tongue and tightened his chest in anger.

Outcasts. That's what his race was, fucking outcasts, and even Arioch's efforts to change the way they fit into the fabric of Aljira didn't make a difference after years of discrimination. It didn't eradicate the way that other Nephilim called his kind dreske, which meant something like "dirty animal", and it didn't change the way that he was reminded of his family's suffering back when they were still alive. So, he pretended like that part of him didn't exist, and leaned into the vicious proclivities that made him a demon that others would tremble before. Because that felt good, having them scared of him. When they were scared they didn't seem to worry about what he was, so much as how they might find his mercy when he broke their skin with his teeth.

But he didn't know mercy. Nor did he care to learn about her. He brought his fingers to his lips and licked them clean.

Hel ... Sweet fucking hel.

He groaned, feeling the familiar sparks at the back of his neck, banding a cord of hot euphoria around his mind. It tasted fucking *alive*.

"Lúc?"

Tariq's voice sounded like Gods damned honey dripping from his tongue, and the way he said Lúc's name made him tense with awareness. But it was more than that. The blood sparked something in him, a cold heat that spread through his body, a slow burn that prickled through every part of him, similar to drinking water after eating mint. Lúc gathered more of it on his fingers and had another taste, keeping his back turned to Tariq, though uncomfortably aware of the Leviathan's movements behind him. He could hear every step, every breath, every swipe of his leathers.

Lúc couldn't focus, as he straightened back up, every fiber in him urging him to run his tongue along the entirety of the floor, to consume every fucking ounce ... He'd never experienced that. Not with Nephilim blood, not with any blood. But Aheia's was consuming him, had him feeling like he might die if he couldn't have more, his vision prickling with white bursts of light that made the room look like it had been lit up with sparkles. His cock swelled in his leathers and he couldn't fucking tell which of the two caused it, Aheia's blood or Tariq's warmth at his back.

He inhaled stiffly, looking at the red on his fingers, such a contrast against his skin, and knew he needed Tariq to taste it too, even though the prospect of sharing it gave him hives. He slipped further and further from his mind and into the Shifter that came out to play when he killed, and when he tore open Nephilim for Arioch. It was a volatile fucking thing that laughed in the face of death and enjoyed pain more than he wanted to admit to himself when reality found him, as it did after every trance. It was a side of himself that he covered up with jokes and grins, especially in inappropriate situations, but he lost the reins on it now. Something about Aheia's blood on his tongue forced him back into a shadowed corner of his own mind while someone else stepped into control. He turned to Tariq, the dark Leviathan towering over him. His black horns glinted in the low lighting, and his expressive eyes amused... until he met Lúc's gaze.

"What are you doing?" He raised an eyebrow, gaze drifting to his fingers. His voice was low and deep and that south Azalam accent pulled and reshaped his words. It was fucking delicious.

"Trying to remember what you taste like," Lúc growled, his vision fraying at the edges, the cold pulsing through his veins. If he didn't know better, he'd have thought his skin was vibrating off his body.

Tariq's lips tilted up one side and his head followed, dark curls falling into his eyes. Lúc watched him reach out his hand and pinch a piece of his own black hair between his fingers, tugging slightly. "Is that right?" Tariq gave it one more pull, before letting go and shoving that hand into his pocket.

Lúc grabbed ahold of Tariq's wrist and pulled him closer roughly, bringing his fingers to the Leviathan's lips, and painting them red. Tariq flicked his tongue and tasted it, his brows furrowing slightly. Those dark eyes wavered and his pupils grew, eating up the rest of his iris as he stared down at Lúc's fingers. For a moment, he looked just as entranced as Lúc felt. But now that Tariq's lips were covered in blood, Lúc didn't seem to care as much about the rest of it on the floor behind him. Instead, Lúc grabbed ahold of Tariq's neck and bruised his lips with his, a mix of tongue and teeth that distracted the Leviathan as the Shifter went for the waistband of his leathers.

"It's sweet when you try to top," Tariq growled, pulling back, his cock twitching against Lúc's hand as he raked it down the center of his seams. Then the Leviathan grabbed onto Lúc's arms and pushed him away with such force that he fell back against the plush couch on his right. "You know that's not how this works," Tariq said roughly, stalking closer, before bracing his hands on either side of his head, forcing Lúc back.

Gods, he knew. He knew Tariq would make him pay for it, but he didn't care about the repercussions as he reached for the Leviathan's waistband and pulled him closer.

"Can't keep it in your pants for one day, little Shifter?" Tariq growled, winding a hand around Lúc's throat as he worked to loosen Tariq's leathers. "*Pathetic*."

Lúc swallowed, the resistance against his throat so tight his vision was starting to darken at the edges, his heartbeat deforming the room with each pulse. He groaned as the towering Leviathan leaned in, running his tongue the length of his jaw, fingers flexing even tighter against his windpipe.

"So fucking needy," Tariq continued, pulling apart Lúc's lips with his thumb and tilting his chin back so he was forced to look up at the Leviathan, his fingers pulling the last of his laces apart.

Tariq leaned closer, his nose brushing against Lúc's, his teeth gritting and bared, his hands hard and bruising, looking every bit like he wanted to finish the job and strangle the Shifter under his touch. The taste of Aheia's blood coursed through him, his cock straining against his own leathers as Lúc snaked his hands into Tariq's pants and slid his palm down his length.

A deep vibrating growl broke from the Leviathan's chest, his fingers flexing. "Did I tell you to touch me, *Lúc*?" he hissed, his cock jerking against Lúc's palm.

Tariq forced his chin back further, pain building in his overextended neck. There was something in those dark eyes that had Lúc squirming–the only Nephilim he'd ever squirmed for, or even submitted to. But when Tariq spoke to him like this, when he dug his teeth into Lúc's bottom lip until it hurt, when he squeezed his cheeks and spit into his mouth, he lost his fucking mind. Especially when he saw the Leviathan's cold exterior around others. It made him think that–just maybe–Lúc had a similar effect on him.

"*Please*," Lúc begged, the word feeling acidic on his tongue. He didn't make a habit of begging, was usually on the other end of those vulnerable words, but at that moment he didn't much care.

Tariq narrowed his eyes and then gave him a tight nod that had Lúc gripping Tariq's cock and pumping his hand. *Fuck*, it was so fucking perfect. He wanted to taste it again, wanted to feel it inside of him, those Gods damned long, and thorough strokes Tariq gave out sparingly until he was crying ... He wanted all of it and he wanted it now.

"*Gods a-fucking-bove*," Shiron's voice pulled Lúc from his haze, seconds from tearing Tariq's leather down his thighs.

The room devolved in shadows as Lúc watched Arioch barrel into the side of the couch across from them, his eyes manic.

"What the–" Lúc jumped from his seat, pushing Tariq out of the way in the process.

"Get the *hel* over here," Shiron hissed, supporting Arioch, who was slipping against the marble. Lúc watched Alshaytan lean over the back of the couch and empty his stomach's contents onto the soft cushion below.

What the fuck.

There was an energy around Arioch that Lúc recognized. What he saw in the demon's eyes as he grasped onto the couch and gagged was something he'd seen before, many fucking times. It reminded him of a night without stars.

Lúc ran across the room, readjusting his leathers and helping Shiron straighten him out while pulling his hair from the vomit splattering onto the couch.

"What is happening?"

Shiron's eyes were unnerved, darting over the wall like he was searching for answers in the gold veins that ran up the marble.

"Get that Čist out of here," Arioch rasped at Tariq who had finished lacing himself up. "Find Aylee. She knows what to do. Now."

"But–"

"*Do it.*" Arioch's face snapped up to the Leviathan and Lúc saw a look that could only be described as helfyre.

"Arioch," Lúc said quietly, pulling Arioch's curls from his forehead, watching Tariq leave the room, his shoulders tense.

"Don't. *Fuck*," Arioch growled, his fingers digging into the cushion.

"What's going on?"

Shiron only shook his head, eyes still darting back and forth.

And that's when he felt a pain in his side. Arioch's shadows had exploded from his body, throwing both of the Nephilim against the wall on opposite ends of the room. Glasses were shattering with the deafening sweeps of the tendrils, furniture was being tossed, and the fire that burned in the fireplace was extinguished, leaving the soft glow of the orbs above. Lúc dove from another violent outburst, a chair narrowly missing him and shattering against the wall, splintering to pieces.

"*Arioch!*" he screamed against the deafening roaring of the smoke around them, trying to crawl closer just as a table scraped across the floor, almost severing Lúc's hand in the process.

He found Shiron, who had made more headway across the room, throwing himself onto Arioch and pulling his arms behind his back. He met Alshaytan's gaze, and it froze his blood. He'd seen that look... he'd seen it when Arioch was holding Sahren's dead body against his chest. And fuck, it was a look that promised a new storm. Lúc shook his head, feeling the claws slide from his knuckles, using them to get a grip amongst the wind and shadows, finally finding enough purchase to edge himself closer. He slid to his knees in front of Arioch, grabbing ahold of the back of the couch to help steady himself before cradling his friend's face.

"Stop. *Ari*, it's us!"

Arioch stared through him like he was nothing, while Shiron grasped one hand onto his shoulder and wrapped his forearm around Arioch's throat, pulling him back against him. Lúc closed the distance and enveloped Alshaytan in a hug, gripping Shiron's shirt in the process, holding on for dear life.

"*Enough,*" Shiron said, into Arioch's ear. "This won't change anything. Don't let them pull you back like this. It's not right."

They stayed like that until the shadows calmed, slowly but surely rolling off of Arioch's shoulders in soft stutters that matched his ragged breathing. Lúc tightened his grip, feeling his friend's rigid body slack slowly, was forced to hold on tighter with Shiron's help to support him, and waited. The anger at whatever had happened passed a new threshold and turned to sorrow in front of their eyes, Arioch's chest shaking with sobs.

"*Who or what are we tearing apart?*" Lúc hissed at Shiron.

"I don't know how to explain," Shiron said. "I still don't understand it."

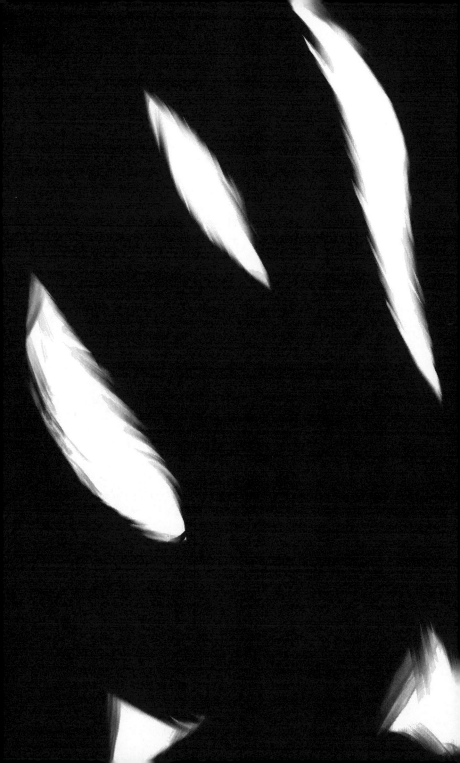

43

Chapter

Aheia

Aheia woke with a start, gasping for air, her head spinning. Nausea hit her in relentless waves, the bile making her gag as she tried to get used to the air that burned her tired lungs.

My soul.

She choked, her entire being sore with its return. Why did it hurt? Why was it so fucking painful?

Her eyes drifted across the ceiling, beige, coarse rock lining her field of vision. She was back in her old room, which confused her. Lúc had brought her to Arioch's room when he took her to see Emryn. The Syraphem had worked on her wounds and given her a sedative, which she was still fighting, the drowsiness pulling her deep into the mattress like it wanted to swallow her whole. But she fought against it, blinking the haze from her eyes, trying to orient herself against the dizziness in her head. Her body was aching as she readjusted, pushing up onto her forearms, the cuts dressed all over her body reminding her of what had happened. Or at least they tried to. When Aheia reached into her mind, she could only summon flashes.

Dead souls and broken bones, pain, the return of her soul, the way Arioch pushed her away once she'd reseated herself in her body. That had hurt more than anything else, and she scolded herself for it. There was no reason why he would have comforted her, had not promised her anything that he didn't provide. But that didn't mean it didn't hurt, and that scared Aheia. It seemed that soul or no soul, the way he'd affected her for the last week wasn't dampened now that things had changed between them. No, it seemed so much worse somehow. Because now there was no constraint, she couldn't tell herself that the

need for him came from their bargain or the situation they were forced into together. What was left in her chest now was all her.

It took her a moment to adjust to the darkness in the room and realized then there was an absence of the familiar light cast by the stars.
She found the soft wisps of shadows curling around the bed, rolling
over the walls and across the floor, and when she squinted into the
dark depths in front of her she saw Arioch's outline. She gasped, her
hand flying to her heart as it leapt, towards him. Like it wasn't being
caged by bones and flesh.

Fuck.

Her chest felt full, too full–like it was straining to accommodate
her, but that wasn't the pain that debilitated her, that had her body
pressing into the mattress like she was shouldering a great weight.
The tears she was doing her best to blink away weren't for the physical,
not for what had happened to her in hel, but for how her heart cried.
It felt like a loss, like someone had wrenched something fundamental
from between her ribs instead of having returned it, and it pulled her
into a dark sorrow. She needed to find a place far away, somewhere she could grieve and hide in a dark corner, away from everything,
away from him, because looking at him hurt, the proximity hurt, all of
it was cutting her open and displaying her insides for the realm to see.

"Say something." Aheia could barely find her voice, her tongue
heavy with emotion.

"Do you know what happened?" he asked, still seated at the foot of
the bed without a single glance in her direction. His voice sounded
tired, and distant like the question was an afterthought.

Aheia bit down on the inside of her cheek until it hurt, trying to distract herself from the pain in her chest with the one in her mouth as
she let herself recall the flashes of memory. "I thought it was a dream.
But then you came for me." She shook her head. "I don't know how I
got there."

Arioch stayed silent at the foot of the bed, his hands clasped between his legs, the shadows stuttering off his shoulders in a slow stac-
cato.

"Where was I?" she asked, shifting onto her knees, slowly, taking
care not to irritate the healing wounds.

The question pulled Arioch's attention towards her, but she wished
it hadn't. Because those eyes were unbearably cold, his irises devoid
of gray, swallowed whole by a black color that made him look like the

demon he was. Aheia gripped onto her thighs, the effort not to shrink back into the headboard overwhelming as he stood.

"I pulled you from Gehenna," he said, his voice rough.

Her mouth fell open, a soft gasp on her lips. "You can't be serious." She hadn't meant to say it. But her mind struggled to wrap around his words. Gehenna. How the fuck had she been dragged into Gehenna?

He stared at her for a moment, watching her face with a calculated look in his eyes before he moved closer, just a couple of steps, and again she had to work not to shrink back. Because her heart fluttered, and her chest tightened, and she couldn't let herself analyze exactly what it meant, because by the way he looked at her, whatever she felt was clearly one-sided. What she saw in his eyes rivaled what she saw when she met him at the border. He looked at her like a burden, like a complication, nothing more.

"Those bodies, Aheia–they shouldn't have reanimated. They were corpses, *are* corpses."

"What does it mean?" she asked, willing her voice to hold steady when all it wanted to do was shake.

Arioch just shook his head and for a moment there was a deafening silence between them that made her feel uneasy. Then he spoke, his voice just as cold as his eyes. "I left some food by the door. Eat."

"Ari, I–" She shuffled closer, but he took a step back. "Don't."

It felt like she hit a pane of glass, the disgust in his voice stilling her in her tracks.

"I have nothing to give you," he said slowly, his shadows dripping onto the floor.

"I'm not asking you for anything." Aheia furrowed her brows, clenching her hands.

"Aren't you?"

She wanted to. Had the question at the tip of her tongue. But before she could open her mouth his shadows slipped onto the mattress and around the back of her neck. They tightened until she went rigid, her eyes widening.

"Did you think this would change anything? That I'd what–" He let his gaze trace down her body slowly before snapping it back to hers. "Keep you?" He pulled her closer, forcing her onto her hands as he stepped in front of her, replacing his shadows with his hand.

"Yes."

Gods. You're weak.

She wished she could take the sad little word back, but what did it matter now. Holding her cards close to her chest would do nothing for her anymore.

"You shouldn't want that, Aheia," he said, raising her back onto her knees by her neck, his face so close to hers she felt his breath on her lips.

A string of anger threaded the embarrassment and sadness. "I'm tired of others telling me what I'm allowed to want."

His jaw clenched. "What you want is destined to hurt you."

He let go of her neck, but she held onto his wrist before he could leave. "Isn't it my right to make that decision?"

He looked down at her fingers on his skin. "It's not your decision to make. It's mine."

She tightened her grip for a second, her heart hammering in her chest. "And you ... won't let me stay? I wouldn't be in your way, could work, live in the city–you'd never have to see me again."

His nostrils flared, and the cold in his stare tempered. "No."

"Why?" she challenged, the anger swallowing her.

"You don't belong here."

That simple phrase shouldn't have run its claws down the inside of her body as it did.

"I didn't think border boundaries were something that held weight for you."

"They don't."

So you just don't want me. It was all my soul.

He narrowed his eyes at her. "You're leaving tomorrow."

Tomorrow.

She felt so fucking stupid. The fact that she had ever believed there may be an outcome that didn't end with him pushing her from his realm, that in seven days she could make enough of an impact to shift his focus.

Listen to yourself, you desperate fucking youngling. Her mind berated her. *There's no relationship here.*

Arioch raked his palm across his lips and held it there for a moment before unclasping her hands from his wrist and stepping back, his shadows forming a thick cloud behind him.

"No—"

But he was already gone, leaving Aheia alone in her bed. She covered her mouth.

Fuck.

She leaned back against the headboard, thankful he couldn't feel her anymore through their bond. Because if he did, he'd know that she was falling apart, breaking silently, biting into her palm as tears fell down her cheeks.

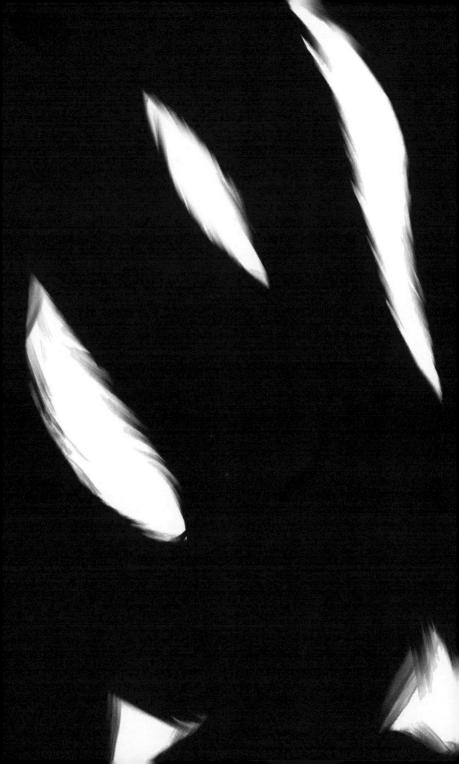

44
Chapter

Aheia

Aheia refused to eat the food Arioch had left or the next tray that a new Leviathan brought to her bedside hours later. She didn't sleep much, but at some point she must have dozed off because she woke on the cusp of panic, nightmares rolling her under. The cold in her chest made it almost impossible to breathe as she sat up in the bed and looked out the window, wondering if she'd slept long enough to pass into the next day. The thought made her throat feel like sandpaper, new nerves settling into her bones. Her wounds felt better, dull and sore, but they must have healed. She peeled back one of the white bandages to find a faint pink line, dark blood dried across her skin.

Her chest was stiff with the renewed presence of her soul, and it didn't help that when she thought about Arioch it tightened, as if it wasn't used to being away from him yet.

She still didn't understand any of it. Not what had happened to her, not how she had found herself in Gehenna, not why Arioch had suddenly been so viciously cold. But the pain in her heart went deeper than him. It felt like losing a game she'd never truly known the rules of.

She couldn't see past her last moments here, didn't know where she'd go or what she'd do. She would run for a while longer if only to prove to herself that she could, but it wasn't a life she wanted, wasn't feasible long-term. And if she knew anything about Ophion, it was that he wouldn't stop. It would be easy for him to keep chasing her, given his resources. If they caught her, she'd face things she couldn't imagine.

She hugged her knees to her chest, unwanted tears rolling down her cheeks. She'd let herself feel the sadness for a moment before she had to lock it away because if she didn't, she'd crumble under the weight of everything.

Her eyes closed, the darkness slipping around her until she thought she felt the light tickle of air across the back of her hand. She looked down to find soft shadows curling around her wrist, but not the tangible kind. They were more smoke than anything.

"Koutávi." She smiled up at the black mass brewing in front of her.

The Varcolac edged closer, dipping the mattress as she wound herself around Aheia, pressing her body against her side. Aheia reached into the smoky void and found soft hair in its depth. She wasn't sure why it surprised her to find something soft at its core when she knew how vicious it could be.

"Why did you help me?" she whispered her fingers stroking down Koutávi's spine, feeling a heavy weight on her knee and the hard ridge of a jaw leaning into her legs. Koutávi made a surprising animal noise, like she was shrugging off her line of questioning, telling her to stop talking. Almost a whine.

A smile pulled at Aheia's lips as she felt the tightness in her chest ease a fraction. She gave Koutávi a couple of scratches before pushing her snout to the side and heading for the adjacent washroom.

She made quick work of cleaning herself, using the gratuitous amounts of soaps and lotions that were lined up in the small alcove, and when she came back to the bedroom, her hair wrapped in a towel, Koutávi was still where she'd left her. Aheia rifled through the closet, finding a black pair of leathers and an oversized black shirt discarded towards the back. No way in hel was she leaving Aljira in a silk dress.

She pulled on the clothing, the pants much too loose, and wound a leather belt around her waist before climbing back into bed, curling herself around the Varcolac.

Aheia leaned into her middle and used her body as a pillow, feeling the strong steady breaths underneath her cheek, getting lost in the rhythm while she listened to the strong heart beating against her ears.

It would have been the perfect moment to drift back into sleep, except her mind wouldn't let her. It started racing through the events of the last six days, half of them feeling like a fever dream.

She felt the remnants of shame string themselves together inside of her chest as she thought about how she'd let Arioch past her defenses with little coaxing. On one hand, she thought herself foolish, but on the other, she didn't see what was all that wrong with it. She wasn't in love with him, even though her heart still felt a little challenged at the thought of him. He'd taken control of her, but she'd wanted him to do so just as much. There was no point in chastising herself when every part of her had burned for what he'd had to give.

Even now, even after all the words, the exchanges, the anger, she'd take more if she could get it—not because she was weak or because she wanted to change his mind, but because she simply wanted. All her life she'd denied herself, had seen other people clamp down on their desires because of a moral construct that was out of date and archaic.

Why was she still adhering to any of it?

Let it go.

Aheia had been staring at the wall across from her for Gods know how long, a new kind of fatigue weighing down her eyes. Now that she'd rested she was tired of sleeping, the thought almost draining. Koutávi was curled around her as the patterns of the rough rock she was staring at started to reveal crooked outlines of animals and shapes the longer she went without blinking. Her eyes were dry and burning and she was unaware of how long she'd gotten sucked into the figures on the wall. She pressed the heels of her palms into her eyes and rubbed, relieving the discomfort slightly.

What a fucking mess. She thought to herself removing her hands.

"Gods!" she gasped, covering her mouth in surprise. Arioch was standing at the foot of her bed. She hadn't heard him, but what felt more foreign was that she hadn't *felt* him. Her hand flew to her chest a little too quickly as Koutávi sat up next to her, the shadows curling around her legs.

Arioch's brows furrowed as he looked between the two of them. "It's time," he said, his voice detached.

She cursed her heart for missing a beat, anxiety rearing its head again.

"What are you wearing?" he asked, watching her crawl from the bed.

"I found it in the closet." She shrugged her shoulders, grabbing her knife and leather pouch from the bedside table. His eyes were on her, hot and cold battling behind the gray.

"You won't take that," he said matter-of-factly, holding out his hand.

"You won't allow me a knife to protect myself with?" She heard the shock in her voice and wished she could have masked it.

"You won't need it."

He waited but she didn't move, her arms suddenly heavy at her sides.

"Why?"

If she was naive, she might have thought he'd changed his mind, but the look in his eyes suggested something completely different, and it made her blood run cold.

"Why won't I need my knife?" she asked an urgency in her voice, her heart hurtling into her ribs.

He didn't answer, just stared, and it was louder than his words could have been.

"You're not..." Words failed her as she let them trail into the room without a conclusion.

He said nothing. He said everything.

He's going to turn me in.

She couldn't bear this. She could run after she left Aljira, no matter how exhausted she was but she couldn't bear this.

"Why?" Her eyes burned as the realization drove a sliver of ice into her heart, like he'd reached into her chest and wrenched. "What is he giving you?"

"Something I can't refuse."

The knife in her hands felt heavy, the darkness inside of her circling her throat, making it almost impossible to breathe.

"Something Alshaytan can't refuse?" She spit the words, sensing Koutávi moving from the corner of her eye.

Again, he said nothing.

Her eyes fell to the marble at her feet, her mind reeling through the scenarios, her options, the different routes she could take. Every single one of them led back to Ophion and Keloseros. Aheia's hand moved before she was consciously aware, the cold blade of her knife hot against the frozen skin of her throat. The movement was so erratic that she cut her skin, pain shooting down her shoulder.

This was going to hurt.

Koutávi had jumped from the bed at the same time and crawled between her and Arioch, who moved closer, his eyes and outstretched hand betraying the ice of his facade.

"*Altajue walaisla*," he said calmly to Koutávi, who growled at him. Growled.

"Stay back," she said, her hand shaking. "I won't let you do this."

"So you'll kill yourself?"

"Yes." And she believed herself when she said it.

Arioch's jaw clenched and Koutávi snarled. It hurt, all of it hurt so fucking much that she had to focus on her intentions, focus through the burning of her eyes, through the tears that escaped them.

Time itself stuttered before darkness swallowed her from all ends and Arioch's hand wrapped around hers, wrenching the knife away, holding his palm against the bleeding cut.

"You won't die like this," he rasped against her temple as he curled his hand into her hair. For a moment, it almost felt tender. Then, Arioch forced her wrists behind her back, tendrils of shadows binding her as he hauled her from the void and into the marble throne room.

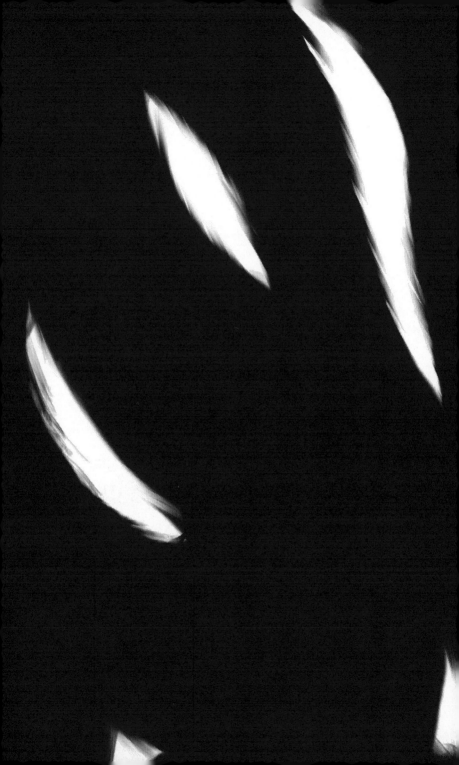

45

Chapter

Aheia

She stumbled and fell, holding on only by his steadying hand. Anger gripped her neck now, every other emotion drowned out completely as she met the stares of his people.

Nephilim were populating the room like it was any other day, relaxed on the couches against the wall, reading, playing games that she didn't understand on marble slabs. All of them were simply living their lives as she watched the sand in her own hourglass run out. Arioch dragged her across the room towards Kar, Emryn, and Shiron—who was holding a dark velvet pouch cinched with gold strings at the top—who were huddled with Lúc and Aylee, speaking in Lujha.

Arioch let Aheia go, his shadows still restraining her wrists. "If you won't let me do it, kill me yourself," she choked, stopping in her tracks as he continued towards the other Nephilim.

"No." He shot her a glare from the corner of his eye. "Not today, little goddess."

"Ari."

His eyes snapped up, darker than she'd ever seen. "That's not my name."

Her chest tightened and it felt like it did when he wore her soul on his sleeve, except now she was intact, though she didn't feel that way when he looked at her with those detached eyes. He looked like a true predator.

"What about Gehenna—everything that's happened?" She tried an angle that didn't involve their relationship.

Relationship.

She shut herself down when the word drifted through her mind.

This wasn't a relationship, this wasn't anything.

He grinned, and it was cold. "It doesn't mean anything." And somehow she felt like he wasn't talking about Gehenna.

Words failed her at that moment, but she stood her ground, no matter how much she was expecting to hurt if she let herself think about anything but the anger that trickled in a cold drip down her back.

"Don't you *dare*," she ground out, taking a step forward.

"What?" he growled, his shadows slithering up her legs.

"Don't treat me like that."

"Like what?" His eyes flashed brightly. "Like your enemy."

"Aren't you, little Dioscuri?" he taunted, the words slicing through her skin.

"I can be if that's what you want," she said.

"You're going back where you belong," he said with finality.

"No."

"There's nothing for you here, Aheia. Nothing. You cannot stay. My people were right, this–" he said, gesturing between them as if it spoke for itself, "this can't stand, not here."

"The people that tried to kidnap and kill me? Those same ones?" She quirked an eyebrow, the truth lighting something bright inside of her.

His nostrils flared. "I took care of it."

"You think that, don't you? I've been here seven days and know this cannot last, none of what you built can last. You have wolves at all of your doorsteps and lion or no, enough wolves will fell a beast your size." She stepped back, intent on leaving with the last word, but he went for her, his hand wrapping around the back of her neck.

"You did this, Aheia, you did this," he said, his breath hot against her lips.

"Stop." She pushed her shoulder into his chest.

"No." He grabbed her waist. "You're going back home, little goddess."

"Don't call me that."

"Oh, but you liked it so much, came around my cock like this."

"Gods, you're–"

"What? A monster?" He grinned. It didn't reach his eyes.

"You're depraved," she groaned, pulling at his hand, trying to run from his words.

"Yes." He leaned in, shadows threading underneath his eyes making him look wrong. Too tired, too angry, too ... dead. "And I remember that got you off too. Such pretty screams, my name on your lips. You begged like a good little whore."

She stilled in his arms. "It didn't mean any more to me than it did to you," she said, her voice measured. And it wasn't the complete truth, but she'd never heard herself be more convincing. Not in all of her life. "You were a distraction, majte." She tipped her chin so she could look down at him even though she was shorter. "One of many."

He tried to keep his expression calm, but she caught the pulse at his temple, the way his jaw tensed.

"Good." Clipped, angry.

He let go of her neck and she stumbled back, feeling him still, a phantom of his hand.

She wanted to say something more, wanted to keep a semblance of power, but the way those eyes around them fell onto her, she couldn't bear it.

That's what you get for slipping into bed with the devil.

Her gaze drifted past him and she noticed Kar staring at her, her brows furrowed. She was grasping onto Shiron's arm, her fingers twisting in the black fabric of her dress. Arioch turned from Aheia and stepped to Kar's side, who flinched when his shoulder brushed hers. Shiron leaned into her ear and whispered something before passing her the bag he was holding.

The anger gave way to sadness, and a feeling of hopelessness she hadn't felt the likes of since her mother died wound itself around her. She swallowed the tears and felt them run down the back of her throat as her chest ached.

For fucks sake, stop it.

She didn't think she'd continue to feel this way, that all of her emotions the last seven days had been largely due to her soul being stripped. Now that it was back, she didn't feel much different, and it hurt. If only she could force her emotions to freeze just as her body did... She felt herself retract, crawl into herself, wished she could just sink into the ground, but instead, Arioch turned and those unfeeling, gray eyes broke her.

He truly didn't care, was trading her in for Gods knew what. He was like all the rest of them, and it was that thought that made her give up the last flicker she held onto.

"*Honey,*" she whispered, the word feeling acidic on her tongue.

You shouldn't have said that. The angry part of her slithered underneath her skin, the darkness inside of her digging its talons into her chest.

Now he knows you're weak. Pathetic.

She swallowed the thoughts just like she swallowed the tears. His eyes narrowed for a moment. "Our game is over," he said, his voice harsh, eyes harsher.

Aheia's heart did something that felt terrifyingly similar to fracturing down the middle, her breathing stuck somewhere in her throat. She hadn't been disillusioned enough to believe he cared for her, but a small part of her had hoped she'd made enough of an impact to sway him with their safe word nonetheless.

The silence fell around them and the longer they stood, the further it pushed the two of them apart until Aheia felt like she was staring at Arioch from across an ocean. She was shrinking, the eyes on her body taking little pieces of her armor with every passing moment, until she felt naked and was fighting the urge to try and run as Arioch continued his casual conversation with Shiron, his words echoing in her mind.

Our game is over.

Arioch took the bag from Kar and mumbled something to her before turning back to Aheia, his features almost deviant in the way his eyes changed, in the way his lips pulled into a smile, in the way his brow arched. She'd briefly wondered, somewhere in between him threatening the demon who'd hurt her and washing the blood from her skin, if he dealt in masks as she did. Because what she saw when they were alone contradicted what she'd seen in public. But now she got the sinking feeling that it was the other way around, that the mask he'd worn hadn't been to mislead others but to mislead her.

He opened the bag in his hand and pulled out a small, fragile pearl, holding the white orb in front of Aheia's face. She gave him a scathing look and fought against the shadows that had her restrained.

"Don't wear yourself out, little goddess." Arioch grinned. "You know how these work?"

"Yes," she ground out, her teeth sawing together until her jaw became painfully tight. The *margaritári* were the pearls that Nephilim emissaries used to travel between realms. Mithra had something similar but dark in color. She'd tried to steal them from Ophion's study once—using one of the margaritári would have enabled her to step into Aljira in the blink of an eye instead of forcing her across Lyria.

But when that proved impossible, she resigned herself to making the journey the old-fashioned way.

Arioch bent down in front of her, setting the orb on the ground while handing the bag back to Kar. He waited until each of his people held one in their hands before he set his own down and smashed it with the heel of his boot.

A blinding white light filled the room in front of him as a rift between the realms opened. It was a chill against her skin, like the wind she remembered ruffling the white leaves of the Callay Forest on cold days.

"*Now*," Arioch commanded, nodding at her pearl as the other Nephilim followed suit, opening five more gateways.

She swallowed, staring at the margaritári. It held her life cradled against its opalescent exterior. A lifeless object, so small and frail could change the course of her future.

The color of it reminded her of the way her soul had been inked on Arioch's skin, and when she brought her heel down on it and crushed the pearl, it felt like she was breaking herself in the process. Her chest constricted as the white light engulfed her, pain beating through her veins with every last pulse of her heart.

This was it. It was over.

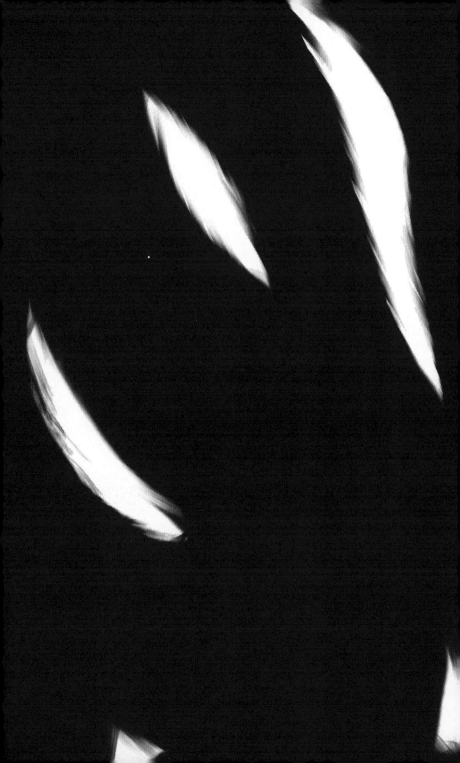

46

Chapter

Aheia

For a moment, she existed in between reality and a dream.

She was nothing but essence, her body vanishing within the dark interior of Arioch's compound. The feeling of weightlessness engulfed her before her consciousness rushed in, and she snapped back together like an overextended bow. The air rushed into her lungs, and she coughed, her body hitting a hard, cold surface, her vision still filled with white light. She tried to blink it away, felt the dryness of her eyes, and wondered how long it would take to clear the rift completely.

That was until she was pulled up by callused hands, and as the world spun she realized that they *had* cleared the rift. The brightness wasn't the crossing instead, it was Keloseros.

Her surroundings started pressing in on her as she realized she was standing on a marble floor, leaning into Arioch to keep from falling over. Her stomach had turned, nausea pulling at her until all she could do to hold it back was swallow her spit over and over again. She stumbled from Arioch's side, the warmth that had imprinted itself on her skin chased away by cold air and a sterile feeling that she knew all too well.

She looked around, the silhouettes and outlines in front of her becoming more clear with each blink. She recognized this place. They were standing between the white pews of a church that she'd attended many times in her years. The church had been erected in honor of Aether, and it was meant to worship him for providing the Mithra with light.

Backward as fuck.

It was always Aether that was depicted, and Theia was treated like

an afterthought even though the Gods had created Keloseros together. Their story was pulled into different narratives but all of them
circled back to a few base facts that all Mithra agreed on. It was said
that Theia and Aether had spent the better half of eternity together,
the Brite Gods that acted as the light for many other beings. Eventually, they became restless and left their worlds behind in search of
something more. They were never satiated, living in a dangerous give
and take; Theia producing so much light she would implode on her
own and Aether needing her light to live as mortals need oxygen to
breathe.

The two of them pulled the realm from the ether and populated it
with a myriad of diverse light creatures; The Maleks with their wings,
the Dioscuri who could bend light to their will, the Nymphs drawn to
the shining waters, the Fae, the Shifters, and the Brite Heretics along
with many others that were scattered across the depths of the Callay
Forests.

But their idyllic life didn't last long as the Brite Gods, who had lived
symbiotically for so long, underwent a vicious shift; Aether suddenly becoming greedier. The God needed more and more light to keep
himself grounded in his mind, and Theia could not support him any
longer. She felt it in her soul, that she wasn't long for this world, as she
watched the immortal bodies outside of their realm pile up against
the border where chaos and death reigned under Manāt and the Kaymaat's ministrations. She could see it in her counterpart, his mania,
the way his eyes shone with need and want, and she knew he'd lost his
mind to obsession.

In the days after Gehenna's creation and Manāt's imprisonment,
Theia was weak. She couldn't give her light to Aether like he was used
to, but the God was restless, strung out to the point of insanity. Aether
took too much from his Goddess when she was still weak, consuming
her completely and eating the last of her essence. Aether went into
a daze that lasted for years but felt like the blink of an eye, and then
he realized what he had done. He wailed in misery so loudly that the
ground shook, and swept through Lyria, his anger burning the barren
lands further. He did his best to try to blame anything and anyone
but himself until he tore himself apart in a cataclysmic explosion that
would reduce him to a hot, burning orb that hung itself in the sky; a
combination of the two Brite Gods.

Aheia had always hated the church—even just standing on the white marble made the hair on the back of her neck stand up. She'd sat through countless sermons, and had recited stories she didn't believe in front of people who she didn't like, all to play into the vision of their perfect family. They'd sat near the altar, her and her sisters, with Ophion and his wives across the way.

She'd rarely gotten to see her "siblings"—she barely knew their names and only met them for church. Most of them lived in their guarded rooms, none of their paths overlapping. Ophion's house had been constructed in a way that saw his families situated as if the others didn't exist.

Her eyes traced the pews, the hard marble lines that had cut into her skin after hours of sitting, that had bruised her knees when they prayed.

The sun was streaming in from the outside, throwing window-grid shadows across the altar that was pushed back, still holding burnt candles, dianthus, and honey. Aheia looked down, concentrating on rubbing her fingers together and searching for that familiar spark, that tingling in her veins that she used to feel when she summoned her light. But nothing but warmth built against her skin, the magyck stolen from her for good.

Her heart was in her throat as she watched a door across the church open, the light streaming inside even more glaring if that was possible. Her eyes were blurry, not having seen brightness like this in weeks. Even Lyria seemed dull comparatively, and she wondered if it was the proximity to the sun that made the light seem much more stifling in Keloseros.

Her palms grew sweaty as she clenched her hands, pulling at the restraints Arioch still had wound around her wrists, her pulse racing with the need to run. She looked around, feeling the panic in her wide eyes, staring at each of the Nephilim next to her. They didn't return the look, just kept their gazes ahead, their black clothing a speck of darkness on an otherwise fresh and new canvas.

Aheia looked up at Arioch as she heard the footsteps draw near.
Clack. Clack. Clack.

The sound scraped over her eardrums while she looked at Alshaytan–every bit the demon that stories spoke of. He didn't spare her as much as a glance.

She was so close, if she could just get out of these restraints, she could try and dive for one of his knives, or maybe Shiron's. He was standing just behind her. If she could get a weapon maybe she could–

What? Threaten six people with a measly knife? And then what?

The self-doubt crept into every little avenue she explored in her mind. She considered that she could run, but she didn't have any powers. She'd be surrounded soon, and couldn't escape Keloseros twice, not as she had before. Doing it a second time would demand a bigger sacrifice than just her light.

This felt like the end of a road, and like before, the thought of death felt... welcome. She'd see her mother again, stop running, and leave all of this behind. Aheia could rest. Then she thought about Arioch and finally leaving him for good, anger digging its claws into her stomach.

She hated him. If she had the chance, she would drive a knife through his heart for forcing her through this, for not letting her end this on her terms, for trading her like an object. But there was a part of her that rebelled against the thought, that still felt that heavy heat imprinted on her soul like he'd returned her tainted, as if she would never quite be herself again. It made her want to scream in fury or pull out her hair with frustration.

This wasn't fair. She had never been on her own, not while she was truly free. She'd never been able to make her own decisions, not without consequence if an outside party deemed it necessary. Her body had been kept in that Gods damned house for years, her mind had been chastised for its thoughts—taught to hate itself because it didn't work as other Mithras' did, and now even after her soul was returned to her a portion of it still ached for Arioch.

None of it was hers.

Her taut skin didn't fit her bones, her thoughts rarely felt her own and her desires were contradicting themselves at every turn.

The coalescing of it brought tears to her eyes and she hated that, too. She hated how she couldn't keep her emotions in check, rein them back in moments like this. The tears spilled down her cheeks, her lips parted in the effort to capture what little air seemed left in the church as she watched white suits shuffle into the open space.

She recognized each one of them. Some were guards, some had held her, some had hit her, and all of them were nothing compared to the sight of Kal and Ophion walking inside together.

Kal was wearing a suit that looked identical to the rest—clean straight lines, his blue eyes shining bright, and his blonde curls combed back. He wore bruises on his skin that made her wonder where he'd gotten them and if they hurt.

She hoped to Gods they did.

Ophion was last, his white jacket a little longer and more ornate, gold cuffs decorating his sleeves, clean, white pants, and dress shoes completing his ensemble. Aheia didn't remember the last time she'd seen him in anything but those exact pieces of fabric.

The air had vanished when she met his eyes, cold blue pulling her into her past. She felt small again like a young child who chose her words carefully for fear of retribution. His gray hair was slicked back, and his smile was deceptive. To Keloseros he looked like the well-mannered *epísimos*, but she knew better. She could see the calculation, the wolf that had itself wrapped in sheep's clothing and was devouring them left and right without them noticing.

Arioch yanked on his shadows, forcing her to move as he approached the Mithra, every step tightening the noose around her neck. She struggled and tripped, pulled on them, but hands gripped her arm and she looked back at Shiron, who was keeping her steady and moving her along. She shot him a vicious look, betrayal acidic in her stomach, but he didn't so much as glance at her, those amber eyes trained ahead.

Gods!

She meant nothing. She meant nothing to anyone, and it was that thought that cracked a fine line down her center.

47

Chapter

Aheia

There were only six Mithra meeting the Nephilim from the opposite side of the church, facing off at some poetic and invisible
line. It was dark and light separated, the suggestion of two perfectly
contrasting factions that were swallowed by the sun above. But Aheia
knew better than to slot any of the two sides into the perfectly just
or the inconceivably wrong. Because for all the things that she hated
about the demon that had her bound at his side, he'd shown her one
thing; there was no pure white and no simply, consuming dark. Both
had their stains, some light, some dark, that muddled them into gray
no matter which side they clung to.

Ophion adjusted his cufflink, and it sent a shiver up her spine that
pebbled Aheia's skin.

"Welcome." He smiled and looked from Arioch to her. "Welcome
home, daughter."

She ground her jaw together, the panic curling her insides into a
tight ball.

"Let's get this over with," Arioch said in a bored drawl.

He can't get rid of me fast enough.

The anger in her chest flared and she held onto it because anger was
easier. Anger hurt less. It prompted the darkness and the ice inside of
her, and she felt them come alive, snaking through her as she looked
at Ophion. His stare was challenging and triumphant, and it made
her want to scratch his eyes out as she yanked at the restraints on her
hands. This time when she shrugged away from Arioch, the shadows
gave way, the force of it tripping her and pulling her onto the ground,
her palms saving her from cracking her head against the marble.

She scrambled to her feet, backing away from Arioch, the nearness jolting something burning and painful in her soul. She didn't have a plan, didn't know where her feet carried her, only that she couldn't stand next to him any longer. The feel of his body was still pressed into her shoulder from when she'd leaned into him, and she would give anything to scrape it from her skin.

Alshaytan stared at her now, and so did everyone else, watching her every move. She looked at the Nephilim's weapons, all of them strapped to their chest where the Mithra had them holstered around their belts. Kal stepped closer but she matched his movement, putting new distance between them too. His eyes were soft, pitiful like he was staring at a child that had fallen and hit its head.

Aheia fucking *hated* that look.

"We'll cast the agreed-upon wards, to shield the doors to the outside. As you know, the church is already protected against Shifter transformation and anything past basic level Heretical spells," Ophion said slowly. "And of course, the realm wouldn't permit any shadow or dark Nephilim magyck to exist, just as yours repels anything Brite," Ophion said, one of the Mithra in their line stepping forward.

"Spare me the lecture. I know how it works," Arioch said gruffly.

Aheia watched as Emryn moved next to Arioch, her wings pulled in tight behind her, facing the Mithra who'd stepped out of line. He held out his hand, a grin curling his lip that reminded Aheia of a serpent that was watching a mouse struggle in his embrace. Emryn didn't smile. She looked him over, shot a glance at Arioch, and then took his hand. Their fingers intertwined as they rotated their wrists, murmurs on both of their lips as a soft hum filled the air, iridescent light dripping from their joined hands. It looked colorful and translucent, coating the floor underneath their feet and spreading like a second skin until it melted up the walls and over the ceiling, changing the light around them into a kaleidoscope of colors. Aheia gaped, watching the Heretics spin what she imagined had to be some sort of protection around them until they were encased.

"There," Ophion said, clasping his hands. "You can trust none of my soldiers can enter through the church doors just as none of you can leave."

Emryn dropped the Heretic's hand, a thin sheen of sweat pearling at her hairline, and backed away, wiping her palm on her leathers, a look of disgust plain in her features.

"You've kept up your end of the deal," Ophion said, his gaze sliding down Aheia's body. "I suppose it's time to hold up mine."

Aheia looked at Arioch, his hard exterior faltering in front of her. It was in the way his eyebrows raised for a moment, the way his eyes softened, almost too quick to catch, in the way he seemed to stop breathing.

She'd asked him what Ophion was giving him in exchange for her and all he'd said was: *Something I can't refuse.*

What made Alshaytan bend like this? Crack like this?

Arioch's eyes found Aheia's, and he crossed the space between them, grabbing ahold of her arm. He dragged her in front of Ophion, his fingers digging into her skin, the softness she'd seen before nowhere to be found. She fought against him, but he didn't seem to notice as he stared down epísimos.

"Stop touching me," she ground out, finally finding her voice.

"Or what ... you'll scream? What will you scream, *Aheia*?" His words were suggestive and fucking mean, and they colored her cheeks a deep red.

"*Gamsió skotá*," she said before spitting at Arioch, her saliva landing on the side of his neck.

He didn't seem to care about that either, as he stared at Ophion. "Now. Don't make me change my mind."

Ophion grinned an easy smile that looked out of place. "Of course."

His hand disappeared behind his jacket and for a brief moment, Aheia saw flashes of him pulling out a dagger and stepping towards her with it. Her vision fractured as day bled into night, and reality and memory flickered back and forth.

She held her breath, stilling against Arioch as she watched, a wave of relief washing over her when Ophion pulled his hand back empty. Or she thought it was empty. He peeled his fingers back and revealed a margaritári. It was a bright white, different from the almost cream that had brought them here. She'd never seen margaritári that color.

He held it out to Arioch, the proximity to his hand sending an army of ants across Aheia's skin. She shrugged back, hitting Arioch's chest, deciding that the evil behind her was preferable to the evil in front of her.

"That's not how this works, Ophion," Arioch growled, his hand dropping her arm and winding around her throat instead. She gasped as he squeezed, her head forced back against him. "Bring him back."

Bring him back.

Aheia watched Ophion's eyes flicker between them, hesitation lingering in his features and for a brief moment she thought she felt something, a familiar warmth slipping around her. But when Arioch spoke, it disappeared almost as quickly as it had appeared. "Give me a reason to break her. It will be so easy." He leaned down against her temple.

"What makes you think that is a deterrent?" Ophion pulled his hand back and arched an eyebrow, the Mithra next to him shifting slightly. "What makes you think her death wasn't the plan all along?"

"You don't think I know what I hold in my hands?" Arioch's thumb rubbed against her pulse, and it made her chest tighten to the point of pain. "You don't think I've figured out why you've been hel-bent on getting her back? Why you went as far as to send your own to barter with me? We slaughtered one of them, locked the other up, and nothing..."

Kal was staring at her, his chest rising and falling quickly, his hand wrapped tightly around his dagger. The bruises on his face and the anger in his eyes were proof of Arioch's words.

Ophion's features tightened visibly as he straightened slightly. "She's an abomination, Arioch. I am doing you a favor, really."

Arioch chuckled into her hair, and then leaned his chin against the top of her head. "You realize your mistake, no? You're handling us with white gloves *epísimos*, when you have grounds to start a war." Aheia struggled in his hold and he tightened his hand. "You made it clear with your lack of actions, that she is *everything*. And I'm inclined to agree with you after seeing what I've seen."

Aheia's mind was threatening to tear itself apart trying to keep up with this new information. She didn't understand what it meant, felt like she was on the cusp of a cliff but couldn't jump.

Ophion dropped his pearl between them. "Enough." He cracked the delicate shell beneath his white shoe and grabbed ahold of Kal's shoulder as the bright light cracked their reality.

So the wards only kept us confined from leaving the church through doors, not the fabric of space.

Aheia recoiled at the vacuum that surrounded them as Ophion shoved Kal through, anger plain on his features now. It took mere seconds, but it felt like hours until Kal returned, holding onto the arm of another.

The male was tall and skinny, with dark tan skin and darker hair. The black mane reached down his back and matched a scruffy beard that hid the features of his face. He wore white pants, his torso exposed. It displayed scars and burns, all of them healed amongst tattoos that wound themselves over his muscles. She recognized the Nephilim glyph on the side of his neck before she noticed his eyes. They were gray. They were Arioch's eyes.

What is Ophion giving you?

"Something I can't refuse."

Arioch's hand fell from her throat, and she felt his heart beating into her back as she stared. She couldn't look away from those eyes across from her. They were placid, glazed over like none of this meant anything to him.

"Kazim, you remember your brother." Ophion clapped the Nephilim on the shoulder, a sick sneer spreading across his lips. "Or maybe you don't—it's been so, so long."

Kazim was unblinking, his naked chest moving slowly as he breathed, no indication that he knew what was going on at all.

"What have you done to him?" Arioch asked, rage blazing from every inch of him.

"He's alive, and I think that's the thing we should focus on."

Aheia looked up at Arioch and watched his eyes closely as he stared straight ahead. She saw the embers flaring, the gray edged out by the black.

"Though you were right, Alshaytan," Ophion continued, and the air seemed to shift around them, "she is important. I can't let her leave, and sadly I can't let you leave either. It's time that the Mithra assimilated that dirty realm of yours, it's time we rid this world of the Nephilim."

Ophion nodded at Kal who pulled Kazim back behind the other Mithra just as a small quake rattled the floor.

Aheia's eyes widened, and she looked around frantically, at the Nephilim behind her, at Alshaytan, at a door that seemingly appeared from the smooth marble wall and opened to reveal more white-clad bodies. New Mithra were pouring out from the hidden hallway, with weapons, drawing near the six Nephilim next to her.

"No," Aheia whispered.

"This could have been avoided if only you'd given her up earlier. Except I must say I'm glad you didn't. This is much better."

"I agree," Arioch said, stepping back with Aheia, his hands now on her shoulders. Ophion's eyes narrowed and just as he turned to his men, a command on his lips, the church lit up with bright light.

48

Chapter

Aheia

Aheia watched in disbelief as Koutávi peeled through another rift between the worlds, carrying a cloaked figure on her back. Aheia turned towards the Varcolac, seeing the figure slipping from her back and discarding the black, thick robe that had been tied around the rider's body.

That's impossible.

She'd never seen one, but had learned about the Ifrit's existence in books, a race of Djynn—one of the creatures brought into existence by the Kaymaat that were said to hold some of the oldest, most raw Calmani magyck in their souls. They'd been a fable, said to reside somewhere in the badlands, *if* they were real. But there she stood: tall, dark skin, cracks of red fire running through her, her hair lit with embers, her eyes just as bright.

The Ifrit stared at her, onyx dress dripping across her body, wet and gleaming; when those orange eyes met Aheia's she felt a jolt in her chest that matched the way the fire in the Ifrit's eyes flared. Her footsteps singed the marble, sizzling around her skin and Aheia wondered if she'd burn at the creature's touch.

"An Ifrit."

"Their magyck isn't bound by the realms, it is descendent of direct Calmani, not Dark nor Brite." Arioch grinned slowly, his eyes sparkling.

That is myth," Ophion said, but his gaze wavered as he looked at the Ifrit.

"Is it?" Arioch tilted his head, Koutávi's tendrils ghosting across him. "Should we find out?"

Aheia's gaze drifted to the ghostly eyes of Kazim, something unnerving in their depths. He hadn't said a word, hadn't shown an ounce of recognition, not even shock or awe at the Ifrit in her full glory. His eyes were trained on Arioch, but not in a way that suggested they were related, and it unsettled her.

"I should have expected this from you," Ophion spat, his people drew in tighter, and the Nephilim slid daggers from sheaths.

A hypocrite until his last breath.

"It's what your father would have done," he chuckled, something sadistic crossing his features, "and we all know it's 'like father, like son' in this family."

Aheia shot a look at Arioch, catching the tail end of his nostrils flaring.

"Should we find out just how alike Sahren and I are?" Arioch's eyes rested on Kazim for a split second.

Ophion ground his teeth together, the calm exterior he'd been clinging to shattered to pieces around him.

She had forgotten to run. Fuck, she'd forgotten to do anything but stare. She didn't know which direction was up, who to trust, what to do. And Gods, did she feel helpless.

Aheia felt Arioch turn towards the Ifrit. "Mazikeen, one last favor?"

She furrowed her brows. "*Sayyid?*"

"*Ant hurun. aid tulum.*"

Mazikeen's eyes widened, the red ink on her wrists shining bright as the last of his words filled the space between them. The air around them seemed to sizzle as Aheia watched the Ifrit's eyes burn, her skin blistering as large cracks ran through her in jagged lines that split and bisected her body.

She couldn't tear her eyes away from what was happening behind her as she watched the Ifrit transform, her dark skin splitting completely, a rolling wave of heat flooding from her. Fire engulfed her in a rage, splitting and coiling, giving way to something new, a being that Aheia had only heard of in lore and legends: an unbound Ifrit.

The space around them filled with the loud pulsing of something invisible as she emerged from the embers of her old skin, a creature with fire for hair and flames for eyes. She was covered in glyphs carved into her with charcoal, tall and sleek wings at her back that spanned further than those of any Syraphem.

The sight shook Aheia to her core and shifted something ancient

427

seated inside of her. The whispers drifted up from the darkness in her veins and spoke to her, the language she'd never before understood.

She had been caught in between reality and her own mind, but she appeared to be the only one. Around her, the Nephilim moved, blood splatters and screams filling the air as the Mithra and the Ifrit descended on one another. It was unparalleled, unmatched, and yet Arioch's people were cutting down Dioscuri and Malek like weeds. She watched Ophion wind his way back to safety and everything inside of Aheia screamed to run after him, wanting to see what *his* blood looked like on her hands for a change, but Arioch gripped her arm and pulled her back as Koutávi snaked around them, soft tendrils of shadows caressing her skin.

"Let go of me," Aheia hissed, wrenching her arm from his grip, but his fingers were tight, ironclad. "*Don't touch me.*"

"Who will you fight with?"

Her lips parted as she stared up at him. "*What?*"

"Choose, Aheia," he said, his voice a low hum that twisted her insides in the most conflicting of ways.

"I don't understand." She shook her head just as he leaned in close, his breath hot and enticing against her skin. She fought a shudder as he continued, his hold on her arm becoming bruising.

"I couldn't risk Ophion seeing into your mind." His free hand found its way onto her jaw, his fingers brushing across her cheek. "To find out I had absolutely no intention of leaving here without you."

She pulled back, a soft inhale on her lips as she met his eyes. But he spoke again before she could answer, the urgency in his voice building with the sounds of blades clashing around them.

"You have a choice."

Her eyes snapped up to his. "*Choice?* Don't use words you don't understand." She clenched her teeth repeating the words he'd told her on her first day in Aljira. He stared down at her, his mouth opening for a brief moment before his jaw shut tight and his eyes darkened to the same black she'd seen before. They stood like that for so long that time felt like it slowed, something new winding its way around them before he continued.

"If you fight with us, you leave with me. If you decide to go back to the Mithra, I will make sure you leave this church alive, though I can't promise the same for the rest of the Čist.

"Why? Why would you do that?" The air rushed from her lungs as his words settled between the broken parts of her, the ones that wanted to tear him apart, to see what his black blood looked like on her hands. "You told Ophion you knew what I was, what was different about me."

Arioch shook his head. "A bluff, Aheia."

"A bluff he played into," she said, her words tumbling from her lips. "Something is wrong with me. Is that why you want me to come back? So you can prod and pull and push and break until you figure me out? Until you find out what's wrong with me?" Her eyes burned as she pulled her arms away, cradling her chest.

Arioch held up his hands, his eyes softening. "They really forced you to believe that didn't they?"

Aheia's gaze snapped up to his. "I'm not stupid, I know something's fucking wrong, Arioch," she hissed, her fingers kneading the skin of her arms, the ice spiraling. "I can feel it. This ... it's not me ... it doesn't fit."

The cold and the dark, the two things she'd lived with for such a long time. They'd always felt like an extra skin, the kind

that was too tight on her bones, didn't belong. "Ruhí–" His voice was low and soft.

"*Stop* insulting me," she yelled, tears welling up in her eyes.

"Insulting? I–"

"It's over. Everything. *Fuck*." Her breathing was coming in spastic bursts now, the noise in the background fading with the erratic beating of her heart.

"Aheia."

"No." She cried, hugging herself, focusing on the blood that was slowly edging into view. Red blood. "*Stop*. Just, stop–"

"It's not an insult." Arioch fingers found the back of her neck again, his voice a low timbre. He pulled her close and for a moment she forgot to fight it.

"What?"

"Ruhí... It means *my soul*."

Aheia's chest tightened further, her heart feeling his words slithering through the thin, broken, little cracks that drew across it. It felt like with that simple statement he'd fractured her just a bit further. It made her feel embarrassed because the sentiment wasn't real, it didn't mean what she wanted it to mean. *Couldn't* mean what she wanted it to mean. So, she pulled herself together, blinking away the what-if's her mind conjured in front of her eyes, and met his dark gaze with as much strength as she could.

"Why are you asking me to come back?" Her face was still wet with tears but her voice held strong as she repeated the question.

His jaw worked overtime to contain whatever lay on his tongue, his eyes dissecting her features.

"You can't give me a straight answer to a simple question?" she asked, gritting her teeth to hold back a new wave of tears. The soul still adjusting in her chest was pulling emotions that no part of her wanted in that moment from the cold depths of her heart.

"No."

She shook her head, dropping his gaze.

"Aheia, I don't have a soul." He said quietly. "My heart works twice as hard for any normal emotion. I can't give you a reason, but I *can* give you a choice. Decide, Ruhí, and I will hear you."

Somehow that sentiment hit her harder than anything else had.

I will hear you.

"If I came back to Aljira, what would it cost me?" she asked, pulling away again. Arioch dropped his hand from her arm and unclasped one of his daggers, taking it by the blade and handing Aheia the leather hilt.

"A chance to prove my worth to you."

It took her a moment to understand the words because her mind was desperately trying to morph them into different answers in front of her.

A chance to prove my worth to you.

"I can't promise you that," she said, even as her body bucked and fought against refusal. And then she took the dagger from his hands because there was no way in hel that she was s going back to Keloseros.

Arioch's gaze dropped to her lips, his jaw clenching; for a moment Aheia thought he might try to kiss her. But instead, he leaned their foreheads together, rubbing the bridge of his nose against hers. "Don't let them touch you, Ruhí."

"Let go of me," she said, trying to preserve some semblance of herself in front of him.

"Save that pretty anger for later. I have some ideas for it," he said with a smirk that had her heart stumbling over itself as he dropped his hands from her body without hesitation for the first time since she'd met him.

"Fuck you." She hated him for making her feel like this, making her think he cared when she thought true emotions were far from why he wanted to hang onto her a little longer. She turned her focus on the carnage ahead.

His grin dropped, but it wasn't her words that had his demeanor changing, it was the sight of Ophion making his way across the church with Kazim and Kal, aiming for the door that had revealed the Mithra now littering the floor.

She swallowed, her heart pounding in her throat as she watched Emryn grapple with two Malek, and Lúc with his hands inside the chest cavity of another, long black claws drawn out over his knuckles. She'd been right, he did use his teeth to fight.

"Come on, little goddess," Arioch said, taking her hand and pulling her through the carnage.

"The wards didn't hold them out," she said, gripping the handle of her knife tighter as Mazikeen swept over their heads, the fire dampening the brightness of the stained-glass windows and leaving them in an amber void, the heat licking at Aheia's skin. She felt it in her chest, something familiar, like a tug and that's when Maz descended on the Mithra that were fighting with the Nephilim, engulfing ten at a time in flames.

"It's part of the structure, must lead somewhere underground. Besides, these Heretic wards are more of a show of good faith. They don't hold up to certain old magyck, Emryn made sure of it," Arioch said, taking her hand and pulling her through the throng of people fighting, narrowly avoiding the Ifrit's wrath as a vile screech left her lips. The sound shattered the windows, glass raining down on them. Arioch pulled her to his chest and groaned as the shards shredded his clothing, blood dripping from his neck and onto Aheia's hair as she steadied him.

"Fuck," he snarled while Aheia looked around his shoulder. Large shards of glass had cracked the marble around the dais, a Dioscuri torn in half, their intestines slung across the sharp edge of what had become a translucent blade, blood running across the floor. Aheia watched Kazim, Kal, and Ophion duck out of sight, blood trailing them. The shards had sliced down the length of the Malek's wing, and it lit a pang of excitement in Aheia's chest. He couldn't fly.

Koutávi skirted into view while ripping off a Mithra's head, her claws exposed from behind the shadows as Arioch whistled. The Varcolac dropped the head with a wet thud and slinked over, bowing down in front of them. Arioch straightened with a groan and gripped Aheia's waist, hoisting her onto the shadow's back. She yelped, feeling Koutá-vi's spine against her as she steadied herself. Her hands disappeared in the tendrils looking for something to hold on to as Arioch climbed on behind her. Then they sprung into action, hurtling after Ophion, through the door and down the white staircase that led deep into the church, darkness broken up by lines of bright, white light that skirted the ceiling, wrapping around them. It lit up her skin, and made even Arioch look sickly as it bathed them in an uncomfortable light.

49

Chapter

Aheia

They'd made their way down a long staircase that had Arioch and her laying down on Koutávi's back so they would fit, the narrow opening at the bottom giving way to a large, open space. Aheia gasped as the Varcolac scraped her claws across the marble floor and jumped onto ground covered in what looked like snow. A white, bright forest spanned in front of them, long, slender leaves falling around them as they raced through the unnatural quiet of their surroundings.

A cold wind bit at Aheia's exposed skin, so much colder than it had been in Aljira. Small pebbles of ice rained down around them, covering the ground in a white blanket, undisturbed save for the footprints they were following. Koutávi growled a reverberating sound that rattled Aheia to her bones as she saw Kal and Ophion winding through the trees with Kazim. He was following them with no signs of being forced along. Aheia's heartbeat drowned out the sounds around her as she watched the Mithra and Kazim grow closer, weaving through trees, Ophion's lame left wing dragging across the cold snow. The Malek looked over his shoulder just as Kal turned to hurtle a beam of light their way, Koutávi twisting at the last moment, narrowly avoiding the blow that sent Aheia and Arioch crashing to the forest floor, both of them powerless. Her elbow hit the ground and her back slammed into the trunk of a tree, knocking the air from her lungs.

"Don't be stupid, *Mithrek Morta*" Ophion breathed, stepping closer as Arioch got to his feet, Koutávi rising back on her hind legs.

"You can't use your Dark magyck here, you can't kill me."

Arioch's eyes were glued to Kazim who stood there as emotionless as when he'd first arrived. His eyes were still glazed over, his skin pebbling from the cold, and his hair a windswept mess. He simply existed, nothing more.

"I'm not the one who will kill you," Arioch said, sliding a glance at Aheia.

She fumbled for the knife that she'd dropped in her descent from Koutávi's back and found strength in the image of sinking it into Ophion's heart. The Varcolac howled, hurtling forwards at Ophion without warning and Aheia ran after her just as Arioch went for his brother, who was still just standing ankle-deep in the cold snow that was surrounding them. Aheia bared her teeth, fighting the cold that threatened not only her skin, but her heart as she ran, her feet screaming against the snow, her breathing ragged.

Kal hissed, hurtling another beam of light their way, manipulating it like it was water, except this time, he slung it around Koutávi and pulled it tight like a rope that constricted around her body. She yelped and fell to the side, her shadows simmering around the light like they were burning.

"No!" Aheia screamed just as something hit her side and knocked her to the ground.

Her head hit the hard underbrush, her vision swimming as she felt a hand on her ankles that pulled her back. She snapped back into reality, clawing at the cold ground while her body was being dragged across it, her fingers red and painful. She could see Ophion going after Arioch at the same time that he was fighting off Kazim, who was wielding a knife against his brother. Koutávi was writhing, the light that bound her feeding into Kal, whose expression was manic.

Aheia twisted and kicked, freeing one of her feet and connecting it with Kal's forearm. He dropped her other foot and jumped on top of her, pinning her wrists above her head.

"*Get off of me,*" she ground out, writhing around underneath him. She could see her dagger just out of reach when she tipped her chin and bucked her hips, trying to throw off the Dioscuri on top of her.

"It's for your own good," he said, breathing heavily as he leaned closer. "It will be better this time, Ophion promised, it will be ok." He almost looked entranced, his pupils too small for his irises. "You'll come back and everything will go back to normal— you and I, we can ..." He paused, his eyes dropping to her lips as he leaned down further.

The proximity turned her stomach, the fact that she felt him pressing into her abdomen was worse. But it gave her a possible way out.

If she let him kiss her maybe she could distract him enough to get to her knife. And then she'd cut out his tongue, the one that had told her all of those pretty lies when she was still in Keloseros.

She held her breath and waited as he closed the distance between them, and felt those soft lips against hers. He was timid even now, made her feel like she might have been his first ever as his tongue slid over her bottom lip. She shuddered, tasting bile in her mouth as he groaned in approval. She opened up to him and pulled his bottom lip into her mouth only to clamp down on it so hard that he convulsed, letting go of her hands.

He tried to pry her away but she bit down harder and harder until his flesh separated and he fell back, blood pouring from his mouth, his lip still between her teeth. He screamed, his hands shaking as she spit the bloody piece of meat out onto the white ground and wiped the blood across her face. It tasted sweet.

His light stuttered, the hold he had on it flickering like a dying candle before finally losing its connection with the Varcolac. Koutávi didn't move, not right away, but was breathing heavily like she was recovering.

Aheia couldn't focus on that. She dove for her blade and got to her feet, her knees still shaking as Kal grappled to get up. He tried to summon the light again, but just as he threw his arm back, Aheia lunged for him, knocking them both to the ground. Kal's head cracked against a snow-covered rock, blood trickling down it as his body went limp. She didn't know if he was dead, didn't have time to find out; she needed to move, couldn't look back.

Her eyes burned as the emotions in her chest overwhelmed every part of her mind, all of them conflicting and painful. She watched Arioch fight off both males, feeling the heat in her chest. She needed him to stay alive, even though a part of her hated him. She knew there wouldn't be a future with him, there couldn't be, but that didn't make the ache for the what-ifs any less vicious in her gut.

Aheia started running, all of her past lingering at her back as she sliced her dagger through the air, narrowly missing Ophion while Arioch attacked him from the other side. She wasn't very good at hand-to-hand combat, but it didn't seem to matter now that it was *her* turn to use a knife on Ophion. She ducked, falling out of Kazim's reach as he jumped for her, barely getting back on her feet. It was a mess–feathers, daggers, and *blood*, both red and black.

She hadn't realized Ophion's prowess with the weapon, not that she had ever seen him wield it in earnest. She assumed he hid behind his wings and guards, but this ... this was trained. Arioch matched him, wielding two of his dark blades, his movements just as fluid, like they were an extension of him, dodging and attacking, his hair starting to loosen from the bun he'd pulled it into, his eyes black. She grit her teeth, her heart pounding in her chest.

Don't die. Don't die. Don't die.

She was hurtling the thought towards Arioch, hoping he'd feel it in his bones, hoping that her soul had left some sort of impression on him, enough for him to feel this last thing that she so desperately needed him to hear as she slid around the fighting males and managed to jump onto Kazim's back. The Nephilim roared like an animal, trying to throw her, but she hung on for dear life as Kazim grabbed ahold of the leg she had slung around him and squeezed her ankle so tight she whimpered, feeling her muscle move around the bone. He'll break it. You need to MOVE. Her mind screamed but she held on to buy Arioch time. She shrieked when Kazim threw them both back, driving his large frame into her. The breath was knocked from her lungs and her chest burned with the impact. There was a sharp pain in her ribs as he leaned in, and she gasped feeling the cartilage move against her muscle.

Her scream had distracted Arioch, she could see it from the corner of her eye as Kazim started to shift off of her. Arioch met her gaze, and with that moment of interference Ophion brought down the blade on his shoulder, burying the knife to the hilt. Arioch groaned, his teeth clenched, the blood dripping down his body as he staggered back.

It all felt so unreal, like one of her nightmares, and at that moment she would have given anything for it to be one of those familiar terrors. Arioch snarled, the dagger still in his shoulder, leaving Ophion without a weapon. Something dark and calamitous flashed in his eyes as he reached for the white hilt and pulled it free slowly. He didn't make a sound, but Aheia did. She felt nauseous watching it, something like a gurgle passing between her lips as Kazim got off of her. She rolled to the side, her ribs screaming, and scrambled for the knife she'd lost. But she was too slow.

She felt a heavy weight pin her down and then a pressure between her shoulder blades. She gasped, the air in her lungs seizing, her fingers stilling midway to her knife as the air whooshed from her. She couldn't breathe, couldn't move, felt a pain cut into her back, the pressure on top of her building. She blinked, trying to understand what had happened as a hot wetness gathered on her skin and dripped down her body, the pain growing, her breathing becoming shallow.

She felt like a fish on land trying to suck in air, every breath was painful and her vision was starting to flicker as light spots consumed her.

A loud, animalistic roar wrapped around her, as the pressure on her back lessened slightly. Kazim was thrown into view, a large, spotted jaguar digging its teeth into the Nephilim's shoulder.

Was she hallucinating?

She blinked, her body refusing to move, red, hot blood trickling over the snow. Her blood.

Kazim had stabbed her.

She couldn't move, not even as she heard the commotion around her, not even as she saw Nephilim running closer from the depths of the forest. She looked up slowly, the world sputtering around her as she saw Emryn sliding into view, Maz melting the snow around them. Kar and Shiron now restraining Kazim, and a large Jaguar holding down Ophion against the snow.

She could vaguely hear things like *We need to go. They're not far behind*, as Arioch dropped to his knees at her side, his hands cradling her face.

"Don't you *dare*," he growled. "I'm not done with you yet." His eyes were frantic, but all she could do was open and close her mouth, the blade in her back keeping her words locked down tight as tears welled up in her eyes and fell onto the cold ground.

"*Go*," she gasped the word. Barely. *Get the fuck out of here.*

Arioch grit his teeth, shaking his head, the black blood on his skin dripping into the pools of her own.

"Fuck no," he hissed, his eyes black, "you can't leave like this."

Aheia's heart jumped. Barely. She was growing weak and was having a hard time focusing on anything but the cold. The ice in her chest didn't ebb with the life that was dripping from her back, no, it seemed to intensify in her veins. She stared at the blood, catching the reflection of herself as it pooled. Her eyes. Though they looked neither like hers nor her mothers in that moment.

She vaguely felt the tug at her side, saw Emryn's wings from the corner of her eyes, and heard Arioch speak again. "Fix this, *please*."

But the darkness was creeping in around her, her eyes losing the

Nephilim around them, losing the forest, losing the light.

Then everything went black, Emryn's voice a soft echo. "I can't."

And in that fleeting moment, death scared her. In that moment, death was unwelcome.

I don't want to die.

Epilogue

Aheia

The darkness was pressing in around her, and it was complete. She couldn't feel her body, couldn't see her hands when she tried to hold them up in front of her eyes, her thoughts drifting like they had no home, like they were existing in the air around her.

It felt so quiet, so absolutely definite, and she wondered for a brief moment if this was what death felt like for everyone. She should have been sad, should have cried, but there was a calm that hugged her tight, an acceptance that she didn't want and tried to push from herself, but couldn't.

The weightless feeling in her stomach had her suspended in the void, a silence that felt loud once again until suddenly a low whisper pierced it.

It surrounded her, too quickly for her to dissect its words as she felt her stomach drop. She was falling, air rushing past her so fast that she was unable to breathe, and at the same time didn't feel like she needed to. The panic that should have tightened her insides never came, not even as she considered where she might be falling to, and if the impact would hurt.

If she was dead, nothing could truly break her.

But then she was thrown through something solid, something that hit her like a wall, her eyes snapping shut tight, a groan leaving her lips and a warmth enveloping her slowly. Aheia blinked, feeling the ache in her bones, the darkness that had held her giving way to something entirely different. She was suspended again, weightless in the middle of a rolling ball of dark gray shadows. It seemed that they were circling, and when she squinted and opened her mind, she was met by eyes that made the blood curdle in her veins. They were black without separation nor variation, like a dark night that held no stars, as dark as the void she'd seen mere moments ago. It was the kind of color that not only blocked out any light around it but consumed it entirely.

Her lips parted, the air tasting heavy on her tongue, her heartbeat increasing slowly.

This, this felt wrong. The calm evaporated in a single swipe of those black eyes, a fear curling around her throat. Without seeing the entity's mouth, she knew it was where the disjointed whisper had come from as the shadows curled around those eyes, hiding the rest of whatever she was facing from view.

"*Finally.*" The voice edged into her mind again, louder this time, sounding exactly how she imagined smoke would. It was the language, a whisper she hadn't understood before, except now she did. And her mind told her that it was Calmani without a single hesitation as if it had learned it and kept it locked away like a secret. She saw the word slipping between them like a tangible thing, as a dark glyph that transformed until she could read it plain as day.

Her chest rose and fell so quickly that she could barely speak. "Where am I?"

A smile penetrated those black eyes while the creature kept itself hidden in the smoke, the hair on her arms standing on end as the glyphs translated in front of her once more when it spoke.

"*Home.*"

Her blood froze, her eyes picking apart her surroundings frantically. She was suspended in the darkness that was occasionally broken up by dull colors, what she imagined living in a thunderstorm might look like, except the colors weren't white lightning strikes, but instead dark reds and oranges akin to the fire that heated the space.

"No." Her throat went dry.

"That panic is delicious," the creature said, its voice scraping across her ears like nails on rough rock. "I can feel it, that power. I've missed that, missed my children oh so dearly,"

Children.

Aheia was frozen, loose tears falling over her cheeks as it spoke, her limbs shaking with how hard she was trying to break free from whatever compulsion had her suspended in the air.

"Who are you?" she managed, in between heaves of air that seemed to do little to calm her down.

"Blood," it said, "same as yours. Darkness, same as yours. Hunger, same as yours." The words repeated over and over again until they ran into each other, the implications choking Aheia where she stood.

"I will see you again when the Gods meet," it continued before a long black, cracked talon stretched from the smoke and wrapped around her wrist. Aheia's eyes snapped down, the contact burning, so painful she wanted to scream. The talons wrapped tighter as Aheia's body convulsed, fire spilling inside of her head, dropping down her body and scorching her skin, an invisible force that shifted her insides. She bowed, her back arching so violently that the crack of it sliced through the air, any and all sounds she'd been making sucked from her mouth like she'd been pulled into a vacuum. That same absence of air suddenly pulled her from those dark eyes and slammed her down so hard that her teeth clashed and her bones shook with the impact. Aheia screamed, cradling her sides, her nails piercing her own skin as she held onto herself in an effort to not split apart. It felt like her skin was peeling, like she didn't fit anymore, every part of her lit up by a cold fire.

To be continued...

ACKNOWLEDGEMENTS

Writing is a journey, and can often be a lonesome one. I recommend to any fledgling author, don't make the mistake of isolating yourself. Sharing your mind is scary, but if you find the right people, those small leaps of faith will fly you to a mountain top you didn't know existed. Pulling the world you've seen in your head and imprinting it onto dead trees in hopes of touching another person's life is the most frustrating, mentally draining, and ultimately exciting thing I've done in my entire life. It takes hard work and discipline, but there's so much more to it. It takes the courage to let others see you— really see you. To tell them how your day went instead of just telling them "it was fine." It takes learning to be open about criticism because no one is perfect. It takes learning to take someone's hand when all you've ever done is fend for yourself.

There's no way to thank you, any of you- not how you deserve. Because the truth of the matter is, is that without you, this book wouldn't exist. The support in the low points, the relentless strength you've lent me when I lost my own, the way you let me vent, listened to my ideas and helped me try and grow past the walls that writers' block solidified in my mind— made the difference. The way you stuck with me when I fell time and time again, made the difference. The way you simply stayed instead of running when I couldn't find the right words to communicate, and pulled my hair out over the feeling of my own stupidity, made the difference.

I want to make this first dedication to you,

Tyler, Cass, Sarah, Car, Taylor, Amy, Elif, Molly & Alyssa. You made the difference for me and I'll never forget that.

The second goes to my Instagram family, to my Heathens, and to everyone who's joined me for this now, 8-month journey. I shared a lot of the highs and lows with you, and it was one of the reasons I kept going when it felt like I couldn't. Because I knew I wasn't the only one who felt this way, and that if others could do it, I could too.

So many of you have lent me your strength, and it means the *fucking* world.

XO,
Murs

Made in the USA
Columbia, SC
08 July 2022

63078385R00269